**KAREN CLARKE** is a Yorkshire-born writer living in Buckingham-shire with her husband and three grown-up children. Her previous books include *And Then She Ran* and *Your Life for Mine*. Karen has also written several series of romantic-comedies and co-writes thrillers with author Amanda Brittany.

## Also by Karen Clarke

*Your Life For Mine*
*And Then She Ran*
*My Sister's Child*
*My Husband's Secret*

## Books by Karen Clarke and Amanda Brittany

*The Secret Sister*
*The Perfect Nanny*

# My Best Friend's Secret

## KAREN CLARKE

ONE PLACE. MANY STORIES

HQ
An imprint of HarperCollins*Publishers* Ltd
1 London Bridge Street
London SE1 9GF

www.harpercollins.co.uk

HarperCollins*Publishers*
Macken House, 39/40 Mayor Street Upper,
Dublin 1 D01 C9W8
Ireland

This paperback edition 2023

1

First published in Great Britain by
HQ, an imprint of HarperCollins*Publishers* Ltd 2023

ISBN: 9780008607562

This book is produced from independently certified FSC™ paper
to ensure responsible forest management.

For more information visit: www.harpercollins.co.uk/green

Printed and bound in the UK using 100% renewable electricity
at CPI Group (UK) Ltd

*For Tim, with all my love*

# Prologue

*The lights will turn red any second. As the car slowed, my heart rate accelerated.*

*I'd been careful for weeks, pretending I was fine to avoid suspicion.*

*It had to be now. I might not get another chance.*

*I turned, to disguise the click of the seatbelt unclipping, and glanced at the child in the back. She was looking out of the window, clutching an ancient teddy bear, and didn't look at me.*

*The car stopped. The traffic light was red, like the blood pulsing through me.*

*I took a breath, jumped out and ran.*

# Chapter 1

*Friday*

I made my way to the school with a purposeful stride, as though I had every right to be there. It was easy in some ways, the setting familiar. Most primary schools looked the same.

Despite the breeze that had punctured the June heatwave, my hands felt clammy, and my upper lip prickled with sweat.

I unfastened the buttons of the jacket I'd pulled on over my knee-length shirt-dress. Combined with low-cut ankle boots, a light coating of makeup, and a band trapping my blonde hair in a ponytail, I hoped I looked a picture of trustworthiness.

Tension pressed on my shoulders like hands as I approached the gates of the low, red-brick building dappled in afternoon sunlight. I wished I really was there to enquire about a teaching job. I'd been hoping to get back to work but hadn't felt ready yet – still lying low as I scraped my way back to the person I'd been before.

Slowing my pace, I scanned the parents and carers gathered at the school gates waiting for their charges to emerge, seeking the face that matched the photo etched on my brain.

It shouldn't be difficult, as the assembled adults were mostly female and the face I sought was male – a lone father among the sea of mothers, grandmothers, and nannies.

Spotting the back of a brown-haired figure, standing apart from the others, nearly a foot taller than most, my stomach cramped with nerves. What happened next required me to act; a feat I was frightened I couldn't pull off.

*I have to get Daisy away from them. She could be in danger. Please help me, Rose. There's no one else I can trust.*

Tightening my grip on the strap of my bag, I reminded myself why I was doing this. Forcing my shaky legs onwards, I arranged my face in a pleasant smile as I came to a stop beside the man I prayed was Isaac Reeves. I couldn't afford to get it wrong.

'Is it a good school?' My voice emerged bright and steady, propelled by an urge to get this part over and done with.

'Not bad.' The man, who had been looking at his phone, turned his head. His gaze swept over my face, which pulsed with heat. 'New to the area?'

'I'm looking for a job.' Best to plunge right in with the words I'd rehearsed in the car on the drive over, repeating them out loud until they lost all meaning. 'I'm a primary school teacher. Year one, so four- to five-year-olds. I'm scoping out a few local schools, hoping one might have a vacancy. It's good to get feedback from parents first.' He was probably wondering why I'd approached him rather than one of the assembled women, or hadn't looked online for reviews and testimonies. 'I've heard this one has a good reputation,' I added quickly.

He turned fully to face me, pushing his phone in his jeans pocket before folding his arms. He was good-looking with a presence that hadn't come across in the photo on the back of his book jacket, but that had been taken a few years ago. There was a wave in his longish hair, and his confident smile was framed by a gold-speckled beard. 'I'm probably not the best person to ask.'

'What do you mean?' I tried to relax the muscles in my face.

4

'You obviously send your . . . child here.' *Remember you shouldn't have any idea who he is.*

'Well, I'm looking to have my daughter home-schooled but haven't found the right person yet.' His words were so on-script that, for a second, I almost laughed as relief swept through me. I wasn't going to have to try too hard.

'Why home-schooled?' Catching the curious glances of a couple of women clustered beneath an overhanging beech tree, I shifted so my back was to them, hoping I looked anonymous.

'My daughter's sensitive,' he said carefully. 'She's had a hard time settling in. She's young for her age and there's been a bit of bullying.'

'I'm sorry to hear that.' Deciding it might sound overfamiliar to ask for details, I said instead, 'Could you or your . . .' I swallowed past the dryness in my throat '. . . your wife home-school your daughter? I mean, the focus is more on learning through fine-motor activities, rather than formal teaching, so she's young enough—'

'It's just me, and I have to work.' As if regretting his abrupt interruption, Isaac Reeves softened his face into a smile. 'So, you're a teacher?'

'That's right.' I pushed down a memory of the class of bright-eyed children I'd abandoned at Chesterfield Primary, whose faces still haunted my dreams – the sense I'd let them down dogging my waking thoughts in the minutes before I forced myself out of bed. 'For nearly ten years. It's all I ever wanted to do, perhaps because my mother was a teacher and my grandmother. I enjoyed school myself, and I love children, especially at that age when they're so receptive.' I was talking too fast – more than I'd spoken to a stranger in a long time. I hauled in a breath, remembering I needed to make a good impression.

*Think of it like an audition. You won't have to do much, believe me. Just smile a lot and keep eye contact. He won't be able to resist.*

'I used to play schools with my dolls and teddies when I was a child,' I went on. 'My dad couldn't understand it, thought I should be outdoors . . .' I trailed off with a surge of sadness at the mention of my father.

'I wasn't keen on school myself, couldn't wait to leave.' Isaac hadn't taken his eyes off my face during our interaction. It was unnerving and took every ounce of resolve I possessed to not squirm away. My instinct for months had been to look the other way, not hook my gaze to a man's.

'I don't suppose you'd be interested in tutoring privately?' Isaac tipped his head to one side, assessing me in a friendly fashion. Recalling everything I knew about him, I felt a prickle of unease at the back of my brain. Was I really willing to put myself at risk, just as I'd been getting my life back on track?

*Please, Rose. I can't live without my little girl.*

'How about a trial, say for a week or two, and if you don't like it, you can walk away.' There was a questioning tilt to Isaac's brow. 'Sorry to put you on the spot.'

'Oh, I . . . I don't know.' I wasn't acting now. Doubt flooded my veins, dragging at my stomach.

Isaac held up a hand as if to halt any objections. 'Come to the house for an interview, at least.' His voice was warm and engaging, his accent neutral.

*He has Icelandic heritage but was born in West London. He takes after his father who was British, so doesn't have his mother's Nordic looks.*

'I'm a pretty good judge of character.' His eyes raked my face once more. My blonde fringe, clear skin, and wide grey eyes gave me a girl-next-door appearance, or so I'd been told; an unthreatening aura that belied why I was really there. Isaac Reeves wasn't *that* good a judge of character.

'Sure, why not?' I shrugged, loosening the grip on my bag, adopting what I hoped was a considering expression.

'Obviously, I'll pay you.'

I gave a quick nod. 'I'd like to meet your daughter.'

'You'll love her – she's a sweetheart.' Isaac's smile widened in a face so pleasant to look at. 'What's your name?' He moved so he was standing in a patch of sunlight, and I couldn't make out his features.

*You'll have to give your real name; he'll want to look you up, but it'll be fine, don't worry. Unlike him, you have nothing to hide.*

'Rose Carpenter.'

'Isaac Reeves.' His hand enfolded mine in a warm grip, holding it a fraction too long, as if divining everything about me through my palm. 'It must be my lucky day.'

'Mine too,' I managed, as the school bell rang.

When he let me go, we turned to face the building, and all I could think over the thudding of my heart was that Isaac had behaved exactly as Elise had predicted.

# Chapter 2

## *The day before*

'I can't believe you're living *here*, in the middle of nowhere.'

'It's not the middle of nowhere.' The area I'd chosen was fairly anonymous, but not isolated. I knew that could be dangerous if I was found. My rented home was in a market town called Chesham, nestled in the Chilterns in the south-east of England. The house was small and unremarkable, set at the end of a short terrace, overlooking a field of horses, hopefully far enough away from my ex that he wouldn't come looking for me.

'I thought you'd end up somewhere exotic, considering you couldn't wait to get away after university.'

There it was: the tang of betrayal in Elise's words, even after all this time, sending the guilt I'd thought long buried shooting to the surface.

'I wanted to put down roots and this seemed as good a place as any.' I wasn't prepared to tell her the whole story yet. Her reappearance was so unexpected after almost twelve years, I was grappling to accept her presence on the edge of my mustard-coloured armchair; a spot of brightness in the otherwise dingy room.

'I thought you'd want to be closer to your aunt and uncle.' As Elise placed the mug of tea I'd made on the faded carpet, her hand shook. 'They're still in Derbyshire then?' she added without waiting for an answer. 'Your Aunt Sarah was very cagey, wouldn't give me your address, despite me putting on my very best, person-in-authority voice.'

The thought of Elise calling Sarah, inventing an emergency to get my number, a number no one else knew, made me go hot, but it made sense of Sarah's worried text the day before, saying the school had called her, needing to contact me urgently; something to do with my pension fund.

'You knew I in worked a school then?'

'An educated – see what I did there? – guess.' She lifted a shoulder in a half-shrug. 'Wasn't that always the plan?'

I leaned forward, the leather sofa squeaking beneath me. 'Why are you here, Elise? Now, after all this time.' She wasn't the only one shaking. I rested my elbows on my knees and pressed my palms together. 'You don't look well.' It was true. The Elise I'd been best friends with at sixth form and through university had been replaced with a version I hardly recognised. I'd barely stifled a gasp of shock when I opened the door, still reeling from her call just after eight to say she was on her way.

Tall and slim, with a fast metabolism that meant she could eat what she wanted and not gain weight, she was all bones and angles now, her cheeks sunken under lifeless eyes, her once-shiny, waist-length hair a brittle brown curtain around her shoulders.

When she'd thrown herself over the doorstep and wrapped her arms around me, it had been like hugging a bird, as though she might shatter if I applied too much pressure. She used to smell of her aromatherapy oils and oddly scented 'cruelty-free' shampoos and soaps, but something sour had caught in my throat, as though she'd been sweating and hadn't washed for a while.

Even her clothes looked wrong, her narrow frame swamped by a shapeless black dress and woollen grey cardigan, feet encased in stompy, round-toed boots – a style that hadn't deviated much from the 'goth-slash-hippy-vibe' she used to carry off with ease, but now made her look like a child playing dress-up.

'What's happened, Elise?'

'I need your help.' Abandoning her half-hearted attempt at pleasantries, after silently watching while I made tea in the kitchen, she got up and dropped to her knees in front of me, taking hold of my hands. Her fingers were cold, sending an icy chill up my arms. She'd always been tactile, her arm linked through mine as we walked to classes or slung around my shoulders; a peck on each cheek when we met, or said goodbye; a nudge with her elbow, or dig in the ribs when she teased me, her touch gentle as she did my eyeliner with a perfect flick. I'd tolerated it then, but was overwhelmed now by an urge to push her away.

'You're scaring me,' I said, part of me thinking *I don't need this*, while a bigger part whispered, *You owe her.* 'What have you done?'

'*I* haven't done anything.' She tugged her hands free and sat back, greenish-brown eyes sparking to life. 'Why would you think that?'

'I'm sorry. I shouldn't have said it.' I reminded myself that Elise was no longer the teenager who'd tended to be theatrical – keen to become an actress, like her mother had been. She was a thirty-three-year-old woman, like me, and clearly desperate if she'd sought me out, the friend who abandoned her to go travelling. 'Tell me.'

The words tumbled out as Elise rose and paced the tiny room, thin hands flailing as she described a marriage gone disastrously wrong, a husband with a manipulative streak – *a monster who wants me dead.*

'Why would he want you dead?' I was appalled, thinking of the man I'd left behind three months ago, after he broke his restraining order. 'Has he hurt you?'

'Not like that, no, not physically, not yet, but he was working up to me having some kind of accident.' She made finger quotes

10

around the word *accident*. 'It's only a matter of time, Rose. I knew I had to get away, even though there was no one to turn to.'

Elise and I hadn't talked much about our tragic backgrounds – the binding factor in our friendship – but I knew the basics: her mother left her father while she was pregnant with Elise, she had a sister who died before Elise was born, her mother was reclusive and drank a lot.

'What about your mum?' I said carefully, recalling their fractured relationship. 'Did you reach out to her?'

'No point.' Elise's lips twisted, with bitterness, or something else. 'She developed early onset dementia last year. She's in a home now.'

'I'm so sorry.'

As if she hadn't heard, more words rushed out – a tsunami of information I could barely digest rattling around in my head. Her mother-in-law had moved in, she had back problems *when it suited her* but tried to take over, and then his sister and her 'degenerate' husband moved in, all of them trying to split up her and Isaac, believing she wasn't good enough for him, an opinion Isaac did nothing to dispute.

'His mother accused me of having an affair, which was absolute rubbish, but it gave Isaac more ammunition against me, even though there was absolutely no proof. He wanted a divorce, but I refused. I haven't done anything wrong, and I didn't see why he should get half of everything.'

It transpired her estranged father, in a fit of guilt, had left her a lot of money in his will when he died, most of which she'd used to buy the house she and Isaac lived in. 'Then I realised he wanted me out of the picture anyway, so he can have full custody of Daisy, which I would never have allowed, and means—'

'Wait, *what?*' I held up a hand, mind spinning. 'You're not making any sense, Elise. Who's Daisy?'

'My little girl.' Elise stopped moving, voice cracking as she said, 'She's four years old, and he has her.'

My stomach churned with dread. 'You need to go to the police, Elise. Tell them everything you've told me.'

'You don't understand.' She dropped into the armchair and covered her face, shoulders shaking. 'I already did that, but because of my past – Isaac had me committed, and tells everyone about my so-called mental health issues – I don't have any credibility, while he and his family have plenty. The police didn't take me seriously at all.'

I stared, out of my depth. I'd thought I had problems, but they paled alongside Elise's. A controlling husband. *A daughter.* She'd sworn she never wanted children, but people changed their minds all the time. She must have fallen for this Isaac, been taken in by him until it was too late, had probably stayed with him as long as she had for the child's sake. Pushing back the torrent of questions jostling for position, I went to her, remembering the friendship we'd once had, how she'd made my life better, brighter, at a time when I'd needed her.

'What do you want me to do, Elise?'

She grabbed my wrists, her nails digging into my skin, eyes huge and imploring. 'You have to get Daisy away from him and bring her to me.'

'What?'

'Please, Rose, I'm begging you.'

'But . . . there must be legal channels, a good solicitor who would fight for you.'

'I can't do it, Rose, don't you see? No one will vouch for me. If I involve any of the authorities, even a solicitor, the family will gang up on me, call me unstable again. And I was the one who walked out.' She paused, letting her words sink in. 'It doesn't put me in a good light.'

I was trying to latch on to some facts, but before I could speak again, she burst out, 'They told Daisy I died. They've told everyone.'

'Died?' My stomach clenched with shock. 'But . . . *why?*'

'To shut me out, make sure I can't come back without confusing Daisy. Because they don't want me disrupting their cosy set-up.'

'How do you know they've told everyone you're dead?' I could hardly believe the words coming out of my mouth. 'Once you'd left, I mean?'

'I called the house one night and asked to speak to Daisy. I wanted to tell her I hadn't forgotten her, that I would come for her one day.' Her chin shook. 'That's when Isaac told me I was dead to her – to everyone – and to stay away.'

'Jesus.' Outrage flared. 'You *have* to go to the police, Elise.'

Her expression darkened. 'I've already told you, Rose. They won't believe me.' Her fingers clutched at my knees. 'Isaac will make sure of that; he's very convincing.'

'But—'

'I meant to go back one night and take her, but I was worried about getting caught,' she broke in. 'They have cameras everywhere. I always felt watched, and Isaac's quite capable of tracking me down. But I can't bear to think of her there without me, I just can't. I need her, and she needs me.' A strangled sob erupted, twisting her face beyond recognition. 'Please help me, Rose,' she begged. 'There's no one else I can trust.'

# Chapter 3

## *Friday*

Shaking, I drove behind Isaac's car, gripping my steering wheel like a lifebuoy. *How had it been this easy?*

'Are you doing anything now?' he'd asked pleasantly, after scooping up his daughter and introducing her to me – a mini-replica of Isaac with wild, brown curls, but Elise's long-lashed eyes. Her face was pale with a pinched expression, and she didn't speak. 'Come back to the house now if you like.'

I'd found myself nodding, smiling inanely at Daisy – *Elise's daughter* – and saying brightly, 'Sure, why not?' as though it was normal to accept an invitation to an interview by a stranger at his home in the middle of the afternoon. 'Where do you live?'

'Beaconsfield,' he said, though I already knew. It was a twenty-minute drive from where I lived and, for a moment after she told me, I'd wondered about my proximity to where Elise had been living for the past five years. Had she singled me out to help after discovering how close I was, or did she really have no one else to turn to?

*He made sure I was cut off from everyone, Rose. It's classic stuff – you read about it all the time. I didn't even realise it was happening. When I tried to talk to my mother, she told me I'd made my bed and should lie in it. That was before she went into the home. She barely knows who I am now.*

Elise's grandmother had spent her final years in a home with dementia, in Derbyshire, where we'd lived. I visited once, with Elise, shocked that Elise's mother Ingrid refused to go. Apparently, it was because she was scared of whatever madness ran in the family and couldn't bear to be faced with it. *And now she was in a home herself.* In High Wycombe, a half hour drive from me, where Elise had been lying low for months. *I couldn't leave her up in Derbyshire, in the old house. At least the money is useful for her care, though she would hate knowing it's paid for courtesy of my father.*

The news had made me sad, and uneasy in a way I couldn't explain. Perhaps it was all the reminders of my own past that Elise had brought with her like unwanted luggage.

Isaac's car was a grey hatchback, a few years old, with dusty bodywork. I remembered Elise saying he didn't have much money and wondered about his career. *A book he wrote years ago.* A failed writer?

I looked at his outline in the driver's seat, wondering whether he was doing the same in his rear-view mirror, sizing me up. In her car seat in the back, Daisy was waving a book as she chatted; probably telling her daddy about her day at school.

I tried to place Elise in the car, turning around to speak to her daughter with laughter in her eyes, but couldn't make the image stick.

Like Elise, I hadn't seen myself as mother material, too aware of everything that could go wrong, but once I turned thirty, something had shifted inside me. I started noticing babies everywhere, and to wonder whether it might be wonderful to raise a child after all. Finding a partner had taken on a new significance, which had led me to Leon.

I refocused on my driving. Beaconsfield was a town divided into two, the old and the new, and renowned for being home to the world's oldest model village. Isaac lived in the old town, which had a well-kept and timeless appearance, its main street of shops, pubs, and estate agencies, housed in historic buildings, their fronts tastefully painted in heritage colours. The cars outside looked equally upmarket and I guessed that, like most areas within a twenty-five-mile radius of London, you needed a sizeable income to live here.

When I met Elise, her mother's acting career had long dried up, her occasional voiceover work only paying enough to keep her in gin – according to Elise – and their ordinary house, a few miles from where I lived, had belonged to Elise's grandparents. It was quite a step up from there to here, but I could understand Elise wanting to invest in property, in a nice area. It wasn't fair that Isaac still lived in the house, while Elise was virtually homeless.

How could he have told his daughter her mother was dead and behave as though it was normal? The injustice hit me all over again, strengthening my resolve to see this through.

I braked as Isaac indicated at a roundabout before turning down a long, straight road and past a church, the scenery becoming more rural as he reached the end and turned again, down a winding track. He finally slowed in front of a set of wooden gates that glided open as if on a sensor. I followed slowly onto a curving driveway lined with mature shrubs, and carpeted pink where a pair of magnolia trees had shed their petals.

Instead of driving into the double garage to the right of the house, Isaac drew up in front of it, between a racing-green Volvo and a silver Smart car that looked like a toy. I parked beside the Volvo, leaning forward to take in the building that Elise had shown me a photo of. It was a classic Georgian stone-built house, rendered a dazzling white, with pale blue shutters that matched the sky, and bursts of lilac wisteria around the porch.

*You know wisteria is toxic to humans? I'm pretty sure that's why I got sick last year when no one else did. He must have put the seeds in my food.*

I tried to picture Elise choosing a house like this. She used to hanker after a New-York-style loft apartment where she could throw parties to entertain her acting friends. She'd wanted to live in a city, to be 'at the heart of things' but, I reminded myself, Elise wasn't that girl anymore and her tastes had clearly changed.

Taking a breath to steady myself, I climbed out of the car, smoothing the creases from my dress. The air was soft and perfumed, birdsong drifting from the trees. Beyond the low roof of the garage, the Chiltern Hills unfolded in a palette of sun-drenched greens and golds. For a brief, dizzying moment, I felt as though I'd stepped out of my life and into someone else's – a feeling I hadn't experienced since my backpacking year after university.

I inhaled again as Isaac emerged from his driver's seat and threw me a sunny smile. 'Not bad,' he said, tracking my gaze, but his eyes didn't linger on the house. 'I'll give you a tour once we've got this one inside.'

Daisy, released from her seatbelt, jumped out and ran over to me, her serious face now brightening into a smile. Unexpectedly, she clasped my hand in her slightly sticky one and tugged. 'I can show you my bedroom.' She tilted her head, one eye scrunched shut against the sunlight, waiting.

'That would be nice.' Something unfurled in my heart that I daren't examine. I was relieved when she let go and charged after Isaac, her rucksack falling off her shoulder.

*Remember, you won't be there long, Rose. Just enough time for him to trust you, so you can get Daisy away.*

As the front door swung open and an older figure appeared, I faltered. Daisy threw herself at the woman, wrapping her arms around her legs, and the woman bent to kiss the top of her head.

This must be the mother-in-law, the one who had hated Elise from the start – or was that Isaac's sister? I was still struggling

17

with the flood of information Elise had unleashed over the course of two hours before collapsing in tears, saying she couldn't go on, and would I mind if she stayed over, because she hadn't slept properly for weeks, had been staying in a soulless B&B in High Wycombe, visiting her mother at Graylands Manor every day, and had walked for miles to reach my house.

The scale of what she was asking me to do sank in as I edged closer to the house, where the woman was looking at me with curiosity now that Daisy had disappeared inside. She was tall and wide-shouldered, her eyes almost comically blue, her white-blonde hair pulled back in a stylish twist. 'Who is this, Isaac?' She had the smallest hint of a European accent, her voice softer and welcoming, like her smile.

*Don't be fooled, Rose. They'll come across as the nicest family in the universe, but they're not. Be on your guard, but don't let them see you're wary. They sense weakness, like those sniffer dogs trained to find drugs.*

'Rose, this is my mother, Cecilia.' Isaac turned, one foot on the doorstep, his gaze appraising me. 'Mum, this is Rose,' he said. 'I'm hoping she can help us take care of Daisy.'

*Take care of Daisy.* The words were inclusive, as if I was part of the family already. Feeling like an actor, spotlit by a beam of sunshine, I stepped towards them. 'Hi!' My cheeks ached from smiling. 'Nice to meet you.'

'Come here, Rose. Let me have a look at you.'

Expecting to hear mistrust, to see suspicion, I was surprised when the woman's smile widened, crinkling her eyes. She held out her hands as I joined Isaac on the step. A tremor ran through me as she took a firm grip of my fingers. Her hands were cool, her gaze clear as we took each other in, though I was certain I was the only one holding my breath. She was probably in her mid to late sixties, with good bone structure, and a rosy glow on her skin, which held laughter lines and faint wrinkles. Her outfit – wide-legged trousers and a buttoned up shirt – was contemporary and unthreatening. 'Come inside, I'll make you a drink.' Breaking eye contact, she let go of me and I obediently stepped over the threshold, expelling a shaky breath.

'I think you've passed,' Isaac murmured beside me. When I looked, his eyes were bright with amusement. 'Not everyone does.'

'Oh, Isaac.' His mother glanced over her shoulder. 'I got your brother-in-law to move the chest freezer, so you should be able to drive into the garage now.'

When her eyes met mine it was a struggle to keep smiling. With a chill of apprehension, I was remembering what Elise had told me: that despite her motherly aura Cecilia once said to her, *You could hide a body in that freezer, and no one would ever know.*

# Chapter 4

Inside the wide entrance hall, the air was spicy with cooking smells and a trace of woodsmoke, and the sound of Daisy's laughter spilled from the depths of the house. Instantly, I was overcome with a painful longing for a time when I'd lived in a home like this.

*It's not real.* My fingernails were sharp in my palms as I tried to focus on my surroundings: the parquet floor, wood-beamed ceiling, and curving staircase; a vase filled with delicate flowers on a polished table next to the cloakroom. Thanks to Elise's detailed description, I knew what was behind each door. A gallery of pictures, mostly mountain scenes, hung along one oatmeal-coloured wall, and an antique mirror opposite reflected my pink-tinged face.

I looked as disorientated and nervous as I felt, not good at hiding my feelings. I imagined Elise's voice in my ear telling me to *Fake it till you make it,* like she used to. *Power posture, Rose – that means don't round your shoulders like you normally do. Make eye contact, and speak slowly and clearly; don't babble. And remember to smile – it's your best feature. A smile like that will get you a long way.*

But this was different to approaching a potential date or going to an interview, and my confidence – before meeting Leon – hadn't been an issue once I'd entered what my aunt had called 'the real world'. In those days, I was used to handling classes of young children with varying needs, not to mention their parents, and happy to make my voice heard at meetings; but now, after months of being jobless and alone, after everything that had happened, I was edgy and out of practice. My motives weren't pure, and I was worried my body language would betray me.

*You have to completely believe in your story, Rose, in why you're there.* That was the actress in Elise talking. *If you do, they'll believe you. I promise.*

Cecilia had vanished through a doorway at the end of the hall, and Isaac was stooping to fuss a black Labrador trotting out of an adjacent room – the living room – tail wagging.

'This is Rocky,' Isaac said, rubbing the dog's muzzle. 'He's getting on a bit now and completely harmless.'

*They trained that smelly old animal to growl at me, then said I was making it up.*

A ghostly Elise, reminding me of all the ways her life at Orchard House had been made hell, but when the dog ambled over to sniff my ankles and fix me with a gentle gaze, and Isaac grinned and said, 'Looks like you've made another friend,' it was hard to reconcile the images planted in my head with Elise's reality. *Manipulative.* That was the word she had used, repeatedly.

After letting the dog sniff my fingers and patting his head, I followed Isaac into a large, bright kitchen with a black and white tiled floor in a diamond pattern, white gloss units and slate worktops, a wall-mounted TV tucked away in a corner.

A family-sized dining table stood in the attached conservatory, which had a domed glass roof and looked out on a country-style garden. Through the open doors I could faintly hear the sound of running water and remembered the house was close to a river, fed by a stream running through the garden.

*It's quite dangerous. The water's fast-flowing, so you have to keep an eye on Daisy when she's playing outside.*

Judging by the footsteps from overhead, Daisy was currently in her room, and though I couldn't hear another voice, I had the sense she wasn't up there alone.

'Sit down, Rose.' Cecilia gestured to a tall, fabric-covered chair with sloping arms at the breakfast bar, while Isaac rounded the kitchen island. He took mugs from a cabinet and slipped one under the nozzle of a chrome coffee machine, without asking whether I drank coffee – another of Elise's predictions come true.

*Arrogant,* she had called him. *He'll expect you to say if you'd rather have something else, but don't. He loves that coffee machine.*

'Mum likes hers strong enough to stand a spoon in.' He gave another of his disarming smiles, before sliding a mug over to Cecilia, who was efficiently slicing a cake drizzled with icing.

'Would you prefer tea, or water?'

Disorientated, it took a second to realise Isaac was addressing me. 'Oh!' Heat flushed my cheekbones as I hoisted myself onto the chair, my dress riding up my thighs. 'Yes. Please. White, one sugar. I know I shouldn't. Have sugar, I mean. It's a hard habit to break.' My face burned as I tugged my hem over my knees and fumbled my bag over the back of the chair. *Remember why you're here.*

'You're doing better than me.' Isaac reached for a silver bowl on the worktop filled with caramel-coloured cubes. 'I take two sugars in mine but tell myself these don't count.' He plucked out a cube with a pair of tiny tongs and dropped it in a mug, which he brought over and placed in front of me with a small jug of milk.

'I tell him he's sweet enough already, but it makes no difference.' Cecilia's voice, warm with fondness, broke the sudden tension. 'Try some cake?'

'Thanks.' I slopped milk into my coffee, certain I wouldn't be able to eat. I'd only managed a slice of toast for breakfast, wrung out after a restless night under a throw on the sofa, aware of Elise's presence above me. I hadn't got around to sorting out the spare room, not anticipating visitors, but Elise hadn't objected when I offered my bed, seeming to fold in on herself with exhaustion as she declined an offer of food and headed upstairs.

She'd left behind the canvas holdall she'd brought with her, and I managed to resist looking through it, half-wondering whether she'd left it there to test me. It was the sort of thing the old Elise would have done, pushing the boundaries of our friendship, testing my loyalty – one of the reasons I'd been glad to leave her behind after I graduated.

Recalling the aftermath had sent fresh guilt through me as I struggled to get comfortable on the sofa, grappling with all that she'd told me. *I owe her this* had been my last thought before drifting off, only to be woken abruptly by Elise in the kitchen, brimming with nervous energy as she set about 'coaching' me for my trip to Daisy's school.

Now, I forced down a mouthful of soft, buttery, lemon-scented sponge. 'It's delicious,' I said truthfully. 'Homemade?'

'I bake to relax.' Cecilia's sat opposite, the rings on her wedding finger chinking against her mug as she wrapped her hands around it. She was clearly intending to sit in on my interview – if that's what it was. Elise would call it a 'power move' but Cecilia was Daisy's grandmother, and clearly invested in the child's welfare. *You'd think she was her mother, the way she carries on.*

Looking at their expressions – Isaac's a mirror image of his mother's – it was hard to believe they were anything but genuine. I'd come across a handful of terrible parents during my years as a teacher, and none of them had been able to hide their intentions this well. But then again, I didn't know Isaac, or his family, and I no longer had faith in the instincts I'd prided myself on before meeting Leon.

'You're probably wondering why we want to keep Daisy at home,' Isaac began, palms pressed on the breakfast bar as if to steady himself. He swapped a look with his mother, who gave a gentle sigh.

'It's complicated.' She cast her eyes to the dark liquid

shimmering in her mug. 'There were a couple of bullying incidents at school that upset Daisy.' Another glance at Isaac. 'She was made fun of because of her mother having had a few . . . issues,' she said delicately.

*Remember, he's going to make out he's a widower, Rose. Less messy that way, more sympathy for him, and not too many questions.*

'I'm sorry,' I murmured, dabbing crumbs from my lips with a paper napkin Isaac produced like a magician. 'Poor Daisy.'

On cue, she rushed into the kitchen like a breath of warm air, trailed by a younger woman, obviously pregnant. One hand rested on her neat baby bump, the other in the small of her back.

'Hey,' she said coolly to Isaac, her blue gaze sliding over me like an ice cube. Her hair, blonde like her mother's but streaked with pink, was caught in a high, tight ponytail, her shoulders tense beneath a loose white shirt. Her stance was sturdy, bare feet planted wide, toenails neon-pink, but her face held none of the warmth that inhabited her brother's.

*Watch out for Lissa. She's a spiteful bitch.*

Lissa – the reason the family had insisted on using Elise's middle name, Ann.

*It was too confusing apparently, and I didn't mind being Ann . . .* Elise had paused then, as if caught by a painful memory. *A reinvention, I suppose.*

*Like playing a part.*

*Maybe.*

Daisy was clutching a half-eaten banana. She'd changed out of her school uniform into flower-patterned leggings and a denim tunic and seemed happier and more certain of herself, a rosy flush on her cheeks. The thought of the part I had to play in getting her away from the house made my insides quake.

Elise had a foolproof escape plan, which she'd outlined. Risky, but doable. There was a cabin in the woods somewhere remote that belonged to a friend. *Best if you don't know exactly where.*

'Can Rose see my bedroom?' Daisy asked.

'When we've finished talking, sweetheart.' Isaac spoke gently, giving his sister an imperceptible nod.

'Let's go into the garden.' Lissa held out a hand and Daisy took it, allowing herself to be led through the conservatory. Rocky followed, claws clicking on the tiles.

'My big sister, Lissa,' Isaac said, watching them go with a complicated look before switching his gaze back to me. I realised Lissa hadn't asked who I was. 'She lives here with her husband, Jonah.'

'We're a close family,' Cecilia added, following her grand-daughter's progress into the garden with an indulgent smile. 'I can't wait to be a grandma again.'

I nodded, not trusting myself to respond as a memory flashed up: two blue lines on a pregnancy stick, a dizzying surge of joy.

'So, tell us about yourself, Rose. How did you end up in Buckinghamshire?' Isaac seemed to relax, finally picking up his mug and taking a sip, watching me over the rim as he leaned against the counter. 'I don't think you're local.'

My smile felt strained. I'd thought my accent was barely detect-able these days, but he'd clearly picked up on something.

'I was raised in Scotland.' No need to mention the move to Derbyshire to live with my aunt and uncle after my parents died. I cleared my throat. 'How about you?'

'Mum was born and raised in Iceland but met my dad in London when she was working as an admin assistant for the summer at the university where he taught,' Isaac said. 'Mum never went back, though we spent a lot of summers over there with my grandparents.'

'My husband was an art historian, quite a bit older than me.' Cecilia's face clouded. 'He died fifteen years ago.'

'I'm sorry.'

Isaac's face flickered. 'We miss him.'

Surprised by his openness, I said, 'I get it. I lost my parents when I was very young.'

'That's sad.' Cecilia reached a hand out though it didn't quite meet mine. 'No one should grow up without their mother.'

'I was lucky in a way,' I said, struck by the irony of her comment. Wasn't depriving Daisy of her mother exactly what the family had done? 'My mum's sister and her husband took me in. They had – have – a little farm in Derbyshire, with lots of animals, and open spaces. Lot of love to give, so—'

'Derbyshire?' Isaac's eyes were questioning. My heart gave a hard thump as I realised my mistake. 'My wife's mother lived there.'

# Chapter 5

'It's a small world,' I said lightly, though my breathing had grown shallow. He'd said his mother-in-law lived in Derbyshire, not *that's where my wife grew up*. Maybe Elise had made out she grew up in Kenya, or New York, or somewhere else exotic, always keen to distance herself from Ingrid. 'I go back to visit quite often.'

Derbyshire – specifically Ripley – was where Elise and I had met, on our first day at sixth form college, when she made a beeline for me and demanded to know if my hair was naturally straight.

I tried to maintain a look of polite interest, but Isaac had moved on. 'As we said, things have been tricky for Daisy. We think having her home for a while will be better for her, emotionally.'

Still his comment about his wife's mother living in Derbyshire reverberated in my head. Could he be subconsciously looking for a link between me and Elise – or Ann, as they knew her – or was my guilty conscience finding connections that didn't exist?

Despite his smiles and apparently relaxed demeanour, Isaac might be suspicious of the woman who had mysteriously turned up at his daughter's school and accepted his interview offer too readily.

Aware of his and Cecilia's scrutiny, I managed a tiny nod. 'I teach primary school children so that shouldn't be too difficult, but Daisy might miss interaction with her own age group?' It sounded like the right thing to say.

'She's struggled since the bullying, and once the baby comes she'll have a ready-made friend.'

*Hardly.* Daisy might love having a baby cousin but wouldn't be able to talk to or play with him or her.

'There's another reason we want to keep her close.'

Cecilia shot Isaac a warning look, but he either didn't see or chose to ignore it.

'Oh?' I was curious about what he would come out with. *You have to remember everything he says, Rose, and take it with a great big pinch of salt.*

He rubbed a hand over his beard. 'There was someone hanging around recently, both here and outside the school.' A look entered his eyes that was hard to turn away from – a fierce intentness, as if picturing a terrible scenario involving his daughter. 'Daisy's very trusting, despite stranger-danger warnings. If someone, especially a woman, spoke to her nicely, she might go off with them.'

*Especially if it was her mother.* Elise hadn't mentioned visiting the house, or Daisy's school, but maybe this happened a while ago. 'You think someone's targeting her?' It sounded like the result of an overactive imagination, but there was no denying the gravity of Isaac's voice, or the way Cecilia's hand moved to cover her heart. 'Why?'

'There are all sorts of strange people about. It's better to be on the safe side,' she said quietly. Her cheeks looked hollow without a smile to prop them up. 'We've just had security cameras installed outside.'

I remembered what Elise had said about there being cameras everywhere and feeling watched. 'Do you have them inside too?'

Isaac shook his head. 'We haven't gone that far, and anyway, we're hoping to move in the not too distant future.' Unease flared. He was clearly banking on Elise never returning if he was planning to sell the house. A smile warmed Isaac's eyes. 'And I'm sure Daisy's completely safe.'

'Absolutely.' Cecilia's smile returned too, but with a trace of anxiety.

Brain spinning, I struggled for the right response. 'Have you informed the police if you think someone's been hanging around?'

Another look was exchanged that I couldn't interpret.

'We don't think it's necessary,' Isaac said firmly. 'Honestly, I just wanted to explain my reasons for taking Daisy out of school.'

'OK, well . . . thank you.'

'We probably seem a bit overprotective of Daisy.'

'Well, I'm sure it's natural.' *When her mother is out there and desperately wants her back.*

'You would need to keep a close eye on her.' Cecilia had put down her mug, her slice of cake untouched. She laced her fingers tightly. 'She's very precious to us.'

'Of course.' I glanced from her to Isaac, feeling as if the walls were closing in. 'But you said you were looking for someone to home-school Daisy, not act as a security guard.'

'Oh God, no, nothing as drastic as that.' Isaac stepped up to the breakfast bar, palms up. 'It's just that, as well as the schooling, it would be great to have someone around to help look after Daisy, to live in even, if that's something you would consider.'

Elise had told me Isaac had wanted to employ a full-time nanny for ages, but she'd resisted. They'd tried it when Daisy was a baby, and Elise believed Isaac had slept with her.

*He was looking for someone to replace me once he'd got rid of me, someone Daisy would have got used to.*

'I . . . don't have any experience of looking after children.' Another flashback, to my failed pregnancy. *A little girl.*

'But you're a teacher.' Isaac smiled. 'You've looked after lots of children.'

'Not in their homes.'

'It's only one child, and she's adorable.'

He was selling it well, but I made myself say, 'I don't know.'

Cecilia was watching me closely and I wondered what she saw. 'Don't you look after Daisy?' I asked her.

'I've been helping out since . . .' She looked down at her hands, as if recalling a painful subject – the supposed death of her daughter-in-law, no doubt – then raised her head. 'But I have to get back to my own life. I work, you see, or I used to. I'd like to get back to it.'

I tried to hide my surprise by nodding slowly. When Elise had said the family lived here, she'd implied they were homeless and jobless. 'I didn't realise.'

'Why would you?' Her smile was slightly strained. 'I'm not ready to retire yet and besides, I love my work.'

'And she'll be even busier when Lissa has the baby.' Isaac slid a glance in the direction of the garden. 'And Lissa won't be available at a moment's notice anymore.' His gaze was optimistic.

'Of course.' I kept nodding, hoping I was giving the impression of taking it all in, considering my options.

'Will you at least think about it?'

Something occurred to me. 'What if I hadn't pitched up at the school today?'

'He's been putting the word round for a while, but no takers so far.' Cecilia brushed a scattering of crumbs into her palm and dropped them on her plate. 'That's probably why he pounced on you.'

'I pounced on him, actually.' My face warmed up as I realised how it sounded. 'I was thinking of applying for a job at the school and asked Isaac about its reputation.'

'You're not working at the moment?'

'No, I'm . . . new to this area, still settling in.'

'No partner?' Cecilia's eyes skimmed my ring finger, as I suspected Isaac's had done already.

I shook my head. 'I'm happily single,' I said, treading down a freeze-framed image of Leon's face the last time I'd seen him, as a police officer snapped handcuffs around his wrists. 'And Daisy's mother . . . ?' I let the question hang, hoping to force an answer.

Isaac's gaze dimmed. He looked at his mother, a tense energy pulsing between them, before snatching up his mug and placing it in the sink. 'My wife—'

'Isaac's a widower,' Cecilia cut in, a hand reaching across the surface between us again, as if to restrain me this time. 'It's difficult for him to talk about.'

Her words shot adrenaline through me. Elise had been right. Her husband had effectively killed her off and yet . . . weren't they concerned, if I was going to agree to look after Daisy, that I would discover it wasn't true? That there hadn't been a funeral – that up until a few months ago, Elise had been living in his house, very much alive?

My heart thudded crazily, and it was an effort to keep my voice steady. 'I'm so sorry for your loss. I understand that you don't want to talk about it.' *I could do this,* I told myself. I could get Daisy away from these people. 'Daisy must miss her mother.'

That strange tension again. It was obvious they were holding back, not telling the truth by some unspoken mutual agreement. Then I caught the sheen of tears in Cecilia's eyes. She seemed genuinely upset. Maybe what they were doing didn't sit well with her. Despite Elise's description of Cecilia, she wasn't coming across as heartless, or someone who would want her daughter-in-law out of the way. But what did I know?

Isaac swung round, making me jump. 'Where did you work before?' He'd composed himself, and I launched into an outline of my time at Chesterfield Primary, hardly needing to force enthusiasm when it was obvious how much I'd loved working there.

'Teaching sounds like a vocation for you,' Cecilia said approvingly, clearly won over. 'Their loss is our gain.'

'She hasn't said yes yet, Mum.' Isaac gave me a friendly eye-roll. 'How about that tour of the house if we haven't scared you off?'

'Good idea.' Cecilia climbed down off her chair. 'I'll let Daisy know she can show you her room.'

'Lovely.' I returned a diluted version of Isaac's smile.

'This is a lot, I know,' he said. 'I promise it won't be as intense as this if you join us. It'll be nice to have someone new around.' *Was he flirting?* Elise had mentioned an affair, that he couldn't resist an attractive female, but I could only detect the same, hopeful friendliness in his face. It was almost as if he believed his own lie about his wife's death.

Before I could fashion a reply, Daisy was rushing through the conservatory trailed by Lissa, whose mouth was set in a narrow line.

'Do you want to see my doll's house, Rose? Great-Granpy made it for me.'

'My father, over in Iceland,' Cecilia said. 'He's a furniture maker or was. He's in his nineties now, but still loves whittling wood.'

'I'd like that a lot.' My spirits lifted at the sight of Daisy's shining face. How Elise must miss her. No wonder she was in such a state, probably pacing my house right now, racked with worry about how I was doing, whether I was playing my part. 'How clever of your Great-Granpy.'

As I followed Isaac out of the kitchen, Daisy leading the way with delighted giggles, clearly enjoying being the centre of attention, a hand closed around my wrist.

Startled, I turned to meet Lissa's disdainful stare. 'Don't get too comfortable.' Her voice was low, though Cecilia was in the garden with the dog, Isaac and Daisy out of earshot in the hallway.

'What do you mean?'

'You don't fool me.' Her voice was like a knife. 'I know exactly why you're here.'

# Chapter 6

My limbs shook with relief as I drove away from Orchard House, Isaac's parting words resounding in my ears.

*We're looking forward to you becoming part of the family, Rose.*

All the way back to Chesham, I checked my rear-view mirror in case he'd decided to follow me, still shell-shocked it had happened – that I really was moving in tomorrow and becoming Daisy's home-teacher and nanny – for a week, at least.

I had the sense I could have stayed if I hadn't needed to go home and pack some things, his relief palpable when, at the front door, Daisy's warm hand in mine, I'd said, 'I would love to be Daisy's teacher.'

'And my friend,' she'd piped up, eyes brimming with faith in a way that melted my insides.

'And your friend.' I hadn't meant to say it, mindful of Elise's warning not to get too close, that in a week's time she would be taken away, so it was best not to form too strong an attachment.

*Obviously you won't in that short space of time, but she's really cute.*

'You can always go home at weekends,' Isaac had said as he walked me to my car, after I explained I'd been renting my home while I explored my options and suggested driving to Orchard House every morning. 'But I'd honestly prefer you to be on the premises during the week. I sometimes work late, and I have a project on the go that eats up a bit of time at the moment. I don't want to keep relying on family.'

I hadn't even thought to ask whether he worked, part of my mind still reeling from Lissa's loaded comment in the kitchen, where my throat had seized up as her eyes tracked mine.

'Why, of all people, did you approach my brother?' she'd demanded to know.

'I suppose because he was the only one standing on his own, not talking to anyone.' The words had felt raspy as I'd wrenched my arm from her grasp. 'It was an impulse.'

'An impulse to approach a good-looking single dad, with a really sweet daughter and a big old house?'

The balloon of fear in my chest had deflated. So that was what Lissa's antagonism was about. She thought I was after her brother.

Finding a spark of anger, I'd said, 'Firstly, this isn't a romcom, life doesn't work like that, and secondly, how would I know who your brother is?'

'You probably heard he wanted to take Daisy out of school and jumped at the chance to worm your way in.'

*Wow.* 'Well, for a start, I don't live around here, and I can promise you, I'm not looking for a relationship.' I'd broken eye contact for the lie that was coming. 'And I'd never heard of Isaac before today.'

Heart thrumming, I'd moved into the hall to see Daisy sitting halfway up the stairs, Isaac leaning over the banister rail at the top.

'I thought you'd got lost,' he'd said, looking past me at Lissa, a cloud of annoyance passing over his face. 'I hope my sister hasn't been putting you off.'

I hadn't dared to turn around to see her expression. It had seemed ironic she was treating me as some sort of gold-digger when she and her husband must be living at Orchard House rent-free. 'Not at all,' I'd said smoothly, hurrying to meet Daisy, who immediately tugged me towards her bedroom.

Now, as I pulled the car down Chandlers Road and stopped outside number seven, I wished I could turn back time, not just to before the call from Elise, but further back, when it looked as though my life might turn out differently.

A glimpse of Elise at the downstairs window slammed me back to reality. She must be going out of her mind with worry. We'd agreed it would be better to have no phone contact that would connect us.

No one had seen her arrive at my house, she'd assured me. The call she made to my mobile had been deleted. She had used an old model she intended to get rid of once she had Daisy back and hadn't revealed the number. *As far as anyone is concerned, right now, you haven't heard from me in years. There won't be any evidence of pre-planning.*

My immediate fear had been getting arrested once it became clear I'd failed to prevent Daisy being 'snatched' by her mother while in my care, but she assured me it wouldn't happen. *Just play the innocent, Rose. You're just as much a victim. Play your part and you'll be OK, I promise. They'll feel sorry for you.*

An image of Isaac on his knees, moving the tiny figures in Daisy's doll's house while putting on funny voices to make her laugh was at the forefront on my mind as I let myself into the house. Already, it smelt different – felt different. No longer just me, taking up space with my comforting routines, moving around the rooms like a ghost, walking into town occasionally to remind myself I wasn't the only person on the planet.

As I removed my jacket and shoes, braced for Elise's questions, I felt a fierce longing for my aunt and uncle, who had been such a strong and steady presence after my parents died. Sarah would be shocked by what I was doing. The thought was sobering.

Elise appeared in the living room doorway, arms wrapped around herself, still wearing the dressing gown she'd been in when

I left – *my* dressing gown – though she must have showered, as her hair hung in damp strands around her face. 'How did it go?'

Her eyes had the fevered brightness of an overtired child, or maybe she'd been crying. Either way, a burst of sympathy burned off my unease.

'It was OK . . . I think.' My mind buzzed with everything that had taken place, trying to arrange it into some kind of order. 'Daisy's fine,' I said, knowing that would be the first thing she wanted to hear. 'She seemed to like me.'

'That's good.' But instead of the relief I'd expected, irritation flashed over Elise's face. 'What did he say?'

Hanging up my bag with my jacket, I chose my words wisely. Of course she would be keen to know whether her plan had worked. 'I'm in,' I said, aware of sounding like an actor in a spy drama. 'He came across as really friendly and, like you said, asked almost straight away if I would be interested in home-schooling Daisy.'

'He interviewed you right there, in the playground?'

'No, at the house.'

She was nodding, teeth digging into her lower lip, no doubt picturing the scene. *Her* house, a home she'd clearly loved.

'It's beautiful,' I said, wanting to take some of the strain from her face, recalling the large, tastefully decorated rooms I'd peered into once Daisy had agreed that Isaac could show me around. 'It doesn't seem fair that you've left.'

'I don't care about the house.' Hearing the snap in Elise's voice, I realised I was focusing on material things instead of her child. I decided not to mention Cecilia's comment about selling up or tell Elise what had crossed my mind as Daisy ran into each room upstairs, pointing out this and that – *My auntie Lissa sleeps in the room down there with Uncle Jonah, but you can sleep in this room, Rose. It has pink flowers on the wallpaper like in a garden, and it's opposite my room* – which was that Daisy would miss living there, and it might be cruel to uproot her from the home and people she loved, even if it meant being reunited with her mother – a mother who, the whole time I was there, she hadn't referred to once.

Blinking away an image of the comfortable, bright bedroom with en-suite bathroom that Isaac had said was mine if I wanted it, the window framing a stunning view of the garden, I realised Elise was standing in front of me, her bony shoulders hunched.

'I know what you're thinking.'

'Sorry?'

'He's got to you, like I said he would. His mother too, probably.' A gust of breath that smelt of bitter coffee. 'I bet there was homemade lemon cake. She loves showing off her baking skills.'

'There was,' I admitted, feeling foolish. I *had* been taken in. Isaac and Cecilia had been so friendly. 'His sister warned me off, though.' My face felt too warm, as if the heating was on high. Inching past Elise, I touched the radiator and snatched my fingers away. It was red-hot. 'She practically accused me of throwing myself at him.'

'Hah!' It was a laugh of vindication. 'That sounds about right.'

'You didn't mention she was pregnant.'

'Didn't I?'

Turning, I saw Elise's face was tense and pale and cursed myself for being insensitive, reminding her she had a child of her own she was currently separated from. 'Sorry, it's not important.'

'At least Lissa's honest about her feelings.' Elise had clearly decided to move on. 'I can almost respect her for that.'

In the kitchen, which looked even gloomier with its small window, dated cabinets and vinyl flooring after the splendour of Orchard House, I switched on the kettle, noticing a trail of crumbs on the worktop, a knife jammed into the butter. Resisting the urge to tidy up, glad Elise had eaten something – wondering whether she'd gone through my drawers and cupboards while I was out – I settled for rinsing my hands at the sink before turning to look at her. 'Well, you'll be pleased to know you were right about everything and I'm moving in there tomorrow,' I said, with forced jollity.

She pressed her fingers to her lips, her tearful gaze locked on mine. She was shaking, and I remembered how she'd always felt 'chilly' – often requesting I feel her hands or touch her cheek to prove it.

'Thank you, Rose.' Her voice was tremulous, and her shoulders sagged as though the tension was leaving her body. 'You don't know how much this means to me.'

'Anyone would feel the same in your situation,' I said, feeling a warm spread of satisfaction. I'd let Elise down badly in the past, but here was my chance to make it up to her in a way that really mattered.

Her fingers moved to fiddle with the belt of the dressing gown. 'Did they mention me?'

'Cecilia told me that Isaac is a widower, and it was difficult for him to talk about, which I took to mean I shouldn't mention you again. No one said how you supposedly died.'

'Carbon-monoxide poisoning.' Her words gave me an unpleasant jolt. 'The old heater in the summerhouse where I used to sleep overnight sometimes. He came in once and switched it on, thinking I'd drunk myself into a stupor. That was the night I knew I had to leave.'

Horror passed through me. 'That's terrible.' I wanted to press for more details, but her eyes shimmered with tears, and I sensed how close she was to losing control. 'Didn't you consider going to the police then?'

She closed her eyes, as if hiding her irritation that I kept bringing up the police. 'No proof,' she said. 'My word against his, at least for now.'

She'd already mentioned that she wanted me to look for, among other things, her journal, which she'd been unable to find before leaving Orchard House. *Everything's in there.*

Elise shifted to the drop-down table in the corner and leaned her hip against it. The dressing gown gaped, revealing her thin, white legs and I felt a surge of compassion.

'There was a photo of you though.'

Her head snapped up. 'What?'

'Well, a photo of you and Daisy,' I amended. 'On a shelf in Daisy's bedroom, next to a rainbow-coloured unicorn.' I smiled at the memory of the cuddly toy, its bright colours reflected in her duvet cover and the curtains at the window.

'Right.' Elise's colour had faded, her lips pinched. 'I'm surprised it's still there when they would like Daisy to forget her mother ever existed.'

'I'm sure they don't want that.' But I was remembering how Isaac's eyes had grazed the picture, the way his jaw had clenched as if it was painful to look at.

'Can you bring it?' Elise's eyes brightened. 'With the other things?'

'Oh, I . . . I don't know, Elise.' The other things were Daisy's passport – she'd grabbed her own but didn't have time to retrieve Daisy's, which she'd hidden – a cookbook that had belonged to her grandmother, and a pair of lost earrings. *I took them out because they were pinching. I was in the garage, getting something out of the freezer, and dropped them when Cecilia crept up on me. She told me the freezer was a good place to hide a body. I'll never forget the look on her face.*

'OK, forget the photo – it doesn't matter,' she said, in a way that suggested it did.

'I'll try,' I promised.

'Oh, Rose.' Her voice was clotted with tears. 'I know I'm asking a lot of you, especially after not seeing you for so long. Look, I don't care about my clothes, or anything else, but it would be nice to have a couple of keepsakes, that's all.'

It was on the tip of my tongue to say that Daisy was all she needed, but I couldn't bear to see her crying again. 'It's fine,' I said. 'I get it.'

'Do you, Rose?' Her eyes were hard, probing mine. 'Do you really?'

I squashed a surge of foreboding. 'Yes,' I said. 'I do.'

# Chapter 7

'Come and look at what I did bring with me.' Elise's expression relaxed. 'I meant to show you last night, but I was too tired.'

I'd almost forgotten that about her; the way her emotions seesawed, sad one minute, giggly the next, rarely anything in between, but she had good reason to be all over the place right now. I wondered what sort of mother she was, tried to picture her with Daisy. I imagined she was fun, prone to impulsive trips out and ice-cream treats before bed, whereas Isaac would be steadier, more disciplined with his daughter, but gentle too, from what I'd seen.

*Gentle.* Not a word Elise had used to describe him, but maybe his difficult side had been reserved for his wife.

I needed a drink and made us each a mug of tea, which I carried through and placed on the worn wooden table in front of the fireplace. Outside, the sky was golden with late afternoon sunshine. My neighbour, an elderly woman I'd only ever smiled at in passing, would be setting out for a walk, as she did around this time every day.

I felt like I'd entered an alternative world, seeing Elise rummage through her canvas holdall, plucking out clothes and discarding them, before holding aloft a framed photograph like a trophy. 'Remember this?' She shuffled over and handed it to me.

I crossed to the window to see it more clearly. It was a picture of us screaming on a roller coaster at Alton Towers – me with fear, Elise with exhilaration. The memory of that day was painted in bright colours in my mind. We'd skipped lessons, at Elise's insistence, something I'd never done before, and I'd been too worried about my aunt and uncle finding out to truly let myself go. Elise had been wild with excitement, demanding I try every ride, eat candyfloss and hotdogs, and *Have fun, for God's sake, Rose. You only live once!* She was sick on the coach on the way home and got into trouble because she'd stolen the money to go from her mother's purse.

Elise had wanted the image and paid for it when we got off the ride. I marvelled at how carefree we looked, how young, my hair longer, hers shorter, but it didn't show the true story of that day. I handed it back with a forced smile. 'I'm surprised you kept it,' I said. 'Do you have any of Daisy when she was a baby?'

She looked disappointed for a second, as though she'd wanted a bigger reaction, then stuffed the picture back and reached for a purse on the floor. She opened it and pulled out a photo that looked tattered, as though handled many times, holding it up in front of me without speaking.

'She's lovely.' My heart twisted at the sight of a baby Daisy, lying on a changing mat in a snow-white romper suit, hands seeming to reach for the camera. 'She's definitely got your eyes.' The picture was replaced, again in silence. Elise's chin quivered and she sniffed. Close to tears myself, I decided to change the subject.

'How did you meet Isaac?' I picked up my mug of tea. 'Where did you get married?'

'I don't want to talk about him.' Her vehemence was alarming after the silence. 'I don't even want to think about that man, to have him in my head.'

'Of . . . of course. Elise, I'm sorry.' I put my mug by my feet and reached out to her. 'I just thought it would help to know as much about him as possible.'

'He doesn't matter.' She grasped my hand in both of hers, face contorting. 'You know, I'll pay you for what you're doing, Rose. I don't think I mentioned that before.'

I pulled back, shocked. 'Elise, I don't want your money.'

'Why not?' Her face smoothed out. 'Teaching's not that well paid.'

'I still have enough to live on.' It was a reminder about the life insurance pay-out after my parents' death and money from the sale of their house – my home. The account had been heavily dipped into over the years – paying for my education, the accommodations I'd shared while teacher training in London, travelling, the house I bought when I returned – but there was enough left to get by without working for a while. 'Anyway, it's the least I can do.'

I wondered whether she would pursue it, bring up that awful time I'd let her down, but her gaze flicked away without acknowledgement.

'Listen, are you sure you'll be able to get away safely?' I persisted. 'Once Isaac calls the police they'll be checking sea and airports, looking for a woman and a little girl. You could easily be found.'

'Do you think I haven't thought this through?' Her eyes rounded, pupils like pinpricks. 'I've planned every tiny detail. I've thought of nothing else for months.' She paused, fingertips pressed together. 'Trust me, Rose – we'll be fine, as long as you can get Daisy to me.'

The pressure weighed heavily.

'What would you have done if I'd said no?' I hadn't meant to ask, and already knew the answer before she opened her mouth.

'I knew you'd feel like you owed me after what happened.' *So, she had understood.* Her hand cupped my knee and seemed to burn my skin. 'Not that I want you feel that way.' She cocked her head, her gaze pleading. 'I forgave you a long time ago, Rose.'

*Forgave you.* I thought how furious Sarah would be to hear Elise say that. *It wasn't your fault,* she had said at the time. *People*

42

*who try to make you feel guilty resent you and want to hurt you.*
*It's emotional blackmail.*

Even so, the effect had been a shroud of guilt I'd carried around and Elise was right: I *did* feel I owed her. Perhaps once I'd returned her daughter, we would be even.

'And I know you always want to do the right thing.'

It was something she'd mocked me about in the past. My sense of fair play, of never letting unethical or unprofessional behaviour go unchallenged. *Why don't you become a prosecution lawyer, Rose, and then you can put all the bad guys in prison?*

I was never sure why that side of me annoyed her so much. It had made me realise she didn't understand me very well.

After an edgy pause, Elise suggested I order in a pizza, which we ate together on the sofa, washed down with a couple of glasses of wine from a bottle I'd bought when I moved in but never opened – drinking alone felt dangerous. We stuck to safe topics for the next few hours. I caught her up with my life, making her smile with some exaggerated anecdotes from the school where I'd worked, and some of the terrible dates I'd been on. Elise stuck to reminiscing, bright-eyed, about being at university – me at London Metropolitan, while she studied drama at South Bank university – as though she wished she could go back, though I knew she hadn't been particularly happy there, and she'd struggled to make friends.

She told me about a few acting jobs she'd had, one in a West End play that I'd heard of, though she only had a small part.

'It felt like the start of something, but when I was beaten to a film role I really wanted, I thought it was time to give up and work behind the scenes. I'd got the money from my father by then, and could have sat about doing nothing, but I went to New York and bagged some theatre work. Terrible pay, but I enjoyed it.'

I wondered how she'd met Isaac but was worried about spoiling the mood. All the same, I couldn't resist saying, 'Isaac doesn't seem your type.' She'd always gone for 'bad boys' falling instantly in love, even though they always let her down.

43

'I suppose I fancied a change,' she said, face darkening. 'More fool me.' After a second of awkward silence, she said, 'You never met anyone serious?'

Instantly, I was back at my aunt and uncle's the day Leon came to value their farmhouse. Sarah had developed a yearning to move to the seaside and wondered how much their house was worth, though the move never happened. When I dropped by after work he was in the kitchen with Sarah, sampling her latest attempt at baking.

'These are good,' he'd said through a mouthful, holding up a half-eaten square of charred chocolate and flour, before washing it down with a swig of strong tea. 'Your aunt's a good baker.'

*He's kind,* I'd thought, liking him, though Sarah wasn't fooled. After one dinner date became two, then three, and I'd started spending the night at the spacious flat he'd told me was his, and I hadn't visited my aunt and uncle for a while, she said, *He's too intense, Rose. He's not what you need. We're worried about you.*

'There was someone, for a while,' I said, aware Elise was waiting for a reply and that my shoulders had stiffened with tension. 'I thought he was good for me because he listened to podcasts and played cricket and watched documentaries about climate change.'

Leon Slater, the smiling, smooth-talking owner of Slater Properties, always smart in a suit and quirky tie, hair combed back in a thick, brown wave. He knew what he wanted and was keen to settle down and start a family with me.

Too keen, as it turned out, rushing to the next stage as if trying to secure a deal. Flattering, in some ways, then exhausting. Finally, frightening. I left him after ten months, but he talked me back. I left him again weeks later, but he wouldn't leave me alone, a bombardment of texts and emails, even letters, and hanging about outside the school, or my house in Finsbury Park, driving by, even shouting through the letterbox, alternately cajoling and furious. No one left Leon Slater. Any woman would be lucky to have him – only he didn't want any woman, just me.

It stopped for a month when I got the police involved, but soon started up again, as if I was an unfinished project he couldn't let go of. I met his family once, and tiny alarm bells sounded when he introduced me as his future wife and mother of his children, and his own mother – a barrister – and doctor father had looked at me unimpressed and his older brother, a surgeon, said darkly, 'You know it's not a competition, Leo.' I knew there were dynamics at work I didn't understand. He'd been angry when we left, though he swore it was nothing to do with me.

The last straw had been discovering his apartment, the one I'd practically moved into, belonged to a friend living abroad for a couple of years. Leon couldn't see why I was upset that he'd lied, said his own place wasn't 'worthy' of me, that he didn't earn as much as he'd made out.

I didn't care about the money. I cared that I'd been deceived.

'It didn't work out,' I told Elise. I wouldn't mention that I still carried a canister of pepper spray in my bag, and that I'd taken self-defence classes – though whether I could ever fight off a thirteen-stone, six-foot man was debatable. Not that he'd shown signs of physical violence, but I wasn't taking any chances.

'I thought you'd have given in and had children by now.' Elise's voice broke up my troubled thoughts.

'I was pregnant for a bit.' The wine had loosened my tongue after all. 'Miscarriage at nearly five months.'

I'd woken in the night, certain Leon was at my front door, putting one of his pleading notes through the letterbox. I jumped out of bed with my phone, ready to call the police, and felt the trickle of blood down my thigh that became a gush, and a sudden pain low down that brought me to my knees.

The only person I had wanted was my mother. *Please, please hang on,* I'd repeated over and over through broken sobs as I drove myself to hospital. I hadn't wanted to call Sarah and drag her down from the farm, had played it down afterwards, though she'd been angry about that. *You shouldn't have gone through it on your own.*

Leon hadn't been near my house that night, he told me, when I forced myself to call him two days later to break the news that our baby was gone. He'd known for sure then I would never take him back. Not without a child to tie us together.

Elise reached out and stroked a strand of hair behind my ear. 'I'm sorry,' she said.

I'd found myself reminded of Elise once or twice during my time with Leon, realising he had that same need to cling and control, but where I'd seen it in her, I'd somehow been blind to it with Leon, at least for a while.

'But lucky for me, I guess.' Elise gave a lazy smile.

I couldn't tell whether she was trying to lighten the mood and decided not to pursue it. 'How did you like being pregnant?' I said. 'Any morning sickness?'

'I'm not going to talk about that.' Her face grew stern. 'Not when you've just told me you lost a baby.'

'What then?'

'I Spy?' It was a game she used to fall back on as a way of making me laugh, coming up with outlandish results I could never have guessed, like G for gusset. *I can see your knickers when you sit like that.*

By the time I went upstairs to pack, there was an almost celebratory feel in the air, a nervous excitement zipping between us as Elise said almost jauntily, 'We'll reconvene at breakfast to finalise plans,' before hugging me goodnight and whispering, 'Thank you, Rose.'

My resolve had strengthened. A mother and her child shouldn't be separated, no matter what. Daisy needed Elise as much as Elise needed her daughter, and I would do everything I could to make it happen.

# Chapter 8

## *Saturday*

'As it's the weekend, I thought it would be a good opportunity to settle in and spend some time with Daisy before lessons on Monday.'

I nodded, swallowing a ball of anxiety. 'Good idea.'

I was alone with Isaac at Orchard House. Cecilia had gone shopping and Lissa had taken Daisy to the park before she was due to pick up her husband from the airport.

'Jonah's mother lives in America and isn't well, so he's been to visit.'

I nodded, trying to square this information with the 'degenerate' Elise had mentioned.

'So, how did the school react to you removing Daisy?' I injected my words with confidence. 'It's a big step, especially in the middle of term.' During my time at Chesterfield Primary, a couple of children had been taken out, in both cases because they hadn't settled well. It had been hard to accept we couldn't handle their needs.

'It was fine; the head understands.' Isaac's manner was relaxed. 'I've spoken to her about it before and she knows how tough

Daisy's found it. She was reassured when I told her you were a teacher and suggested having a chat if you'd like that?'

'Of course.' It made sense, but I wanted as little interaction with people as possible while I was here. 'Oh, I brought this,' I said quickly, pulling the CV I'd printed out the night before from my laptop bag.

'He's probably looked me up online,' I'd fretted to Elise. 'He might think it's odd that someone my age isn't constantly on Twitter or Instagram.' I'd almost deleted my accounts after Leon, but a streak of resistance had stopped me. Even so, I hadn't posted anything since moving to Chesham. I didn't want him guessing where I was, or to put myself back on his radar.

'At least you have accounts,' Elise had said, in a way that told me she'd looked me up before. Of course she had. She'd probably kept tabs on me for years, while I'd barely given her a second thought once I'd dealt – or thought I'd dealt with – my guilt about her suicide attempt. 'And you're on LinkedIn, which is the important one in terms of your career.'

Luckily, despite my abrupt departure, the head of Chesterfield Primary had provided a good reference, saying she was sorry to see me go, and that I'd been an asset to the school – words that had fuelled my hatred of Leon, and despair at myself for letting him drive me away.

'It all looks great,' Isaac said, as his eyes skimmed the text in a way that suggested he wasn't taking it in. He must assume it was pointless for me to lie about my qualifications when he could easily check them with a phone call. 'You were obviously highly thought of.'

'Thanks, I . . . I was sorry to leave.'

'Why did you?'

*Stick to the script.* 'I needed a change.' Spoken firmly. 'Bad break-up, but I'm over it now.' Light laugh, accompanied by a glance around the living room we were standing in. 'This is even nicer than I remember.'

Dazzling sunshine poured through the window, interrogation-bright. The room was high-ceilinged with sturdy, mushroom-coloured walls that gave an air of generations having lived there before, hung with landscapes in heavy frames, and clusters of family photos – Daisy as a toddler with Isaac on a beach, dramatic clouds overhead, a formal black and white picture of Daisy in Cecilia's arms as a baby.

I looked for a wedding picture, something of Elise, but found nothing, no hint of her anywhere. Had she chosen the furniture, clearly bought for comfort; big, bouncy sofas in a soft shade of lilac, a creamy, deep-pile rug in front of the brick fireplace, that invited the touch of bare feet? Had she picked the flowers, spilling browning petals from a ceramic jug on top of the baby piano by the patio doors? I'd forgotten Elise played piano, and pictured her there, hair falling forward, slender fingers dancing over the keys, though she'd never taken it seriously when she was younger, forgoing music in favour of drama.

'Let me show you to your room.'

Isaac's voice startled me out of my discreet examination of a heap of *National Geographic* magazines stacked beneath the window, next to a basket filled with Daisy's toys. Elise had mentioned Isaac's love of mountains, so it seemed likely to be his choice of reading material.

The family were a puzzle I couldn't decipher. Elise hadn't been forthcoming with information about them beyond how they'd made her life a misery.

'Don't go playing detective while you're there, Rose,' she'd said, huddled into the baggy grey cardigan again as though she couldn't get warm, before I set off. 'Just bring me Daisy.'

'What if it doesn't work?'

'I have faith in you.' A smile had surfaced, though her eyes were ringed with tiredness. I doubted she'd slept any better than I had.

'And you'll be OK here on your own?' I'd felt a sudden pang at the thought of leaving the house that had been my sanctuary for the past few months, even if it hadn't exactly felt like home.

'You've got Netflix, there's plenty of food, and if I need anything else I can order it in.' She'd given me one of her fierce hugs followed by a gentle shove. 'Go,' she'd instructed, the word undercut with steel. 'It won't be for long.'

Next Friday morning, I was to offer to take Daisy to the park, to the café there, where Elise would be waiting. I was to go to the café toilet, telling Daisy to wait, and Elise would leave with her. I was to leave the café, behaving normally, giving them time to get away, before calling Isaac to raise the alarm.

'What if he doesn't want me taking Daisy to the park on my own.'

'He will because he'll trust you.' Elise had seemed completely certain of this. 'And it's Daisy's favourite place.' Her gaze had grown wistful. 'I used to love pushing her on the swings, higher and higher. It was our happy place.'

'But what if something goes wrong and we can't make it?'

'You have to make it happen, Rose. The flights are booked.'

We'd gone over it twice already.

'Daisy could be ill, or Isaac might have other plans.'

'Well, you'll have to think of something.' I'd homed in on her black-flecked irises as her eyes burned into mine. 'Our flight's at 6 p.m. so you'll have plenty of time.'

I'd nodded, stomach churning with nerves. 'Remember to lock up every night.'

'I'll lock up as soon as you've gone,' she'd said with a familiar touch of impatience.

'The latch on the back door doesn't always work properly. You have to give the bottom a bit of a kick.'

'Don't worry, Rose.' She'd rolled her eyes, in what I supposed she thought was an affectionate way that didn't quite come off.

'Should I tell my neighbour you're housesitting?'

'I'll tell her myself if she asks, which I'm sure she won't if you haven't spoken to her since you moved in.'

I'd checked no one was around before shoving my suitcase

into the back of the car, failing to hold back a tide of worry as I'd driven away.

Back in the present, I slipped past Isaac into the room that Daisy had said could be mine, taking in the king-sized bed with its mountain of plumped-up pillows and cushions, and the off-white walls that complemented the one behind the bed that was papered with blush-pink roses. The bank of mirrored wardrobes reflected us side by side, Isaac's face angled towards me as though checking my reaction, my own face plastered with a smile that looked genuine.

'It really is lovely,' I said, comparing it to the bedroom Elise had inhabited for the past couple of nights, where light struggled to infiltrate the small window that looked onto the road at the front, the furniture cheap and basic, home-assembled. 'Thank you.'

'It's not my choice of décor to be honest.' He scratched the back of his head with a rueful expression. 'My, er, wife was a fan of the country-garden look, if that's what you'd call it.'

I caught the stumble in his words, the almost imperceptible tightening of his features, and wondered what phase Elise had been going through when she chose the floral wallpaper, and the crimson, velvet curtains that skimmed the dark oak floorboards. Perhaps she'd thought she was providing Isaac with the kind of home he wanted, ignoring her own preferences.

'Have you lived here long?' I reached for my suitcase, which Isaac had insisted on carrying upstairs, pretending to buckle under its weight to make me smile.

'A few years,' he said easily. 'I won't miss it, if I'm honest.'

'Too many bad memories?' When he cut me a sharp look, I realised I'd chosen the wrong word. 'I meant sad,' I amended, face prickling. 'I'm sorry.'

'No worries.' His smile returned. 'When you're ready, come downstairs and have some lunch,' he said, not answering my question. 'You can tell me all about yourself, before the girls get back.'

*The girls.* It sounded so innocent and light.

He left with a friendly smile, bare feet pattering down the

stairs. When he'd answered the door earlier, face bright with welcome in a way that warmed my insides, I'd noted his casual outfit – khaki shorts and black T-shirt – and damp, tousled hair that suggested he hadn't been up long.

Nerves circled my stomach as I quickly unpacked, hanging my clothes in the empty wardrobe, pushing my underwear in the top drawer of a white-painted chest, mind circling all that I wanted to ask, and all that I had to do.

My hands shook as I dumped my toilet bag in the en suite, which was darkly tiled but cosy, pots of trailing ferns lining the windowsill, and a roomy shower I felt like diving under so I could wash away the grime I imagined coating my skin.

Aware Isaac was waiting downstairs, I checked my hair in the wardrobe mirrors, smoothed my fringe and tugged my long-sleeved top down over my trousers. Most of my clothes were practical, from my teaching days, but my tops were bright and patterned – flamingos in this case – to entertain the children.

*You don't need to dress up or pretend to be something you're not, Rose. You're female. That's enough for Isaac.*

Had he been having an affair? Another reason, perhaps, for wanting his wife out of the way, especially as she'd refused to divorce him?

There was no sign of Isaac downstairs, but as I passed the half-open door of the dining room, I heard his voice.

'As soon as you find out, let me know. It's important.'

I froze, arrested by his tone. Not friendly, but clipped and cold.

There was a response, tinny and faint on the other end of his phone call, but I couldn't make out the words. Scared he might walk out and catch me, I shot into the kitchen, pulse racing.

Rocky, lying in a puddle of sunlight near the industrial-sized oven, heaved to his feet and walked to the back door, casting me a pleading look. I opened it, and he ambled into the garden, lifting his leg against the base of a pot frothing with herbs.

I spun around, intending to put the kettle on, make myself

useful, trying to work out whether Isaac's call could be linked to Elise. What if he'd set someone after her, to track her down? Or perhaps it was simply a work call.

As I forced air into my lungs, my gaze landed on a row of cookbooks lined up beneath the cabinets. The title Elise had asked me retrieve leapt out: *The Art of Cooking* by Linda Merriweather.

Checking I was still alone, I slid it out, shoulder blades rigid with tension. On the inside cover were the words, ***To my darling Annelise, I hope you find it useful. Love Mummy xxx***

The book given to Elise's grandmother by her mother and passed down to Elise, who had been named after her.

How could I possibly sneak it into my suitcase? I couldn't do it now. It was too big to slip under my top, and anyway, it might be missed, the sort of detail Cecilia would pick up on, even if no one else did.

I sild it back with fumbling fingers, pausing as I spotted a notepad wedged by a fruit bowl filled with grapes, bananas, and apples – the sort used to jot down shopping lists. The words, neatly written in black ink, wobbled in front of my eyes.

*Rose Carpenter, 33*
*Born?*
*School?*
*Parents?*
*Boyfriend?*
*Work history?*
*No social media presence since last year – why???*

Light-headed, I crossed to the sink, gripping the porcelain as I tried to calm my breathing. Was it an innocent list of questions designed to get to know me better, or was someone suspicious and wanted to catch me out?

Sensing Isaac's approach, I turned, arranging my mouth into a smile. 'So,' I said brightly, as he entered the kitchen. 'What would you like to know?'

# Chapter 9

It didn't take long to run through the history of my life, edited, but not so much that red flags would be raised.

No siblings or living grandparents, mother and father killed in a car accident on holiday when I was eleven, which was tragic, yes, but as I'd said the day before, my aunt – Mum's older sister, Sarah – and her husband Roy had taken me in and looked after me like the daughter they'd never had.

No need to mention my parents' holiday had been a make-or-break trip after months of arguing over the long hours my father worked as a GP, and Mum's suspicion he'd been seeing another woman – arguments I'd listened to with my ear pressed to my bedroom carpet, face wet with tears – or how my life had fractured when Sarah, looking after me while they were away, came into my bedroom and broke the news of their fatal accident, or how I'd convinced myself they must have been having a row and that's why my father wasn't concentrating. He'd been driving on the wrong side of the road.

No need to tell Isaac how, for months, I'd longed to step back into the past when my mother was alive and happy, my father the man I'd looked up to. How I'd yearned to be back in the house in Scotland, but when I returned with Sarah had found too

54

many memories there, and visiting the graveyard where they were buried, I kept flashing back to the funeral, and the knot of people crying and clutching each other, and me. I couldn't wait to leave.

Thank God for Sarah, no children of her own, but who had an innate understanding of how to be a mum. For a long time, life had felt unreal, insubstantial, like a dream I couldn't wake up from, but Sarah – even while grieving the loss of her younger sister – had made it valid again, given me structure and warmth, an abundance of love, and brought back the colour and sound. There would always be a well of grief at my core, that my parents would never witness my journey to adulthood, but Sarah had made me – almost – whole again.

'I suppose I was a bit odd in that I loved going to school,' I told Isaac, skipping over the early days after my parents' funeral, starting somewhere new, when I'd felt apart from everyone else, inhabiting a different space, and had focused on lessons instead, until I was top of the class in every subject. 'I enjoyed learning new things; it gave me a buzz. I had some great teachers, too. I was lucky.' *Lucky.*

I supposed I had been, in a way. I'd settled, made friends, which boosted my confidence through to sixth form college, where I met Elise, and on to university in London, where I'd met new people that Elise had resented because they took me away from her.

Better not to think about Elise in case I inadvertently gave something away.

'How about you?' I said quickly, my mind flicking back to the list of questions I'd seen, wishing I'd had the nerve to mention it and make a joke, instead of accepting his proffered invitation to sit in the conservatory while he made some coffee. 'I didn't ask what you do for a living.'

He brought his mug to his lips, seeming to consider my question. He was perched on the edge of a rattan chest, while I practically melted into the cushions of a wood-framed sofa in an effort to appear relaxed.

'I used to be a bit of an adventurer,' he said, after a swig of his coffee. 'Mountaineering mostly – and I was a ski instructor for a few years. Not exactly a career, but as long as I had enough money to get by, I didn't mind.' He shrugged. 'I gave it up when I met my wife and got married, turned to writing, something I'd done in between the other stuff.'

'Fiction?'

He nodded. 'Commercial, adventure, with a bit of crime. Drawing on experience, I suppose. Not the crime part, I hasten to add.' His mouth twisted into a smile. 'I had a bit of success with my hero, Scott Ripley.' He said it in a film announcer voice. 'I based him on my great-grandfather, who was a polar explorer.'

'Impressive.'

'My great-grandfather?'

'Both,' I said, smiling in spite of myself. 'Maybe I'll read your book.'

His smile faded. 'There was going to be a series but I kind of dried up. Things weren't going so well at home and after Daisy was born . . . my wife struggled a bit, so I became a sort of house-husband, I suppose.'

'So . . . you don't work?'

'Well, I've actually finished a new book recently and have sent it to my old agent, so I'm waiting to hear from her.'

'That's great.' So Elise's disappearance had reignited his creativity? Maybe he'd incorporated a dead wife into his plot.

'And I'm pretty involved with an indoor ski centre I set up a few years ago, though it's taken a long time to get up and running.'

'Indoor skiing?' I'd noticed the way his face had lit up. 'Is it as good as the real thing?'

'It's pretty close actually, proper snow and everything.'

I decided to leave that for now. 'Do you miss the mountaineering?'

'Nah.' He put down his mug, rested his elbows on his knees. 'A friend was killed climbing Everest. It was a bit of a wake-up call. I don't want to be risking my life. I want to be around for Daisy.'

'Of course.'

'The ski centre, Snow Zone, also offers disadvantaged teenagers the chance to learn for free, gives them somewhere to go and keep out of trouble.'

'That sounds . . . great.' It did. Commendable. Wanting to be close to his daughter *and* help young people? To someone who didn't know better, he sounded almost saintly.

'Trouble is, although we have a couple of generous donors, we mostly rely on fund-raising to keep going. There's no government grant, and although we've had some lottery funding, it's not a regular thing.' He spread his hands. 'If this book deal comes though, it'll be a massive relief, and once I sell the house . . .' He glanced around. 'I don't need a place this size for me and my daughter, and money left over from the sale can be put to good use.'

*Money that Elise was surely entitled to a share of.* It was as if Isaac truly believed his wife was dead, and that what belonged to them both was his alone. 'It must be frustrating,' I said, tracing a fingertip around the rim of my mug. 'Not to be able to immediately do what you want.'

His gaze sharpened in a way that made me catch my breath. It was the first time in months I'd been alone in a man's company, and I hadn't felt threatened until now. Isaac was looking at me in a way that made the hairs on my arms stand up.

'Sorry,' he said, standing abruptly and crossing to the open door, filling the frame so I couldn't see past him. 'You sounded like someone else for a moment.'

*Elise.* I didn't speak for a moment, a pulse beating in my throat. I straightened, pulling my top away from my skin. It was another warm day, sun pounding through the glass conservatory, so it felt like a greenhouse. 'I imagine it's tough being the boss.'

'It's the business side I'm not so keen on, rattling the money tin for the ski centre like some charity mugger.' He swung round before I could speak. 'Listen to me, banging on.' He sat back down.

'Anyway, if I'm not around as much as I should be, you know why. Finances are a distraction, but I've also got a new book to write.' His smile invited me to join in. 'Oh, and don't mind my sister, by the way.'

'Sorry?'

He lowered his voice. 'She's suspicious of any woman who comes near me these days, thinks they're auditioning to be my next wife.'

So, he hadn't missed our exchange.

'Don't worry – it's understandable.' I managed not to jerk away when the back of his hand brushed my knee as he bent to pick up his mug. 'She's bound to be protective of you.'

'She has a few issues,' he began, the rest of his sentence interrupted by a volley of barks from Rocky. Daisy came running through from the kitchen and hurled herself at Isaac.

He pretended to fall backwards, flailing his arms, then picked her up in an easy movement. 'You're back,' he said, feigning amazement. 'And you smell like chocolate.'

'I had a brownie at the café and Auntie Lissa told a lady to eff off for rubbing her baby tummy without asking.'

Lissa came in, her stripy top stretched tight around her belly, the waistband of her slouchy jogging bottoms pulled low. 'Being pregnant doesn't give people the right to touch you,' she said. 'And don't worry, brother dearest. I said "eff", not the actual word.' She slid him a smile that transformed her face. 'I'm not trying to corrupt my niece.'

'I'm glad to hear it.' Isaac put Daisy down. She smiled at me, suddenly shy, one hand clutching the hem of his shorts. 'Are you sure you don't want me to go and pick up Jonah?'

Lissa shook her head. Her hair was in a loose topknot today, strands floating down, pink as candyfloss. 'I can still squeeze behind a steering wheel,' she said. 'I quite fancy a change of scenery.' When her eyes swivelled coolly to mine, I knew it was a dig.

'Hi.' I gave her a silly wave she ignored.

'Lissa, be nice.' Isaac's tone had an edge. 'My sister's bark is worse than her bite,' he added, directing the words to me.

I made myself smile as I rose, feeling too formal in my trousers and top, with my neatly brushed fringe, beside Lissa's exposed flesh and floaty tendrils of hair, silver bangles encircling one arm, her makeup-free face glowing.

*Would I have looked that good as my pregnancy progressed?*

'My bark is as loud as it needs to be.' Lissa fired me a smile that held no warmth.

'Only dogs bark, Lissy,' Daisy said, frowning up at her aunt.

Keen to escape, I held out my hand. 'Shall we go up to your room, Daisy?'

To my relief, she nodded. 'Can we do sums? I'm good at adding up.'

Isaac's eyebrows shot up. 'For some reason, my daughter loves maths.'

'That's good.' My teacher voice provoked an eye-roll from Lissa. 'You can show me how much you've learnt at school.'

Low voices trailed after us – an argument? I couldn't hear properly as Daisy chattered brightly, crouching to pat Rocky on our way past him.

Then, Lissa said more loudly, 'I'll be home in an hour,' and the back door slammed, followed by silence.

Unsettled, I let Daisy run ahead, watching her swipe her hair off her face with an impatient gesture that reminded me of Elise. Upstairs, she disappeared along the landing and through the open door into her room. I paused, eyes drawn to the room at the end of the landing, the oak-wood door shut tight like a coffin lid. It must be the master bedroom. My insides thumped as I remembered I had to go in there and find Elise's journal and Daisy's passport before I left.

A noise made me start and I turned, heart jumping into my throat when I saw Cecilia approaching. I hadn't heard her come home and wondered how long she'd been in the house, whether she'd listened to my conversation with Isaac.

'Hi, Cecilia.' I gave her a confident smile to hide a rising uncertainty. She didn't look friendly, like she had yesterday in front of her son. It was as though her mask had slipped, her mouth a hard line in the softness of her face.

She came close – too close. I was enveloped in her perfume as I backed up against the banister; something musky. She was wearing a denim dungaree dress over a white T-shirt that emphasised the almost unnatural hue of her eyes.

'Daisy's everything to us.' Her voice was completely calm, as though commenting on the weather. 'There's nothing I wouldn't do for that child.'

I brought a hand to my throat, tried to laugh. 'Of course you would.' Nerves choked my words. 'I completely understand.'

'Do you, Rose?' She tilted her head, scanning my face as though trying to decipher a code. 'I hope so.' Her wide hand, knotted with veins, rested on the wooden rail by my arm. 'Because if anything happens to our darling Daisy, I'll make sure you regret ever setting foot in this house.'

# Chapter 10

In Daisy's room, I tried not to show how rattled I was by Cecilia's warning as I listened to Daisy reciting her sums. *One plus one is one. Two plus two is four. Three plus three is six.*

It was only natural she would have her granddaughter's best interests at heart, but I couldn't help wondering whether she'd picked up on something, a sixth sense telling her there was more to me than met the eye.

Or maybe that's just how she was – had certainly been with Elise, undermining her abilities as a mother, according to the details Elise had let slip about her mother-in-law.

*All sweetness and light on the surface, but there's a lump of granite where her heart should be.*

Not where Daisy was concerned. It was obvious Cecilia adored her, just as it was clear that she loved her own children – which could make her a dangerous enemy. Now I'd glimpsed a different side to her, it wasn't hard to believe she'd hated her daughter-in-law.

A headache pushed behind my eyes. I needed to talk to someone I could trust, but I couldn't call Elise, and there was no one else since I'd lost touch with old friends. Talking to my aunt would only cause her to worry. Uncle Roy had had a small stroke last year, and I was certain my situation with Leon had played a part. He'd recovered, but I didn't want to cause any more stress.

'You really do know your numbers,' I said as Daisy waited for my response, her eyes questioning. She was sitting at her child-sized desk on a small wooden chair, while I perched on the side of her cabin-style bed. 'You clearly work very hard.'

The beam that spread over her face made my chest feel warm. 'I can read you a story if you like,' she said. 'I know *all* the words.'

'Wow, I'd love that.' As she jumped up and crossed to her overflowing bookshelf, my eyes landed on the photograph I'd seen before, next to her cuddly unicorn. 'That's a lovely picture of you and your mummy.'

Daisy tipped her head, curls bobbing. 'Hmmm,' she said in an offhand way, before dropping to her knees, tilting sideways to examine the rows of books. 'My mummy's an angel in heaven now, but it's OK 'cos I have Daddy and Gramma and Auntie Lissa and Uncle Jonah, and they love me very, very much, and I might have a new mummy one day.'

Shock briefly blanked my mind. It sounded rehearsed, as though she'd been coached on what to say if anyone mentioned her mother. Aware I was treading on dangerous ground, I glanced at the open doorway, checking no one was outside.

'You must miss her,' I said softly, masking my horror that she believed her mother was dead.

A quick glance at me, forehead furrowed. 'Not really.' She gave a tiny shrug, face clearing. 'Daddy says she was poorly for a long time.'

Was that the line they were spinning, to turn Daisy against Elise? How long had it been going on before Elise left? Daisy spoke about her as though she barely knew her, not like a child who desperately missed her mum.

I longed to tell her she would see her mother again soon. And when she did – what would the shock do to her when she realised that, far from being an 'angel', her mother was alive and well?

Anger rose, thick and fast. The sooner I reunited them, the better.

I took a few deep breaths to settle my heartbeat, and as we sat back on the bed, Daisy leaning into me with a well-read copy of *How to be a Lion* open in her lap, Isaac appeared.

'Drinks for the ladies,' he said in a stage whisper, creeping in with pantomime steps that prompted giggles from Daisy.

He winked at me as he placed a glass of orange juice and mug of milky coffee on the desk before backing out wide-eyed, a finger pressed to his lips. Daisy chuckled with delight while my heart raced. How had we looked to him, snuggled together on his daughter's bed – me taking the place that rightfully belonged to Elise – the mother he'd callously told his daughter was in heaven?

'Daddy's silly,' Daisy said fondly, her words triggering an unexpected flashback to my own father, kneeling by my bed, pretending to be the bear in one of his made-up stories while I huddled under the covers, deliciously scared, begging him to stop while hoping he'd carry on.

'Daddies are special,' I said, not wanting my view of Isaac to transmit to her. 'Mummies are too.' Daisy nodded, her head coming to rest against my arm, and the gentle weight of it made something inside me unspool. 'Now, are you going to read me this story?'

Several books later, as my eyelids were growing heavy – adrenaline seeping away, and my sleepless night catching up – Rocky barked downstairs, jerking me upright. A door slammed, followed by voices all talking at once in the hallway.

'Uncle Jonah!' Instantly, Daisy was up and off the bed, books slipping to the floor in her wake. I followed, heart in my throat as she dashed towards the wide, steep stairs, but she was clearly used to them, holding on to the rail as she descended at speed.

The man who had entered turned, dropped his bag, and held out his arms. 'Hello, Jellybean!'

Cecilia, Lissa, and Isaac moved aside as Daisy skipped over

and threw herself at her uncle who wrapped her in a bear hug and swung her around, before depositing her gently down. 'I've missed you,' he said, in a heartfelt way, attention swinging between the assembled group before settling on me.

'You must be Rose.'

'And you must be Daisy's Uncle Jonah.' I stepped forward and took his outstretched hand, feeling the needle-like prod of Lissa's gaze. 'Nice to meet you.' I wondered what she'd told him about me – or rather, her feelings about me – and realised with fresh shock that he must be a party to the lie about Elise's absence from this house.

'You too.'

His voice was well-bred and gentle which, along with his appearance, didn't fit the image I'd formed. From the way Elise had spoken about him, I'd pictured Jonah as a stereotype: red-faced, balding, and pot-bellied, eyes glazed from too much booze, tattoos snaking from the sleeves of a faded T-shirt.

Instead, he gave off a hippy vibe the old Elise would have appreciated: greying, curly brown hair pulled back in a bun, dark eyes and beard. He was wearing a soft, round-necked shirt, and baggy linen trousers with the hems rolled up, feet pushed into Birkenstocks.

'I'm sure Daisy's lucky to have you,' he said, warm fingers slipping from mine to rest briefly on his niece's curls.

'Rose is my friend,' she piped up, her words so guileless I felt close to tears as I joined in the smiles that lightened everyone's face but Lissa's. Cecilia did a good job of finding the comment adorable, darting me a genuinely warm look that filled me with confusion.

'I thought we could eat lunch on the patio as it's a lovely day,' she said, nodding to Jonah as she placed a hand on his shoulder. 'Ready in five minutes if you want to freshen up.'

It sounded like a line from a novel, and I had the feeling again of being a player in a drama I hadn't learnt the lines for.

'I was sorry to hear about your mother,' I said to Jonah as he picked up his rucksack while the others moved in the direction of the kitchen. Daisy clung to Isaac's hand, head angled towards him as she chattered.

'It's hard when she lives so far away.' Sadness settled in the lines around Jonah's eyes. He was a few years older than Lissa, maybe forty, and seemed to have the weight of the world on his shoulders. 'I've begged her to move over here, so we can help take care of her, but she has good friends in Florida,' he said. 'At least that's something. Oh, and the cancer treatment is working, so . . .' He lifted one shoulder, a smile returning. 'That's my sad story,' he said. 'I look forward to hearing yours.'

Lissa had turned, was heading back.

'What makes you think I have one?'

He pulled his head back, eyebrows lifting. 'Everyone has a sad story, Rose.' He glanced towards his approaching wife, adding almost to himself, 'This family more than most.'

Sitting on a wooden bench around a rustic table, under the stylish parasol Isaac had cranked up with Daisy's 'help', it was hard to not become swept up in the easy warmth of it all: delicious food dished up by Cecilia – glistening olives, honey-drizzled slices of salmon, homemade sausage rolls, fresh, crusty bread, and a bowl of pasta salad – and the chatter that flowed easily back and forth. Isaac, seated beside me, took care to include me with a look or a smile as I soaked it all up while helping Daisy with her food, agreeing that olives were 'Yuk!' which earned a laugh.

It was a version of the meals I'd experienced at my aunt and uncle's, and hadn't realised until now how much I'd missed. They had been so eager for me to spread my wings – experience life, the world, before 'settling down' – that little value had been placed on what I already had, the solid ground that had launched me into university life in London, and to my trip to Thailand, where I would sometimes slip out of whichever rat-infested hostel I was staying in with my co-travellers, or away from a Full Moon beach party, wishing I was back in Derbyshire, watching TV with Sarah and Roy.

Even Lissa had thawed, eating as though half-starved, catching my eye to joke, 'I feel like I'm eating for twelve. This baby's permanently hungry.'

'When's it due?' I managed to ask without too much of a pang.

'Beginning of October.' Jonah hooked an arm around his wife's shoulders, his other hand spreading over her bump. 'An autumn baby, like I was.'

They complemented each other, her light, him dark, and were clearly in love, Lissa softening like butter under Jonah's smiling gaze, one hand resting on his as she continued pushing olives into her mouth.

'Have you thought of names?' *I would have called my baby Meredith, after my mother.*

'Zac,' Lissa said, decisively.

'Holden.' Jonah spoke at the same time, pretending to cower as Lissa threatened him with a chunk of bread.

'He's showing off his literary chops,' she said, almost as though she was enjoying having a new audience for their charade.

In spite of myself, I couldn't help a spark of pleasure. 'I love *Catcher in the Rye* but naming your child after the main character means they'll always be explaining it to people.'

'Exactly,' said Jonah, nodding. 'He'll stand out from the crowd.'

'Not in a good way,' Lissa protested while Cecilia shook her head, chuckling softly in a way that made me wonder whether I'd dreamt her stony expression from earlier, her words of warning.

'It's nice to have a name that's a bit different.' I was flushed with warmth, from the food and the zesty fruit punch, the sunshine slanting across the patio, and Isaac's interested gaze. 'There were four Emmas and three Jacobs in my very first class, ten years ago, and three Noahs in the last class I taught.'

'At least Zac is timeless without being too popular,' Lissa said, studying me through narrowed eyes.

'I like it,' Isaac said. 'But it's nothing to do with me.' He held up his hands, throwing Jonah a grin. 'You guys need to sort it out.'

'I hoped you might name him after your father,' Cecilia said to Lissa, bringing out a dish of strawberries and a jug of cream. 'It's about time Ignatius was brought back into fashion.'

I smiled at the groans of laughter – clearly not the first time they'd had this discussion – and wondered whether Elise or Isaac had chosen Daisy's name.

'I still have his name as my phone password,' Cecilia said. 'A way of keeping him alive.'

'Mum, you know that's not safe.' Lissa threw her a frown. 'You should change your password every few months, for safety.'

'I use my date of birth with a hashtag at the end for all my devices,' I admitted. 'It's just easier.'

'I've had the same one for years,' Isaac admitted. 'Let's just say a certain canine features.' He eyed Rocky who was snuffling around the table. 'Easy enough to remember.'

'Naughty boy,' Daisy scolded, as the dog tugged a half-eaten sausage roll from her hand.

Isaac ordered him to lie down, and Jonah bent to pat his glossy head, while Lissa tipped a pool of cream into her bowl.

It didn't feel as if they were putting on a friendly front for my sake, but how could I be sure? I tried to insert Elise into the scene, to imagine her beside Isaac, and the temperature seemed to dip as though the sun had gone in.

'It's lovely you all being under the same roof,' I said, caving in to an urge to dig deeper, to reveal some hidden truth that made sense of Elise's experience with this family. 'Have you lived together long?' I addressed the question to Jonah, half-expecting the atmosphere to subtly change, a sticky silence to fall. He merely paused his spearing of a strawberry and waved his fork.

'It's been longer than we anticipated.'

'They were going to build their own place,' Isaac explained, elbows on the table, a scrunched-up napkin in his hand. 'Got fed up with living in a broken-down caravan in a farmer's field, pair of hippies that they are.'

'Oi, just because we used to live in a commune,' Jonah protested, darting a look at Lissa. The humour had left her face while I wasn't looking. 'We loved that caravan.'

'Any*way*,' Isaac continued. 'It didn't really get going.'

'Yeah.' Jonah's eyes clouded. 'All our savings gone.'

'We were scammed by a dodgy landowner, who took off with the cash.' Lissa's jaw clenched around the words. 'We were screwed after that.' Her gaze flicked to Cecilia's and away so fast I might have imagined it.

'That's awful,' I said.

'I suggested they move in here – there's plenty of room – give them time to save up and make their next move.' Isaac spoke lightly, but I had a feeling it wasn't the full story.

Lissa made a noise in her throat that Isaac ignored but won her a sharp look from her mother.

'Mum moved in just before Daisy was born,' Isaac went on swiftly. 'The old neighbourhood wasn't what it used to be, and the old house needed repairs.'

'It was never the same living there after your dad died,' Cecilia said quietly. 'It was a relief to leave in the end.'

There must have been plenty of money from the sale of a house in London.

'It's nice to have Mum around to help with Daisy.' Isaac's voice was strained and there was no mistaking the undercurrent of tension that rippled around the table. Even Rocky lifted his head and let out a whine.

I imagined Elise as a ghostly presence at the table and wondered what she would make of it all. Perhaps they were thinking of her too.

Daisy, bored, slid to the ground. 'Can I go on the swing?' She spoke too loudly, as if trying to break a spell. 'You can push me, Rose.'

'Not when you've just eaten.' Cecilia switched on a smile as Isaac said, 'Good idea.'

'She'll make herself sick.'

'Maybe show Rose the stream first,' Isaac instructed. 'But remember to hold her hand.'

I pushed my bowl aside, forcing down all the questions I wanted to ask. 'That was a lovely meal, thank you.' I made to stand up, light-headed all of a sudden.

As I gripped the edge of the table while everything spun, Jonah's voice reached me as though from a distance.

'Rose,' he said, in a musing way. 'What did you say your surname was?'

*I didn't.* Vision clearing, I met his curious gaze. 'Carpenter,' I said. 'Why?'

'It sounds familiar.' His brow crinkled. 'Have we met before?'

# Chapter 11

My heart rate was off the scale as I pretended to consider Jonah's question. 'I don't think we've met.' I held on to a smile. 'I'm sure I would have remembered.'

Lissa's gaze had sharpened. 'Where do you think you know her from?' *Her.* Relegated, once more, to stranger.

'It's the name, more than anything.' Jonah drummed his fingers on the table while he thought. 'It rings a bell for some reason.'

'Maybe you're thinking of that actress you like.' Isaac's eyes were fixed on Daisy as she jumped along the patio. 'She was in that film about fostering kids.'

'Very helpful, bro.' Lissa's voice dripped sarcasm, but her face relaxed. 'Or, The Carpenters,' she added. 'Jonah doesn't like people knowing he loves their music.'

Cecilia smiled, smoothing a lock of hair behind her ear. 'Nothing wrong with liking The Carpenters,' she said. 'I saw them play at the Royal Albert Hall with my parents in 1971. They flew over specially for the weekend. Of course, I was more excited about seeing London.'

'Maybe it's a combination of both.' My smile became strained as the dizziness returned. The sun had moved, hot on my neck, sending prickles of sweat along my brow. 'I need some shade,' I said, rising. 'Let's go, Daisy.'

When we were standing side by side on the miniature hump-back bridge that spanned the narrow stream, Daisy peered over into the bubbling water while I waited for my pulse to slow.

'I sometimes paddle when it's summer,' she said hopefully, chin resting on the curved wooden rail. 'But there are stones on the bottom.'

'You need to wear jelly shoes.' My breath caught, as though I'd been running, despite strolling down the garden as though I hadn't a care in the world. 'They'll protect your feet,' I said in response to her quizzical look, wishing I could switch off from Jonah's question.

Elise had said that Isaac and his family knew nothing about me, that she hadn't mentioned me to them – *no offence, Rose* – but what if she had and forgot? She might have drunk too much one night and opened up to Jonah about the friend who abandoned her, and my name had lodged in his memory.

If that was the case, he couldn't have mentioned it to the others; they'd seemed genuinely puzzled.

I thought again of the list of questions, wondering who was responsible. *Lissa?* If she had shared her concerns with Jonah, he might have put them together with a name he thought he recognised, and . . . Acid burned my throat. I wasn't cut out for this. I'd been raised to believe in honesty, a trait I'd tried to instil in the children I taught, but here I was, lying to everyone.

But these were exceptional circumstances, I reminded myself, letting Daisy lead me over the bridge to a meadow-like area. The emerald grass was overgrown, sprinkled with colourful wild flowers, and the trees were loaded with fruit, branches bowed beneath the weight of apples, pears, and plums.

'Fairies live here,' Daisy sang, skipping ahead, her arms stretched wide as if embracing the world. I envied her – wished I really was here as her nanny, or teacher.

A thought crashed in. *Had Elise's mother mentioned me?* Ingrid was Isaac's mother-in-law. She must have met the family, would

71

have been at the wedding, although . . . Elise hadn't got on with her for years. It's probable she hadn't invited her, or even introduced her to Isaac. She would have worried about Ingrid getting drunk and showing her up. And of course there was the dementia – when had that started?

There was so much I didn't know. But did it matter? A week from now, Elise would be out of my life, Daisy too. The thought brought a pinch of panic, but as for what came after – I couldn't let myself think about that now.

'Peaceful here, isn't it?'

I jumped as Isaac appeared at my side, realising I'd stopped walking and, to all intents and purposes, was staring into space while Daisy, crouched in the grass, had set about making a daisy chain.

'This is like my name.' She held up one white flower for approval.

'A beautiful name,' I said.

'You're a flower like me.' She grinned. 'Rose and Daisy, Daisy and Rosie.'

A rush of emotion caught in my throat. 'Will you make me a bracelet?'

She nodded. 'Can you watch me, Daddy?'

'I'm watching.' He pretended to focus a pair of binoculars using his fingers. 'Make it a good one, bunny.'

She concentrated her attention, biting her bottom lip, drawing smiles from us both.

'Having second thoughts yet?' he said, keeping his attention on Daisy.

'Of course not.' Wrong-footed, I bent to pluck a blade of grass so he couldn't see my face. 'Why would I be?'

'Families can be difficult.' Sunshine slanted through the trees, burnishing his hair. 'Sometimes, I wish . . .' He paused and shook his head, as if changing his mind about what he was going to say. 'They've been a big help though, with Daisy.'

'You're lucky,' I said, adding quickly, 'But I can see it might be a bit much at times.'

'If there's anything you want to know, just ask.' He slid me a sideways look, concern settling over his face. 'I mean it, Rose. It's a big ask, joining a family you've never met. If you were considering working for a company you would do your research first, find out as much as possible about who they were.'

I kept my expression still as I thought of the all the things I already knew about them.

'I guess it is a lot different, coming into a family environment rather than joining a company, or a new school in my case.' I mustered a smile, winding the blade of grass around my finger. 'At work, I got to go home at the end of the day and switch off.'

It was meant to be a joke – and not strictly true as I often took work home, and rarely switched off completely from thinking about the children in my care.

'If you would rather do that, we can think again about our arrangement,' Isaac said, apparently taking me seriously. 'Maybe see how you feel at the end of the weekend.' His eyes met mine. 'There would be no hard feelings if you changed your mind about staying.'

'Oh no, I didn't mean that.' I felt a wave of panic. 'Everything seems great, and Daisy . . . well, she's lovely.' At least that much was true. 'Will you all, I mean, the others . . . will they be around all day?'

Isaac shook his head. 'Jonah does shifts at an organic café in town while he studies counselling, and Lissa will be in her studio most of the time, or should I say the summerhouse in the garden. She makes sustainable jewellery.'

I thought of her multiple bracelets and wasn't too surprised. And Jonah, training to be a counsellor? It made sense somehow, chiming with the gentleness I'd perceived. It just didn't fit with Elise's description of her brother-in-law, but I reminded myself that he – along with the others – were no doubt behaving differently now she'd gone.

73

'She's good but has a bit of a chip on her shoulder about not going to university.'

'She didn't?'

'She and Jonah met young, wanted to live off-grid and do the whole commune thing, until they got fed up a couple of years ago and bought the caravan with some money Jonah's grandparents left him.'

'It's a shame about what happened,' I said.

'Jonah's not very good at holding on to cash.' *Interesting.* 'His father paid for him to go and visit his mother in Florida.' A nerve twitched at the corner of Isaac's mouth.

'Won't they want their own place eventually?'

'Maybe.' His tone drew a line under the topic, and I decided to move on. 'And your mum?'

'She works with a local baker, decorating cakes. She got into it years ago, after giving up admin work. She took a break for a while to help out with Daisy. She loves it but standing up all day doesn't do her back any good.'

*She has a bad back when it suits her.* 'What happened to it?'

'She was hurt on a skiing trip with my father back in the day and has had recurring pain ever since, but she tries not to let it stop her doing what she wants.'

*Making her daughter-in-law's life hell?*

'I'm sorry,' I said. 'That's why I've never been skiing. I'm pretty clumsy and would probably break a leg the first time I tried.'

'It's actually not that difficult with the right instructor.' He pulled his gaze from Daisy. 'We're going to Iceland later in the year. I could teach you,' he said – the last thing I'd expected.

'Iceland?'

'Plenty of ski resorts there.' When he smiled, his resemblance to Daisy was strong. 'Daisy wants to learn, and I can't wait to show her where my ancestors lived. She's at an age where she can appreciate it.'

'It sounds . . . wonderful.' It did. Idyllic, in fact. Only, Daisy wouldn't be in Iceland later this year. She would be somewhere else entirely. With her mother.

Uncertainty bubbled up. The idea that Daisy belonged anywhere but here with her family seemed suddenly ludicrous.

'Why aren't you two helping me?' she said suddenly, training her attention on us. 'I can't do it all by myself.'

Isaac chuckled. 'I'll leave you with Rose,' he said, turning to me with an enquiring look. 'If that's OK?'

I nodded, light-headed once more, and shivery despite the sun.

'I've a couple of calls to make, but come back up to the house whenever you're ready and help yourself to anything you need.' He briefly touched my shoulder. 'This is your home while you're here.'

I watched him blow Daisy a kiss before striding away, combing a hand through his hair, and joined Daisy in the long grass, admiring the crooked chain she'd created.

'Try it on,' she suggested kindly. 'I think it might fit you now.'

I sucked in a breath and tried to focus, nausea unfurling in my stomach. I must have eaten too much, food mingling with fruit punch to produce an acid mix. Or maybe it was the conversation with Isaac I was finding hard to digest.

Luckily, Daisy was tired of grappling with the delicate stems and, after admiring my flower bracelet, jumped up and headed back to the little bridge. 'We can look for butterflies,' she called over her shoulder.

I followed slowly, taking deep breaths, and almost left my skin when a woman appeared from behind an apple tree, her glasses nestling in a crown of black hair that couldn't be her natural colour.

'Lovely little girl.' Her voice had a rasp and her eyes, like shards of jet in a walnut-like face, pinned me to the spot. 'You looking after her?'

'How did you get in here?' My heart jackhammered in my chest. 'You're trespassing.'

She produced a raspy laugh. 'I live in the cottage through there.'

A crooked finger pointed at the tall leylandii hedges screening the orchard and I noticed a gap, big enough for a small person to fit through.

'Mr Bennet finds his way in here most days.'

I glanced around, half expecting to see an elderly man lurking among the greenery.

'My dog.' The woman, her toothy grin suggesting she knew exactly what I was thinking, let out a piercing whistle. 'He's taken a fancy to Rocky, can't keep away.'

As she spoke, a small, white-and-tan terrier snuffled out of the undergrowth, tail wagging, and reared up to dance on his back legs.

'Get home, you naughty boy.' The dog turned and ran for the hedge, vanishing through the gap. 'Little devil, he is.'

My heart was still racing. 'You know the family?'

'Not really.' The woman, who looked to be in her seventies, tugged at the grey hooded top she was wearing with mud-stained jeans and wellingtons. 'The houses aren't exactly conjoined,' she said. 'Just this bit of the garden, and the family ain't exactly friendly.'

She sounded like a Londoner, but despite the accent and casual outfit, the rings around her bony fingers looked expensive, a spray of diamonds catching the sunlight.

'That poor woman, though.'

Ice ran down my spine. I almost said *Elise?* but caught myself in time. 'You knew her?'

'I spoke to her a few times, and I heard plenty.' The woman tapped the side of her nose, her thin lips wrinkled like a drawstring purse. She took a step closer, lowering her voice. 'There was an accident, you know.'

I caught sight of Daisy on the patio, talking to Jonah. They would be wondering where I was, but I was transfixed by the stranger. 'I heard about that.'

'My name's Thora, by the way.' She studied me for a second,

as though weighing up what to tell me. 'It was tragic, the way she was treated. No wonder she spent most of her time in there.' She directed her gaze towards the summerhouse. 'Told me some horror stories about them.'

'Ro-*ooose!*'

Daisy was calling. 'I'm coming!' I shouted back, adding to the woman, 'I have to go.'

Her hand landed on my arm in a claw-like grip, her breath sour in front of my face. 'You be careful.' She gave a sharp nod at the house. 'There's something not right about that lot.'

# Chapter 12

'Did you get lost?' Daisy ran to me as I joined the family at the table, a smudge of strawberry juice on her chin. 'I play hide-and-seek sometimes.'

'There are a lot of good places to hide,' I said, a silly grin on my face, Thora's words racing around my head.

There was no sign of Isaac, but the others hadn't moved. Lissa was idly stroking Rocky's back with her foot, sipping rose-coloured liquid from her glass, while Cecilia and Jonah huddled over a newspaper crossword. It seemed too studied and I suspected they'd been talking about me.

As I sat down, Cecilia scrunched a piece of paper into her fist, but not before I recognised the list of questions I'd spotted earlier. Pretending not to notice, I said, 'I spoke to your neighbour.'

Startled glances were exchanged.

'Was it Mrs Nosy Parker?' Daisy's nose wrinkled as she hopped from foot to foot in front of me. 'She looks like a witch.'

Lissa snorted, widening her eyes when Cecilia threw her a chastising look.

'Her name's Thora,' Cecilia said then turned to me, shading her eyes with her hand. 'Why was she in our garden?'

'Being a nosy parker,' Daisy piped up and giggled with an edge of hysteria, perhaps sensing something in the air.

'I love the unicorn in your bedroom, Daisy.' I raised a smile, trying to disguise my unease. 'Could you draw a picture of one for me?'

She nodded eagerly. 'I do good drawings.'

'I'll come and help in a minute,' I said, but she was already skipping indoors and didn't look back.

'Daisy must have picked up on me calling the old bat names.' Lissa sounded unrepentant. 'What was she doing?'

'Looking for that mutt of hers I expect.' Jonah clicked the pen he was holding on and off with his thumb. 'He finds his way in here nearly every day.'

'She said he's taken a shine to Rocky.'

The dog lifted his head at the mention of his name.

'Shame he doesn't feel the same way.' Lissa shifted, putting her glass down and spreading her palm across the small sphere of her bump. 'We need to fix that gap in the hedge. Mr Bennet's a nuisance.'

'I thought she was talking about her husband,' I said.

'Ha.' Lissa arched her back. 'The old man died a few years ago. He had a lucky escape if you ask me.'

'I think she's lonely.' Cecilia's pale skin was splashed with pink, her composure ruffled. 'Her children hardly ever visit.'

'Not like us then.' Lissa's voice hardened, eyes flicking to me like lasers. 'Did she say anything else?'

Sickness rose and I swallowed. 'Just what a lovely child Daisy is.'

Lissa made a dismissive noise. 'She was always asking to babysit when Daisy was younger, probably because she wanted to snoop around the house.'

Not *your* house, I felt like saying. They probably hadn't wanted their neighbour seeing how things really were. Had Thora voiced her concerns to Elise, tried to help her? Elise hadn't mentioned it, but the neighbour probably wasn't top of her list while she was condensing her life here for me.

'Oh, and she mentioned an accident?'

I didn't imagine the stillness that fell, as though someone had frozen the scene with a remote control.

'That's Thora for you.' Cecilia spoke first, accompanying the words with a short laugh, the patches of colour on her cheeks deepening. 'Can't resist trying to make everything her business.'

That seemed a bit mean after she'd just defended Thora, suggesting she was lonely.

'She doesn't like that we've never invited her round for afternoon tea, or whatever.' Lissa directed the words to her belly, as if addressing the baby. 'She's a conspiracy theorist. Given half a chance she'll tell you the moon landings were faked, and that we're a bunch of murderers.'

'Don't be mean about her, Liss,' Jonah said, but his gaze was soft as he looked at his wife. 'She's harmless enough.'

'Just can't keep her opinions to herself.' Cecilia rose, gathering plates, indicating the conversation was over, declining my offer to help with clearing up.

As if proving a point, Lissa stood and picked up some glasses, eyes still trained on me. 'Aren't you supposed to be watching Daisy?'

'Give her a break, Lissa.' Jonah pushed back his chair and stood with an eye-roll in my direction. 'Rose will be doing a runner at this rate. We won't see her for dust.'

From the look Lissa gave me, that would suit her just fine.

It was cool indoors, where Cecilia was loading the dishwasher in the kitchen. Her smile faded as I hurried past, my stomach turning over.

'Are you OK?'

'Too much sun,' I managed, as the feeling of nausea strengthened.

Rocky followed me in and nudged the living door open with his nose. I caught a glimpse of Isaac pacing in front of the window with a hand in his hair, his phone pressed to his ear. He didn't see me shoot by or run up the stairs, where I made it to my bedroom and the en suite toilet just in time for my stomach to empty.

Eyes watering, I sank to the floor. Maybe I'd caught a bug. Working in a school for so long, my immune system was pretty robust, but I hadn't been around people for months.

After rinsing my face at the sink and brushing my teeth, I headed for Daisy's room, guiltily relieved to see that she'd fallen asleep on her bed, dark lashes feathered against her cheeks.

She must have worn herself out, unless . . . My heart jumped. I crossed to the bed and gently touched her forehead with the back of my hand. It was cool, her breathing slow and even. No fever, thank goodness.

I watched her for a moment, in her rumpled dress, dark hair spread across the pillow like a child in a fairy tale. 'I'll have you back with your mummy soon,' I whispered, resisting an urge to kiss her cheek in case I was infectious, though I felt a lot better now whatever it was had left my system.

I glanced around, heart squeezing when I saw Daisy's desk, which was scattered with chunky crayons, and a sheet of paper where she'd started sketching her unicorn before drowsiness took over.

I leant closer and studied her heart-shaped face. Was it natural to sleep this deeply? She seemed almost sedated. I recalled my bout of sickness. Something tugging at my subconscious, just as Daisy turned, flumping onto her side. A puff of breath escaped as she settled once more, hands tucked underneath her cheek.

*She was fine.*

I debated whether to stay until she woke, or return to my room and have a nap myself. Sleepiness washed over me, as if it was catching, and I backed towards the door. Perhaps I should alert somebody first, let them know Daisy was resting.

What would normally be happening on a Saturday afternoon?

My eyes landed on the photograph on the shelf of Elise with Daisy, looking into each other's eyes. On impulse, I went to my room and got my phone, and took a snap of the photo. It would have to do. I couldn't take the real thing but would have a copy printed for Elise. Checking the image had gone into my Google cloud, I deleted it from my phone.

Stepping onto the landing, I left Daisy's door ajar. My room was opposite, so if I left my door open, she would see me when she woke up.

*Just one week,* I told myself, putting my phone down and kicking my shoes off, head swimming as I bent to tuck them neatly under the bed. *A few more days and this would be over.*

Straightening, I rubbed a hand over the back of my neck, which came away moist with sweat. My reflection in the wardrobe mirrors showed my red face, hair damp at the hairline ... I craned forward, noticing a gap at the edge of the bank of mirrors. One of the wardrobe doors wasn't shut properly. I hadn't left it like that.

I crossed the room with a feeling of vertigo and tugged the door all the way back along its runner. My empty suitcase was where I'd left it, but the zip hadn't been pulled back around properly, and the laptop bag I'd left on top wasn't straight. Details someone else might not notice, but indicated to me that someone had been in here, looking for . . . *what?*

A shiver of fear whispered through me as I recalled the short list of items to retrieve from the house. Elise had urged me to memorise them, but I'd kept the Post-it note, worried I might forget the title of the cookery book, or what the earrings she wanted me to find looked like. I'd tucked it into a notepad I kept in my laptop bag, fastened inside a pocket, but if someone was looking for something specific, they might have found it.

My stomach contracted as I crouched and opened the bag. I pulled out the notepad, fingers trembling as I flicked through it. The slip of yellow paper was where I'd left it, but that didn't mean it hadn't been read.

Pushing out a shaky breath, I glanced at my neat handwriting, then crumpled up the note and looked for somewhere to hide it.

Panic rose. Just having it in the house was a problem, but what could I do? *Eat it?* Hysterical laughter fizzed in my chest. This was ridiculous. Even so . . . I glanced once more at the note, then tore it into confetti-sized shreds and flushed them down the toilet.

I woke from a dreamless sleep, just as Daisy bolted into the room, eyes as bright as stars.

'Come and play with us, Rose,' she cried, before darting out again.

'Be there in a minute.'

The sun had shifted, slanting across the floor. Blinking, I checked my phone to see it was three-thirty. I wished I could text Elise to let her know Daisy was fine. It seemed wrong to not have any contact.

I climbed off the bed where I'd lain to 'rest my eyes' wondering how Elise was passing the time. I pictured her on my sofa with the curtains drawn, chewing her nails as she pretended to watch something on Netflix. Would she go out, even into the garden, for some fresh air? The grass needed cutting. I normally kept it neat, like I did the house, imposing order. It seemed trivial now.

As I slipped my shoes back on, it hit me how readily I'd thrown myself into this scheme after months of being so careful. To help Elise, yes – the feeling I owed her hadn't gone away – but maybe it was more than that. For months after losing the baby and the mess of Leon, my heart had felt like a flattened battery, worry a constant hum in the background. I'd reduced myself to a state I could easily manage because I didn't want to risk being hurt again. I was barely interested in even making a home, beyond the most basic requirements, but Elise's reappearance had jolted me back to life and imbued me with a sense of purpose. Despite the weirdness, I was glad to be doing something that mattered.

I scooped my hair back into a ponytail and checked my top wasn't creased. I paused, meeting my gaze in the mirror. A week from now, Isaac would be going out of his mind with worry, and

I would have another part to play; one I had to pull off before I could move on. There wasn't much to feel good about just yet.

The rest of the day slipped by with old-fashioned games – Snakes and Ladders, Jenga and Monopoly – stretching into dinnertime, the conversation light, everyone seemingly focused on letting Daisy win and making me feel welcome. There was no hint of unfriendly undercurrents as Lissa praised my Jenga moves, and Cecilia teased out some details about my teacher training, Isaac listening with apparent curiosity from the floor. He was sitting with his back against the sofa, a smile hovering, though I noticed now and then his attention would shift and wondered who he'd been on the phone to earlier. *His agent?* Nobody talked about his writing, and I didn't like to ask more questions than I had already.

After dinner, Lissa and Jonah took Rocky out for a walk and Cecilia chose a book to read on the patio. Isaac ushered Daisy upstairs for her bath and bedtime routine, and I offered to read her a story, but she wanted her daddy to do it.

'Relax, watch TV if you like,' Isaac called from the top of the stairs. 'I'll be down shortly.'

'I think I'll go and phone my aunt for a catch-up,' I said, trying not to feel rebuffed. I could hardly waltz in and displace normal routines, established over time – and Isaac had spoken nicely, almost regretfully, when Daisy had insisted on him reading to her.

*How can he behave as though nothing is wrong?*

The voice in my head persisted as I went to my room and stared out at the garden, at the swing set and slide Daisy was almost too big for. Maybe it was easy to keep up a pretence in front of someone who – as far as Isaac knew – had no inkling about him, his family, or their past.

Across the landing, I heard Daisy's bubbling laughter and Isaac's voice, the sounds increasing my tension. However strongly I believed that Daisy ought to be with her mother, there was no doubting how much she loved her father.

I unplugged my phone from its charger, trying not to think about someone being in my room, going through my things.

'Hey, Sarah, it's me.'

'I know it's you, sweetheart – your name came up,' my aunt replied, as she always did. 'How are things?'

'Good,' I said lightly. 'Just having a quiet night in, ha ha.' It was what I always said.

'You sound better.' Warmth suffused her voice. 'More like your old self.'

'I'm feeling good.' The temptation to tell her the truth was overwhelming, but I bit back the words and asked what she and Roy had been up to. If anyone was listening outside the door there would be no cause for alarm – in fact, I'd left the door open slightly for that reason. Clearly, someone in this family didn't trust me, despite their earlier displays of friendliness.

'How's Roy?'

'He's bought a couple of pigs,' she said. 'Named them Pinky and Perky.'

I laughed, relieved my uncle was well enough to be out and about, obviously used to the stick he'd needed since his stroke, which left him with some weakness in his right leg. Sarah sounded relaxed, and although I hated not being honest with her, I was glad she didn't know that I was back in touch with Elise.

As I finished the call, Isaac poked his head around the door. 'Fancy a drink?'

I hesitated, trying to read what he wanted my answer to be, and shook my head. I was tired too, despite my nap. It had been a long day and playing a part was exhausting. Not to mention the sickness, which had left me with a queasy headache.

'I'll have a shower and an early night,' I said, unfurling from the window seat, feeling self-conscious about my bare feet, and mussed-up hair, freed from its ponytail. 'If you don't mind.'

'Not at all.' He flashed a smile. 'Have a good night's sleep, and don't get up too early tomorrow. Sundays are usually lazy.' It was hard to imagine Elise being lazy on a Sunday, or any other day. Maybe it was a new thing since they'd killed her off.

I managed to smile and nod. 'Goodnight, Isaac.'

'I'm glad you're here, Rose,' he said. 'Daisy likes you a lot.'

I tried to unpick his tone as he left. He sounded genuine, as though everything was as it should be. It was easy to believe I was the only one looking for suspicious behaviour, but the truth was, I was hiding something too: the real reason I was there.

# Chapter 13

*Sunday*

'Sunday's a relaxing, family day.' Cecilia tipped a golden loaf out of the bread maker as I entered the kitchen apologising for rising so late. It was gone nine-thirty, but I'd waited until I heard movement, not wanting to be the first downstairs, embarrassed to catch Isaac emerging from his bedroom at the same time, his hair damp from a shower.

I'd tried to see inside his room as we exchanged 'good mornings' but he pulled the door shut behind him, enquiring politely whether I'd slept well, and whether I'd found the bed comfortable.

I said yes to both, still surprised I'd slept so deeply, waking just after eight refreshed, and oddly free from the angst of the day before. The feeling had been heightened by a long soak under the shower before dressing in jeans and a thin cotton shirt. Perhaps if I pushed aside the reason I was staying, I would get through the week more easily.

'Help yourself,' Cecilia said, moving around the sun-filled kitchen, which smelt of yeast and coffee. 'Breakfast is through there.' She nodded to the table in the conservatory, loaded with jars of honey, marmalade, and jam, alongside dishes of scrambled eggs, crispy bacon, and plump, fried tomatoes. 'We have the full works on a Sunday,' she said, when I made appreciative murmurs, her smile as warm as the loaf she placed on a wooden board with a bread knife and carried through.

Isaac seated himself beside me again, the sun illuminating his face. Close up, he didn't look rested, a hint of pink marbling the whites of his eyes. Maybe a guilty conscience kept him awake at night.

'Thanks for this, Mum.'

Even his voice was weary, though he switched on a grin when Daisy rushed in from the garden and held out a snail in her palm for him to admire.

'Maybe you should put him back, so he can carry on with his journey,' Isaac said, his face close to hers.

'Is it a boy or a girl?' I asked, slipping into teacher mode.

Daisy studied the snail, her eyebrows drawn. 'How will I know?'

'Ah, well, it's a trick question.' I glanced up to see Lissa lowering herself onto the chair opposite, her face a little puffy. 'It's both.' I paused for effect. 'A boy *and* a girl.'

'Really?' Daisy's look of astonishment was gratifying. 'That's 'mazing.'

'I didn't know that.' Isaac looked mildly impressed. 'How come you know so much about snails?'

'Is that what you learn at teacher training?' Lissa was hacking into the loaf, her eyes fixed on me. It was as if overnight, whatever doubts she'd had about me had returned.

'I'm full of fun facts,' I said, adding when she didn't smile, 'It was actually my dad who told me that and it stuck.'

Lissa opened her mouth, as if to say more, but maybe mindful of the fact that my parents were dead, closed it again and focused on spreading honey on her slice of bread, glancing up when Jonah came through, tousling his hair with his hands.

'I think I'm still jet-lagged.' He nodded at me as he sat beside his wife.

Lissa stiffened suddenly, then grabbed his hand and rested it on her bump. They exchanged private smiles, no doubt feeling the baby move, and as Cecilia leaned over and asked if she could feel it too, I caught Isaac's eye. He made a face, as though apologising for their intimate display. I offered a shrug and a smile in return. *It's fine! I don't mind being transplanted into the middle of your dysfunctional family, pretending to be nice while until I return Daisy to her mother.*

My smile faltered, but Isaac was rising to accompany Daisy on her mission to 'release' the snail and didn't notice. Lissa snuggled closer to Jonah, softening in his presence, and talked about some of the other parents-to-be at their antenatal group until Isaac and Daisy returned. I let myself surf the tide of normality. This must be their usual Sunday routine – at least since Elise had left. It struck me how upset she would be to see Daisy sitting on Isaac's lap as he fed her some scrambled egg, Cecilia urging her to try the tomatoes while Jonah made encouraging *nom-nom* sounds as he ate. Lissa playfully punched his arm and agreed with Daisy that cooked tomatoes were *disgusting*. It was as if the wound of Elise's absence had already healed and become invisible.

My appetite waned, but I forced myself to eat, not wanting to draw attention to myself. I wondered what would happen if I asked outright who had been in my room the day before and looked through my things. It might have been Daisy, who had gone upstairs before me, and wouldn't have been too careful about covering her tracks. The thought was strangely reassuring, and my stomach unclenched enough to accept a slice of bread and honey from Lissa, even though I wasn't keen on honey.

'Locally sourced,' she said, shaking back her hair, which flowed down her back. The pink streaks matched her strappy dress, which revealed a sun tattoo on her upper arm. 'There's a farmer's market in town every week.'

There was something almost too avid about the way she watched me raise the bread to my lips and as I took a tentative bite, I remembered how ill I'd felt the day before. Elise's words ricocheted in my head. *You know wisteria is toxic to humans? I'm pretty sure that's why I got sick last year when no one else did.* Instinctively, I dropped the bread on my plate with an apologetic wince. 'It's a bit too sweet for me.'

'It's fine, I don't like it either.' Isaac held up a hand, refusing Lissa's offer. 'And Daisy's not allowed, because too much sweet stuff will rot her teeth.' His tone was playful as he deposited his daughter on the floor, where she crouched to make a fuss of Rocky.

'Dogs can't eat sugar,' she said in a wise-woman voice.

Cecilia nodded. 'That's right, but a little now and then won't do any harm.'

Lissa had eaten her honeyed bread with relish, so would hardly have poisoned it. I was being ridiculous, Elise's warnings colouring my thoughts and clouding reason. 'I still haven't had my unicorn picture,' I said to Daisy, keen to switch focus. 'How about—'

'I thought we could go for a walk by the river with the dog,' Cecilia cut in, glancing through the window as if trying to find a distraction. 'We should make the most of the sunshine.'

'Good idea.' Jonah stretched his arms above his head. 'I could do with some fresh air.' He patted the tiny paunch beneath his faded T-shirt. 'And some exercise.'

'I have a meeting,' Isaac said.

'On a Sunday?' Cecilia swivelled to look at him. 'You didn't say.'

'*Please*, Daddy.' Daisy cocked her head, hands on hips. 'I want you to come too.'

'Next time, bunny, I promise.'

'We can take Rose to the park one day,' she said, brightening. 'She can push me on the big swings, can't you Rosie? They're better than my one in the garden, 'cos that's a baby swing.'

'It's big enough,' Cecilia said mildly.

My heart started racing at the mention of the park, where I was to take Daisy the following weekend. 'I'd love that,' I said, glancing at Isaac for confirmation. He nodded but seemed distracted.

'You're working too hard,' Cecilia told him, not quite a reprimand. When I looked at her face there was sympathy there, as if she believed he had no choice.

Jonah got to his feet and placed a hand on Isaac's shoulder. 'Good to hear you're unblocked, mate.' He winked at me. 'I'm talking in a writerly sense.'

Isaac looked embarrassed. 'I was keeping it quiet for now, until I hear from my agent.' He looked pointedly at Lissa, who feigned interest in her fingernails.

'You've been holed up in your study, every minute you're not at your spiritual home—'

'She means Snow Zone,' Jonah said round the side of his hand.

'—so it's obvious you've been in there writing up a storm,' Lissa finished. 'It would be nice to be properly self-sufficient again, for sure.' I couldn't interpret the look she gave Jonah, but all the humour left his expression. 'Shall we?' she said, into the awkward silence, extending a hand to Daisy. When her gaze skimmed mine it was clear that, this time, her anger wasn't directed at me.

Daisy insisted on taking my hand as we trooped down the garden and over the bridge, and onto the narrow path that bordered the river, which was a chalk stream rather than a river, sparkling innocently in the sun – not quite the fast-flowing body of water Elise had led me to believe.

Cecilia strode ahead with Rocky, his leash wrapped in her hand, the hems of her trousers rolled up to reveal sturdy calves. Her hair was secured with what looked like a pair of chopsticks, the back of her neck tanned golden.

Lissa and Jonah brought up the rear, chatting quietly. For a moment it felt as if I'd forgotten how to walk as I imagined their eyes on me. I forced myself to breathe deeply and focused on Daisy's stream of chatter as she pointed out the ducks waddling on the bank, and told me their names, and how she went on a boat once when she was little, and that her daddy taught her to swim when she was a baby, but she couldn't remember. It was tempting to ask her about her mother, but I suspected Lissa was tuned in to every word. Now and then, Cecilia glanced over her shoulder, as if checking we were still there. I hoped she saw it as a good sign that Daisy was happy in my company, that she would remember it when we were gone.

'Can I hold him, Nanna?' Daisy let go of my hand and ran ahead, making a grab for the leash.

'Hang on, Daisy.' I picked up pace and Daisy turned, stumbling against the dog, who yelped and leapt forward, pulling free from Cecilia's grip.

'Rocky, come back!' she called as he charged for the stream and leapt in, seeming delighted with his unexpected freedom. There was a flurry as several ducks fled the water with angry quacks, and Daisy screamed and clutched her grandmother's leg as they headed towards her. I lurched for the water, intending to grab Rocky's collar just as Jonah shot past, wading knee-deep as the dog floundered, head bobbing beneath the surface.

'Have you got him?' Lissa pushed roughly past me to enter the water. Caught off-guard, I teetered, flailing my arms, and toppled forwards. I managed to save myself, hands and knees thudding into the gravel at the bottom of the stream. The water wasn't deep, but chilly, soaking through my jeans and shirt sleeves and splashing my face and hair.

I made a scramble for the bank, feet slipping in my canvas shoes. I scrabbled at the grass and hauled myself up, ignoring Cecilia's outstretched hand.

'I'm fine,' I managed, teeth chattering with shock as Rocky paddled past, shaking himself hard. Water drops flew from his coat, soaking me further; Cecilia too. Scolding him gently, she slipped his lead back on, while Daisy stood open-mouthed, her expression hovering between laughter and tears.

'You're wet,' she observed, wide-eyed. 'Did you hurt yourself?'

'No, I'm OK,' I reassured her, producing a laugh as I wrung out my shirt tails. 'I'm wetter than the ducks.'

'It was funny.' Daisy allowed herself to smile. 'Your bottom was in the air.'

'Sure you're all right?' Cecilia's face lacked emotion, as if hiding her feelings.

'No harm done.' I turned to see Jonah had waded back to join Lissa, who was speaking to him in a low, angry tone. 'I'd better go back to the house and get changed.'

'What happened?'

I looked at Cecilia, sweeping back my sodden fringe. I knew what had happened. Lissa had meant me to go in the water. She'd shoved me on purpose.

'I don't know,' I said. 'I must have slipped.'

# Chapter 14

The first thing I saw when I entered my room was broken glass on the floor. I hurried over, still panting from my half-jog back to the house and dash upstairs, praying Isaac wouldn't see me.

It must be the tumbler from the en suite. I crouched to pick up the jagged shards, wondering how it had got in the bedroom and smashed so comprehensively – almost as if it had been thrown down, hard.

I'd drunk from the glass after brushing my teeth the night before, but I hadn't been so out of it that I wouldn't have remembered bringing it through or knocking it over.

*Had Isaac done this?* He was alone in the house, but it didn't make sense. If Daisy had run in, she could have been hurt. The thought made my back stiffen, as I recalled turning to leave Cecilia and Daisy, and Lissa calling after me, 'Where are you going?' There had been an edge to her voice I'd read as frustration that I was somehow spoiling their walk – Jonah was wearing knee-length shorts and had sensibly kicked off his sandals before going into the water – the implication being that I was a clumsy nuisance.

Had Lissa done this earlier, intending Isaac to find the broken glass, or 'discover' it herself, once we returned, so she could reveal my 'incompetence' to her brother? She was obviously still struggling to hide her dislike of me, hence the shove into the river. Poor Elise if this was the kind of behaviour she'd had to put up with.

My spinning mind struggled for answers as I wrapped the glass in toilet paper and ran downstairs to deposit the package in the recycling bin. I decided not to mention it. The only person who would notice it gone was the one who had smashed it and I doubted they would want to bring it up.

My heart raced as I headed back to the stairs, damp jeans cold around my legs. I let out a yelp of fright when a man burst out of the living room and slammed the door behind him. Leaping aside, I pressed a hand to my chest as he swerved past me.

'Sorry,' I said. 'I didn't know anyone was here.'

He paused, face clearing of annoyance as a polite mask slid into place. 'James Parry.' He stuck out a hand, gaze dropping to my wet clothes. He looked to be in his late fifties, tall and grey-haired, rounded shoulders under an expensively tailored jacket. 'I take it you're the new girlfriend.' His tone was sardonic, eyes narrowed behind heavy-framed glasses.

'I'm not a girlfriend.' I pulled my hand from his. 'I'm Daisy's home tutor and . . .' I hesitated over the word *nanny*, knowing I wasn't one, but James Parry didn't seem to notice. His thick brows knitted together.

'You're here for Daisy?' He pushed out a sound that wasn't quite a laugh. 'They tried that before, didn't they? Not long after she was born. Didn't quite work out.'

*He knew about that?* Did he know Isaac had supposedly slept with the nanny? He seemed angry about something.

'Postnatal depression, or so they said. Her mother wasn't coping, needed help.' He nudged his glasses with a long finger, gaze softening. 'How much do you know about this family . . . ?'

'Rose,' I supplied, reluctantly. 'They seem lovely.' I glanced at the door, imagining Isaac behind it, listening.

Tracking my gaze, James puffed air through his nostrils. 'He's in the garden,' he said shortly, adjusting the leather portfolio tucked under his arm. 'He's got a lot to think about.'

The way he said it – his whole attitude, which lacked any kind of respect – was a shock. If he disliked Isaac so intensely, why was he here? 'Are you a doctor?'

His laugh sounded genuine this time, warming his eyes. 'I'm a property agent,' he said, a slight slur to his words. 'Nothing for you to worry about, Rose.' His aftershave, strong and spicy, was making my eyes sting. 'You look like you've been swimming in your clothes.'

'An accident by the river,' I said. 'I . . . fell in.'

He grew still, gaze sharpening in a way I didn't like. 'Things happen here, Rose. Isaac's wife, she . . .' He glanced at the door, then back at me. 'I knew her for a long time. I was a friend of her father's—'

'Her father?' The words shot out before I could stop them.

He gave me a strange look. 'That's right.' He hesitated, then plunged on, perhaps deciding as he'd already been indiscreet he might as well continue. 'She was a troubled soul, I understand that, but she loved this house, which I helped her find, and I hate that he wants to sell it. She would be devastated.'

I could hardly tell him that Elise didn't care about the house. 'Is that why you're here?'

'When I heard he'd been making enquiries about the value, I thought it worth having a chat with him, let him know that I . . .' He paused. 'There's nothing I can do legally – it's out of my hands, I'm afraid.' James Parry trapped his bottom lip with his teeth for a second, then sighed. I caught a waft of alcohol, and understood why he was being so spectacularly careless.

'You knew his . . . the wife?'

He nodded, a wistfulness entering his eyes that made me wonder whether he'd had feelings for Elise that were nothing to do with his job. 'A beautiful woman.'

'But troubled?' I wanted to ask him so much more. Why did

he talk about Elise as if she were really dead?

'She loved that little girl, whatever they would have you believe.'

*She still does,* I wanted to say. 'Of course.' I took a step back, one eye on the living room door. Isaac could reappear at any moment. 'It's such a shame what happened to her,' I said carefully, trying to think how to word things in a way that wouldn't arouse suspicion. 'So sad for Daisy.'

'Tragic, more like.' Seeming to realise he'd not so much crossed a line as leapt over it with both feet, James Parry cleared his throat and produced an apologetic smile. 'Forgive me for talking like this. It was a, er, difficult meeting, shall we say?'

'No problem.' I returned his smile with an overly bright one. 'It won't go any further.'

'Take care, Rose, if you decide to stay.' He gave an odd little salute, seeming suddenly desperate to escape. 'I'd better get back. My wife's cooking Sunday lunch . . .' He trailed off, running a finger around the inside of shirt collar. 'Anyway, nice to meet you.'

'You too.' I managed a feeble wave as he hurried out, just as Isaac opened the living room door.

Frowning, he glanced around. 'I heard voices.'

'I bumped into Mr Parry.' No point lying. 'He seemed annoyed.'

Isaac's smile was grim. 'I bet he did.'

A car engine revved on the drive. I hoped it was a taxi and the man wasn't driving.

'Not a good meeting?'

Isaac dipped his head. 'Pretty good for me, actually.' When he looked up, his face had lightened. 'Let's just say, it was an issue he couldn't fight, as much as he wanted to.'

I tried to ignore how fast my heart was beating. 'Sounds complicated.'

'He had a soft spot for my wife.' Isaac spoke with surprising candour. 'He's reluctant to concede I have rights in certain areas,' he continued. 'He insists my wife wanted the house put in trust for Daisy, but she never got around to putting it in writing.'

My smile felt tight. He had no right to sound so pleased. 'Good news.'

When his expression changed, I thought I'd struck the wrong note, but he was looking at my outfit with raised eyebrows. 'What happened to you?'

*Your sister shoved me in the river.* 'Rocky wanted to chase the ducks.' I tugged at the hem of my dirt-smeared shirt. 'I went after him and fell into the water.'

'Poor you.' He made a sympathetic face. 'I'm surprised Mum let him off the lead.'

I didn't have the energy to explain, my head too full.

'It must have been a shock.' His gaze deepened into concern. 'Are you all right?'

I nodded and gestured at the stairs, feeling awkward. 'I was on my way to get changed.'

'Good idea.' He nodded too, but absently, as if his mind had returned to other matters – like selling his wife's home. When I looked back from the top of the stairs, he was standing at the bottom, staring after me with a blank expression that sent goose bumps across my skin.

I changed quickly into the dress I'd worn the day I went to the school – which already felt like months ago – and after blasting my fringe with a hairdryer I eased out onto the landing, the pale carpet soft beneath my soles.

There was no point going back to the river. I'd told Cecilia I would see her and the others later and guessed they wouldn't miss me.

My gaze was drawn to the door at the end of the landing: the master bedroom. I could sneak in and look for Daisy's passport and Elise's journal before everyone came back – sneak them into the hidden compartment at the bottom of my suitcase. I might not get another chance.

I drew in a breath, trying to instil a feeling of bravery as I crept along the landing, treading carefully to avoid any creaking floorboards. I tried telling myself this was more exciting than anything I'd done in ages. On a normal Sunday, I went for a run to stop myself lying in bed all morning, phoned my aunt, forced myself to cook something healthy for dinner, read a bit, watched a film, and thought about what to do with the rest of my life – a rut I'd fallen into that felt safe.

But sneaking into someone's bedroom – a private and intimate space – didn't feel brave or exciting, and my heart was in my throat as I rested my fingers on the cold brass knob and turned it. The door swung open with a groan of hinges that made me freeze. How would I explain if Isaac appeared? I waited, but nothing happened. Exhaling, I shot into the room, barely registering the neatly made bed, and smell of freshly washed linen as I headed for the narrow chest, which had nothing on top but a lamp with a stained-glass shade. This must have been Elise's side of the bed. On the other, as well as a matching lamp, were a couple of paperbacks, a wood-framed snapshot of Daisy, a phone charging cable, and a set of keys.

Checking no one had come into the room, which was carpeted like the landing, I slid open the top drawer of the chest to find it empty. I pushed my hand inside and felt the wood underneath for the passport. I couldn't remember exactly where Elise had said it was hidden.

Breathing fast, I closed the drawer and opened the one underneath, which rattled with a selection of pens, a reel of Sellotape and something else. Tucked at the back was a battered-looking notebook, smaller than I'd expected. *Brown leather cover,* Elise had said. *The word 'journal' embossed in gold on the front, so you can't miss it.*

Peering over my shoulder once more, I pulled it out, hands clumsy as I flicked it open. The handwriting was small on the yellow-tinted page, densely packed into the middle, blank spaces above and below. The next page was the same, and the next. It made the writing hard to read, but perhaps that was the intention.

Clutching the book, I shut the drawer, resisting the urge for now to search for Daisy's passport.

After checking everything was as I'd found it I crossed the room, the notebook in my hand, and paused by the wardrobe. It was old and traditional, made of solid wood. I tugged open one of the doors and peered inside, half-expecting to see a rail of clothes belonging to Elise. There were only men's outfits inside: a few shirts and pairs of smart trousers, one suit, some folded sweaters on shelves, several pairs of jeans, a pair of black boots at the bottom that looked barely worn. Everything smelt fresh, with an undertone I recognised as Isaac's.

Did Cecilia do the laundry? It was hard to imagine Elise engrossed in something so mundane, but Isaac gave the impression he knew his way around a washing machine, and surely Lissa and Jonah did their share? No housekeeper, no gardener either, as far as I could tell. Perhaps that was Cecilia's domain too.

I gently closed the wardrobe door and, emboldened by the sound of Isaac moving about in the kitchen below, looked for signs of Elise, but the room was plainly decorated with few accessories; deep blue walls, complementing the lamp shades and rug by the bed, grey blinds at the window, black and white prints on the walls, mostly of mountain scenes. Had Isaac insisted on a masculine look for this room, or redecorated after Elise left, getting rid of anything that reminded him of her?

I hurried back to my room, hardly able to believe I'd got away with it, that I had the journal. *A record of my marriage.* Adrenaline had made me hot, my palms sticky as I dropped onto the edge of the bed and opened the notebook, a shaft of sunlight picking out the words *. . . whenever I turn he's there, watching and waiting, for what I don't know. For me to slip up, to prove I'm not worthy of being his wife? This feeling is nothing new, not now. Hard to believe I once loved this man with all my heart, when it's clear in his every look and touch that he despises me.*

The tone was oddly formal. I'd never seen Elise's handwriting. She hadn't been one for birthday or Christmas cards, and certainly not writing letters – not that she'd needed to. It was almost as if she intended her outpourings to become a play, or a drama she hoped to star in one day.

Ashamed of the uncharitable thought, I turned the page, eyes jumping over the words.

*This family is not what I thought. Their welcomes, their smiles, they hide dark thoughts. They like to control, and I think that's where he gets it from; it's in his blood. I can't stay. I have to think of my little girl, but where can we go where we'll be safe, where he/they will never find us? I have to go, to save our lives.*

A knock at the door made me jump so hard, I dropped the journal.

'Rose?' It was Cecilia. 'Are you OK?'

I hadn't heard them come back. 'Fine,' I said, too loudly. I retrieved the book and shoved it beneath my pillow with feverish haste, before hurrying to open the door. 'Did you enjoy the rest of your walk?'

'Daisy was sad that you left and wanted to come back.' Cecilia looked me up and down, seeming satisfied that I'd been drying off and getting changed and not doing something I shouldn't have been, like snooping around the house. 'Would you like a drink in the garden before lunch?'

'Sounds good.' I followed her out of the room, fresh determination straightening my spine. The journal was proof Elise had suffered in this house, banishing the tiny doubts that, in spite of everything, had begun to grow after James Parry's revelation about her being a *troubled soul*. Of course she was troubled, living with a family hell-bent on destroying her.

I had to keep my focus on the end goal: returning Daisy to her mother.

# Chapter 15

'So, are you staying, or would you like to leave?'

'Speak now, or forever hold your peace,' Jonah said, in response to the question Isaac had thrown at me. 'Run while you can.'

We'd just finished dinner, a relaxed affair in the wake of whatever news Isaac had extracted from his visitor, though he'd chosen to play it down when Cecilia asked how his meeting had gone, saying simply, 'I don't think I'll be seeing him again, let's put it that way.'

I'd stuck close to Daisy throughout lunch and most of the afternoon, absorbing myself in her world of drawing, reading and chatter, helping to build a Lego ice-cream truck and enjoying a picnic on the lawn with a selection of toys. The rest of the family were within my eyeline, reading the papers and chatting while classical music drifted from a speaker, until Cecilia produced a roast leg of lamb and all the trimmings just after six.

Now, as a pin-drop silence fell, I wished Isaac hadn't asked me in front of his family, though it gave me a chance to see their expressions as I replied, 'Of course I'm staying, if you'll have me.' I wondered whether he'd asked in front of Daisy, to make it less likely I would say no.

I smiled when she let out an excited squeal and clapped her

hands. I imagined a spy, or undercover police officer, forging connections in order to extract something, and felt the burn of guilt.

'And you're happy staying here, or would you prefer going back to your own place at night?'

'Stay, stay,' Daisy chanted, and when I nodded, gratitude flooded Isaac's face. He seemed genuinely thrilled in a way I hadn't expected. Although the others were smiling and nodding, their faces were harder to read. Cecilia was stacking dishes and Lissa looked watchful, while Jonah's eyes remained fixed on his wife, as if he too was looking for her reaction.

'I'm glad,' Isaac said simply. 'I'm happy to cover your rent for now.'

'No need.' Remembering Elise was at my house, and that I would be returning once the week was over, my face grew hot. 'I'll pop back there this evening and pick up a few more things if that's OK.' I needed to talk to Elise. I could give her the journal and tell her about Isaac's meeting with James Parry and let her know that Daisy was fine.

Replaying the way Daisy lit up around her father, hugged her grandmother spontaneously, demanded piggybacks from Jonah, and was gentle around Lissa, excited to meet her cousin, I knew I wouldn't go into detail.

'Of course it's OK.' Isaac's smile widened as he stood to help his mother clear the table, a teasing light in his eyes. 'You're not a prisoner here.'

'Can I come?' Daisy pleaded, eyes bright, her cheeks splotched red.

'Early night for you.' Isaac smiled at his daughter's upturned face. 'Lessons in the morning.'

'That's right,' I agreed lightly. 'You need a good night's sleep.'

'I'd like to come.' Lissa's voice cut through Daisy's protests. 'I haven't been to Chesham in ages. I went to the market there one Wednesday. Have you been?' Her expression was neutral, but I knew she was doing what I'd half-expected Isaac to do: check out where I lived. She wanted more clues, or answers to the questions she still had.

'I have,' I said, truthfully. I'd acquainted myself with the town soon after moving there, more for Sarah's sake than mine, so I could tell her about it. 'There's a nice library too I was thinking of joining. And a great little chocolatier's called Sophie's. I bought some truffles for my aunt's birthday.'

'It'll be nice to see the bit where you live.'

'Great idea.' Jonah stretched a smile between us, revealing a speck of broccoli between his teeth. He ate like a barbarian, tucking away more than the rest of us put together. 'You'll be doing her a favour,' he said to me, a directness in his brown eyes that I hadn't seen before. 'Soon, she'll be too big to get a seatbelt around the baby.'

'Rude.' Lissa playfully slapped his arm. 'Ready when you are,' she said to me, and my gaze went to her bump as she rose from the table, her decisive movement suggesting the matter was settled. She was coming, whether I liked it or not – to the house where her sister-in-law was hiding out.

Aware my panicked silence was attracting odd looks, I summoned a weak smile. 'Great,' I said, failing to find a reasonable excuse to say no. 'As long as you don't go into labour in the car.'

Cecilia's burst of laughter seemed excessive, while Jonah's tiny shoulder slump told me he'd expected a refusal. When a flicker of triumph crossed Lissa's features, I understood that none of them trusted me yet – apart from Isaac, who was negotiating Daisy's bedtime, promising an extra story if she allowed either him or Cecilia to wash her hair, an activity she wasn't fond of.

'Rose will be here in the morning,' he said, his smile flicking on. When his eyes met mine, I had a strange sensation again, as though about to fall.

*Women fall for him all the time.*

Not this woman.

I ran upstairs to get my bag and keys, promising Lissa I wouldn't be long. I couldn't even call Elise to warn her. I already knew Lissa would insist on coming in the house to have a look around. She was on a fact-gathering mission, searching for ways to discredit me. Coming face to face with her sister-in-law would certainly fit the bill.

With sweaty hands, I grabbed my things, trying to reactivate the problem-solving side of my brain, the part that had helped me deal with difficult situations at work. It seemed to have deserted me since leaving the school – since Leon turned my life inside out.

I would have to think of something on the way.

'Sorry it's a bit small,' I heard myself saying as Lissa strapped herself into the passenger seat of my Mini five minutes later. 'Are you comfortable?'

'I'm fine.' She settled back, teeth snapping on the chewing gum she'd folded into her mouth – *to stop me feeling carsick* – as we left the house.

My movements felt unchoreographed as I swung the car around the driveway under the weight of Isaac, Cecilia, and Jonah's gaze. They'd come out to wave us off, as if we going on holiday. Daisy blew kisses that Lissa returned, her face unguarded as she fluttered her fingers at her niece. She looked younger, happier – until she fixed her gaze through the windscreen and said, 'Don't drive too fast, or I might throw up that dinner we've just eaten.'

'Your mum's a great cook.' My breath was tight in my throat as I eased through the gates and onto the lane, Isaac's words rushing back to me. *You're not a prisoner here.* So why did I have the feeling I'd been released from jail, under the care of a prison warden?

Hard to believe a few days ago, I had no idea of Lissa's existence.

'It makes Mum feel good to feed the family,' she said, hands resting on her stomach. Her protruding belly button pushed at the thin material of the stretchy top she'd changed into before dinner. 'Isaac's good in the kitchen, Jonah too, when they get a chance.'

'Not you?'

'I can boil an egg – that's about it. I keep meaning to learn, especially as I'm going to be a mum, but as long as Jonah doesn't mind cooking we'll be fine.'

The way she softened when talking about her husband made me say, 'You two have a good relationship.'

'Gee, thanks for your seal of approval, woman-I've-only-known-for-two-days. It means a lot.' Pressing her palm to her chest, she blinked wide eyes at me.

Embarrassed by her sarcasm, I accidentally pressed the brake instead of the accelerator after leaving a junction, and Lissa squealed as she jolted forward, hands shooting out to the dashboard. 'Jesus!' Now her eyes were wide with fear. 'Are you trying to kill us both?' One arm moved to protect her bump.

'I'm sorry,' I said, desperately trying to focus as I drove through the deserted town. 'I'm not used to having a passenger in the car.' I risked a glance to see her staring at me, her face the colour of milk. 'Are you OK?'

'I'm fine,' she said, but her posture was rigid, and her jaw had stopped moving, as if she was too tense to chew her gum. Guilt flooded my insides, curdling the food I was struggling to digest. Imagining her baby, curled inside, jolted by my careless driving, made me want to cry.

'So, why don't you want a relationship?'

The bluntness of her question threw me. Without the restraining presence of her family, she was clearly going for broke.

'I was in one for a while, but it didn't work out.' The words were like glue in my throat. 'I moved here for a fresh start, but don't really know anyone. It hasn't been easy.'

'OK.' Surprise had loosened Lissa's features, as if she hadn't expected me to be honest – or, as honest as I was going to be. 'I'm sorry,' she said, sounding it.

It was my turn to be surprised. 'Meeting you all has helped.'

I slid her a sideways look. 'It was unexpected, but I really am looking forward to teaching Daisy.'

'Won't it be weird when you're used to having a class full of kids?'

'Probably,' I admitted. 'A lot of them would have benefitted from one-to-one attention, but it wasn't possible.'

She was silent for a few minutes, looking out at the scenery, bathed golden in the evening sun. Maybe she was reassessing her opinion of me.

As we approached Chesham, my nerves fired up again. Should I insist she wait in the car, tell her the house was a mess? But I already knew that nothing was going to put her off coming in, and any attempts would confirm whatever suspicions she had.

'Here we are,' I said, mock-cheerful, as I turned down Chandlers Road, to the little row of buildings that would probably fit inside Orchard House.

'Nice,' Lissa observed, eyes alert as she peered at the white façades before turning to the field opposite, which was dusted with buttercups, horses grazing, and rabbits hopping in the long grass. She was no doubt taking mental snapshots to feed back to Jonah. 'Cosy.'

'Do you think you'll carry on living at Orchard House after the baby's born?' I slowed the car outside number seven, desperate to prolong the moment when we would have to get out.

'Not if it's sold.'

'Wouldn't you rather have your own place?'

'You've probably gathered that money's an issue,' she said. 'We can't all afford a mortgage.'

'No, of course not. I'm sorry.'

'Not your fault, is it?' She pushed out a breath.

I stopped the car, heart racing. 'Did you get on with Isaac's wife?' I revved the engine, hoping Elise would hear it and see that I wasn't alone. 'Sorry,' I said, switching off the ignition. 'I don't mean to pry, but I get the feeling something wasn't quite right there.'

Lissa's blue eyes flicked to me and away. She shook her head, waves of hair swinging around her shoulders, before resting her head against the seat. 'She was a nightmare, OK? Isaac would hate me for saying this, but she was a total headcase. And a terrible mother.'

Shocked by the unfairness of her comment, I said, 'I'm sure she loves . . . loved Daisy very much.'

'I'm sure she did in her own way.' Lissa turned to face me. 'But I hated the way she used her against Isaac.'

'How do you mean?' I wasn't sure I wanted to hear what was coming.

'He wanted a divorce, and custody of Daisy, but she wasn't going to let that happen, even though she barely had anything to do with Daisy. She just didn't want Isaac getting his own way.' Lissa's face was taut with remembered bitterness. 'Also, she had all this money her father had left her, but wouldn't spend a penny to support Isaac, and this was after telling him to give up writing because he couldn't get another book deal – which was probably down to the stress of being married to her, by the way – and she'd been all keen on him setting up the ski centre, which he was passionate about, then pulled the plug because he wasn't spending enough time at home, and all because she thought he'd slept with the bloody nanny.'

Lissa's colour had risen, and she shifted in her seat as anger spilled over.

'And he definitely hadn't?'

'She was twenty-two, Irish Catholic and a virgin. Even if Isaac had wanted to sleep with her, she would have turned him down.' She curled her lip. 'She just didn't want him having what she saw as hers.'

Buffeted by shock and confusion, I didn't know how to respond.

'That's where all Mum's money went after she sold the house in London.' Lissa pulled a tissue from her bag and spat her gum into it. 'Helping Isaac out, and paying off ...' Her sentence drifted. She pushed the crumpled tissue back in her bag. 'Helping me and Jonah. Because we were broke after being scammed.' When I failed to respond, she said, 'Anyway, at least Isaac can sell the house now, plus there's publisher interest in the book he's been writing, so hopefully things are turning around.'

'Maybe she was worried about him being with her for her money.'

Lissa's laugh was incredulous. 'Isaac's always paid his own way, but she made it impossible for him to earn a living. She loved having that power, making him feel small.' Before I could reply, she shook her head. 'I'm sorry if that sounds awful and lacking in compassion or whatever, but you've no idea what she put my brother through. That's why we're there, really.' She fixed me with a pin-sharp gaze. 'He needed help. She didn't want us around, even though Mum helped look after Daisy, but we couldn't stand seeing him suffer.'

My head spun as I tried to absorb what Lissa was saying. 'It sounds ... bad.'

'It was.' Lissa's face was stony. 'She couldn't help it; I get that. It was an illness, not obvious at first – Isaac really fell for her – but after Daisy was born it got worse—'

'Postnatal depression?' I remembered James Parry's assumption.

'No, it was something else.' A nerve twitched in Lissa's jaw. 'Paranoid delusional disorder, according to a specialist Isaac took her to see.' *Elise hadn't mentioned that.*

'Did any of you try to help?' The words were out before I could stop them.

'Are you kidding?' Lissa's incredulous tone was tinged with anger. 'Why do you think Jonah ended up training to be a counsellor, and that Isaac was continually persuading her to see doctors and specialists, and therapists, always online, or on the phone, looking for answers, why mum took over with Daisy so Ann could have the time to herself she craved?' The use of her name was a shock. *You mean, Elise,* I wanted to say. *Did you not think about how she might feel, being denied her birth name?* 'Of course we tried to help. We didn't enjoy seeing her suffering, but to be honest, it was hard to sympathise because she was so full of hate a lot of the time, and Isaac didn't want Daisy exposed to that; none of us did.' She took a quick breath, shook her head. 'She believed we were all out to get her, that Isaac was unfaithful. She went somewhere for a while for treatment, but nothing changed.'

*He had me sectioned, so nothing I said was taken seriously. I was the crazy lady.*

My stomach was a ball of anxiety. Lissa sounded so convincing, and she had no reason to be making this up. It was an explanation, as far as she was concerned, about why she was so protective of her brother, and why they'd all moved in with him.

But what if Isaac had fooled them? No one really knew what went on inside a marriage. I knew that from my own parents who, to the outside world, had been happily married.

So many things weren't adding up, I barely knew where to begin.

'How did they meet if you don't mind me asking?'

Lissa took out a bottle of water and had a drink. 'Some theatre bar in London where she was playing piano,' she said, wiping her hand over her mouth. That fitted, though I'd thought Elise had been in New York. 'She was good actually, but I got the impression she didn't take it that seriously. Anyway, Isaac was there, his book was out in the world and so was he, having drinks with friends, and he got talking to her.' Her face suggested it was the worst thing he'd ever done. 'He fell pretty hard. I think he hadn't met anyone like her before, none of us had. Next thing, they were getting married over in Iceland because he wanted our granddad to be there, and she didn't want her mother anywhere near, then they bought Orchard House, and then she was pregnant and everything went to shit.'

'Right.' I couldn't think of anything else to say.

'Anyway, sorry to come across as a bitch, but now you know why,' Lissa concluded, with another shake of her head, smoothing her bump as if brushing away her words. 'I'd prefer if you didn't tell Isaac we had this conversation. He doesn't like us talking about Ann. Well, none of us do. It's been good to get back to something like normal.'

'I won't say anything,' I promised, surprised to see a gleam of tears in her eyes. 'Thank you for telling me.'

'I don't want my brother to get hurt when he's doing so much better.' She blinked and gave me a hard look. 'He's not looking for a relationship.'

'Like I said, neither am I.' I returned her stare. 'You've no need to break any more glasses to try to make me look bad.'

Her eyes widened in apparent confusion. 'Is that a euphemism?'

'It doesn't matter.' As if she was going to admit what she'd done. I risked a look at the house. The curtains were open in the downstairs window, no sign of life. 'I'll run in and pack a bag,' I said, fumbling with my seatbelt. More than ever I needed to talk to Elise, but how could I, with Lissa tagging along? I felt as if she'd pushed my head underwater and I couldn't get air in my lungs.

'Do you want to come in?' I said, opening the car door. I wondered whether to 'accidentally' blast the horn in case Elise wasn't yet aware of our presence, but to my surprise, Lissa was pulling a bottle of water from her bag and shaking her head. 'I'm going to say hello to the horses.' She nodded at the fields with a longing expression. 'It reminds me of the commune near the New Forest, when ponies were part of the family.'

I couldn't even begin to dissect that statement, almost dizzy with gratitude. 'Oh, they're really friendly,' I gushed. 'I call the big one Chestnut, which isn't very original. He comes up to the fence so you can stroke his nose, but the other two are a bit wary.'

'I can relate to that,' Lissa said dryly. 'No rush,' she added, after taking a swig of her water. 'It's nice to be somewhere different.'

She got out, and after a long look at my house over the top of the car, made her way across the narrow road to the verge on the other side. From behind she didn't look pregnant at all, but like a teenager in her leggings and flip-flops, her long, pink-tinted hair swinging.

Not trusting that she wouldn't change her mind and follow me in, I scrabbled for my key and jammed it in the front door. It was unlocked, despite Elise promising she would keep the place secure.

Heart rate rocketing, I slipped inside and called her name. 'I'm sorry, I know this wasn't part of the plan, but I need to talk to you. Lissa insisted on coming with me. She wanted to see where I lived.'

There was no reply. 'We need to talk, Elise, but we'll have to be quick.'

Making sure the door was locked behind me, so Lissa couldn't burst in, I headed into the kitchen where plates and mugs were scattered along the surfaces. Elise clearly wasn't spending her time cleaning up. There were takeaway cartons spilling out of the bin, and the place smelt stale, like somewhere that had been sealed up too long. There was another smell that I couldn't place that made the hairs on the back of my neck stand up.

'Elise?' I moved to the gloomy living room, where the throw from the sofa lay in a rumpled heap on the floor with a pair of cushions, and dust motes danced in the light around the edges of the curtains. The television was on, the sound muted, an episode of *Countryfile* playing. A half-empty wine glass stood on the pile of textbooks I used as a side table.

'Are you here, Elise?' Maybe she was hiding upstairs.

I ran up to my room, wrinkling my nose at the smell of body odour pervading the small space, my double bed a mess of tangled sheets and duvet, one of the curtains hanging off the end of the pole as though yanked back too hard.

Elise's canvas bag was there, her clunky old phone beside it, the cardigan she'd been wearing flung on the end of the bed. A pair of red Converse sneakers lay on their sides on the floor, but there was no sign of her boots, which she tended to wear all the time once she was dressed.

Stupidly, I opened the built-in clothes cupboard, as if she might be in there. 'Elise?' After glancing through the window, where I could see Lissa apparently communing with the big, brown horse, its nose nuzzling her palm, I grabbed some clothes and stuffed them in a rucksack I rarely used, along with a couple of books. I'd already taken what I needed to play teacher to Daisy, but it would look odd to return with nothing.

After checking the bathroom, and flushing the toilet, I turned off a dripping tap and ran downstairs, panic building.

'Elise!' I flung open the back door, which led round the side of the house into the small back garden, where grass was growing over the concrete path of slabs embedded in the grass. There was nowhere to hide, and I couldn't imagine her going for a walk.

I pressed a hand to my mouth, my breath coming faster, heart slamming against my ribs as I faced the only possible conclusion.

Elise was missing.

# Chapter 16

'There you are.'

The voice from next door shocked me into a cry.

I stared at the woman on the other side of the waist-high fence between our gardens, realising it was my neighbour who had spoken. Having only ever seen her in passing, it was odd to hear her voice, which was high and soft, younger than her years – somewhere close to eighty, judging by the fluff of white hair and crinkled skin.

'Sorry, you scared me.' My mind was scrabbling about. Should I call the police to tell them Elise had vanished? But if I was wrong, and she'd simply gone out . . . *barefoot?* Maybe she'd brought more footwear. She couldn't have borrowed anything of mine – her feet were too big.

'. . . about your friend,' the woman was saying, knobbly fingers pressed across her chest, causing her blouse buttons to gape slightly. 'It must have been such a shock.'

I tuned back in. 'Sorry, what?'

'I'm sorry about your friend,' the woman repeated, dark brown eyes, like shiny buttons, taking me in. 'I knew you had someone staying. I saw her drinking coffee, or maybe it was tea.' Her sparse eyebrows puckered. 'She was sitting on the doorstep, looked like she'd been crying, but went back inside when she saw me. Anyway,' the woman continued, the lines around her eyes crinkling, 'The walls are quite thin you see, but I've never heard a peep out of you, so when the noises woke me up, I knew something was wrong.'

'Noises?'

'I thought it was you at first, when I looked through the letterbox, lying at the bottom of the stairs.'

I couldn't make sense of what she was saying. 'Stairs?'

'That was the noise. A sort of strangled shout, and then the banging, like someone falling. Your friend must not be familiar with the layout – that's what I thought. I knew you couldn't be there, or you'd have heard her.' Her fingers were like claws at her throat as she relived the moment. 'I could tell something wasn't right; I used to be a nurse. She wasn't moving.'

'Not moving?' I sounded like an echo.

Realisation dawned in the woman's eyes. 'You didn't know, did you?'

'I . . . I just popped back,' I said. 'My friend was, she was house-sitting for me, just for a week. I meant to tell you, I have this job, but I—'

The woman cut through my jabbering. 'It's OK. I called an ambulance, and they took her to Stoke Mandeville Hospital. I couldn't tell them who she was, just that she was a friend of yours, only . . . I didn't know your name either.'

'Rose Carpenter.' It was too much to take in. Elise was in hospital. She'd fallen down the stairs. *She was in hospital.* The words circled my mind, wouldn't settle. 'I'm sorry I didn't introduce myself sooner.'

'It's fine, Rose. I keep to myself too, I prefer it that way. At least I did, but when I heard her fall . . .' The woman's voice trailed off. 'I called the hospital earlier and they said she's going to be all right, but she hasn't regained consciousness yet. They were hoping to contact next of kin. The police were here earlier to talk to me. I thought that's why you'd turned up.'

I thought of the bag upstairs, the burner phone. No ID, no details. 'I'd better call them.' My nerves were spiky with panic and confusion. 'Thank you so much . . .'

'Beatrice Miller.' The woman blinked, as though coming back to the moment. 'I gave a statement, but it wasn't much. I couldn't really tell them anything.' The barriers were down, and she couldn't stop talking. 'In all the years I've lived here, there's never been any drama. It's shaken me up if I'm honest. Pete Thomson, two doors down, he invited me in for a cup of tea. We're not close, but seeing an ambulance – well, that sort of thing draws people together. If nothing else, I feel as if I've made a couple of friends—'

'I have to go.' I was shaking, mind sparking in different directions.

Beatrice, noticing, gave a fierce nod. 'Let's not be strangers,' she said, reaching a hand over the fence. 'You keep me posted, won't you? Let me know if there's anything you need. I can give you my number.'

'I have to go.'

She blinked again, hand pulling back. 'Of course you do. Take care, Rose.'

I stumbled inside with a feeling of unreality, as though I was in the plot of an Agatha Christie novel, but the voice on the end of the line when I got through to the hospital confirmed it was real.

'Your sister has a lot of bruising and is still unconscious,' the nurse, or maybe it was a doctor, informed me. 'She's in recovery, and stable.'

I'd barely thought about what to say but the words *I'm her sister; her name's Elise Carpenter,* had left my lips before I knew they were going to, a distant part of me shocked at the easy lie. 'We don't have any living relatives, and she doesn't have a partner,' I continued. 'I'll be there as soon as I can.'

'Try not to worry, Rose. Your sister's in good hands,' the nurse or doctor said. 'She's lucky her injuries weren't worse.'

'My stairs aren't that steep,' I said, stupidly. As if that made a difference. She could have fallen awkwardly and broken her neck. 'Sorry, I just meant . . .'

'It's fine, no worries.'

Next, I had to talk to the police, which took longer as I couldn't seem to get my words in the right order. By the time I'd given a garbled explanation of who I was, lied again about my connection with Elise, and why she'd been alone in my house, confirming it wasn't unusual for her to have been drinking – her blood-alcohol levels were high – Lissa was banging her fist on the front door.

I let her in as I ended the call and sagged against the wall.

Lissa grabbed my arm, her face a mask of alarm. 'What's happened?'

'I've had some bad news about an old friend,' I said, incapable of censoring my words. 'She was in an accident. She's unconscious in hospital.'

'Jesus.' I found myself being ushered to the stairs and seated. Lissa looked down at me, fists pressed into her hips. 'I'm sorry, Rose.'

'I have to go and see her.' I pulled my knees up and pushed my hands through my hair. 'She's got no family.' Tears hovered. 'She had me down as her next of kin.'

'Of course you must go.' Lissa dipped to one side and picked up my rucksack, which I couldn't even remember bringing downstairs.

'You shouldn't be carrying that.'

She nudged my hand away. 'I'm pregnant, not an invalid,' she said crisply. 'Which hospital?'

'Stoke Mandeville.'

Lissa's eyebrows rose. 'Your friend lives locally?'

'High Wycombe,' I said, compounding the lies. 'It's partly why I chose to move to the Chilterns.'

Her brow cleared. 'I'll come with you.'

117

'No, it's fine.' My smile felt wobbly. 'I might be there a while.'
'I don't mind.'

'I'll drop you back at the house.' My voice had steadied. 'No offence, but I'd rather go alone.'

'Of course you would. You hardly know me.' Her tone prodded me with guilt. 'Would you like one of the boys to drive you?'

'No, but thank you.' A shudder rippled through me as I realised I was sitting where Elise must have lain, unconscious, the night before. If I hadn't come back – if Beatrice hadn't woken in the night, alerted to something strange – Elise might have died, here, in my house. Without ever seeing her daughter again.

My stomach crawled. 'We should go.'

Lissa already had the door open, casting a curious gaze around the narrow hallway. My heart lurched as her eyes skimmed over the floor, and a silver hair-slide by the skirting board that must be Elise's. She didn't show any sign of recognition, eyes lifting to the old-fashioned lightshade before snagging on a framed photo I'd hung up, of me with my parents, aged about eight, taken by Sarah on a trip to Edinburgh, the castle visible in the background. At least it confirmed to Lissa where I was born, assuming she recognised the landmark.

I rose shakily and took a last look around, something niggling. For a split second, I had the sense I'd missed something crucial before reality bounced back.

Elise needed me more than ever.

It was odd, seeing her so still. In my mind, Elise was always moving, smiling, crying, hands shifting, hair swishing, eyes darting around. Seeing her motionless, hooked up to hospital machinery, a livid bruise on her pale, hollowed-out face, made my body contract with shock.

'You can talk to her,' the nurse said, a tiny woman, about my age, with cropped brown hair and pale, freckled arms. Her name badge said Nikki. 'She can probably hear you.'

'Do you know when she's likely to wake up?'

The nurse pocketed a pen. 'Not for certain, but we're hopeful it will be soon.' She checked Elise's blood pressure. 'Does your sister have any clinical conditions we should know about, any medication she should be taking?'

My heart lurched. 'Not that I know of,' I said, adding quickly, 'She lived in America for a long time, only came back recently, but as far as I know . . . no.'

Nikki's smile produced a dimple in her cheek. 'You don't look at all alike.'

It took me a moment to realise what she meant. 'Oh, we get told that all the time,' I said, feeling my face redden. 'We looked more alike when we were younger.' I'd never lied so much in my life but was gripped by a sudden conviction that my future, and Elise's, depended on me navigating this detour in whatever way felt natural. Not that it did feel natural, pretending Elise was my sister. I'd never felt that way about her, even when we were friends – that she was the sibling I'd longed for but never had because my parents decided to stop at one child. Sometimes, I'd been guiltily relieved that I *wasn't* related to Elise and could walk through my own front door and leave her dramas behind. Except here I was, caught in another, much bigger, and potentially more dangerous drama than I'd ever imagined.

'Elise, it's me,' I said softly, moving closer to the bed, shivering at the thought of Lissa's reaction had she insisted on staying with me. After dropping her back at Orchard House, I'd asked her to explain to Isaac, and tell him I would be there for Daisy in the morning.

'Take as long as you need,' Lissa had said, a less guarded look in her eyes as she bent to look at me through the passenger window. 'Lessons can wait.'

'I can't believe this has happened,' I murmured now, placing my clammy hand over Elise's cold fingers. Her thin body made hardly any impression on the sheet, while her dark hair was a stark contrast to the whiteness of the pillow. 'I can't believe you were drinking . . .' I looked up to see the nurse watching me.

'Probably not helpful to give her a hard time right now.' Her smile took away the sting. 'Maybe save that for later?'

'Sorry.' A flush of shame spread through me. 'It's been a shock.'

'No judgement here.' The nurse touched my arm as she passed. 'We've seen and heard it all, believe me.'

'Thank you for taking care of her.'

'Hey, that's what we're here for.'

Tears swam to my eyes. It was on the tip of my tongue to tell her Elise had a young daughter, but I caught myself in time. There would be implications, questions raised about her daughter's safety.

'It's going to be OK,' I said, bending closer to Elise so she would feel my breath on her skin. 'You'll soon be home where you belong, with the person you love most in the world.' I was deliberately ambiguous for the nurse's sake but squeezed the icy fingers underneath mine so Elise would know I meant Daisy. There was no response, but I hoped my words had filtered through whatever darkness was preventing Elise from opening her eyes.

The nurse smiled and moved away, as if to give us some privacy. 'Daisy's going to be so happy to see you again.' Leaning in, I lowered my voice as I said, 'I came back to see you, Elise. Thank God I did, or the police would have come looking for me. I'd have had to tell them the truth.'

The tiniest movement, a flicker of her eyelid, made me catch my breath. 'Can you hear me, Elise?' I checked the nurse was occupied – chatting now, to a porter in the doorway. 'Squeeze my fingers if you can.' I gently reached over and took hold of her other hand, warmer as though her blood had pooled there. I waited, nerve endings tingling, but nothing happened. 'Try to blink if you can.' I waited a beat. 'Everything's going according to plan,' I whispered, close to her ear. 'I've even got your journal.'

No mistaking it this time: a flicker of the almost translucent skin covering her eyes, as though trying her hardest to come back from wherever she was. 'I'll try to visit when I can.' I kept my voice low. 'You might not be able to fly at the weekend, but don't worry. I'll stay with Daisy, I promise. I'll be there until I can get her safely to you.'

Another flicker, and definite movement this time in her fingers. 'Elise?' I remembered the flights she had booked, how imperative she'd made it sound that she get away on that day. 'We can discuss it when you wake up.' I tried to sound reassuring though my reserves were running low. I was so far out of my comfort zone. 'Try not to worry.' I forced a bounce into my voice for the nurse, as much as Elise. 'Everything is fine,' I said. 'There's nothing for you to do right now but get better.'

The nurse hurried over, as if seeing something in my expression. 'What is it?'

'She moved her hand and tried to blink.' There was a hopeful note in my voice. 'I think she's trying to wake up.'

The nurse peered at Elise, before checking her vital signs again on the monitor. 'Her blood pressure's up a little, which is good.' She gave a satisfied nod. 'We'll be keeping a close watch on her, don't worry.' Keeping her fingers pressed to the inside of Elise's wrist, she said softly, 'Do you know what happened?'

'She fell down the stairs at my house while I was away.' The nurse would know this already, the police must have told her, but I hoped somehow, Elise could hear me too.

'Drinking?' She almost mouthed the word, as if worried about offending Elise, though she must have known that too from the tests they'd done.

I nodded. 'She's separated from her husband.' I felt an urge to defend Elise, though I couldn't understand why she'd left herself so vulnerable, however anxious she was about me getting Daisy back. 'She's having a rough time.'

After checking Elise once more, the nurse motioned for me to follow her into the corridor, which smelt like all hospitals did. It tumbled me back to the day I lost my baby, and I felt a disproportionate horror that the nurse was about to say something terrible.

'What is it?'

'Could her husband have done it?' The nurse's breath was minty. 'Hurt her, I mean.'

For a confused split second, I pictured Isaac at the top of my stairs, watching Elise crash to the bottom, his face a triumphant sneer. I shook my head. 'No, no. Nothing like that,' I said. 'They've been separated a while. He doesn't know where she is.' Something tugged at my subconscious – my stairs, a figure . . . Elise falling – but vanished before I could grasp it. 'It's the first time she's visited,' I added, needing the nurse to understand that this wasn't a case of domestic violence. The last thing we needed was a police investigation. I could already feel hysteria rising at the thought of how many people were now involved in our lives. 'I would know,' I added, without the usual pinch of shame. 'Not violence, but . . .' I pressed my lips together, wishing Leon didn't keep intruding, even here, in my supposed 'fresh start', but the nurse was nodding, her fingertips resting lightly on my arm.

'It's fine,' she said. 'I believe you, but we have to make sure. We don't want unwelcome visitors turning up.'

'Of course not.' I suddenly wished I hadn't told Lissa the name of the hospital, but even as I pictured her arriving to check I hadn't been lying, an inner sixth sense told me she wouldn't. Something had shifted between us this evening. We weren't friends, but she no longer saw me as an enemy. *She will soon. She'll wish she'd trusted her instincts.* The treacherous voice in my head brought another swirl of panic.

'I'd better go.' I glanced back to Elise, who hadn't moved. 'I'll visit when I can, but it's . . . it's difficult. I've just started a new job, and—'

'Don't worry, we'll call if there's any change and you can phone whenever you need to,' the nurse said, her goodwill fading slightly as she pointed down the corridor. 'Leave your number at the nurses' station before you leave.'

I wanted to say more, tell her Elise and I hadn't been close for years, we weren't sisters, or even best friends, and I couldn't be here every hour until she woke up because I had to look after her daughter. But I'd already said too much.

'You should pop into the police station, in Aylesbury, let them know you've been in,' the nurse continued over her shoulder, heading back to Elise. 'They'll want to talk to your sister when she wakes up.'

My upper lip prickled with sweat. *Don't lose it.* I had to stay calm. 'Of course.' I clutched my bag as I hurried to the desk to leave my number, getting it wrong the first time, my heart speeding and skipping.

I only hoped that when she did wake up, Elise's story matched mine.

# Chapter 17

## *Monday*

I woke from a dream about Leon, the first I'd had in ages. In it, his smile was tinged with menace, the way it was the day I told him I was pregnant – not as a prelude to celebrating, but because I thought he deserved to know, even though we weren't a couple anymore.

'We have to stay together now,' he'd said, as though I'd handed him a gift. 'I have rights.'

'Not over me you don't.'

In the dream, he sprang up from the table, where he'd been nursing a beer, swelling in size until he was towering over me, smothering me like a cloud of toxic smoke until I couldn't breathe and jerked upright, fighting for air.

'Did you have a nightmare, Rose?'

Still in the jaws of the dream, I turned to see Daisy in the doorway, holding an action figure by the arm. 'You looked funny.'

'I'm fine, Daisy.' I forced a smile as I smoothed my hair, my forehead damp. An advantage of working in a school was that pupils didn't get to see their teacher dishevelled and sweating before breakfast. 'I'm getting up now.'

'Come and get dressed, Daisy.' Isaac appeared, wrapped in a dark green dressing gown. 'Sorry,' he said, resting his hands on his daughter's shoulders. 'She's been waiting for you to wake up.'

My smile fixed, I pulled the duvet up to my chin, despite being well covered by an old T-shirt nightdress with *Let Me Sleep* on the front. 'No worries,' I said, engineering a cheerful voice. 'I won't be long.'

He hovered after Daisy had ducked away and raced back into her room. 'Are you OK?'

He'd asked the same thing the night before, after I'd driven back from checking my house was locked and taking the set of keys I'd left Elise, unnerved by the silence that had settled over the place. I'd sped back to Orchard House on autopilot, replaying the scene at the police station, where I'd seen the officer who had spoken to my neighbour.

'She thought she heard a male voice, but couldn't be sure,' he said, reading from his notes. 'It might have been the TV, which had been on loudly earlier.'

Beatrice hadn't mentioned that, and the television volume had been muted when I got there. I'd felt a prickle on the back of my neck. Had Isaac somehow discovered Elise was there? As far as I knew he hadn't gone anywhere unless he'd sneaked out in the middle of the night.

I'd looked for some sign as I confronted the family in the kitchen – all but Daisy, who was sleeping – searching his face for a hint of guilt, but he only looked concerned for me, saying he understood if I wanted to put our arrangement on ice and go home. 'You can always come back when your friend's recovered,' he'd said, which reassured me he only knew what Lissa had told them. Cecilia had agreed it was up to me, while Jonah nodded, struggling to stifle a yawn, blaming jet lag once more when Lissa gave him a prod.

'Honestly, it's fine,' I told them, eyes stinging with tiredness, desperate to escape their questions. 'The hospital will keep me up to date, and I can visit again tomorrow evening.' I'd hesitated, then added, 'We haven't been close for a long time, but mine was the only number they had.' *Liar, liar.*

'That's sad.' Cecilia had pulled a sympathetic face that exactly matched Isaac's. 'She's lucky to have you, Rose.'

Later, as I lay in bed, muscles bunched and tense, I'd sifted through the things Lissa had told me about Elise, trying to match them to the version of herself Elise had presented to me.

Seeing her unconscious had wiped it all from my mind, but in an accelerating spin of anxiety, I wondered: *which Elise is real?*

Was she the terrible wife and mother who needed psychiatric care, using her daughter against her husband because she was mentally ill, or had Isaac made them believe Elise was unstable, so if she died in suspicious circumstances, her mental state would be blamed?

I looked at him now, his hair flat on one side where he'd slept on it, dressing gown gaping to reveal a grey T-shirt and boxers underneath. Was he capable of harming anyone, let alone his wife, the mother of his child?

According to Elise, he was, and that was all that mattered.

'I'm making pancakes for breakfast,' he said now, breaking the heavy silence that had fallen, pushing away from the door with a brief smile. 'Ready in fifteen minutes.'

'I'll be there.'

Once showered and dressed, I called the hospital, keeping my voice low so as not to be overheard using Elise's name. She hadn't woken up but was otherwise stable and part of me was relieved. As long as she was asleep – as I preferred to think of it – she wasn't worrying, and I could get on with what I was here to do.

The pancakes were delicious with yoghurt and blueberries. I resisted the honey once more and surprised myself by eating a sizeable portion. When breakfast was over, eaten in an oddly companionable silence, Cecilia departed for Kitchen Mixer, the cake baking company, workmanlike in dungarees, with a canvas bag over her shoulder. Jonah, seeming more alert this morning, set off for a shift at the café, promising Daisy he would bring back a gingerbread man. Lissa, pale and puffy-eyed when she came downstairs, asked if there was any news, and after repeating what I'd told the others, she nodded before drifting through the conservatory with Rocky at her heels.

'She doesn't eat much first thing,' Isaac said, as if some explanation was required, watching his sister wander down the garden, a hand in the small of her back. 'She'll be going to the recovery centre near Aylesbury today.'

'Sorry?' Startled out of watching Daisy eat, I looked at Isaac. He was still in his dressing gown, holding a pan under running water.

'It's for young women with drug and alcohol problems. She runs jewellery-making sessions there once a month.' Seeing my raised eyebrows, he shrugged. 'What can I say? She believes in the healing power of creativity.'

Not a totally spiteful bitch then. Or maybe Lissa had only started since Elise had gone, just as Cecilia had returned to work, their lives running on smoothly while hers had stalled.

'Some of them have joined the ski centre,' Isaac went on. 'It makes a real difference having a focus that's also fun.'

'And Jonah's training to be a counsellor,' I said, the slide-show inside my head shifting and rearranging. 'It all sounds very wholesome.'

Isaac switched off the tap and studied me for a moment. 'You make it sound like a bad thing.'

'No, no. It's admirable.' I watched the little tower of blueberries Daisy had been building collapse. 'Not many people are so selfless.' *And neither are you, according to your wife, who, by the way, is unconscious in hospital.*

'I wouldn't say selfless.' Isaac, frowning, dried the pan with a sheet of kitchen roll. 'It's nice to do good.' He rolled his eyes at the sentiment. 'I know how that sounds. But you must get that being a teacher.'

I nodded, the children from Chesterfield Primary flashing behind my eyes. 'I get it.'

'It's good for the family to be able to pick up where . . .' He paused and placed the pan on the worktop. Daisy, growing impatient, looked from Isaac to me with her arms folded, as though watching a tennis match. 'Things we liked to do were let slide before, because of . . .' He glanced at Daisy and changed tack, clearly unwilling to bring her mother into the conversation. Maybe he wasn't as comfortable telling lies in front of her. 'Aren't you pleased you don't have to wear school uniform?'

Daisy scowled. 'I like school uniform.'

'You can wear it if you want to,' I told her, lifting my eyebrows at Isaac.

He nodded. 'Of course you can, bunny.'

'I don't want to,' Daisy said, contrarily. 'Can we do schools now?'

Isaac laughed, seeming happy in that moment. Because of my presence, and knowing his daughter was in good hands, his family getting on with their lives? Or because his wife was no longer around? Either way, it was an effort to turn my frown into a smile.

The morning passed smoothly. Daisy was an easy pupil, delighted to have my undivided attention, though she insisted Rocky be present in the playroom, which was doubling as a classroom.

'It used to be a dining room, but we rarely ate in here,' Isaac explained, before disappearing with a cheery, 'I'll be in my study across the hall if you need anything.'

It was a comfort to push everything aside and get back into my old routine, falling back on the planner I'd brought with me, with all the tips and tricks I'd used since starting out, and updated regularly. Though I didn't really need it, it helped to make the switch from guest to teacher.

I started with some warm-up exercises, which I'd devised to get the children in my class limbered up and breathless, and usually smiling by the time they sat at their desks. Daisy giggled through the star jumps and knee bends, but seemed keen to learn, head cocked to one side as she sat behind the traditional school-style desk that had been put there, presumably by Isaac, as I showed her how to write the letters of the alphabet before she copied them carefully with her pencil. She clearly had a good grasp of letters and numbers already, and there was a sense of freedom in knowing I could adapt the class to suit her ability, rather than stick to a curriculum.

*This isn't real,* I reminded myself. Even so, I owed it to Daisy – and Elise – to do my best.

While having a mid-morning break of milk and cookies for Daisy and coffee for me, Isaac came through to say he had to go out for a couple of hours.

'You've got the place to yourself,' he said. 'Is that OK?'

'Of course.' I noticed he'd changed into outdoorsy clothes, a lightweight, short-sleeved top with a zip-up neck and cargo shorts, his lower legs brown and muscled. It was easy to picture him either scaling a mountain or skiing down one with the wind in his hair, without a care in the world.

'Rocky will protect us,' Daisy declared, brushing crumbs from her front. The dog's tail thumped in response.

'Rose will take good care of you,' Isaac told her, looking at me for confirmation.

'Of course I will.' A weight of responsibility settled as my mind turned back to Elise.

'Let me give you my mobile number.'

I passed him my phone and his fingers flew over the screen before handing it back. 'Call if you need to or want to. I mean it.'

I nodded mutely, his smile sending an unexpected arrow of heat through me.

He kissed Daisy's head, smiling fondly when she squirmed away. 'See you later, bunny.'

'My mummy used to call me that,' she said unexpectedly when Isaac had gone. 'That's what Nanna says. Auntie Lissa says it's a silly nickname, but Daddy says it's nice and I don't mind.'

'I like it.' It was the perfect opportunity to get her talking about her mother, but something stopped me. It felt too manipulative.

Kneeling on the rug in front of the unlit open fireplace, I looked around while I sipped my coffee, admiring the décor and the row of Daisy's drawings stuck to the wall. I thought that Elise would love them and wondered how easy it would be to take one down.

'Good news.'

I jerked round, hand flat to my chest in shock and almost dropped my mug. 'Isaac!'

He was holding something, smiling at Daisy. 'I bumped into the postman on the drive,' he said as she leapt up from where she'd been stroking Rocky and ran to him.

'What is it, Daddy?'

'Your new passport's arrived.' He caught her with one arm and swung her up. 'We won't have to leave you behind when we go to Iceland,' he teased.

I scrabbled to my feet. 'Passport?'

'We couldn't find Daisy's anywhere, could we?' He kissed her ear as she wrapped her arms around his neck with a squeal of joy. 'Had to order a new one in the end.'

I thought of the bedside table in his bedroom and the passport Elise had taped to the underside of one of the drawers. *I couldn't risk him hiding it to stop me from taking her out of the country.*

It looked like her plan had backfired.

I managed a strained, 'That's great,' but all I could think was, *How am I supposed to get hold of it now?*

# Chapter 18

Daisy couldn't settle once Isaac had left for the second time. She wanted to talk about Iceland, where her daddy was born, so I fired up my laptop and we talked about how it stayed light all the time in summer and how the country originated from a volcanic eruption a long, long time ago. 'There are around two-hundred volcanoes there,' I explained.

She nodded solemnly. 'But it's very cold because it's near the Artic Circle.'

'Arctic,' I corrected with a smile. She was well informed already, no doubt having heard stories about her great-grandfather's place of birth since she was old enough to understand. I was surprised she hadn't been over there sooner to visit, but perhaps Elise hadn't allowed it. Had she been there herself at some point with Isaac, maybe on honeymoon? I wished I'd asked Lissa for more details – or Elise herself – though more and more I was starting wonder how much of what she'd told me was the truth and not her version of it.

But maybe Lissa's version couldn't be trusted either.

My mind grew muddled, apart from one clear thought: someone was lying.

It was a relief to break for lunch at twelve-thirty. I made us both a sandwich, and we ate on a bench in the garden, Daisy feeding bits of crust to Rocky, her bare legs swinging. She'd settled for a red gingham dress in the end, not unlike the summer uniform for girls at Chesterfield Primary.

I pointed out a pair of blue-tits darting in and out of a bird box, but Daisy was looking down the garden.

'It's the witch's dog,' she cried, as a white-and-tan terrier bolted up the grass. She dropped her remaining sandwich and squeaked, as if the dog was about to attack.

'Don't be scared; he won't hurt you.'

As Rocky retreated inside the conservatory, I got up and shut the door so the smaller dog couldn't get in, making a grab for his collar.

'Come on, Mr Bennet,' I said, making Daisy giggle as she jumped down off the bench. 'Let's get you home.'

'He belongs to the witch,' Daisy repeated, bolder now.

'She's not a witch,' I scolded gently. 'Her name's Thora.'

We found the old woman searching around the fruit trees, but I had a feeling the dog's escape had been manufactured.

'There you are.' She spoke to me, rather than the dog. 'I'm sorry he's such a nuisance.'

Daisy turned shy, staying close to me as the dog shot past the woman, through the gap in the hedge and out of sight.

'Hello, sweetie.' Thora's glasses were on her nose today, magnifying her eyes. She bent at the waist, hands on trousered knees, sunshine bouncing off the sequinned lightning bolt on her sweatshirt. 'You've grown so big,' she said.

Daisy took a step back, chewing her knuckle.

'Why don't you go and check on Rocky,' I said, a hand on her silky hair. 'I'll be there in a minute.'

She looked at Thora a moment longer, then turned and skipped up the garden.

'The dog scared her,' I said when Daisy was out of earshot. 'Maybe you could fix up the hedge from your side?'

'To be honest, I like to keep an eye on her when I can.' Thora's words froze me. 'Make sure she's OK, you know?'

'What do you mean?'

'Her mum used to worry the family didn't treat her very well.'

I didn't like the gossipy note that had entered her voice. 'I haven't seen any signs of that.' It was true, though I wasn't sure why I was defending them. 'She's a happy little girl.'

Thora bristled. 'You haven't been here long.'

'People can't hide their true selves for long,' I said, though it struck me that was exactly what the family was doing, by keeping up the pretence that Isaac's wife was dead. 'They wouldn't have invited me to stay if something sinister was going on.'

'Good cover, I suppose.'

My senses prickled. 'Cover for what?'

Thora pushed her glasses up into her hair, her eyes shrinking. 'You know . . .' She glanced around, checking no one was listening. 'I sometimes wonder whether Ann is really dead.'

Her words sent an icy chill down my back. 'What are you talking about?' Had Elise outlined her plan to Thora or hinted she wanted to leave?

'Oh, it's nothing, just a silly feeling.' Thora seemed to deflate, her shoulders. 'Only, if she was alive and I knew where she was, I'd get that little girl to her myself.'

The tension knotting my stomach pulled tighter, but before I could respond, Thora continued, 'She loved her so much, but I know she'd had enough of the rest of them. She wanted a divorce, she said, but was scared of something.'

I knew I should go back to the house and check on Daisy, but I could hear the creak of the swing now, and the sound of her high voice singing, *Row, row, row your boat, gently down the stream* . . .

'Did they tell you how she . . . how she died?' I tried to convey only casual curiosity. 'I've wondered, but don't like to bring it up.'

When a gleam of satisfaction brightened Thora's eyes, I wished I hadn't asked. 'One day she was there, in the summerhouse, like

133

she often was, then I went on holiday – I've a caravan in Norfolk; I go every year with my sister, take Mr Bennet with me – and when I came back she'd gone.' I started when Thora snapped her fingers. 'I didn't see her for a couple of days, and I got worried, after everything she'd told me. I got my nerve up and went to the house, asked the sister-in-law. She was very rude, said it was none of my business, but him – the husband – he did have the decency to come to the door and tell me Ann had died but he didn't say what had happened. It was all a bit dodgy if you ask me. I thought maybe she'd killed herself and he didn't like to say, or was covering for the fact that she'd left him, though it seemed a bit drastic.'

She paused for breath, or dramatic effect. 'There's no one else to ask,' she continued. 'We don't have neighbours as such, and the family aren't exactly the life and soul around here. I even checked the papers and looked on the internet to see if there was any news, but nothing. Anyway, I was thinking of talking to the police when I caught the mother-in-law, Cecilia, down here one morning, while I was searching for Mr Bennet. She looked awful, like she'd been crying, her face all red, but when she saw me she almost ran back to the house.' Thora paused and brought her voice down. 'I figured Ann must be dead if she was in that state, so I left it. Probably a guilty conscience, because if she took her own life, it was down to them.' She gave me a piercing look. 'Does Daisy talk about her mother?'

'What?' I looked at Thora's weathered face, her narrowed eyes brimming with morbid curiosity, and wondered how much of a friend she'd really been to Elise. 'Not much, no.'

'Probably traumatised, poor pickle.' Her voice oozed senti-mentality. 'It's good she's got you now.' She pulled her glasses back down as if to see me more clearly. 'I'm here if you need anything, remember that.'

Maybe she really was concerned about Elise, or maybe she liked the drama, but our exchange had made me feel grubby. I hadn't learnt anything about the family I didn't already know.

As I made my excuses and walked away, certain I could feel Thora's eyes on my back, I realised that the only member of the family she hadn't mentioned was Jonah.

At dinner, I let the others do most of the talking, some of the anxiety that had lingered throughout the afternoon melting away as Daisy claimed enthusiastically that I was her 'best teacher', earning me a grateful smile from Isaac that looked sincere.

He'd returned around five with Cecilia, both seeming buoyant after some time away, closely followed by Lissa and Jonah, his arm tight around her shoulders.

Lissa had seemed almost manic, a frenetic energy to her words as she helped herself to the mountain of spaghetti Cecilia had cooked, while talking about her session at the recovery centre.

'You can see their attitude change when they're occupied. It's like . . . they need to feel absorbed in something, as if they have a purpose.' Her stance was warrior-like as she turned from the countertop holding her cutlery aloft. 'Some of them are just kids, brought up believing they're not worth anything, but they are. Some of them, anyway. Some have real promise and could do something with their lives if they could just get clean.'

I guessed it was a conversation they'd had many times, maybe repeated for the benefit of a new audience. I chipped in to say it was the reason I loved working with very young children.

'It's good to get involved as early as possible,' Jonah approved. He smelt vaguely of coffee and vanilla after his day at the café, and there was a groove of stress between his eyebrows. There'd been a power cut, which had caused havoc with the tills.

Isaac nodded his agreement. 'We need to feel a sense of pride in something,' he said, patiently showing Daisy how to wind spaghetti around her fork. 'I just wish I could get the extra funding for the ski centre sooner rather than later, or we might have to close.'

'Just be patient a little longer,' Cecilia said.

At the word *patient*, my mind crashed back to Elise alone in her hospital bed. Pricked with guilt for stuffing my face, hoping Daisy wouldn't mention our encounter with the neighbour, I refused dessert – a pavlova that Cecilia had brought home – and made my exit.

The drive to the hospital seemed quicker now I knew the way. I sat for a moment in the car park absorbing the silence. Cecilia had thrust a bunch of plump, black grapes into my hands before I left.

'I know it's a hospital cliché, but when she wakes up, she might appreciate them.'

'Try playing her some music,' Lissa advised, antagonism on hold. 'Do you know what she likes?'

It struck me that no one had asked my friend's name. Perhaps they weren't that interested. 'Not these days,' I'd admitted, a memory flaring of Elise on a dance floor, jumping around to trance music. I preferred pop, or R&B back then, and her energy had made me feel older than eighteen as I tried my best to join in. *You're so boring, Rose. You need to let go.* She would drag me up, twisting and turning me so that I couldn't help laughing and joining in – until she got so drunk she could barely stand, crying and begging me not to leave.

Why had I stayed friends with her for so long when she'd often drained me so deeply I could barely speak? It wasn't pity, not really. She mostly seemed so confident, sure of herself, with the way she came alive on stage, and was full of plans for her acting career. Her enthusiasm had carried me along in its wake. Maybe it was those times that kept me pinned; the hope that they would eventually outweigh the times her mood would dip, and I'd find myself on the end of a verbal attack, or subtle put-downs about my clothes, my weight, my hairstyle, the friends I'd made, masking her insults with an apology – *sorry, but I'm only looking out for you* – telling me I needed to cut the apron strings and stop seeing Sarah and Roy as often as I did.

My choice to be a teacher amused and infuriated her – she

136

thought I was 'settling'. She accused me of wanting to make my mother and grandmother proud, even though they were dead and would never know. The cruelty of her comments were soon followed by more cringing apologies: it was her time of the month, she was jealous because I still had friends who were 'genuine', not hangers-on, and family I loved, when her own mother barely registered her presence and her grandmother had dementia.

Maybe that was why I didn't ditch her, even when better friends told me I should. I saw through the barbed, often nasty digs, to the child who had been abandoned by her father and blamed for it by her mother.

I got out of the car and locked it, shivering as a breeze sprang up. The sky was heavy with clouds. Rain was forecast, the heatwave due to break.

Pulling on my jacket I made my way through the sliding doors, and down the corridor to Elise's room.

'I'm here to see Elise Carpenter,' I said at the nurses' station. 'Has she woken up yet?'

It was a different nurse, older, with deep lines around her eyes. 'Not yet.' Her cheerful voice was at odds with her severe fringe and thin-lipped smile. 'No reason why not, as far as we can tell, unless she's not ready yet.'

'What does that mean?' I said, following her, soles squeaking on the floor.

'It means there's no obvious medical reason why she hasn't woken up. No swelling on the brain, which is good news. Could be related to the amount of alcohol she had in her system.' The nurse's voice turned brisk. 'Try talking to her about family, books, films, anything that's special to her.'

'You make it sound like she has a choice.' I knew I sounded annoyed, but she seemed to be making it my responsibility to wake Elise up.

'The nurse stopped so suddenly, I almost bumped into her. 'That's not what I meant,' she said, more gently. 'Just keep talking to her, or even read to her. Just the sound of your voice could be enough.'

I entered the room, to see Elise exactly as I'd left her the night before. It felt oddly like a rebuke, like the sort of stunt the old Elise would have pulled.

*Work hard if you want me back. I won't make it easy for you.*

But surely her daughter was reason enough to wake up.

'She was moving her fingers yesterday,' I said.

'There has been brain activity, and eye movement,' the nurse said, checking Elise's blood pressure. 'We know she's in there.'

At the door, she turned and beckoned me out. 'Just to let you know, a man was seen hanging about on this floor by Nikki – that's the nurse you saw yesterday. She mentioned your sister had come out of a bad marriage, so—'

'A man?' Fear swelled my chest. 'Did he say who he was?'

'No, he didn't get that far. When he saw Nikki approaching, he smiled and said he was in the wrong place and left.' The nurse's fringe lowered as she raised her eyebrows. 'Nikki thought it was a bit dodgy.'

My heart was hammering. 'What did he look like?'

'Nikki left a description in case he came back.' She tightened her eyes, remembering. 'Brown eyes, a beard – quite well-spoken, wearing ordinary clothes, trousers, black top, a navy baseball cap.'

It could have been anyone, but my heart still raced. 'He didn't ask for anyone by name?'

The nurse pursed her lips. 'Like I said, he didn't get that far.'

'OK, thank you.' I turned to look at Elise and made myself breathe out slowly. 'Please make sure that no one but me comes in here.'

'She's safe, don't worry. There's CCTV everywhere anyway, and no one's getting past us without our say-so.' The nurse gave a reassuring smile. 'It might be worth talking to the police if you're worried.'

That was the last thing Elise would want. As the nurse left, I walked over to the bed, my hands ice-cold. 'It's me,' I managed, a single thought swirling through my mind: Isaac had gone out earlier. I'd assumed it was business, but what if he'd been keeping track all along, and knew exactly where Elise was?

# Chapter 19

I sat by the bed and chatted to Elise as though she could hear me, my voice strained and unnatural. I told her about my lesson with Daisy, and how bright she was – as if Elise didn't know. I mentioned the garden and how the weather was set to change, and resorted to reminders of our past, when we'd hung out, putting a glossy spin on them.

After a lull, checking her eyelids for movement, I began telling her about my volunteering stint at an elephant orphanage in the Chiang Mai province of Thailand, recalling with nostalgia the misty mountains where the sanctuary had nestled, then stopped. She wouldn't want to hear about the trip that broke our friendship, and didn't need a reminder of that awful time, when I came home and discovered how close she'd come to dying, because of me.

I pulled the journal from my bag and opened it towards the end. 'Your writing's not how I imagined,' I told Elise, peering at some of the words and deciding not to read them aloud.

*I've thought of a way I could go. He likes to drive, doesn't trust me behind the wheel of the car of course, thinks women shouldn't be drivers. At the traffic lights in town, I'll jump out and run. I'll take just a few things – some money, my bag, and passport. I could do it! It would mean leaving my darling girl behind, but I've thought and thought, and there isn't another way. I'll go back for her once I've got settled somewhere. I'll book a place to stay, I'll use a different name. I can be a different person. The person I was meant to be.*

It was hard to read what she'd been through, and how much it had cost her to get away. I shoved the journal back in my bag.

I wanted to ask her about the disorder Lissa had mentioned, if it was true, and why she hadn't told me. Then I realised . . . she'd tried to tell me once before how she'd been feeling; a cry for help I'd deliberately ignored.

'I'm sorry, Elise,' was all I could think to say.

When the nurse popped her head round the door and gave me a funny look, I realised I was sitting there, staring into space.

'I'll bring a book to read to her next time,' I said guiltily, touching Elise's fingers as I stood to leave, though I had no idea of the sort of books she liked. She'd never been a big reader, other than learning lines for a play.

'She might be awake before then.' The nurse bustled around, checking the monitor, and smoothing the sheet. 'I know it's hard,' she said as I hovered. 'Not natural, talking to someone who doesn't talk back.'

'We never had a lot in common,' I admitted.

The nurse's mouth drew down. 'I can relate to that.' She looked up with a wry smile. 'I don't get on with my sister but in this situation, we do what we can.'

'Of course.' I felt flustered and useless, certain the nurses would have something to say about how Elise had no one to sit by her bed all day, talking to her lovingly, brushing her hair, playing her favourite music. There were no flowers, or balloons, no get-well cards. She had nobody but me.

'I brought these,' I said, producing the bunch of grapes from my bag, realising too late there was nowhere to put them.

'They look tasty.' The nurse managed to sound kind. 'I'll take them, shall I?'

Back in the car, rain pattering on the roof, I began to cry. I desperately wanted to talk to Sarah, hear some clear-headed advice, but I couldn't. And anyway, her advice would be simple: *come home.* I wished for the hundredth time I'd stayed in touch with friends instead of letting Leon scoop me away and wear me down, until they gradually stopped calling, messaging, and inviting me out. After it was over and I lost the baby, I was too embarrassed to get back in touch, to admit that, yes, I'd become one of those women we'd read about: a statistic. And that it still wasn't over because he wouldn't take no for an answer, and I was taking drastic action and moving away.

I thought of Isaac and Daisy at Orchard House, music playing quietly as they chatted about their day – though she would be ready for bed now, perhaps asleep already, the rest of them watching TV, or reading. I'd noticed they didn't seem attached to their phones, preferring to talk or to play a game with a glass of wine. The longing I felt to be with them was intense. I missed the connection – that was all – having a family to go home to.

After blowing my nose, I started the car, turned on the windscreen wipers and drove away from the hospital. Approaching the roundabout, something that had been lurking at the back of my mind came sharply into focus.

When I went home last night, after visiting the police station, the back door had been unlocked, which made sense because Beatrice had seen Elise sitting on the doorstep with a drink, but I hadn't checked the latch had dropped properly. And something had caught my eye in the living room that hadn't properly registered. There had been two mugs on the floor, one by the sofa, another by the armchair, as if two people had been there. The police officer said Beatrice had mentioned hearing a man's voice, but couldn't be sure it wasn't the television, which was turned down low by the time I got there.

Unsure why I needed to check, when Elise had left mugs lying everywhere in the house, I turned the car in the opposite direction and headed for Chesham, images surfacing in my mind: Isaac turning up late last night, demanding Elise let him in; a reunion of sorts. Why else make him a drink? Then, an argument that turned physical; Elise running upstairs to get away from him, Isaac going after her, a struggle, him pushing her down the stairs and leaving her; driving home as if nothing had happened. It wouldn't have taken much skill for him to find the house. Perhaps he'd been checking it out and spotted his wife inside.

Something wasn't adding up, but I didn't have the brain capacity to work out what it was. My eyes were swollen from crying, my stomach a tight ball of nerves. I eased off the accelerator as a speed camera loomed at the side of the road.

The steady rain and darkening sky made it seem later than eight o'clock, and the house looked unfamiliar when I parked outside. I'd got used to seeing it in sunlight recently, its façade cheerful and bright if I bothered to look. I felt like a visitor letting myself in, as if I should announce my presence.

As soon as I closed the front door, goose bumps ran over my skin. Something was off; there was a subtle scent, the one I'd detected the day before and couldn't place, but stronger and vaguely familiar in a way that made my legs feel heavy.

I pulled the door open again, the urge to escape strong. Maybe it was just that the air in the house was too concentrated, holding on to the heat of the past few days. But as I edged along the hallway, phone in my hand, ready to call the police, I knew.

Just as he'd been in my dream, he was sitting at the table in the kitchen, the tiny one that pulled down from the wall. When he saw me he jumped to his feet with both hands up as though I was holding a gun.

'What are you doing here, Leon?' I wished I hadn't left my bag in the car, with the pepper spray inside.

'I was waiting for you to come back.' His face had a ghostly pallor above the beard he'd grown to conceal a childhood scar, now too long and peppered with grey, giving him a homeless look.

'How did you get in?'

'The back door wasn't shut properly.' His voice sounded hoarse as he pointed. I could see from where I was standing the latch hadn't quite dropped into place.

'How dare you.' Something odd was happening. Instead of fear, anger and outrage flared, twin flames spreading through me. 'How dare you let yourself into my house.'

His palms came up, shielding himself. 'Rose, wait. I can explain,' he said as I began to jab my phone. 'I promise it's not what you think.'

I paused, looked at him properly. It was like seeing the 'after' photo of the man I'd thought I was in love with. And now, he was in front of me again, breaking his second restraining order.

'You're in big trouble.' I pressed the second nine. 'You must be crazy coming here.'

'I had to, Rose. I wanted to tell you I . . . I've been having therapy. I needed to apologise, in person. I'm so, so sorry for the way I've behaved, and I wanted to tell you to your face, to say that you don't have to run away, or keep looking over your shoulder.' His words came at me in a rush, as though he'd been saving them up. His light brown eyes were wide with a plea for understanding I'd never seen before. 'Because I do care about you, Rose,' he continued, and when I started to speak, he added quickly, 'And that means letting you go, letting you be happy, even if it's without me.'

'That's big of you.'

'I know you hate me, and I don't blame you. I never meant things to go as far as they did.' He slumped down at the table, as if his bones had shattered, and cradled his head in his hands. 'When I think back, I don't know . . . it wasn't me, Rose.'

'But it was.' I lowered my phone. 'That was all *you*, Leon. The stress . . .' My voice cracked. 'I lost the baby because of the stress.'

'Our baby.' He raised his head, his gaze tortured. 'It's what pushed me over the edge.'

'This is nothing new, Leon.' I fought back tears, not wanting to cry in front of him ever again. 'I've heard it all before.'

'I mean the fact that it was *my* fault. It destroyed me.'

That was a first. Accepting responsibility, instead of blaming me for letting myself get 'worked up' after turning up at the house after I called him to break the news, making the worst time of my life so much harder. 'Maybe you are having therapy, but you're still breaking the law by being here.'

'I know, but I had to come; I had to, Rose. One last time and you'll never see me again. I'm moving to Canada,' he said when I started to protest. 'I've an old friend who lives out there, remember I told you about him? Carl Jennings, he's in property development. He's offered me a job.'

My phone was slippery in my hand. 'How did you find me?' I said, after absorbing words I never thought I would hear. *He was going away.* 'I chose this place at random.'

He rubbed his hands down his face, pulling it out of shape. 'I'm not proud of this, Rose, but when I saw you'd sold your place I hung about on moving day and followed you here, but I swear that was the first and last time.' His hands were flat on the table now, as if pressing home his intent. 'It was such a wake-up call. I went back and started therapy the very next day, an emergency appointment.'

Now I felt boneless, cortisol draining away. Making sure I kept the table between us, the doorway close, I braced myself against the worktop. 'What happened here?'

'Oh, God, it was crazy.' He shook his head, his voice a groan. 'No one answered the door, but I'd seen you – someone I thought was you – moving about inside. I went round the back and knocked there, and this woman opened the door, said you weren't here and that she was housesitting. I told her . . . and I'm sorry about this, but I so badly needed to see you . . . I told her I was your boyfriend, and she let me in. She changed, became sort of . . .' he screwed his eyes up, as if trying to find the words '. . . flirty, or something, I don't know. Said you told her you were single. She'd been drinking; I realised that straight away. I felt bad for taking advantage of it but thought she might at least tell me when you were coming back.'

I felt a slump inside, imagining too easily this version of Elise, who had been equally intrigued and jealous if a man was interested in me, demanding details, searching for something she could latch on to, a chink to put me off them.

'She made me coffee – I've stopped drinking – but poured wine into her mug, and when I told her why I was here . . .' He paused, shaking his head, as though he couldn't quite believe it. 'She seemed to think it was funny.'

'You told her the truth?'

He nodded, leaning back on the spindle-backed chair that was too small for him. He looked thinner, his fleecy black top hanging off a frame that used to be gym-toned. He'd tried to persuade me to join his gym, but it wasn't my thing. I preferred walking – until he started coming with me, turning it into a 'hike' with backpacks and a thermos.

'That's why I'm here,' he repeated. 'You know how in AA one of the twelve steps when getting sober is to make amends to the people you've hurt—'

'You hurt Elise.' The realisation hit hard. 'You pushed her down the stairs.'

'No – no, I didn't, I promise.' He was on his feet, the chair falling back, but he made no attempt to come towards me as I darted to the doorway. 'She started telling me how you'd gone to get her daughter back or something, that you were staying with her family. She said I should go away until it was over, whatever "over" meant.' His gaze locked on mine. 'She got a bit weird, saying she shouldn't have said anything and told me to go, then she ran upstairs. I heard her being sick.'

He shook his head again. 'I felt terrible for upsetting her, without meaning to. I had no idea what she was talking about. I went up to see if she was OK and she rushed out of the bathroom and started screaming. She begged me not to kill her, and I said of course I wasn't going to hurt her, but she rushed at me.' He mimed reeling back. 'I side-stepped, and she went down.' Horror rippled over his face. 'It was awful, Rose. I thought she was dead.'

I couldn't speak, my mind a jumble. It sounded a lot like he was telling the truth.

'I was in shock. Then someone came and looked through the letterbox. She called out, said she lived next door and was going to ring for an ambulance. I knew I couldn't be here. If the police found out . . .' His voice dropped. 'I'd go to prison.'

'You should have thought about that before.' In my head, the words were a roar, but came out as a whisper. 'You went to the hospital,' I said more loudly, horror blowing across my mind as I took in his top, the trousers, and trainers. *Ordinary clothes,* Nikki the nurse had said, which was pretty general. I'd worried it was Isaac.

'No, no, of course I didn't.' Leon was shaking his head. 'I didn't even know which hospital she would be at. I phoned around a couple to find out how she was but didn't go there.'

My mind took a dizzying swing back to Isaac. Or maybe Nikki had got it wrong, over-vigilant because of the story I'd told, and whoever was on that floor of the hospital hadn't been looking for Elise at all.

'I could turn you in, right now.' I held up my phone. 'You've broken the law.' I sounded like a third-rate actress in an old TV show and had to squash a hysterical urge to laugh.

'Rose, are you OK?'

For a second I stared at Leon, wondering how he'd spoken without moving his lips – barely visible through his tangle of beard – then realised the voice was behind me. Leon stared over my shoulder with a look of such fear, I whirled round, heart jumping into my throat. A familiar figure had appeared, as though I'd conjured him up.

'Isaac.' I hardly recognised my voice. 'Why are you here?'

# Chapter 20

Isaac moved to stand beside me, keeping his eyes on Leon. 'Do you want him to go?' His tone was artificially light.

Despite my banging heart, I managed to say, 'He was just leaving.'

'I owed Rose an apology,' Leon said at the same time, and something about the way he spoke, squarely meeting my eyes, convinced me he was being serious. There was a witness now. Isaac could confirm that Leon had broken the terms of his restraining order if I asked him to. 'You won't ever see or hear from me again.'

I held his gaze a moment longer; the man I'd once thought I might have children with – almost had – and the man who had driven me away from my home.

'Go.' I pocketed my phone.

For a second he simply stared, as if he couldn't believe I meant it, before moving slowly from behind the table with a single nod. As he passed me, I tried not to shrink away. The scent I'd recognised when I came in was the bodywash he used: Molton Brown's Black Peppercorn, which I'd once loved but had grown to hate.

'I really am sorry for everything.' There was a tremor in his voice. For a second, I thought he might mention Elise and my shoulders tightened, but he only said in a sombre voice, 'Goodbye, Rose.'

Isaac stood aside to let him go. I sensed a tension inside him waiting to spring free. Once the front door had shut his shoulders dropped, and he turned to look at me.

'What was that all about?'

Hardly breathing, I wondered how long he'd been there – whether he'd heard me accuse Leon of pushing Elise down the stairs. *Had we mentioned her name?* Hating that this was my uppermost thought, I rushed to the window in time to see an unfamiliar dark car drive off down the rain-slicked road – a car I hadn't noticed when I pulled up outside.

'He's my ex.' I wished I didn't have to explain Leon, to bring him back into my life. But he'd inserted himself there yet again, and Isaac . . . I spun round to face him. 'I asked you why you're here?' My tone was defensive. 'Have you been following me?'

'What?' Disbelief crowded his face. 'God, Rose, no. Of course not.' He took a step towards me then stopped. 'But I can understand why you might think that, after what I just heard.' His eyes narrowed. 'He's been harassing you?'

'He . . . he was.' I briefly closed my eyes, everything rushing at me, my mind slipping around as it tried to make sense of Leon's story. Elise had talked to him, told him things she shouldn't have done, then accused him of trying to kill her. *Paranoid delusional disorder.* It was suddenly easier to believe that Lissa hadn't got it wrong after all, that Isaac hadn't lied about Elise's illness. If so, and she wasn't taking medication, what did it mean for Daisy? I was gripped by the horrible thought that it wasn't Isaac who was a threat to his daughter, but Elise.

Then I remembered the journal . . . all those things she'd written, about how he didn't like her driving, and the only way she could think of escaping was to jump from the car and run, leaving behind her precious daughter. And now she was in hospital because of me. I should have told her the truth about Leon. If he hadn't turned up looking for me, if she hadn't let him in—

'Rose?'

I jumped at the sound of Isaac's voice.

'I thought he didn't know where I lived.' My voice wobbled. 'He's the reason I moved down here.'

He studied me for a moment, taking it in. 'You're not going to call the police?'

I shook my head, a violent shudder rippling through me. Shock, I supposed. I was cold and wrapped my arms around myself. The morning's lesson with Daisy seemed light years ago.

'Hang on a minute.' Isaac ducked out of the kitchen, and I heard the front door click shut. He came back through and gestured to one of the dining chairs. 'May I?'

I nodded, seeming incapable of nothing but head movements.

He pulled out a chair and sat down. I looked at the other, where Leon had sat, and couldn't bring myself to move. 'Why are you here, Isaac?'

He hesitated, as if weighing up what to say. 'Are you sure you're OK?'

I managed another nod, telling myself I had nothing to fear from Isaac – as long as he knew nothing about my connection to Elise.

He took a breath. 'I had a phone call earlier, from the head of Chesterfield Primary School in Derbyshire.'

My head snapped up. It was the last thing I'd expected to hear. 'Helen Larch?'

He nodded. 'I was following up your references because Lissa . . .' He paused, looked at his hands. 'It's a long story, to do with my wife, but I had a good feeling about you as soon as we met. I knew that Daisy would be in safe hands.' As he spread his palms in a gesture of sincerity, Elise's warning rang loud in my mind. *Don't be fooled, Rose. They'll come across as the nicest family in the universe, but they're not.* 'Everything looked great on paper, and I was happy with that, but my sister's a lot less trusting I'm afraid.' He raised his eyebrows. 'You've probably noticed.'

'It's fine.' I felt flattened under the weight of his admission. Of course Lissa was right to not trust me, just as I was right to not trust her. 'You have every right to check my references.'

He pressed his lips together, seeming undecided about how to continue. 'She wasn't very happy,' he said, with that same air of apology that made me hate myself. 'Claimed you left mid-term, leaving them without a replacement and, although you were well liked and good at your job, she was disappointed by your behaviour, that you'd proved to be unreliable.' It sounded exactly like the sort of thing Helen Larch would say – trying to be fair, but incapable of embellishment. 'But actually this—' Isaac glanced around the kitchen '—the situation I walked into explains it,' he said, his smile brushed with relief. 'You left because of him. Is that right?'

'I took out a restraining order and he broke it.' My voice was drained of emotion now. 'Even the threat of a prison sentence didn't put him off, and I couldn't bear that I would always be looking out for him, so I left. I suppose it was a sort of breakdown,' I added, only then acknowledging what I'd denied was true at the time – to my aunt, and to the school. 'I had to get away, start over.'

'I'm so sorry that happened to you, Rose; I really am.' It was hard to make out his expression in the gloomy kitchen. Rain splattered the small window, the sky outside slate-grey. 'I had a meeting with an investor in Amersham this evening, and on impulse drove over here.' As if reading my mind, he added, 'I know what that sounds like, and after what you've just been through I hate the idea of being the sort of man sitting outside your house in his car, looking at where you live, but . . . it was a long shot. I thought if I could talk to you here about the phone call it was better than doing it at home. When I pulled up, I noticed the front door was open.'

'It's OK.' I unwound my arms and gripped the back of the dining chair, the lingering scent of Leon catching in my throat. I was exhausted, wanted nothing more than to sink into bed and sleep. 'How much did you overhear?'

'Something about him going to hospital.' Aware of my own hypocrisy, I was glad that he didn't pretend. 'To see your friend?' He made a dismissive gesture as I opened my mouth, though I hadn't a clue what to say, struggling now to remember the lies I'd told. 'It makes sense, I suppose, that he tried to get to you through someone you know.' His eyes seemed very bright as they focused on me. 'Do you honestly believe that he'll leave you alone now?'

Without hesitation, I nodded. 'Yes.' Tears blurred my vision. 'I actually do.'

In the pause that followed, something flowed between us. I sensed that he wanted to reach for me but wouldn't, maybe out of respect, and was hit by a wave of confusion. *Who was Isaac Reeves?* It didn't matter. Just a few more days, and I would be out of his life.

# Chapter 21

## *Tuesday*

Daisy had a check-up at the dentist's the following afternoon; the first day of July.

Cecilia came into the playroom after lunch wearing cropped linen trousers and a pale green tunic top. 'I thought we could go and see the new *Minions* film afterwards,' she said to Daisy, who squealed so loudly Rocky staggered up and lumbered out.

Cecilia winced and said with a smile, 'I think that's a yes.'

After they'd gone, Isaac looked in at me clearing up and suggested I take the afternoon off, his smile kind and concerned in a way that heightened the confusion I'd felt the evening before.

'Go and visit your friend or take a walk, or whatever you like. Have some time to yourself.'

After I'd followed him back to Orchard House, assuring him I was fine, he'd advised me to head straight upstairs, offering to tell the others I had a headache and needed an early night. 'Our conversation won't go any further,' he'd promised, holding my car door open as I got out. 'It's no one else's business.' His words had

154

twisted a knife of guilt that seemed to have lodged in my throat. 'I'll bring a drink up for you.'

I'd almost cried when I came out of the shower to find a mug of milky hot chocolate on the bedside table, which I drank standing up, before crawling into bed and falling instantly asleep, waking at seven to sun streaming through the window.

I'd phoned the hospital from the en suite to be told Elise had stirred and murmured in the night. 'We're hopeful she'll come round fully soon,' the nurse had said, promising to call me the second she did.

Eating breakfast, my mind had returned to the night before, and I'd felt something approaching a tentative peace where Leon was concerned for the first time in months. The nightmarish situation was over, but I couldn't relax and enjoy it with everything that lay ahead.

Then Daisy rushed in and asked me to do her hair in plaits, and my heart filled as she rested against my knees and let me brush out her curls. Seeds of hope took root as I pictured Sarah and Roy's reaction to hearing Leon was no longer a threat. I wouldn't tell them he'd been to the house – they were bound to call the police – but would say he'd sent a letter of apology via the school, informing me he was moving abroad and that I wouldn't hear from him again. If they wanted to see the letter as proof, I would tell them I threw it away, that I wanted no reminders of him in my life. Sarah knew me. She would be able to tell from the pitch of my voice I believed it was truly over.

The image had carried me through the morning, lifting my mood, and now, I gave Isaac a grateful look.

'A walk would be nice,' I said with a smile. 'Thank you.'

'I'm cooking tonight, but don't feel obliged to rush back.'

'Sounds good.' *Don't be taken in by him.*

Left alone, I phoned the hospital once more. 'I'm checking whether there's been any change in Elise's condition,' I said, when I was put through.

'I'm afraid not, Miss Carpenter, but all her vitals are normal.'

'I'll be in this evening.'

'I'll tell her.' I wondered whether I was imagining a reprimand in the nurse's voice.

As I ended the call, a sound made me turn. Isaac had left the door open, probably because Rocky had a tendency to whine outside until he was let in.

I moved quickly across the floorboards and yanked the door wide, peering into the hallway. A sound came from somewhere above: the soft click of another door closing.

I edged out, glancing up the staircase to the sunlit landing. Maybe Isaac had run up there as I finished my call. A feeling of dread turned my stomach. I'd asked after *Elise*, her name audible to anyone lurking nearby. Why hadn't I gone outside?

I jumped as Rocky exited the living room, casting me a baleful look as he headed past. Maybe it had just been the dog roaming around.

On impulse, I walked to the patio doors and let myself out, jogging across the grass in my flat sandals until I reached the summerhouse, partially hidden by a spreading laurel. I slowed, hearing music; an old Kate Bush song that took me back in time, to Mum watching a repeat of *Top of the Pops* on TV, singing along as she ironed my school uniform, then rummaging for an old cassette tape of tracks that Dad recorded for her when they were dating. *Running Up That Hill* had been her favourite tune.

Out of breath, I crept to the closest square of glass and peered inside, cupping my hands around my eyes. After the brightness of the garden, last night's rain already forgotten, it was hard to make everything out, but I could see a tall craft light angled over a wooden workbench crammed with tools, including a tiny hammer, and a neat row of small metal buckets hanging on the wall behind, filled – presumably – with crafting implements. Twisting my head, I saw a small sofa that dipped in the middle, covered with an orange blanket, and two mugs and a kettle on a shelf running along the wall at the far end.

'What are you doing?'

My body jerked with shock. I spun round to see Lissa approaching from the house, a covered plate in one hand, the other resting protectively on her bump. *Had she been in the house the whole time?*

'You scared me.' My laugh was shaky as I glanced at the window behind me, mind racing in time with my heartbeat. 'Daisy's gone to the dentist's with your mum, and I was . . .' I cleared my throat, turning to face her. 'I was curious about your work but didn't want to disturb you.'

'So you thought you'd sneak around outside instead?' I couldn't tell from the glint in her eyes whether she was angry, or teasing. 'I could have gone into premature labour if I'd spotted your face at the window.'

'It's not that bad, is it?'

To my relief, her expression relaxed. 'Not scary at all.' She moved past me, trailing a spicy smell that mingled with her perfume. 'I was getting some lunch. I sometimes forget to eat when I'm working.' She opened the slatted door and turned, one foot over the threshold. 'Come in then.' She inclined her head, and I had no choice but to follow her inside, greeted by a slight smell of burning.

'That smell is from soldering.' Lissa moved aside a pair of safety goggles to make space for her plate. 'I mostly work with silver.' My gaze skimmed a shelf displaying a selection of jewellery, some of it chunky, some delicate, a few pieces studded with brightly coloured costume jewels. A chrome hand, cut off at the wrist, wore multiple rings and bracelets beside a silver tree, its branches hung with necklaces.

Lissa sat on a curvy-backed swivel chair and tugged open one of the drawers in the desk, where gemstones glittered, catching the light. 'Fiddly to work with, but I like the challenge.' It was clear from her tone, the narrowing of her concentration, that she loved her work.

'Do you sell to local businesses?'

Lissa shrugged, leaning to peel the foil from her plate, which contained a wedge of leftover lasagne, along with a fork. 'A couple of places. I sometimes sell at the market but now I'm pregnant, my back aches if I stand for too long. I'm turning into Mum.' I smiled at her horrified expression. 'It brings in a bit of cash, not much. I mostly get commissions through the website.'

'You have a website?' I hadn't meant to sound surprised.

'You need one if you're self-employed.' Fixing her blue eyes on me, Lissa began to eat, unselfconsciously. 'How are you today?' she asked when she'd swallowed, grabbing a tissue from a box on the bench and passing it over her mouth. 'No news about your friend?'

*Was there something loaded about the question?* I became engrossed in a tray of wires cut to different lengths. 'There was some movement last night,' I said. 'The doctors think it won't be long before she wakes up.'

'Hey, that's great.' Through a mouthful of food, Lissa sounded pleased. 'What will happen when she's released? Won't she need you to look after her?'

'We'll need to talk, but I expect there are other people in her life she's close to.'

'So why have you down as her next of kin?'

'She never really got on with her family,' I said, as a thought snuck into my head. 'But there might be a partner, or even a work colleague she's closer to than me these days.'

'Yet no one has come forward, wondering where she is?' Her gaze seemed too intense. 'Don't you *want* to take care of her if she's your friend?'

'Like I said, we haven't been close for a long time.'

Lissa put down the almost empty plate. 'How long?'

I was pressing the palm of one hand with the thumb of the

other but stopped when I saw Lissa watching. 'Years, really. We didn't keep in touch after university.' Was Lissa working out a possible timeline? Maybe it had been her, listening outside the door. She knew it was Elise and this was a trap.

'I've got a friend like that.' Lissa reached up to release her knot of hair and retied it more firmly. 'She only ever gets in touch these days when she wants something.' She delicately wiped the corners of her mouth with the tip of her little finger. 'You shouldn't feel bad if you don't want the responsibility.'

'No, you're right.' A flood of relief weakened my knees. 'But I'll help if there's no one else.'

'At least she has no serious injuries. Apart from the concussion, I mean, though you don't know what state she'll be in when she wakes up.' Lissa had turned to her workbench, eyes moving busily over her tools as if itching to get back to work. 'She might have to move in with you if it turns out there is no one else.'

That tone again, almost taunting. Or was I imagining it? 'Hopefully, she'll be fine,' I said, a tightness in my throat.

'I suppose she could recuperate at your place while you're living here, if she has nowhere else to go.'

I couldn't read her at all. 'I'm sure it won't come to that.' I glanced at the rough wooden walls, seeing a faded space where there might have been an old boiler-type heater. *Carbon monoxide poisoning.* 'It must get cold in the winter.'

Lissa's head shot up. She looked around and nodded. 'I haven't spent a winter in here yet.' She picked up a pair of pliers and put them down again. 'Anyway, I'd better get on.'

'Of course.' I replaced a Celtic-style ring I hadn't been aware of picking up. 'That's nice,' I said, fingering a silver starfish on a short chain. 'Maybe I could commission something.'

'Please do.' Her gaze fixed on the necklace as I backed towards the door, perhaps checking I hadn't slipped it into my pocket.

'Thanks for letting me in.'

Her eyebrows rose. 'You practically let yourself in, remember?'

Uncertain how to respond, I mumbled an apology and left her there, trying not to stumble as I headed up the garden, pausing as I caught movement in an upstairs window. *Isaac?* I shielded my eyes, but whoever was there had gone.

I continued inside to get my bag and keys, pushing aside the double-edged tone of my conversation with Lissa. The thought I'd had while we were talking had stuck in my head. I was going to High Wycombe to visit Elise's mother.

# Chapter 22

As I drove through Beaconsfield towards the A40, I glimpsed a familiar figure exiting a café along the high street. *Jonah.*

His phone was pressed to his ear, and he was tugging a black apron off as though an emergency had arisen. I slowed and lowered my window. Seeming to notice me, he stopped. I prepared to wave, to ask if everything was OK, but he spun abruptly, his back to me as he carried on talking into his phone.

The car behind me beeped. Thinking the sound would attract Jonah's attention I waited a beat, but he remained motionless, apron dangling from one hand. I drove off, heart bumping. Had Jonah ignored me, or been so engrossed in his call he hadn't recognised me?

Shaking off a sense of unease, I turned on the radio as I headed to High Wycombe, trying to imagine Ingrid's reaction on seeing me. Perhaps she wouldn't recognise me, but Elise had said her mother sometimes remembered things from decades ago, even if she didn't know her own daughter these days.

As I drove, my heart sped up as my mind tumbled back to the last time I'd spoken to Ingrid. I'd just returned from Thailand to discover from my aunt that Elise had taken an almost fatal overdose, according to her mother, who had stormed round to the house a few days earlier, blaming me. My blood had chilled with shock as I finally listened to the messages Elise had left on my phone – messages I'd deliberately ignored, not wanting her intruding on my time away or to get dragged into whatever drama she'd constructed. Her increasingly distraught pleas for me to call, to talk to her, had filled me with a deep shame. *I need you, Rose. I don't know what I'll do if you won't talk to me. I'm so unhappy. I don't think I can go on.*

When I rushed round to see her, recuperating at her mother's, Ingrid had launched into a drunken tirade about what a nerve I had, showing my face *after what you've done*, and I'd felt as guilty as though I'd been personally responsible for forcing the pills and vodka down Elise's throat. *Some friend you turned out to be.*

Elise, clammy-skinned with purple-shadowed eyes, on the chaise longue in her old bedroom, had turned away when I reached for her. *Elise, I'm sorry.*

*Just go, Rose.* She'd sounded so bitter, and I could hardly blame her. *You've made it clear you don't care about me.*

*I should have been here.* I'd felt desperate seeing her so pale, a shadow of the friend I'd left behind, had wanted to do something, anything, to raise a smile. *I'm here now. Talk to me.*

*Honestly, Rose, I'm fine now.* Her tone had hardened, her chin lifting. *I won't make the mistake of thinking you're my friend ever again. You're free.* She'd wafted a hand towards the door. *Off you go.*

*Elise, please—*

*Just leave me alone, Rose.* She'd turned her head to look out of the window, so I could no longer read her expression. *Like you have for the past year.*

Knowing I deserved the barb, I'd let it go. *Give me another chance.*

When she hadn't replied, I'd stared at her tense shoulders, skinny beneath a thin, grey top that looked like it needed a wash. *At least promise me you'll get some help, Elise. Please.*

*I suppose that would ease your conscience.*

*I'm worried about you.*

*If you were that worried, you wouldn't have gone away without me.*

Ingrid had appeared then. *You heard her.* Her tone had been vindictive, as though she'd won something, and it had struck me that she'd never liked me, even though I hadn't – until then – given her a reason not to. *Run off back to your perfect life.*

*Ingrid, I'm so sorry I wasn't there for her, but—*

*You're the one who has to live with it,* she'd cut in, eyes narrowed. *Elise will be OK.*

If Ingrid remembered telling me to stay away as I left in tears, it was doubtful she'd want to speak to me now, but I had to let her know Elise was alive. I had no idea whether Isaac had told his mother-in-law about her daughter's 'death' or whether Ingrid was capable of understanding; but even if she wasn't, she had a granddaughter she probably knew about – might even have been asking after. Though, if I was being honest, it wasn't so much that I thought Ingrid deserved any truths after the childhood Elise had endured. More that I was looking for clues, hoping she had answers, even if I wasn't sure of the right questions to ask.

Entering High Wycombe, I slowed at traffic lights. Glancing in my rear-view mirror, I jolted to attention. A couple of cars behind was a vehicle I recognised, sun bouncing off the bonnet. It was the racing-green Volvo belonging to Lissa and Jonah.

I couldn't make out who was behind the wheel, but it had to be Jonah. He'd driven to work that morning. And what were the chances of there being another Volvo in that particular shade on the exact same road, right now?

In fight-or-flight mode, I swung the car towards the town centre and into the nearest car park. Sliding into a space, I switched off the engine and checked my wing mirrors while feigning interest in my phone. Sure enough, the Volvo pulled in, coasting past to park at the opposite end, shielded by a yellow delivery van.

163

My heart was speeding as I got out of the car and paid for parking using the app on my phone, hoping I looked a lot calmer than I felt.

Without glancing back, I headed into the shopping centre, making sure to stop and browse in shop windows as I passed, before darting into Primark, where I made a point of picking up several tops. I held one up while keeping an eye on the entrance. Jonah sidled in and pretended to examine a rail of T-shirts, casting me covert glances. He was a terrible spy, almost laughable, except I didn't feel like laughing.

Had Isaac or Lissa called to tell him I'd gone out and asked him to trail me, or had he spontaneously jumped in the car after seeing me drive past?

Either way, he'd be disappointed to discover I'd simply fancied a shopping trip and bought a couple of cheap tops. I took a handful to the till, and after paying, headed for a coffee shop further down, where I ordered a latte and a muffin. Taking both outside, I sat at a vacant table and took out my phone, making sure my head was lowered as he walked by, feet dusty in the Birkenstocks he wore daily, even with his work outfit of stone-coloured chinos and white Polo shirt.

'Jonah!' I nearly laughed at his look of fright when he pivoted automatically towards the sound of his name. 'What are you doing here?' I jumped up, gathering my bags and coffee, faking surprise with a wide-eyed smile. 'I've been doing a bit of shopping.' I lifted the paper bag. 'Daisy's gone to the cinema with Cecilia.'

'Oh, that's right.' Jonah did a good job of appearing bemused. 'Sorry, I was miles away.'

'I thought you were working at the café today.' My tone was a little too matey, but Jonah rallied and tilted his head with a friendly grin.

'I ducked out early,' he said, scratching behind his ear with a bashful air. 'It's Cecilia's birthday soon and Lissa's not up to wandering around the shops at the moment, so I said I'd pop down

164

and look for inspiration.' He eyed a nearby jeweller's. 'Can't go wrong with a pair of earrings, though I'm bound to get it wrong.'

'Surely Lissa could make her something if you're looking for jewellery?'

I was almost enjoying baiting him, 'Unless she prefers gold.'

'She does.' Jonah gave an easy nod, but curls of hair clung to his damp forehead. He wasn't as relaxed as he was making out. 'She'd like a watch actually. Old-school, I know. I use my phone to tell the time.'

'Oh, I like a watch.' I took a sip of coffee, hoping I looked casual. 'I have one my parents bought me for my tenth birthday. It still works, though I don't wear it.'

He nodded again with a thin smile, then raised a hand. 'Anyway, I'm on a late lunch-break, so I'd better get back.' He'd clearly forgotten he was supposed to have finished early for the day. 'Might be easier to look for something online.'

'Good point.' I wiggled my fingers at him as he turned to leave. 'See you later.'

He raised his arm in acknowledgement as he strode away, his phone to his ear before he'd exited through the double doors – no doubt letting his wife know my outing was perfectly innocent.

Graylands Manor looked more like an upmarket hotel than a care home; two storeys of smooth honey-coloured stone and sparkling windows, set behind tall gates in landscaped grounds. The previous night's rain had unleashed the scent of honeysuckle, which floated through the open car window, pulling me back to Sarah and Roy's, where trumpet-like flowers grew up a trellis on the front of the house, scenting the air all summer.

The benches positioned around a circle of deep, green grass, where a stone fountain spouted water, were full of elderly people chatting, or staring into space. An old man under a pinewood pergola watched a pair of fighting pigeons, his shoulders shaking with laughter.

Elise had clearly thrown money at the problem of her mother, placing her in the most luxurious care home she could find. Maybe she felt she owed it to her, though Elise had never subscribed to doing things out of duty. At least, not when I'd known her. I reminded myself she was a mother now, and perhaps something had shifted. Maybe she'd uncovered some sympathy or understanding for Ingrid even if it appeared to be too late.

Inside didn't smell as I'd imagined it would – the reception area could have passed for a five-star spa – but it was hot, and something about the quality of air made me think of the reptile house at Edinburgh Zoo, the image compounded by the sight of a man with scaly skin, shuffling past, with a walking frame, in a pair of furry slippers.

'Careful now, Edwin. The floor's been polished.' A dark-haired woman in a lilac tabard, with a lanyard around her neck, hurried to catch him up. 'Let's go into the café,' she said, ushering him away from the doors.

I took in the board behind the glossy white desk, displaying all that Graylands had to offer: a book club, cinema, hairdresser's, church services, and something called a reminiscence room, presumably for the dementia patients – or clients as they were no doubt referred to. 'I wouldn't mind staying here myself,' I said to a woman wearing crimson lipstick looking at her computer behind a protective wall of Perspex.

Her brief smile said she'd heard it before, and that if I was at the stage of needing to be there, I probably wouldn't enjoy it. 'You'll have to sign in,' she said, enunciating clearly as though I was deaf, pointing to a visitors' book attached to a pen on a chain. 'Who are you here to see?'

'Ingrid Lockwood.'

The woman's expression morphed from professional interest to open curiosity. 'First visitor she's had in a while.' Her hands were poised over her keyboard. 'Are you a relative?'

'An old friend of her daughter's.' It was a relief to be truthful, though I couldn't help a shiver as I imagined what would have happened if I hadn't noticed Jonah following me. 'I haven't seen her for a long time.'

'Such a shame about Ann,' the woman said, forehead crumpling.

So someone *had* passed on the 'bad news'. 'Yes,' I said carefully. 'Actually, Elise is her real name.'

The woman's eyes widened. 'She mentions that name a lot,' she said. 'Marnie – that's her one-to-one carer – said Ingrid often asks after Elise. One of her lost girls, she calls them.'

I remembered the daughter who had died before Elise was born and wondered whether that was where Ingrid's problems had started. 'Where can I find her?'

'Down the corridor, first on your right.' The woman leaned forward, pointing with a manicured fingernail. 'She's in number five,' she said. 'I'll let Marnie know you're here.'

I hurried away, past a bustling café and what looked like a bar, cooking smells prickling my nostrils – not the boiled cabbage and stewed meat variety, but fragrant and spicy. Maybe they employed a Michelin-starred chef.

The door of number five was ajar, sunlight slanting across a teal-coloured carpet. I pushed it open and entered a large room, decorated in shades of blue and cream, where a woman was sitting in a high-backed chair by the sash window. It was open at the top, a light breeze ruffling the lining of the velvet curtain.

'Ingrid?'

The woman turned at the sound of my voice, and I was struck at once by her likeness to Elise, which hadn't seemed so obvious in the past.

'Who are you?' Her voice was sharp, edged with suspicion. 'What are you doing here?' Her hands curled around the arms of the chair as she hauled herself to her feet. 'I don't know you.'

'I'm Rose.' I didn't move, not wanting to alarm her further. 'Rose Carpenter.'

Ingrid stared at me with watery eyes, as if trying to bring me into focus, her mouth working. She looked much older than seventy, in a different class to my aunt who, at sixty-eight, still went running two or three times a week and belonged to a yoga group and had a large circle of friends. Her naturally grey hair was usually coloured a light, ashy blonde, but Ingrid's hair was white and cut too short, revealing large ears, making her nose look bigger. It was more hooked than I remembered. She was tall and whip-thin, her loose, floral dress like a shroud.

'Do you remember me?' I risked stepping further into the room. 'Elise's friend?'

At the mention of her daughter's name, a cry emerged from Ingrid, raw and guttural. She dropped back in the chair, running the material of her dress through her fingers.

'My lost girl,' she cried, mouth gaping. 'My lost girls.'

Despite the open window, the air was dense and seemed to stick in my lungs. Would it help to tell her Elise was alive, or only confuse her more?

I'd read somewhere that if people with dementia believed something to be true, it was best to agree, to avoid upsetting them more – but her daughter wasn't dead. Then again, if she no longer recognised Elise, maybe it was better to leave it that way. Apart from anything, Elise wouldn't thank me for coming here and raking up the past.

'It's a lovely room,' I said, desperate to distract her, taking in the framed oil paintings of the Chilterns on the walls, wondering whether they belonged to Ingrid, or came as part of the package. 'Do you like it here?'

'It's my home,' she said in a haughty tone. She lifted her chin, her anguish apparently forgotten. 'Who let you in?'

'I wanted to see how you were doing.' Taking a chance, I dropped onto a velvet-covered armchair, the same shade as the carpet. The cushion was stiff and unyielding, and I shuffled to the edge, my bag in my lap, wondering why I'd come. It was clear that Ingrid inhabited another world, only drifting occasionally into this one.

A head poked round the door – the woman from reception. 'Marnie will be in shortly.' She flashed big, white teeth. 'I'll bring you some tea.'

'No need,' I said, but she'd gone.

'Rose Carpenter!'

I looked at Ingrid, whose face was transformed; softer, smiling, a flush on her pale cheeks, as though possessed by her younger self.

'What are you doing here?'

Unsettled by her lightning change of mood, I said, 'I came to see you.' I leaned forward slightly. 'Do you remember me?'

'Of course I do.' She pulled her chin back. 'You're Elise's friend.'

'That's right.' Suddenly, my heart was pounding. 'It was a long time ago.'

Ingrid shook her head, eyes clouding. 'It wasn't nice, what she did to you.'

'What she did?'

'Blaming you when she took those pills.' Ingrid's lips pulled tight. 'It was that boy she'd been seeing. He finished with her on Christmas Day, and she couldn't get over it. She used to call me, crying down the phone, saying she didn't want to live anymore.' When her eyes met mine, they were filled with distaste. 'That's a horrible thing for a mother to hear.'

I nodded, dry-mouthed, wondering what she was talking about. Elise hadn't said anything to me about a relationship break-up. She'd let me believe her breakdown was due to my leaving, her needing me.

'I wasn't a very good friend,' I admitted, wondering whether Ingrid was remembering wrongly. 'You were angry with me when I came to see her, remember?'

'I was always angry.' Ingrid flapped a hand. 'I drank a lot. Not her fault but I couldn't forgive her, you see.'

I frowned. 'Forgive her for what?'

169

Ingrid pitched forward suddenly, hands clasping her knees. 'The women in this family are cursed.'

A chill ran through me. I didn't know what to say.

The neck of Ingrid's dress dropped, exposing a slice of flesh-covered bra. 'Do you know I have a granddaughter?' A sparkle entered her eyes. 'Her name is Daisy.'

'Yes, I know.' I tried to match her tone, still grappling with her previous comments. 'Does she come to see you?'

Ingrid was looking around, eyes darting past me to the door, then the window. 'Have you brought her to see me?' A sun-spotted hand shot out. 'I have rights, you know.'

'I've got a picture.' I dug a hand into my bag, remembering the picture I'd taken of the photo in Daisy's room. 'She looks like her mum.' My bag slid to the floor, spilling the contents: the canister of pepper spray, the journal, a pack of tissues, and my coin purse and keys. 'Sorry.' Flustered, I bent to pick up the items, but Ingrid beat me to it.

'Where did you get this?' Her voice was shrill, shot through with disbelief. She was holding up the journal like a talisman. 'Did you steal it?'

'I . . . I found it,' I stammered. 'I was looking for it for Elise. She wants it back—'

'It belongs to me.' Ingrid flicked wildly through the pages, a tide of crimson rising to her face. 'I had to leave.' Her voice was high. 'I had no choice, not if I wanted to live. I couldn't stay with him – he would have killed me. It's all in here.' She waved the journal. 'I hated leaving her behind, my little girl.' She made a keening sound. 'It was the only way, but I didn't know what it would be like. I couldn't forgive her.'

I tried to hold her hand, but she snatched it away. 'Ingrid, I don't understand. This journal belongs to Elise.' But as I spoke, certainty seeped away.

Ingrid snapped the book open and held it in front of me, finger jabbing at the inside page. Two letters I hadn't noticed

before, written in the same black ink as the words inside. *IL.*
*Ingrid Lockwood.* I stared at them until they began to dance, and
Ingrid snatched the journal away.

The journal wasn't Elise's. It belonged to her mother.

# Chapter 23

At Orchard House, I parked beside Jonah's Volvo. The garage door was open, Isaac's car inside. *I got your brother-in-law to move the chest freezer, so you should be able to drive into the garage now.*

Was it really only days ago that Cecilia had uttered those words?

I got out of the car and headed for the garage, not stopping to check whether I was being observed. If anyone asked, I would say I thought I'd spotted a scratch on Isaac's car bumper.

The garage smelt warm and woody with a tang of petrol. There would be room for another car if it weren't for the wide freezer, now pushed up against the side wall, beneath the casement window.

I dipped my eyes to the concrete floor, hooking my hair behind my ears. Elise had dropped her earrings when Cecilia crept up on her and hadn't had a chance to retrieve them. They could still be here. It seemed imperative now that I find them. The shock of discovering the journal didn't belong to Elise had thrown everything I thought I knew into doubt. Once Ingrid had pointed out her initials, she'd thrust the book at me as though it was on fire.

'Take it.' She'd made shooing motions, twisting her head away as though she couldn't bear to look. 'I don't want to read all those bad memories. They're locked in here.' She slapped the side of her head. 'Do you think I don't have regrets, Rose?' Her eyes had blazed with sudden fury, reminding me of the temper she'd unleashed the last time our paths crossed. 'I have regrets, but *she* should too. She wasn't the daughter I wanted. I just didn't know until it was too late.'

The casual cruelty of her words had swung my feelings back towards pity for Elise. No wonder she was messed up, when the woman whose love she was supposed to take for granted had seemed to despise her. Even Ingrid's defence of her daughter back then – when I thought about it – had seemed theatrical, as if she was putting on a show of being an aggrieved parent, rather than feeling it. And all along she'd known Elise wasn't so much heartbroken about me leaving – which fitted with her cold sneer and parting shot of *Go and 'have fun' while the rest of us work for a living. You always were a selfish cow* – as distraught because another boyfriend had dumped her.

'Who are you, anyway?' Ingrid had said as I stuffed the journal into my bag with trembling hands, relieved beyond measure when the woman from reception returned with a rattling tea tray.

'I'm afraid I've upset her,' I said, already retreating from the overheated room. 'She doesn't know who I am.'

Not waiting for a reply, I'd fled, barely aware of driving back to Orchard House as I struggled to remember whether Elise had actually said the journal was hers, or only implied it. *Record of a bad marriage. Proof, if you like.* She'd clearly wanted me to believe she was documenting her own life, but why? I felt as if I'd been shoved in deep water with nothing to hold on to. Maybe if I found the earrings, it would prove Elise had been honest.

As I bent over, a glimmer caught my eye by the flat tyre of a pink and white tricycle stashed by the freezer. I dropped to a crouch and picked it up, dropping the delicate earring into my palm. It had the patina of age, bronze with a screw back, shaped like a flower. My heart raced in response. Clutching it, I knelt and pushed my other hand under the edge of the freezer, running my fingers along until they felt something sharp-edged. I managed to tease it out, hardly able to believe my luck as the matching earring shot into view, the petals bent out of shape. It was a small triumph but didn't do much to address the swarm of questions buzzing around my head. I pushed the earrings into the pocket of my jeans and sneezed. It was dusty and cobwebby at this level. I jumped as a spider scuttled from under the freezer and darted past.

As I made to stand up, car tyres crunched the gravel and came to a stop outside the garage, followed by doors opening and slamming.

'I'm going to tell Rose about the film, Nanna.'

I ducked behind Isaac's car, realising I'd left mine unlocked, my bag on the passenger seat and the key in the ignition. It would look odd if Cecilia glanced inside.

'Can I have ice-cream for pudding?'

'You've just been to the dentist,' Cecilia called, her tone warm with affection. She didn't sound as though she was following Daisy, so I stayed where I was, holding my breath. I imagined Cecilia's stare burning through metal, spotting me crouched like an intruder.

Daisy would be charging around the house, looking for me. I swore under my breath as I looked around, hoping there might be a door leading into the house, but the garage was separate from the main building.

About to risk a glance around the side of the car to see if the coast was clear, I heard another voice.

'What is it?'

Every part of me went rigid. *Isaac.* It sounded as though Cecilia had asked him to come outside. Whatever she had to say, she didn't want anyone overhearing.

'No sign of anything suspicious?'

'I've told you so many times, Mum, I don't think she'll be back. Not if she's got any sense. I'll have the police involved in a heartbeat if I see her. I promise.'

174

'I still think she might have a case if she persists. That she could convince someone she has rights where Daisy is concerned.'

'She has no more rights than her mother does.' Isaac's voice tightened with anger. 'Thank God at least one of them is locked up.'

Panic squeezed as I tried to process what I was hearing.

'She's in a care home, Isaac, not that far from here. She could come over if she was having a good day.'

'Dementia doesn't work like that, Mum. She barely knows what day of the week it is.'

'But Elise—'

'She won't dare show her face. I'm certain of it.'

Hearing Elise's real name was like a slap. They were talking about her as though they knew she was alive. About Ingrid, too. I pressed a hand to my mouth.

'That's not how you felt a couple of weeks ago when you thought she'd been in the house.'

*Elise or Ingrid?*

'I feel more positive now.'

'Because of Rose?'

I closed my eyes, breath held.

'I trust her, Mum.' His voice warmed. 'You should too.'

Guilty heat spread through me.

'We can't take our eye off the ball.' Cecilia's voice was gentler too. I had to strain to hear. 'It won't always be like this.'

'Not if I have anything to do with it.' The words, heavy with intent, made me crouch lower. I shivered as a gust of air grazed my arms, though it wasn't cold. Overcome by the urge to sneeze, I pinched my nose with my fingers. When the feeling passed, the voices had stopped.

I shuffled onto my front and peered beneath the car. No signs of life outside the garage. After scrabbling to my feet, I dusted myself down and ran to my car, throwing myself inside as Daisy dashed out of the house.

'There you are!' She skipped over and grabbed my sleeve as I reached for my bag. 'Where did you go?'

'I saw you come back and wanted to hide, to see if you could find me.' The skin on my cheeks flamed. 'Then I remembered I'd left my bag in the car.'

'Silly Rose.' *Idiotic, more like.* 'Where were you hiding?'

Praying she wouldn't pick up on my apprehension, I managed a secretive smile. 'I can't tell you that, or I won't be able to hide there next time.' I widened my eyes at her. 'Did you enjoy the film?'

She nodded eagerly. 'Brilliant,' she declared. 'But Nanna said it was too noisy.'

'Do you want to tell me about it?'

'I'm helping Daddy make dinner if I want to have ice-cream for pudding.'

'That's OK.' My guilt levels rose at her torn expression. 'We can play tomorrow,' I said, remembering Isaac had said he was cooking tonight. 'You go and help your dad. You can be his sous chef.'

'What's that?'

I explained as we made our way indoors, my heart rate slowing a little as I realised no one was waiting to grill me about where I'd been, or what I'd been doing.

I wondered what Jonah had fed back to Lissa, and whether I would be able to tell by her demeanour.

Isaac was slicing mushrooms at the kitchen island, face furrowed in concentration. 'Nice afternoon?' He glanced up with a smile and rubbed the back of his hand across his forehead.

'Bit of shopping.' I held up my bag, feeling every inch the fraud I was. 'Bumped into Jonah,' I added, figuring it would be odd not to mention it.

'He said.' As Isaac's smile grew, it was hard to imagine his conversation outside with Cecilia had really happened. 'Came home empty-handed so Lissa's commandeered him for foot-rubbing duties this evening.'

'Uncle Jonah doesn't like feet.' Daisy, who had been rinsing her hands at the sink, scrunched up her nose as she turned, dripping water onto the floor. 'He tickles them so that Auntie Lissa tells him to stop.'

'Clever.' I raised my eyebrows at Isaac. 'Smells good.' I eyed the skillet pan on the hob, filled with sizzling chunks of chicken.

'My specialty.' Isaac spung round to turn down the heat. 'Chicken, mushroom and broccoli bake.'

'Yuk, broccoli,' Daisy muttered.

'You won't even know it's there.' When Isaac dropped me a wink, something wrenched inside me. I couldn't bear the small talk after what I'd overheard, and everything I knew.

'I'll go and get changed,' I said, stamping down the instinct to help Daisy tie her little apron. 'Back soon.'

Cecilia was coming downstairs and gave me a friendly nod, nothing in her expression to suggest she didn't trust me. 'Been shopping?' she queried politely, though she must know already. They all did.

I nodded. 'Just a couple of summer tops.'

In my room, I shut the door and stood for a moment, trying to corral my thoughts. If they truly believed Elise was alive – and Cecilia in particular was still 'on her guard' as she'd put it – I was starting to doubt that they would agree to let me take Daisy to the park on my own. And I still had no idea whether Elise would be awake by then, or fit to travel.

For a shameful second, I imagined a situation where she decided her plan was ridiculous, and that she was going to leave the country alone, after letting me know I could stay and take care of Daisy for her.

I gave myself a shake. I was trying to absolve myself of any blame, unwilling to face the consequences, instead of focusing on the reason I was here in the first place.

'Get a grip,' I told myself through gritted teeth, throwing my bag on the bed. I would have a quick shower and change into one of my new tops and put everything else out of my mind until it was time to visit Elise in hospital.

As I crossed the room, something caught my eye on the bedside table. I retraced my steps. It was a necklace; a tiny starfish on a delicate silver chain, coiled in a patch of sunlight. 'Oh,' I breathed surprised and touched that Lissa had left me a gift. Maybe she felt bad about the way she'd treated me after our recent conversations.

Once showered and dressed – I hadn't realised while covertly watching Jonah that the top was covered in tiny pink hearts, more suited for someone younger – I fastened the necklace around my neck, the starfish resting just below my collarbone. I rarely wore jewellery and would have to resist the urge to fiddle with it. It looked pretty, but I would leave it behind when I left. I didn't want gifts from this family.

By the time I returned downstairs, everyone was gathered around the table in the conservatory, Cecilia doling out plates.

'You look nice,' she approved as I approached, self-consciously smoothing a hand over my fringe, which was refusing to lie flat.

'I like your top,' Daisy said. She was kneeling on a chair, spooning some steaming chicken bake from a serving dish into a bowl. 'I mashed the potatoes,' she said proudly, dropping the serving spoon with a clatter.

'It looks great.'

I noticed Isaac staring at me and stopped, eyes darting to the others. Lissa was frozen in the doorway and Jonah, already seated with a fork in his hand, looked from me to his wife with a frown etched into his forehead. 'What's wrong, Liss?'

'Sit down,' Cecilia instructed as she pulled out a chair and signalled something to Lissa that I didn't understand.

'Daisy, could you pop upstairs and fetch my cardigan?' Lissa's voice was brittle. 'The white one on the bed.'

- Daisy gave an exaggerated sigh but got down and ran through the kitchen, into the hallway.

'Where did you get that?'

It took a second to compute that Lissa's coldly furious tone was aimed at me.

'I'm sorry?'

'That necklace.' Her finger stabbed the air. 'It doesn't belong to you.'

# Chapter 24

All eyes were on me, but I couldn't look away from Lissa's accusing stare. 'It was by the bed in my room.' I heard the rising tension in my voice. 'I thought it was a gift.'

'It was in your room?' Looks were exchanged. 'How did it get there?'

I shook my head, anxiety fluttering like a trapped bird in my stomach. 'It was on the bedside table,' I said. 'I assumed it was from your workshop.'

'It is.' Her cheeks were scarlet, the hand on her bump curled into a fist. 'But it belonged to someone else.'

Discomfort prickled along the back of my neck. I looked over to see Isaac's gaze fixed on the starfish.

'Honestly, it was just lying there, as though meant for me to wear.' I lifted my hands and fumbled to unfasten the clasp. 'I thought it was a gift and wore it to be polite.'

'It belonged to my wife.' Isaac's voice held a dangerous undercurrent that didn't seem directed at me. As his gaze flicked between Lissa, Jonah, and his mother – who was standing silently, hands clasped around a dinner plate – something began to brew in my subconscious. *There's more to that lot than meets the eye.* Thora's words echoed in my mind, but I couldn't place specifically what felt off, when nothing about the scene was right.

I held out the necklace to Isaac, who took a step back as though it was a grenade. 'I would never have worn it if I'd known.'

'But you must have taken it.' Lissa seemed unwilling to let it go as she advanced towards me and snatched the necklace from my fingers.

'Lissa, that's enough.' Cecilia sprang to life, banging down the plate and rearranging some cutlery. 'Rose has explained how she came to be wearing it.'

'I didn't realise the necklace was still in the house.' Isaac's eyes met mine, confusion scored into his brow. 'It was on your bedside table?'

I nodded, wanting him to believe me.

'She gave it to Lissa, back before they fell out.' Jonah's words were quietly spoken. 'I'm surprised she kept it.'

'That's enough.' Cecilia's voice sliced the air like a blade. 'We don't need to discuss this in front of Rose.'

'I don't like being made to feel I've done something wrong.' I was aware of my own hypocrisy but annoyed to be called a thief.

'Sorry, Rose.' Lissa almost sounded as though she meant it. 'Family stuff.'

'Honestly, you can leave any time you want. We wouldn't blame you.' Jonah's jokey tone seemed strained, his smile not meeting his eyes. It seemed they would all prefer me to leave, except Isaac, who was turning to greet Daisy arriving back with Lissa's cardigan.

'Thanks, sweetie.' Lissa pushed her arms in the sleeves, even though her forehead was pearled with sweat.

'Are you OK?' Noticing her discomfort, Jonah jumped to his feet and pulled out a chair. 'Sit down,' he ordered.

Lissa obeyed, twitching away when he laid a hand on her shoulder.

'My dinner will be cold soon,' Daisy announced, immune

to the tension in the room as she sat down, wriggling herself comfortable. 'Can I start now?'

'Of course.' Isaac motioned to me to sit too, eyes semaphoring an apology. Part of me was desperate to escape to my room, but I made myself join the family, focusing my attention on Daisy, who wanted to tell us in detail about the film she'd seen. Her descriptive narration gradually dissolved the heavy atmosphere, eliciting smiles, even from Lissa, who was pushing food around her plate.

Isaac's gaze kept returning to me, but I couldn't work out whether he was checking I was OK or replaying the sight of me wearing his wife's necklace, and no matter how hard I tried, I couldn't work out which one of them had wanted me to wear it. As it was only hours since I'd been in Lissa's workshop, she seemed the mostly likely candidate, yet her shocked reaction had seemed as genuine as Isaac's. She hadn't expected to see it – none of them had. At least, that was the impression they gave. But one of them must be acting. *Cecilia?* I caught her concerned expression as she passed me a bowl of peas, the quick smile that flashed over her face. I sensed unease lurking beneath the surface, but had the feeling it wasn't about me, unless I was reading things wrongly.

It was a relief to finish dinner and be able to escape to the hospital, even though I knew I would be the topic of conversation after I'd left; at least once Daisy was in bed.

Entering the hospital, I held my breath against the astringent smell of cleaning fluids and hurried to Elise's room, only to find it empty.

'Where is she?' I asked at the nurses' station. Nikki was there, her eyes widening when she saw my expression.

'Don't worry, your sister's fine,' she reassured me, coming round from the behind the desk. 'We've moved her to a private room as she's been stable for a couple of days.'

'She still hasn't woken up?'

A fleeting look of worry crossed Nikki's heart-shaped face. 'Not for any medical reason,' she stressed. 'Her brain scan was normal.'

'So . . . you think she's *choosing* to not wake up?'

'You'll need to speak to the consultant.' Nikki led the way down a different corridor, lined with open doors I didn't want to look through. 'Maybe your sister needs to hear your voice to bring her back.'

'I'll do my best,' I said, as Nikki stopped at the final door and gestured for me to enter. 'I'm sorry I haven't been here as often—'

'No need to apologise to me.' Nikki's interruption made it clear that, in her eyes – and probably the rest of the staff's – my apparent lack of support for my 'sister' was becoming indefensible. 'Just talk to her,' she advised in a warmer tone. 'Give her a reason to wake up.'

I felt redness bleed into my cheeks and was relieved to be left alone in the sterile room, which at least had a padded chair by the bed, and a decent-sized window. Even though it overlooked the soulless car park, evening sunlight fell in golden strips along the wall.

Despite the monitor measuring her vital signs, and a drip attached to her arm, Elise looked to be sleeping peacefully. Dark lashes fanned the skin beneath her eyes in a way that reminded me of Daisy, and her skin was no longer waxy. Her hair had been swept over one shoulder, and looked freshly brushed, though her lips were dry.

'Elise?' I moved to her side and took hold of her hand. Unlike last time, it was warm, as though her blood had been heated up. 'I'm sorry this happened to you,' I whispered. 'I should have told you about Leon, but I didn't know he was going to turn up.' I waited a moment, certain her breathing had changed. All the things I wanted to ask her crowded my mind. I tipped forward, breathing in the faint odour of sanitiser. 'Can you hear me, Elise?'

Glancing at the monitor, I saw that her heart rate had increased. When I looked down, Elise was staring right at me.

A cry of fright flew out before I could stop it. I let go of her hand, my own heart beating fast. Leaping back, I knocked into the chair. 'Elise, I'm sorry. I wasn't expecting you to suddenly wake up.' I edged forward, pulled by the intensity of her charcoal gaze. 'I'll go and get the nurse.'

'No.' Her voice was low, scratchy from lack of use. Her tongue flicked over her lips. 'Thirsty.'

I darted to the table at the end of the bed and poured some water into a plastic cup. 'I'm not sure I should be doing this.' I held the cup to her mouth and let water dribble between her lips. To my surprise, she shifted, hoisting herself onto her side with a series of grimaces, before draining the cup.

'I've been awake a while,' she said, dropping back on the pillow, swiping her hand across her mouth. 'I was waiting for you to come in. I didn't want to answer their questions.' Her hand reached for mine. 'I think that man turned up at your house to kill you, Rose.'

I felt my blood drain. 'No, Elise, he didn't.' I tried to take in the fact of her being awake, her wide eyes unblinking as they mapped my face, the essence of her apparently restored. 'What do you remember?'

She pressed her fingertips to her forehead and closed her eyes. 'I'd been drinking.' Her voice – less grating now – was laced with remorse. 'I know it was wrong, Rose. I wouldn't have let him in if I hadn't been drunk. We talked, then . . . I got sick, and he tried to help me, but I didn't want him to. I pushed him, then slipped and fell.' She knocked the heel of her hand against her head and muttered, 'Bloody stupid. I could have ruined everything.'

The tension knotting my shoulder blades loosened a fraction. It was a relief to know for certain that Leon had been telling the truth, but odd she didn't remember accusing him of trying to murder her. *Paranoid delusional disorder.* Would it be a good time to ask her about it? Maybe I should check her bag at the house for pills. I could bring them in and explain to the nurses that I hadn't realised she was supposed to be taking them.

'I had no idea he was going to turn up,' I said, refocusing. 'I've spoken to him since your . . . since the accident. He was worried about you and wanted to apologise. He's gone now, and won't be back.'

'Did he call an ambulance?'

'That was my neighbour, Beatrice.'

'It would have been better not to involve anyone else.'

'She heard you fall.' Irritation surged at the cloak-and-dagger nature of it all. 'She probably saved your life.'

'I wouldn't have died.' Elise was wearily dismissive. 'I bashed my head, big deal.'

'You were unconscious,' I pointed out. 'You could have choked on your own vomit if she hadn't come round.' I liked to think Leon would have done the decent thing and called for help but couldn't be certain.

'OK, so thank her for me then.' Her gaze didn't waver.

After a loaded pause, I said, 'I'll go and tell the nurse you're awake.'

'We need to talk first.' Her eyes darted to the doorway behind me. She struggled to sit up again, and I reached to steady the drip on its stand as it toppled. 'This doesn't change anything, Rose.'

'Elise, of course it does.' I looked over my shoulder, willing a nurse to come in. They must do regular check-ups. 'You can't leave the country until you've properly recovered,' I told her, firmly. 'It could be dangerous.'

'I'm fine, a bit of a headache, but that's nothing.'

My mind raced. 'There are so many things I need to say—'

'I'm sure they've got to you, Rose.' She sank back, what little colour she had draining away. 'I warned you, didn't I?'

'It's not that, Elise.'

'Daisy, how's Daisy?' Her forehead crumpled. 'What have they done to her?'

'They haven't done anything,' I said, alarmed at the change in her. 'She's absolutely fine.'

'I promised,' Elise said, though it sounded more like a groan. 'I promised I would go back for her.'

*Had she promised Daisy that?*

'I spoke to Thora.' I wasn't sure why I said it. 'The neighbour.'

Elise's gaze sharpened. 'That old witch?'

'I got the impression you were friends.'

'No one there is my friend.' Elise spoke through clenched teeth.

Shocked by her callousness, I opened my mouth and closed it again, recalling how she'd rejected me when I went to her after her overdose, thinking again of Ingrid's version of what had happened back then.

Elise shut her eyes, her voice becoming plaintive. 'Please don't deviate from the plan, Rose.'

A burst of laughter from down the corridor made my heart jump. I longed to be out there, chatting with the nurses – better still, away from here altogether, at Orchard House, reading Daisy a bedtime story. Elise wasn't thinking straight. She'd been injured, unconscious for forty-eight hours, was on intravenous fluids and probably strong painkillers.

'Look, of course I'll stay with Daisy until you're better.' I adjusted my tone, as if coaxing a fractious child. 'You can go back to mine once you're discharged. Leon won't be returning – you don't have to worry about that. I'll come and see you, and we can talk. There's so much we need to discuss. We have to work out what's best for Daisy.'

'I already know what's best.' The words were ground out. 'I have it all worked out.'

Feeling an urge to please her, I dug a hand in the pocket of my jeans. 'I found the earrings.' I held them out like a prize. 'They were in the garage, like you said.' I thought of the necklace and decided against mentioning it, or the journal that wasn't hers. 'I'm afraid the passport you hid won't be any use,' I continued, slipping the earrings back in my pocket when Elise didn't respond. 'Isaac realised it was missing and ordered a new one.' I wouldn't mention the proposed trip to Iceland either. *So many things I couldn't say.* The back of my skull tightened. 'I'm sorry, Elise.'

'You have to bring it.' Her breathing was fast and shallow now.

'You have to get her to the park like we arranged.' Her hand grasped mine, surprisingly strong. 'Promise me, Rose.'

'Elise, I don't know if I should.'

She released me and hooked her forearm over her head, fingers clawing her hair. 'Please, I beg you.' Her face was distorted with misery. 'Please, Rose. You promised.'

How was it possible that I was here, having this terrible conversation? 'I'm going to fetch a nurse.' I made my voice strong, even as my insides shook. 'I'll come back tomorrow, and we'll talk then.'

'No!' The cry seemed to come from her depths. 'You nearly had a child once, Rose.' Her words froze me. 'A little girl.' Her voice sank to a whisper. 'Wouldn't you have done anything for her?'

The world slowed down. 'That's not fair.'

She blinked a couple of times, childlike. 'I found the scan print,' she said. 'I was looking for a pair of socks and came across that little envelope. I know I shouldn't have looked, but I couldn't resist.' She must have dug deep to find it, wrapped in white tissue paper, hidden at the back of my underwear drawer beneath the delicate woollen blanket Sarah had crocheted. 'Why didn't you tell me, Rose?'

Anger rose, hot and fast. 'You had no right to look. It's private.' My jaw hardened. 'And don't you dare emotionally blackmail me.'

'I'll tell them you're not my sister.' Tears leaked from her eyes. 'How could you say that?' she said. 'You're not my sister.' She pressed the back of her hand to her mouth, stifling a sob. I wondered uncharitably what else she'd heard while supposedly unconscious.

'I told them I was your sister so I could see you.' I strived to stay calm, to hold on to my last shreds of sympathy. 'The situation was suspicious enough as it was. The police are involved, Elise. They'll want to interview you.'

'I'll tell them your ex-boyfriend shoved me down the stairs.'

I felt winded. 'And if I tell them you're planning to take Daisy away?'

'You can't, not without implicating yourself.'

I swallowed the ball of misery in my throat. 'It's up to you what you do, Elise.' Maybe it would be a relief to tell the truth. Get it over and done with. Except . . . Daisy's face, her giggle, the shampoo scent of her hair and the way her hand felt in mine. How could I abandon her with nothing resolved? 'If you really want your daughter back,' I countered, 'it can't happen without me.'

She fixed watery eyes on my face. 'I'm sorry, Rose. I didn't mean any of what I just said. I'm desperate.' She sniffed, wiping her cheeks with her fingers. 'The truth is . . . I wasn't going to tell you, because I didn't want to scare you, but I had a message from him before I came to yours.'

The hairs on my arms rose. 'A message?'

'It's on my phone, my old one that I had before. I don't know why I kept it. It's in my bag at your house. You can check if you don't believe me. The passcode's my date of birth.' She gestured me closer, voice dropping to a ragged whisper. 'He said I would never see Daisy again, and if I tried, he would make sure we both disappeared for good.'

# Chapter 25

## *Wednesday*

I woke with a start the following morning, a nightmare spinning away, leaving behind a feeling of dread. Hearing movement downstairs, I reached for my phone to see it was almost eight. I'd had a message from Sarah. *Come and visit soon. Roy's bought a hammock and wants to sleep in it under the stars! Xx*

Tears pooled in my eyes at the normality of it, her voice clear in my mind. Not so long ago, my life had been stable, predictable, comfortable, if not exactly exciting. I wished I was there, in the bedroom that Roy had redecorated when I turned sixteen to be more 'grown up' even though I'd secretly loved the faded lilac walls and sunshine-yellow window frames.

*He must be feeling better,* I replied, picturing where Roy would have fixed the hammock; between the ivy-cloaked trunk of the old oak tree round the back of the house and the concrete post with a washing line attached that had been there for as long as I could remember. *Hope to see you soon xx*

What would they think when it came out that I'd wormed my way into Elise's family to return Daisy to her mother? How could

I ever tell them the truth? The fact that I couldn't picture it was surely proof I no longer believed in what I was doing, despite Elise's revelation about Isaac's message.

She'd begun crying when I asked why she hadn't mentioned it before, and how did she know he hadn't followed her, or had her followed. She could only stammer that he'd assumed she was 'out there' somewhere, banking on her checking her phone at some point. She promised she hadn't replied or switched her phone on since.

'I wouldn't have let you go to the house if I thought for a second there was a chance he knew I was planning to take Daisy away,' she insisted, her gaze so forceful I ended up agreeing it didn't change anything.

When the nurse came back, she'd been astonished to see Elise awake and talking, and turned a beaming smile on me, as though I'd brought her back from the dead.

'I was coming to get you,' I said lamely, while Elise deployed her acting skills, transforming into a smiling, grateful patient, marvelling about being out for so long, joking that she'd been enjoying some much-needed sleep but couldn't wait to go home. 'No offence,' she said, when the doctor hurried in after presumably being alerted that his patient was conscious, 'but I need some proper food.'

I'd stayed while various checks were carried out, silent as a ghost in the corner of the room, meeting her eyes every so often while my own head throbbed, full of disjointed thoughts. She wanted to be discharged right away, but reluctantly agreed to stay one more day on the doctor's advice.

As she kept up a stream of inconsequential chatter, I could see they were charmed by her, the old Elise magic working wonders, even though the seam of desperation beneath the bubbly veneer was obvious – to me, at least.

'I'm so grateful to my little *sister*,' she said at one point, enveloping me in her smile, but only I appeared to notice her emphasis on the word *sister*.

When told the police would need to speak to her, she clutched a fist to her chest and said with a sober expression, 'I know I drank far too much that night, and I'm *so* sorry for wasting everyone's time.'

When I moved in to say my goodbyes over a cacophony of reassurances and offers of counselling if she needed it, she'd pulled me into a hug and murmured, 'I'll get a taxi to yours tomorrow. You don't need to come back here. I'll see you on Friday. Remember Daisy's passport.'

'Elise, I—'

'My life won't begin again until I have Daisy, and that's down to you.'

I closed my eyes. 'I have the spare keys to my house.' My voice was a whispered squeak. 'And you don't have any fresh clothes here.'

'I'll wear what I had on when I came in. I was even wearing my boots,' she said. 'You can leave me the keys.'

I'd fished them out of my bag with a feeling of powerlessness, as though I was under a spell, all the questions I needed answers to falling away.

Back at Orchard House, it had taken a gargantuan effort to join the family in the living room, my own acting skills strained to the limit as I told them my friend had woken up and was fine.

'She was a bit embarrassed to discover I'd been summoned to the hospital, considering we haven't been in touch for so long,' I added, inventing an on-off boyfriend who had been contacted and was on his way to collect her.

Isaac had been perched on the arm of the sofa when I came in, showing Cecilia some paperwork, but stood as I approached, a line of concern between his eyebrows. 'Hadn't he missed her?'

'They were on a break, apparently, but, er, I think they'll probably get back together now.' Guilty heat had crawled across my skin.

'Well, that's great.' Cecilia swivelled to look at me properly. 'And now the two of you are in touch again, so it's a happy outcome all round.' There was something unnerving about her blue stare, but her tone was placid as she rose and offered me a drink. 'You must need one.'

Lissa and Jonah, who had been sitting outside, came in and wanted to know what was happening. As I repeated my lies, I noted Lissa was distracted and Jonah slightly annoyed, his narrowed gaze shuffling from Lissa to the floor. Maybe they'd had an argument. 'So, basically, I won't be shooting off to the hospital anymore.'

Once I'd forced down the camomile tea Cecilia brought me – a flavour I'd never liked – and I'd asked after Daisy, I headed up to my room, where I had to resist the urge to pack and drive away. It was the sight of Daisy, sleeping soundly, a hand curled by her cheek, that swung things into perspective. Soon, I could leave. Whatever happened next, I would deal with it, but Daisy would be with her mother, the pair of them far away, my part in it over.

The thought had left me feeling oddly empty and now, as I swung my legs out of bed and reached for my robe, I wondered what would happen if Elise was wrong about Isaac and he *did* go after them. He had a persuasive manner that he could use to his advantage, and if he'd convinced people that Elise was mentally unstable in the past, he could easily do it again. I had no real clue what Isaac was capable of.

After I'd left the hospital I checked Elise's bag at the house. No pills in any of the pockets, which supported the fact that she wasn't taking medication, but didn't prove that she shouldn't be. Even so I'd been relieved. Her mental state, the drinking, was nothing more sinister than the result of her being separated from her daughter. I'd found an older model iPhone tucked at the bottom of the bag, the battery flat. After locking up I'd called at Beatrice's to tell her Elise was OK and would be back tomorrow.

'And I'll be home at the weekend,' I added, interrupting a flow of questions. 'No, really, you don't need to do anything, but she wanted me to tell you how grateful she is that you called for help.'

Elise hadn't seemed grateful at all, but I reminded myself she wasn't capable of rational thought, and probably wouldn't be until Daisy was with her once more.

*You almost had a baby once, Rose. What wouldn't you have done for her?*

It was a calculated move, knowing how much her words would hurt, but Elise was right. I couldn't envisage a situation where I would willingly be parted from my child, and I knew first-hand the pain of losing a mother. It didn't matter whether or not Elise had been a perfect parent, what mattered was that – now – she wanted more than anything to be with her daughter, and would do anything to make it happen, including roping in an old friend I wasn't certain, even now, she'd ever really liked.

Part of me didn't want to check the phone message from Isaac, to be faced with proof that he wasn't the man he seemed, which was why I'd left the iPhone in my bag overnight, trying to ignore its presence as I tried to sleep.

My hand shook as I retrieved it and plugged it into my charger.

By the time I'd showered, brushed my teeth, and dressed in fresh clothes, there was enough charge to key in the passcode. Elise's Christmas Eve date of birth was easy to remember. The screen showed no WhatsApp icon, or email, or any social media apps. I wondered whether she'd deleted them, or never had them in the first place.

On impulse I checked Google Maps, but her search history was empty. There was nothing in her calendar, no notes. Her contact list was empty too. She'd been thorough in wiping away all traces.

Holding my breath, I clicked into her texts, heart racing as I saw a string of them, from an 'unknown' number.

*I know you're out there.*
*You've been seen near the house. STAY AWAY.*
*I could call the police and get you locked up.*
*You have no right to even see Daisy. Leave her alone, you mad bitch.*

And the one she'd told me about, the date a couple of days before she arrived on my doorstep.

*You'll never see Daisy again and if you try, I'll make sure you disappear for good.*

Not quite the same, I realised, reading it again, a pulse beating in my throat. I was sure Elise had said *I'll make sure you both disappear for good*, but she would say I was splitting hairs. Maybe she'd read it that way or got it wrong, but the tone of the text was unmistakable. It was a threat.

I could hardly look Isaac in the eye over breakfast, making sure I focused on Daisy, who wanted Rocky to wear a bow tie during our morning lessons and persuaded her dad to help her fasten it while the dog sat patiently. To my immense relief the others had already left, and Isaac himself seemed preoccupied, constantly checking the time when he thought no one was looking.

'If you have to be somewhere, you can leave us to it,' I said, as he leaned against the worktop, looking at his phone, one hand smoothing his beard over and over. 'We'll be fine, won't we, Daisy?'

'We'll be fine, Daddy,' she parroted. 'We're doing times tables today.'

'Thanks, Rose.' He put down his phone and flashed me a grateful smile that made my stomach squeeze. 'My agent wants to meet up, but I can put her off.'

'No way, it's probably good news if she wants to see you in person.'

He smiled. 'If you're sure?'

'Positive.'

He dropped a kiss on Daisy's hair on his way out of the kitchen, as she carefully loaded her cereal bowl into the dishwasher. I got up to help and noticed Isaac's phone on the worktop. Hearing the front door close, I moved over to see the screen was still showing.

I touched it to stop it closing and after nodding yes when Daisy asked if she could let Rocky out in the garden, I quickly tapped open his text messages, pushed on by an urge to see for myself the one he'd sent to Elise. There wasn't much there, just a couple of appointment reminders. He probably used WhatsApp for family exchanges, and email for everything else, and had probably used another phone as the number had been unknown.

I heard the click of the front door opening, and footsteps approaching. I switched off the phone and moved to the back door, heart thudding as I watched Daisy ordering Rocky to do a wee as she had to get to school.

'I'll forget my head, one of these days.'

I glanced round as though surprised to see Isaac waggling the phone at me with theatrically wide eyes. 'See you later.'

'Bye.' I summoned a smile and a wave, and as he left for the second time, I hoped he really was meeting his agent, and not out looking for Elise.

# Chapter 26

It was an effort to focus after Isaac had gone, knowing Daisy and I were alone in the house. It was a chance to find Daisy's new passport, but I had no idea where to look, and wouldn't involve her in my subterfuge. Just the thought of it made me feel sick. If an opportunity arose, I would take it, but otherwise, I was sticking to the lesson plan, using the tried and tested times-tables poster I'd brought with me. It would have been helpful to speak to Daisy's teacher and find out exactly what stage she was at, but I would have to rely on my instincts, and on Daisy herself. Not that any of it would matter this time next week, I reminded myself with a pang.

Watching Daisy write out her numbers, I wondered where she would end up going to school. Was Elise planning to teach her at home? Where would home even be? The thought of Daisy being somewhere in the world with her mother should have brought a measure of relief, but a panicky feeling gripped my ribcage. Should I persuade Elise to tell me where they were going and insist we keep in touch, or would it be better to have a clean break? Could Elise be trusted to do what was right for her daughter?

I wished my head wasn't filled with conflicting stories about her, but should it matter? Elise had come to me for help, to get her daughter back. Achieving that would go a long way to restoring the part of her that had been broken by her life with Isaac at Orchard House. And now I'd seen for myself the messages he'd sent, I had to remember he was dangerous, and could turn that side of himself on his daughter one day. The way he appeared to be with Daisy could be an act, a show for my benefit. He'd been quick enough to hand over her care to someone he barely knew, despite his family's concerns. *I have a good feeling about Rose. I trust her.* What if he'd known all along I was hiding in the garage and had meant me to overhear – to be flattered enough to stay? Just because I couldn't figure out an alternative motive for him wanting me around didn't mean there wasn't one.

By lunchtime, my head was spinning with unanswered questions and Daisy was complaining that her eyes hurt. Despite the patio doors being open, bringing in waves of air, her face was flushed, her eyes heavy. 'I need to go to sleep.'

My stomach gave a lurch of concern. 'Do you feel sick?'

She propped her head on a hand and raised a shoulder. 'Maybe, a little bit.'

'Let's get you upstairs,' I said, standing. 'Maybe you need a drink of water.'

'Not thirsty.'

*Should I call Isaac?* It wouldn't look good for Daisy to get sick on my watch, but more importantly, I was worried about her.

'Don't be sad,' she said, leading the way out of the playroom, not bothering with Rocky who stood to watch us go. 'I'll be better soon.'

'Does this happen often?'

'Sometimes.' Another little shrug. 'Nana says sleep is the best medicine.'

'That's true.' I recalled Daisy's deep sleep of a few afternoons ago. 'Did your eyes hurt before when I was here?'

She paused at the foot of the stairs and nodded, rubbing her eye sockets with her knuckles. 'I have some medicine too, that Nana gives me.'

'Not Daddy?' Seeing her face drop, I said quickly, 'It doesn't matter, sweetheart.' I was about to add that I would go and get the medicine, but something stopped me. At Chesterfield Primary, we had only been allowed to administer prescribed medication via written consent, dispensed by a pharmacy with the child's details attached, so I probably shouldn't risk giving her anything.

'My mummy had poorly headaches, and that's why I do too.'

'Oh?' Elise hadn't mentioned it – unless it was a recent development. Or had Daisy been made to believe that as some sort of smokescreen?

Aware once more of a rising paranoia, I helped settle Daisy into bed, making sure the window was open, and tucking her unicorn beside her when she sleepily pointed to it.

'I'll fetch some water,' I whispered, stroking her hair from her forehead, but when I returned, she was already asleep. Putting the cup down, I knelt by the bed and watched her, in case she woke up, but her breathing was deep and steady.

I got up and headed into the family bathroom, a pulse of unease lodging in my chest as I opened the glass-fronted door of a cupboard tucked into an alcove, searching for a bottle with the familiar Calpol logo, or a brown bottle with Daisy's name on the label. There were only tubes of toothpaste, toothbrushes still in their packaging, and bottles of shampoo and shower gel. Perhaps medicines were kept in the kitchen, or a first-aid box.

Checking once more that Daisy was sleeping, her features smooth, I edged along the landing, pausing outside Cecilia's room. I pushed open the door and stuck my head around. It was as clean and tidy as the rest of the house, a pair of cotton pyjamas folded neatly on her pillow, the surfaces clutter-free apart from a book with a pair of reading glasses on top, and a family photo on her bedside table in a simple, gold frame. I recognised a much younger Isaac and Lissa, posed in front of an older couple, all in ski-wear.

Cecilia was instantly familiar, a wide smile crinkling her bright blue eyes, and I assumed the handsome, blond-haired man with a moustache by her side was her husband. All their faces were open and relaxed – an ordinary family on holiday, caught in a flare of sunlight, the brilliant sparkle of snow in the background. It was probably the same place they were going on holiday, except . . . of course they wouldn't be going. Not without Daisy.

*You have no right to even see Daisy. Leave her alone, you mad bitch.*

Not the words of a man prepared to give up on his daughter, no matter what Elise believed. When Isaac realised I'd let Daisy go, I imagined the full force of his fury switching to me. Was I ready for that? Could I cope? I lengthened my spine, took a deep breath, and shook out my hair, which was sticking to the back of my neck. I couldn't let my mind go further than reuniting Elise and Daisy.

I went into my room and ran cold water over my wrists in the en suite, then looked out of the window at the picture-perfect landscape of green and golden fields, framed by unbroken blue sky. How could things be so wrong in this beautiful setting?

Back on the landing, a gasp of fright flew out. Rocky had come upstairs and dropped down on the carpet outside Daisy's room as though on watch.

'Good boy.' I passed, pulse skittering with nerves as I ran downstairs and into Isaac's study before I changed my mind. It was bright and airy, light flooding through windows on two walls, and there on his desk was a folder, a passport on top.

Catching my breath, I hurried over and picked it up, scanning the photo inside. An involuntary smile sprang to my lips at the sight of Daisy's serious expression.

I could hardly take the passport now; it would be too obvious it was missing. I would have to leave it until the very last minute.

I thought of the earrings that Elise had barely taken any notice of – the only things I'd managed to salvage, along with her mother's journal. I was considering taking the cookbook and slipping it into my suitcase but as I entered the kitchen, Cecilia came in, bringing the scent of the garden with her.

'Oh,' she said, as though surprised to see me standing there empty-handed. She put down the cake box she was carrying, and placed her bag beside it, brushing a hand over her hair. 'Where's Isaac?' she said. 'His car's not here.'

Recalling their conversation the day before, I understood the snap of concern in her voice. 'He's got a meeting with his agent,' I said evenly.

She cast her gaze around the kitchen, as if he might suddenly appear. 'Where's Daisy?'

'Her eyes were hurting, so she's having a sleep.'

Cecilia's expression changed. 'I can't believe we didn't mention it.' Her face had paled. 'She hasn't had one for a while, but I think the excitement of the cinema yesterday and trip to the dentist, plus the change of routine, and you being here—'

'Hasn't had what?' I cut her off, trying to ignore the charge of accusation in her tone. 'Is Daisy ill?'

'Migraines.' She moved to one of the cupboards and reached to the top shelf, pulling out a bottle of medicine. 'If the headache hasn't gone when she wakes up, we give her some of this, but we prefer to let her sleep it off.'

'Daisy has migraines?' A memory flickered like a shadow: Elise, prone on my bed in my university accommodation, insisting she couldn't go home as she had one of her 'heads' and would need to sleep it off. I'd grown sceptical about her headaches, which were never officially diagnosed as anything serious, as they seemed to come on when it suited her. Perhaps they had been migraines.

*My mummy used to get a poorly head, and that's why I do too.*

'It starts behind her eyes,' Cecilia said, placing the medicine bottle on the worktop. 'We thought at first she might need glasses but her eyesight's fine. The next time it happened she was sick, and the doctor said it was probably a migraine. It's likely she'll grow out of them.'

Shame flushed through my chest at the thought of how quickly I'd assumed the worst, when there was a simple explanation. 'She told me her mummy used to get headaches.'

Cecilia's face tightened. 'Migraines were the least of Ann's problems.' She gave a hard smile that didn't touch her eyes. 'I pray that Daisy's inherited more of her father's traits.' As if regretting speaking her mind, she picked up the medicine bottle and replaced it in the cupboard. 'I'll go and check on Daisy.' She moved past me, eyes averted.

It dawned on me that I would have to take the medicine with me, just in case, and make sure Elise knew the signs to look for. A heaviness descended, constricting my chest. 'I'm sorry,' I finished. 'I wouldn't want to do anything to make Daisy unwell.'

'Well, to be fair, Isaac was the one who brought you here.' Cecilia swung out of the kitchen, leaving me staring after her, my mind foggy and slow as I tried to pull my thoughts together. Cecilia wasn't a threat to her granddaughter, she was a tigress who would do anything to protect her cub. If Elise should be afraid of anyone, it was her mother-in-law.

# Chapter 27

Thankfully, Daisy woke full of energy a couple of hours later and insisted on finishing her lesson while her grandmother watched. I tried not to squirm as Cecilia positioned herself in a chair by the patio doors, Rocky curled at her feet. I'd been observed before while teaching, but it hadn't felt this personal. To her credit, she applauded and murmured her approval when Daisy faultlessly recited her two times table before shooting into the garden.

'You clearly have a gift for teaching,' Cecilia said, getting to her feet with a wince, one hand moving to her lower back the way Lissa's often did.

'Isaac told me about your skiing accident.' I closed my laptop and gathered my teaching materials, and Daisy's page of numbers, into a neat pile. 'When my aunt hurt her back a few years ago, she found acupuncture helped.'

'I've tried everything,' Cecilia said, but not unkindly. She seemed subdued since admitting she'd forgotten to tell me about Daisy's migraines, though nobody else had either. 'I usually take a couple of painkillers and wait for it to pass.'

When Isaac returned twenty minutes later and learnt of Daisy's 'poorly head' he took me to one side to thank me for taking care of her. 'I can't believe we didn't think to mention it, but like Mum said, she hasn't had one for a while.' He hesitated. 'You mustn't feel bad that you didn't know,' he went on. 'It's entirely our fault.'

I felt my face flush. 'Thank you,' I said, wishing I could work out what his agenda was. He was looking at me with what appeared to be genuine gratitude, as though I was the answer to his prayers – as though he hadn't killed off his wife and sent her threatening messages. His acting skills were off the scale. 'How did your meeting go?'

He couldn't stop the smile that filled his face. 'There've been several offers for my book, good ones. A bit of a bidding war.'

'That's amazing.' So, his money worries might be over too. He would soon have the life he'd wanted – the one without Elise. 'Maybe you won't need to sell the house after all,' I couldn't resist saying.

The smile dimmed. 'Oh, I'm selling the house,' he said, softly. 'No matter what happens.'

I was desperate to escape to my room after dinner – Jonah came home with a selection of pizzas because Lissa had a craving for cheese – but Daisy requested I read her a story after her bath, which I couldn't refuse.

'You're an honorary member of the family now,' Isaac said, once Daisy was swaddled in a towel and brushing her teeth at the sink. 'She goes through phases where she only wants my mother, or Lissa – never Jonah, for some reason; I think he made up a ghost story once and it scared her – but it's usually me.'

'Not her mother?'

I shouldn't have said it. Braced for an angry response, I was surprised to see a cloud of sadness cross his face. 'Her mother wasn't too keen on bedtime stories.'

'Oh well, it's nice that's she's read to,' I said, my stomach churning with guilt, as though Isaac's sadness was real. But maybe it was – for Daisy. 'A lot of parents don't bother these days; at least that's what I gathered from my previous job.'

'I still like being read to.' Isaac's smile returned. 'I listen to audiobooks in the car.'

'Me too.'

He held my gaze until I had to look away, reminding myself once more of the texts he'd sent Elise. *I'll make sure you disappear for good.* He wasn't a nice man, despite appearances.

Soon, Daisy was in her pyjamas, sitting up in bed with *The Last Wolf*.

'I'll leave you to it,' Isaac said, after returning Daisy's goodnight hug. 'I'm going to have a look for ski-wear in the attic, check there's nothing we need to buy before our holiday.'

'When are you going?'

'Not until late August, but best to be organised.' He was cheerful now, still riding the wave of his meeting and the news about his book.

'Can I look too, Daddy?'

'Not tonight, bunny. Enjoy your story.'

For a while, I managed to forget everything else as Daisy snuggled against me, smelling sweetly of strawberry-scented shampoo, her hair curling as it dried. She read along with me every now and then. It was a story she'd obviously heard before, and I felt a pull of sorrow that I was the one reading to Daisy, instead of Elise. She would make a production of it, doing the voices and actions, getting Daisy to join in – but there would be plenty of time for that, once they were back together. It was a comforting image that carried me through *Rhinos Don't Eat Pancakes* and *The Bumble Bear* until Daisy slid under her duvet, thumb edging towards her mouth, and Cecilia came in to say goodnight. I had the feeling she'd been standing on the landing, listening for some time. I blew Daisy a kiss and left them alone, murmuring about calling my aunt.

Back in my room, reality bounced back. I rang the hospital to check Elise hadn't relapsed.

'Your sister's fine, been quite chatty. She ate some dinner, and now she's sleeping,' said a cheery nurse whose voice I didn't recognise. 'She's quite a character.' Elise had always flourished with an audience and was no doubt trying to prove she was fit to go home. 'She's being discharged in the morning.'

'Give her my love,' I said, to make up for the shameful second I'd wished she hadn't yet woken up. *You're not Daisy's mother,* I reproached myself. *You have a family.*

I thought about phoning Sarah, then remembered it was her monthly book club night, and Roy wasn't good at chatting on the phone. Instead, I took Elise's earrings from my pocket and slipped them into my toilet bag, then pushed Ingrid's journal into the concealed compartment at the bottom of my suitcase, arranging some underwear on top. I couldn't discount someone searching my things again.

Downstairs, voices rose and fell. Isaac called Rocky in from the garden, and Cecilia said something that provoked an outraged 'Mum!' from Lissa, followed by a peal of laughter.

I felt a burst of loneliness. I could go down but felt I would be intruding. And my head was aching with a mish-mash of jumbled thoughts.

After drinking some water from the tap in the en suite, I got ready for bed and mentally planned tomorrow's lesson with Daisy. I tried to read, but my eyes kept slipping over the same paragraph. I gave up and stared through the window, replaying the last few days on a loop until the sky outside grew dark.

I was woken sometime later by a tap on the door and sat up, alert, senses quivering. 'Hello?'

Nothing.

The room was dimly lit by the moon, hanging outside the window like a child's drawing, outlining the furniture and pictures on the wall.

Pushing my hair back, I glanced at my phone: 2 a.m.

Certain I hadn't imagined the knock, I got out of bed and

opened the door, half-expecting to see someone outside. The landing was empty, the only light a pinkish glow from the night-light plugged into the wall in Daisy's room. Her door was open. I tiptoed barefoot across the carpet and looked inside. Her bed was empty.

'Daisy?' I whispered. Maybe she'd gone to the toilet, but when I checked the bathroom it was empty too. The closed doors of the other rooms looked sinister, not a hint of light bleeding around the edges. I tried to picture everyone sleeping, but could only imagine Jonah and Lissa, Cecilia, and Isaac standing with their ears pressed to the wood, waiting to hear what I was going to do next.

I gave myself a shake, wishing I'd at least put a robe over my pyjamas. I felt exposed, and a cool breeze surged through the open landing window.

Perhaps Daisy had needed something, like a drink of water, and when I didn't answer her knock, she'd gone into Isaac's room, or Cecilia's, and snuggled up with one of them.

Turning to go back to my room, I noticed something at the foot of the short stairway that I knew – thanks to Elise – led to the attic room. It was Daisy's unicorn, its glass eye shining. As I moved to pick it up, I noticed the hatch to the attic was open, the ladder pulled down. My scalp prickled. Was Daisy up there? I remembered her asking to go with Isaac earlier, her little pout of disappointment when he refused. Maybe she'd decided to explore and had wanted me to go with her.

Without stopping to think, I ran up the few stairs and climbed the steep wooden ladder. At least it was sturdy, but why had Isaac left it down and the hatch open?

I poked my head through the gap, and reached my hand around, feeling for a switch. When my fingers encountered a piece of hard plastic on the nearest beam I pressed, blinking in the dull, yellow light that came from an overhead bulb hanging from the rafters.

No sign of Daisy. I looked around, curiosity stirring. The attic was obviously a dumping ground, stacked with cardboard boxes, redundant chairs, and other small pieces of furniture, Christmas decorations, bags of clothes and heaps of books.

Satisfied Daisy wasn't hiding, and deciding she was probably in her dad's room – perhaps the noise I'd heard was his door closing – I hoisted myself up, drawn to a small wooden trunk with the word ANN crudely marked in black on the side.

Timber flooring had been laid, as if the space had been earmarked for conversion into another room at some point, and there was enough space to stand upright. My heart squeezed at the sight of a highchair and pram in the corner that must have been Daisy's – perhaps kept for a baby brother or sister – and an open bag of tiny clothes I couldn't bear to look at; the sort of outfits I'd dared to started buying once I was three months pregnant.

Turning back to the trunk, my foot caught one of the skis propped against the wall, sending it clattering to the floor, hitting a box spilling goggles, thick gloves, and insulated hats – the ski-wear Isaac had presumably been looking through.

I waited a moment, blood pounding in my ears, certain I'd woken the whole house. When nothing happened, I crouched by the trunk and gingerly touched the walnut-wood lid. It was surprisingly dust-free, as if recently opened. I lifted it and peered inside, breathing in the slight mustiness of long-stored clothes.

There wasn't that much: a thick, camel coat, good quality, that smelt faintly of perfume, heavily floral – not Elise's type, or not when I'd known her – a couple of cashmere sweaters in pastel colours, some soft black leather boots with a slender heel – surely too small for Elise, but I'd only ever seen her wearing what Sarah had called her 'clod-hopper boots' – a pink and green satin robe with an elaborate, cherry blossom design, a couple of pairs of aviator-style sunglasses and a navy, designer swimsuit. I shuffled my hand underneath, hoping to find some photographs, or letters – though who sent letters anymore? – something more concretely Elise's, but only encountered a selection of silky scarves in primary colours that I couldn't imagine Elise wearing.

I pulled one out and trailed it through my fingers, and as I pushed it back, felt something in the pocket of the camel coat. I tugged it and checked, but the pockets were empty. I checked the lining and saw there was another pocket, something tucked inside. I pulled out a small notebook, brown leather, *Journal* on the front in gold lettering. My heart leapt. I dropped the coat back in the trunk and held the book to the light. Was *this* Elise's diary; the one she'd asked me to retrieve? But why say it was hidden it in the bedroom, exactly where I'd found it, rather than here, in the attic?

I opened it randomly to a page of blocky, almost childlike writing, and read: **He'll kill me if he finds out, but if it's OK for him to have an affair, why shouldn't I? Maybe he'll realise how it feels, or maybe he doesn't care. Did he ever? Does anyone?**

*Elise had an affair?* I turned a few pages, heart thudding with trepidation.

**Being a mother is hard. She looks at me sometimes as though I'm the devil when we both know who the real devil is in this house.**

I shuddered, flipping the page to see a school photo of a girl in uniform I recognised – though she was younger than the sixteen-year-old I'd met at sixth form. She was smiling, not shy about her braces, long, dark hair gleaming, wide eyes gazing beyond the camera, maybe at the photographer. I turned it over. **Elise Ann Lockwood aged 13** was written in blue ink on the back and I couldn't help smiling at this more innocent version of the girl I'd known. She told me once her mother hadn't bought any of her school photos after the age of seven, because she found them too 'posed' but Ingrid had obviously kept this one and given it to Elise. Inserting it back in the journal, I read a bit more, smile slipping at the tone of desperation leaking from the page.

*How can I go on like this? It feels as if my head is too big, too full. I have to be on my guard all the time. I know I'm being watched; there are cameras hidden. I don't know what they'll do next, what they're capable of. They all hate me, HATE ME.*

On an earlier page, the words: *They've trained the dog to hurt me. He growls whenever I walk past, but seems to love everyone else* jumped out, on another: *They might throw Daisy in the river and say she drowned, and no one would ever know the truth but me, and how would I prove it??* It must have been exhausting for Elise to have lived with this constant worry. The next page detailed her wish that Isaac would pay more attention to his daughter.

*Sick of relying on his mother. She can't stand the sight of me, but he really thinks he can be famous by making up characters, just because he once had a publisher. I told him I need him to be present, but he never listens. He thinks his needs are more important than mine, than his daughter's . . .*

The next page had three lines written on it, and one word: *Elise, Elise, Elise* over and over, pressed hard so the page had torn in the middle. I imagined her, desperate to be herself again, using her birthname. Anger rose. Despite her assertion that she hadn't minded being someone 'new', Isaac shouldn't have insisted on using her middle name, especially as his sister went by Lissa and not Elise.

I looked for more references to Daisy, but only found one.

*. . . happiest at the park because we're free there. On the swings, pushing her higher. She always wants to go higher, my brave little girl. Then HE comes along and ruins it, tells me it's dangerous – she might fall off. Anything to make her afraid of me.*

Flipping to a page further on, I read *. . . came into the summerhouse thinking I'd passed out and fiddled with that old heater. I know it's only a matter of time before I have a terrible 'accident' and that's why I have to leave—* A sound made me freeze.

Instinctively, I snapped the journal shut and tucked it into the waistband of my pyjama bottoms and pulled down my top to cover it. Another sound, behind me; the squeak of pressure on a floorboard.

Someone was up here with me.

# Chapter 28

'What are you doing?' Jonah's voice sounded muffled in the crowded space. I could only stare as his eyes, dark and alert, scanned the scene – the toppled ski at an angle across the floor, the skiing goggles, and gloves – before settling on the trunk. He was wearing a crumpled grey T-shirt, twisted as though he'd hastily pulled it on, his shins pale and skinny beneath jersey shorts.

Dumbly, my heart a hollow drumbeat, I followed his gaze. Although I'd closed the trunk, the scarf I thought I'd dropped back in was trailing down the side in an emerald cascade.

Before I could speak I heard movement on the ladder, and Lissa murmuring sleepily somewhere beneath, 'What's going on?'

Isaac's head appeared through the hatch. 'Rose?' He looked almost comical, just head and shoulders and sleep-tousled hair, eyes wide with confusion as he looked from me to Jonah. 'What's going on?'

'I heard a noise.' Jonah turned, scratching his shoulder. His hair, freed from its bun, sprang around his head in a mess of greying curls. He looked older, or maybe it was the way the light shadowed his face. 'I think Rose was going through Ann's things.'

When Isaac's gaze moved to the trunk, then lifted to my face,

I felt an irrational flash of anger at Jonah that curdled almost immediately into embarrassment.

'I heard someone knock on my bedroom door, or I thought I did.' I was horribly aware of the notebook tucked beneath my top. 'When I came out, Daisy's bed was empty, and her unicorn was at the bottom of the stairs.' My voice was breathy and high. 'The hatch was open. I thought she might have come up here to explore.'

'She came into my room, said she'd heard a funny noise.' Isaac hauled himself though the opening, and sat on the edge, legs dangling. 'I closed the hatch earlier.' Puzzlement was etched on his brow. 'There's no way Daisy could have opened it and pulled the ladder down.' Like Jonah, he was wearing a T-shirt and shorts, and the sight of us all in the attic in the middle of the night in our sleepwear might have been funny if I hadn't been struggling for words. My mouth was so dry I could only swallow in a dry gulp.

'I promise you it was open,' I said. 'I wouldn't have noticed it otherwise. And Daisy's unicorn . . .' I jabbed my finger in the direction of the landing. 'It was on the floor.'

'Maybe she dropped it on her way into my room.' Isaac ruffled his hair with both hands. 'I didn't see it.'

'Me neither,' Jonah said. His eyes softened into understanding. 'It's OK to admit you were curious.' He folded his arms and cocked his head to the side, as though conducting a counselling session. 'Bit risky though, with everyone in the house.'

'Exactly.' Despite my guilt, I wanted to defend myself. 'Why would I come up here without a good reason?'

'What's going on?' Lissa's voice was louder. 'I'll come up if you don't tell me.'

'What on earth's happening?' Now Cecilia was awake, her voice sharp with alarm. 'Is everything OK?'

'It's fine, Mum,' Isaac called down, his jaw set, knuckles white either side of his knees. 'Go back to bed.'

'Not until you tell me what's going on.'

It was like a scene from an old-fashioned sitcom, with me as the butt of the joke. Someone had intended me to come up to the attic, looking for Daisy, had banked on me going to the trunk marked 'ANN', guessing I wouldn't be able to resist looking inside. *But why?* To discredit me in front of Isaac? Unless it was Isaac himself, but that didn't make sense. His bafflement seemed real.

'Let's go down, before Daisy wakes up,' Jonah suggested, looking once more at the trunk, before sweeping his arm out to let me go past.

Isaac rubbed the back of his neck. I met his quizzical look with a shake of my head, words rushing out before I could stop them. 'I'm sorry I looked in the trunk, it was unforgivable, but I promise that isn't why I came up here.' His eyes were level with my lower half. I prayed he couldn't see the shape of the journal in my waistband, but he merely gave a tight-lipped smile and dropped down through the hatch in a fluid movement. I heard a flurry of loudly whispered questions from Cecilia and Lissa.

Gritting my teeth, I came down the ladder, feeling like a burglar caught red-handed. I joined them, standing stiffly while Jonah clicked off the light and paused to pull the hatch cover over before descending with clumsy steps. 'I'll leave the ladder down until the morning. It makes a bit of a racket.'

'I'll go and check on Daisy,' Isaac murmured, moving to the master bedroom, leaving behind a silence heavy with questions.

'I thought she was up there,' I offered, beginning to shiver with nerves. Any trust I'd built up was now shattered. I didn't know how to put it right. *Things* aren't *right*, an inner voice cried. *You are an intruder.*

'Look, it's fine,' Isaac said in a low voice when he returned. 'Daisy's sleeping and no harm's been done.'

'Apart from Rose snooping about in the middle of the night,' Lissa said abruptly.

'Like I said, I thought Daisy had gone up there.'

'You did have a good look around though.' Cecilia sounded less

213

angry than I'd expected, arms belted around her waist, cinching in her knee-length nightdress.

'Isaac already said, he closed the hatch.' Lissa turned on her mother, her thin robe flaring open over a vest top and flimsy shorts, the visible skin across her stomach as taut as a drumskin. No one had switched on the light, so we were a series of shadows, flashes of teeth and eyes, and scents – musky, floral, coffee and alcohol, a whiff of garlic breath I thought might be coming from Jonah – with me in the middle like a sacrificial lamb.

'Maybe I thought I closed it, but forgot,' Isaac conceded, sounding tired. He rubbed his forehead with the heel of his hand. 'It doesn't really matter.'

'But I would have noticed it was open when I came up to bed,' Lissa hissed, eyes gleaming as she looked at me. 'Find anything interesting up there?'

'I saw clothes in the trunk, that's all.' I folded my arms across my waist, the journal I'd hidden seeming to burn my flesh. 'And some of Daisy's things from when she was a baby.' To my horror, my voice shook. 'I was pregnant, this time last year.'

The silence shifted. I sensed their shock as this information was absorbed, and wished I'd kept my mouth shut. 'Sorry,' I began when I felt a warm hand on my arm.

'I'm sorry, Rose,' Isaac said.

'Not really an excuse, but yeah, that sucks.' Lissa's words were grudging. Her teeth gnawed her lower lip.

'A miscarriage?' Cecilia's voice was close, the whites of her eyes very bright . . .

I nodded, brushing a hand across my cheek. 'Five months.'

'I'm so sorry,' she said softly. 'I lost two, before Isaac was born.' The lack of surprise in the resulting silence told me this was old news. 'You never forget those babies.'

'No.' My throat thick was with tears. After a pause, I said, 'I didn't go up there intending to snoop.'

'I believe you.' Isaac's voice was gentle. Huddled with the family on the landing in semi-darkness felt too intimate. Only Jonah hadn't spoken, as if he was still digesting what was happening. 'We kept some of Daisy's stuff in case . . . well, they'll be useful for Lissa's baby,' Isaac continued. 'And I kept some of her mother's things in case Daisy would like them, one day.' So he hadn't completely written Elise off.

'Of course.' I still had a patchwork quilt my mother had made me out of my old baby clothes and some of her favourite Agatha Christie novels, as well as a woollen scarf my father had loved. Precious things that meant nothing to anyone else.

I sensed Lissa wanting to speak. Her mouth opened, and she glanced at Jonah, then rubbed the end of her nose with her knuckles and the moment passed.

Isaac let out a long breath. 'We should get some sleep.'

I hadn't realised his hand was still on my arm until he moved it. The skin there felt cold, and I covered it with my fingers.

'I'm so sorry.' My stomach writhed with mortification as I flashed back to Jonah materialising like a ghost, the tell-tale scarf dripping from the trunk. I shouldn't care what they thought of me, but somehow I did. 'I'll understand if you want me to leave.'

'Of course I don't.' Isaac spoke firmly, threading his fingers through his hair again. 'None of us wants that.'

'Let's forget it happened.' Cecilia spoke in a whisper, so I couldn't gauge her tone, but she briefly touched my shoulder as though to reassure me. 'Tomorrow's a new day,' she added, rubbing Isaac's arm before making her way back to her room, the door closing softly behind her.

Without speaking, Jonah and Lissa followed, and even through the gloom, I saw how she shrugged him away when he tried to drape his arm around her shoulders. She was angry with me, not Jonah, but he was the one who would suffer.

Left alone with Isaac, I was aware of his breathing, and the heat emanating from him. My heart swelled with some emotion I didn't understand, and it spread, flooding my veins. I had an urge to reach out and touch his hair. *What was wrong with me?* 'I really am sorry,' I murmured, trying not to buckle under the weight of his gaze, readying myself for whatever it was I sensed him trying not to say.

In that moment, on the edge of a precipice, I was certain I was about to understand something vital, but all he said was, 'Goodnight, Rose,' before walking away.

# Chapter 29

## *Thursday*

I barely slept for the rest of the night, after shoving the journal under the mattress, burning with alternating anger and guilt as I replayed the scene in the attic over and over.

Why had Jonah blurted out that I'd been going through the trunk? Perhaps it was the shock of finding me there, or maybe he'd still been half-asleep, though he hadn't looked it. He must have heard the ski fall over, perhaps thought he'd find Isaac up there. Recalling how he'd followed me the day before – probably at Lissa's request – I reminded myself that Jonah wasn't my ally, and neither was Lissa. I'd sensed a softening in Cecilia after I mentioned the baby – *why had I done that?* – more like the woman who'd been open and friendly the day I was interviewed, before Lissa filled her mind with doubts. I thought again of the list of questions I'd found. There was no doubt in my mind that Lissa had written them.

Regret rose like a wave as the voice in my head reminded me, *They're right to suspect you, even if they don't know why.*

I jerked from a fitful doze just after seven-thirty to sunlight and birdsong and forced myself out of bed on legs that felt heavy. My stomach was a ball of nerves. If only last night hadn't happened. Then again, at least I now had Elise's actual journal, as well as the school photo, so it hadn't all been for nothing. I knew I should read more, look for specific details of her apparent affair, Isaac's too, and all the other things she hadn't revealed to me – *had she worried about casting herself as the villain?* – but I couldn't face the anguished tone, the palpable distress scratched into the pages. It was like watching someone suffer and being unable to help. I knew at some cellular level I wasn't going to find the truth of what exactly had happened at Orchard House in Elise's journal – if I found it at all.

An engine revved at the front of the house. I recognised the sound of Jonah's car driving away. He must be doing an early shift at the café. Relief loosened the ache of tension in my neck. One less person to face over breakfast.

Hearing a child's laughter in the garden, I looked out of the window to see Daisy running in circles after Rocky, who had a tennis ball in his mouth. Isaac was sitting on the grass watching with a smile, arms looped around his knees. He and Daisy still had on their nightclothes, but Cecilia – emerging from the orchard with a basket of fruit in her arms – was dressed in what must be her work outfit of dungarees over a short-sleeved shirt, espadrilles on her feet. She swerved passed Rocky, smiled at Daisy, and paused to say something to Isaac, who tilted his head to look at her as he replied – something that made her laugh and ruffle his hair, as though he was a small boy.

Seeing her tender expression melted my tension further. They didn't appear angry, though I hadn't seen Lissa yet. Knowing it would be worse to put off a confrontation, and assuming I was still expected to play teacher to Daisy, I dressed after a hasty shower, fussing with my hair, and moisturising my hands until I couldn't decently put off going downstairs.

Cecilia was on her way out, checking her reflection in the hall, but smiled and said pleasantly into the mirror, 'Good morning, Rose.' As she moved, she winced, a hand shooting to her back.

'Are you OK?'

'It's a bit painful this morning. I shouldn't have gone fruit-picking. Then that damned dog appeared through the hedge, and I chased him away.' Her face tightened. 'I'll be fine.'

She managed another brief smile and let herself out. At least there hadn't been any hostility towards me. My spirits lifted fractionally then sagged when I walked into the kitchen. Lissa was crunching into a slice of toast as she leaned across the work surface, scrolling through her phone.

'Hi,' she said, glancing up. Her eyes were pink-rimmed, as if she hadn't slept or had been crying. 'You OK?'

Taken aback by her tentatively friendly tone, I managed a weak smile. 'Better than I deserve, after last night.' No point skirting around the issue.

The doors were open, and warm, sweet-smelling air surged in. Isaac and Daisy were still in the garden with Rocky, Daisy's voice high and excited as Isaac called, 'Catch it this time, butterfingers.'

'Daddy, you have to throw it in a straight line.'

Lissa put down her crust and straightened, brushing her hands together. 'To be honest, if I'd seen an open attic in a house where I was staying, I doubt I could have resisted having a peek.' Her tone was almost conspiratorial, but tension began to creep along my shoulders. Had Jonah – or even Isaac – asked her to go easy on me, or she was trying to catch me out?

'Like I said, I thought Daisy was up there when I realised her bed was empty.'

She widened her eyes in a mildly teasing way. 'You're sticking with that line?'

Unsettled, I took a clean cereal bowl from the dishwasher and picked up a box of muesli. 'Only because it's the truth.' I matched her tone, determined not to be cowed. I inclined my head towards the garden. 'Looks like they're having fun out there.'

'Well, it's about time,' Lissa said, lacing her fingers over her belly as she watched me pour out cereal. She was wearing a loose, white cotton dress that highlighted her tan, her hair scraped up in a ponytail. 'There wasn't enough fun in this house for too long.'

Unsure how to respond, I scooped some spilled muesli into my hand and transferred it to the bin.

'Are you working today?' I asked politely when it became obvious she wasn't leaving. As I took milk from the fridge, she started telling me about a couple who'd commissioned a pair of wedding rings and how she was worried about messing things up.

'Imagine them getting to the crucial moment, and the rings are too big, or too small and I've ruined the service.' She leaned over the breakfast bar, chin resting on her palm, fingernails digging into the skin of her cheek. 'I'll probably never work again.'

'Have you not made wedding rings before?'

'Only my own.' She stuck out her other hand so I could see the thick, silver band. 'It was more about the engraving. Our initials and wedding date so, you know, we never forget our special day.'

There was something in her tone I couldn't work out. 'Did you have a traditional wedding?' I climbed on a chair and began eating my breakfast. I much preferred this chattier version of Lissa but didn't entirely trust her. *Maybe she feels the same about me.*

'God, no.' She straightened, hands moving to her back in a reflexive way. 'It was a woodland ceremony in the New Forest, just close family, and friends from the commune.' Her gaze grew wistful. 'We could hear birds singing, wind in the leaves, that sort of thing. I carried a bunch of wild flowers, and Jonah wore a tweed suit that belonged to his father. We had a picnic after the ceremony, around a bonfire, and friends provided the music, mostly acoustic guitars.'

'Sounds perfect,' I said, picturing it. 'Isaac was there?'

Lissa blinked, as though landing back in the present. 'Yeah, of course he was there.' She traced a tiny scratch on the work surface with her finger. 'It was just before he met Ann, and my friend Jules kept trying it on with him, but he was all, *Ooh, no, I'm leaving the country on Monday; I can't get involved.* He was leading a team up Everest or trekking barefoot across the desert or something macho.' There was a hint of affectionate eye-roll. 'He came back off a trip especially for the wedding, but that's my brother.' She gave a small smile. 'Loyal to the core.'

Another description of Isaac that didn't tally with Elise's version, but Lissa was his sister, bound by blood. And she couldn't have been privy to everything that had happened between her brother and his wife, even after she and Jonah moved in.

'I'm sad my dad didn't get to be there.' Lissa's eyes were cast down. 'It's a shame he never got to meet his grandchildren.'

'I feel the same about my parents.' I lifted my spoon, milk dripping into the bowl, and wished I'd chosen toast. 'All the things they've missed and will never experience.'

When Lissa looked up, I could see red blood vessels in the whites of her eyes. 'Now and then I think it's a blessing.' As she reached for her phone I thought of Leon and losing the baby. Maybe it *was* a blessing my parents hadn't seen me suffer, but wasn't that part of life?

'I'm glad Dad didn't live to see the shitshow that was my brother's marriage,' Lissa said. 'It probably would have killed him.'

The mood soured. I replayed the desperate words in Elise's journal. 'No one really knows someone's marriage apart from the people in it,' I said, before I could stop myself.

'Get that from a book, did you?' Lissa exhaled a scornful laugh. 'I told you what she was like and you're still defending her.' She shook her head. 'We lived it, you didn't, so I don't think you're qualified to pass an opinion.'

My heart was suddenly pounding. Sensing I was inches from disaster, I took a breath. 'You're right. I'm sorry,' I said calmly. 'It's none of my business.'

'Look, I feel bad for what you've been through, but we don't need anyone else's baggage in this house.' Lissa grabbed her discarded crust and tossed it into the bin. 'We've got enough of our own.'

My mouth fell open, but no words came out. Not that it mattered as she was already walking away, through the conservatory and into the garden, stalking towards the summerhouse, where Elise had spent most of the final, miserable weeks of her marriage.

I sat, spoon in hand, staring at nothing until Daisy raced in.

'Rosie, I'm going to get dressed and then it's time for school, so finish your breakfast.'

I smiled and nodded, as though she was the grown-up and I was the child. When Isaac came in and asked if I was OK, his gaze a force I could feel, I managed a single nod before getting up to empty my bowl, refusing his offer of coffee.

'I think I'll head to the classroom.'

'Are we good?'

Unable to bear his solicitous tone, I curled my fingers over the edge of the sink. Instead of the anger I knew I should feel on Elise's behalf, humiliation warmed my chest.

'We're good.' My voice was small. 'Thank you.'

*What the hell are you thanking him for?* Elise's voice in my head made me wince. I hurried out of the kitchen, grateful to slip into a semblance of my former self. Flinging open the patio doors, I prepared to greet Daisy, who was banging about in her room above.

Moving to the table, I noticed my laptop had been moved slightly, the work on top not aligned the way I'd left it. I sat down, heart tripping as I remembered revealing how I used my date of birth and a hashtag to access all my devices as it was easy to remember.

I lifted the lid, gripped with foreboding. The home screen appeared, and I typed in the password. A document appeared, one sentence marching across the page in bold black letters. **YOU SHOULD DO THE DECENT THING AND LEAVE.**

I snatched my hands back. Someone had touched the keys, if not last night, then this morning. I looked around, as if the culprit might be waiting, watching, observing my reaction.

Was this why Lissa had been friendly at breakfast? To cover her tracks? But she'd soon reverted to her sceptical, slightly bitter mode.

I had an urge to show Isaac, but couldn't rule him out, even if I couldn't imagine him typing such a warning – not after going to the trouble of checking we were 'good'. I was sure he wanted me around his daughter, so why would he urge me to leave?

If I brought it to anyone's attention, it would cause chaos. Accusations would be thrown around, defences would go up. I would be seen as a pest, at best, more trouble than I was worth. *We don't need any more baggage in this house*, Lissa had stated baldly. She couldn't have made her feelings plainer but maybe she wanted to put it in writing in case I was in any doubt.

I deleted the words and closed down the page, just as Daisy came in, wearing her gingham dress. There was no point instigating a confrontation now.

One more day and Daisy and I would be gone.

# Chapter 30

I tried to train my mind on the present as I taught Daisy some facts about the local area, using one of my printouts, explaining the differences between a city, a town, and a village.

'Ten thousand, six hundred and seventy-nine is a *lot* of people,' she said of Beaconsfield's population, eyes widening when I told her how many people lived in London. 'How many are where you live, Rose?'

'Chesham is bigger than Beaconsfield, so even more people live there.' I brought up a geography learning page on my laptop, trying not to think about the message I'd deleted. 'So, what is the difference between a city, a town, and a village? Can you remember?'

'What's it like where you live?' Daisy tilted her head, tapping the desk with her pencil 'Have you got a big house?'

'Not as big as this one.' I smiled at the way she scrunched up her face, preparing another question.

'Have you got a garden at your house?'

'A small one.' I knew I should steer her back to the lesson, but couldn't resist adding, 'But over the road there's a big field with horses in it.'

'Horses!' Daisy dropped her pencil and clasped her hands under her chin. 'Can we go and see the horses, Rose, *pleeease*?'

'It's Rose, and . . . I'm not sure, Daisy.' I shouldn't have mentioned the horses. 'I don't know who they belong to, and sometimes there's only one there anyway, and—'

'But I can stroke him, can't I, Daddy?'

I turned to see Isaac in the doorway, a quizzical smile on his face. 'What's this?'

'There's some horses near Rosie's house and she said we can go and see them, and I can stroke one.' Daisy practically vibrated with excitement as she scraped her chair back and ran to Isaac. 'You can come too.'

She turned pleading eyes on me, dancing from foot to foot. 'Please say yes, please say yes.'

Isaac came in, laughing and shaking his head. He perched on her small chair, causing her to shriek with laughter and try to pull him up. 'I don't see why not.' He raised his eyebrows at me. 'If Rose doesn't mind,' he said. 'Daisy loves animals, as you can probably tell.'

'I wouldn't have guessed.' I hoped my smile masked the panic raging through me. 'Though I can't guarantee they'll be there today,' I added. 'How about later we visit somewhere I've never been, like the model village? I'd love to see it, especially the little railway.'

'But I've been there loads, haven't I, Daddy?' Daisy appealed. 'I want to see the horses.'

'Well, I suppose there's no harm in looking.' Isaac allowed himself to be pulled to his feet, feigning difficulty, while Daisy laughed with delight.

'What about the lesson?' I said.

'Maybe when you've finished?' When Daisy began to protest that she wanted to go now, he said firmly, 'Finish the lesson first, bunny, and then we can see the horses.' He glanced at me, eyes dancing with humour as Daisy shot back to her chair and sat down with a studious expression. 'I'm looking forward to it,' he said quietly. 'Give me a shout when you're ready. I'll be in my study wrestling with a new chapter of my next novel.'

'Intriguing.' A string of swear words flew through my head as he left, my concentration shot. *Why had I mentioned the horses?*

Thinking quickly, I asked Daisy to draw a picture of her favourite place, then took my phone out onto the patio.

'I'm going to ring up my neighbour and check the horses are there today,' I told her, hating myself for the lie.

I rang the hospital, praying Elise was still there.

'Oh, hi, Rose. It's Nikki.' The nurse on the other end sounded cheery. 'It's such great news about your sister.'

'It's wonderful.' I tried to squeeze the impatience out of my voice. 'Can I—'

'Are you coming to collect her?' Nikki cut in. 'We can cancel the taxi.'

'What?'

'She's been discharged.'

'Oh, no, I'm afraid I can't, but I do need to speak to her urgently.' Into the pause that followed, I added, 'She hasn't got a mobile phone.'

'Of course.' Nikki's tone had cooled. 'You're lucky to catch her.'

There were muffled sounds, then nothing for a full minute, and I jumped when Elise eventually hissed in my ear, 'Why are you calling me, Rose?' I assumed Nikki couldn't be listening or she wouldn't sound so rattled. 'I've spoken to the police this morning and told them what happened, that I was drunk . . .' She paused. 'What's happened?'

'You can't go back to the house yet.' My heart kicked against my chest. 'Daisy wants to look at the horses in the field and Isaac's coming too.'

'What?' She sounded as panicked as I felt. 'Why the hell did you agree to that?'

'I mentioned the horses – I don't know why.' I pressed my fingers to my forehead, feeling dizzy. 'Daisy was so excited to go and see them, and I couldn't think of a reason to say no that

226

wouldn't sound odd.' I glanced into the playroom to see Daisy, head bent over her drawing. 'She loves animals.'

'All kids love animals, Rose.' *All kids*. But this was *her* kid we were talking about. 'You should have said no, for God's sake. You're supposed to be her tutor.'

Something inside me hardened. 'The point is, we'll be there within the hour, so it's best if you don't go back right away.' I waited. 'Is that OK?' Only the sound of breathing at the other end. 'How are you feeling?'

'I've got a headache, and I'm desperate to see my little girl, but otherwise I'm fine, thank you for asking,' she bit back. Her voice softened. 'Sorry, Rose. I'm scared that something will go wrong.'

'It won't,' I said, even as my mind flooded with doubt. 'We just have to get through today.'

'Right.' She blew out a breath, sounding weary now. 'I suppose I could, I don't know, go into town, to a coffee shop or something.'

'You shouldn't be doing that, not straight out of hospital.' In a rush of guilt, I said, 'Look, go back to the house and stay in the bedroom. I'll make sure we don't come inside.'

'No.' She was decisive. 'I won't risk it, Rose. Not after getting this far.' As I opened my mouth to protest, she said, 'I'll see you tomorrow, as planned, OK?' When I stayed silent, she added tersely, 'Promise me, Rose.'

I felt a tightening across my chest. 'I promise.'

It took a few seconds of silence to realise she'd ended the call.

# Chapter 31

As Isaac drove, Daisy chatted happily in the back seat, buzzing with excitement.

He'd insisted on us going in his car, saying it wasn't fair to use my fuel when it had been Daisy's idea to see the horses. It had been a relief, not only because I couldn't imagine focusing on the road with Isaac and Daisy in such close proximity, but because I had a reason to leave my keys behind. If Daisy wanted to look in the house, I would be able to truthfully say I couldn't get in. My only worry now was that Beatrice would see me and come out to ask about my friend who had fallen down the stairs, keen to tell Isaac how she'd called an ambulance and probably saved her life. In an attempt at disguising myself, I'd put on a sun hat I didn't remember packing and a pair of sunglasses that covered half my face.

'I'm a bit allergic to horses,' I told Isaac when I came out of the house. 'It helps to keep my eyes covered.'

'Did you hear that?' He looked at Daisy scrambling into the car. 'You're a very lucky girl that Rose doesn't mind, even though horses make her sneeze.'

'It's the least I can do after last night,' I said in a low voice. His grin only heightened my feelings of deceit. Although, if he'd left the hatch open, intending me to go up there, he could probably afford to appear forgiving.

*You have no right to even see Daisy. Leave her alone, you mad bitch.*

I had to keep those texts at the forefront of my mind and remember what Elise had told me about Isaac not being who he seemed. Someone capable of sending those messages didn't develop that kind of mentality overnight.

No wonder she'd had an affair. Although I would have preferred to have known, I could understand Elise keeping it from me, perhaps not wanting to taint herself in my eyes. And, whoever the affair had been with, he clearly wasn't in the picture anymore, unless . . . could he be the person who owned the cabin where she planned to live with Daisy? Perhaps she had a stepfather already lined up.

My head was a churning mass of thoughts as we arrived in Chesham, my cheeks aching with the effort of smiling, and responding to Daisy's questions about the 'ponies' as she called them, and her story about a roundabout horse she once rode on – *a fairground carousel,* Isaac clarified – when she nearly slid off. I wondered whether Elise had been there but asking Daisy about her mother felt dangerous.

I let out a quiet sigh of relief as we drove down Chandlers Road, pointing to the space outside number seven. Hopefully, Beatrice was in her garden at the back, rather than near her window or, better still, out shopping. She might recognise Isaac's car, I realised, remembering how he'd turned up at the house while Leon was there – though, as far as I knew, she hadn't seen him that night.

'There they are, the ponies, look!' Daisy was uninterested in the house when we emerged from the car. She tugged my hand and held out the other to her dad. Isaac took it and we crossed the road with Daisy between us, looking like a happy family to anyone observing. The thought made my throat ache.

I resisted the urge to glance over my shoulder, hoping Elise hadn't changed her mind and was, right now, looking out of the bedroom window, overcome by the sight of her daughter. What if she couldn't stop herself rushing out? And seeing Isaac . . . no, she wouldn't risk a confrontation, under any circumstances. Not this close to getting away.

'Maybe you should give him a name,' I said as we reached the fence and the chestnut horse trotted over. Isaac hoisted Daisy up, and she reached out to stroke the horse's nose.

'He should be called Spirit.' She looked at Isaac for approval. 'Like Lucky's horse.'

'It's from an animated kids show on Netflix called *Pony Tales*,' Isaac explained, tipping Daisy forward so she could touch the horse's ear. 'She got a bit obsessed with it earlier this year.'

'I wanted to have a pony, and Nana said they cost a lot of money, but maybe when I'm bigger I can do riding lessons.'

'That sounds like a good plan.' My stomach twisted. Would Elise agree to riding lessons once they were living together? I made a mental note to add Daisy's love of horses to the list of things that might help Elise bond with her daughter once they were alone. Recalling her throwaway comment on the phone I felt a momentary kick of panic. *All kids love animals.* It had sounded so dismissive, but – I reminded myself – Elise was bound to be wound up after waking up in hospital, an unwelcome deviation from her plan. Once she and Daisy were together, things would fall into place. I had to believe that.

I paused my spiralling thoughts, aware I was staring again, with my jaw clenched. I made myself pat the horse's side, agreeing with Isaac that it was a stunning setting, the field a vast carpet of green beneath a soft, blue sky. 'Lots of good walks around here,' he said, eyes on the hulk of hills in the distance. 'No mountains, but still.'

'The others are coming!' Daisy bounced against Isaac as the pair of smaller horses padded over, flicking their tales.

'We could be here all afternoon.' Isaac smiled at me. 'Thanks for this.'

'It's nothing, I—' Someone was calling my name. I spun round. Beatrice was on the kerb, about to cross the road. 'It's my neighbour,' I said, as Isaac twisted to look. 'I'll go and see what she wants.'

'Daddy, can I sit on Spirit's back?'

As Isaac returned his attention to Daisy, I hurried across to Beatrice, hoping my smile didn't look deranged. 'How are you?'

'I thought it was you.' Beatrice peering more closely, seeming puzzled by my appearance. 'I can see myself in your lenses.'

Heart thumping, I took off the sunglasses – so much for my 'disguise' – and moved to the path that led to her front door, so she had to follow me. 'The horses make me sneeze, so . . .'

'Who's that then?' She nodded to Daisy and Isaac.

Not knowing how else to explain them, I said, 'It's the little girl I've been helping look after this week.'

'The reason you've been away.'

I nodded. 'My friend's coming out of hospital today.' Better to say it now in case Isaac came over and she let something slip in front of him. 'She's staying tonight, and I'll be home tomorrow.'

'That's good.' Beatrice seemed distracted, her brow wrinkled. 'I'm glad I caught you,' she said. 'I made a call this morning and didn't know how to let you know about it.'

My heart jerked. 'A call?'

'To your landlord, apparently.'

I'd rented the house through a letting agency and hadn't met the owner; a woman called Andrea Kenning. 'I don't understand.' I jumped as a white cat ran out of Beatrice's open front door. If Daisy spotted him, she would want to come over. 'Can we go inside for a second?' I touched my forehead. 'It's a bit hot out here.'

'Of course, dear.' Beatrice led the way, shooing the cat upstairs, her awkward gait suggesting a painful hip. I stood in her doorway, attention caught by a vase of pink and white roses on a shiny console table. The hallway was identical to mine, but bright and cared for. 'Would you like a glass of water?'

'No, I'm fine thank you.' I smiled, though it didn't feel natural. 'You were saying?'

She paused, one hand on the post at the bottom of the stairs. 'A card had been put through my door with a number on the back, asking me to call, so I did. A man said he'd come round to your house after getting wind that you had somebody living with you, which would be breaking the terms of your contract. You weren't in and he couldn't get hold of you, and no one was answering their doors.' Her lips pursed. 'Anyway, he asked whether I'd seen signs of someone moving in.'

I felt as though I was falling. 'Do you have the number?'

She moved to the console table and picked up a business card for the letting agency. The number on the back in blue ink was different. 'Can I keep this?' She nodded and I slipped it in my pocket. 'What did you say?'

Beatrice pulled herself taller. 'I didn't like his tone,' she said, a prim set to her mouth. 'Pretending to be oh-so-nice, to get information.' She tapped her temple with a bent finger. 'I still have all my marbles.'

'Of course you do.' My nerves were jangling. 'And I *don't* have someone living with me.'

'Well, exactly.' Beatrice bent to scoop up the cat winding around her swollen ankles. 'You have someone visiting, and that's entirely different.'

'Is that what you told him?' The walls tilted closer.

'Of course not.' She looked affronted, the lines around her mouth like brackets. 'I said I hadn't seen anyone but you in the house, and he should confront you directly if he has any issues.'

'Thanks, Beatrice.' I felt light with relief. 'I'll give this number a call later on.'

'I found the whole thing odd.' Beatrice rhythmically smoothed the cat's head, its purr like a ticking engine. 'I know the house was advertised through an agency because of the To Let sign outside. I never met the owner.'

'Did he have an accent?' I thought of Leon, though it didn't stack up that he would call Beatrice attempting to uncover a house guest he already knew about.

'Not noticeably.' Beatrice screwed her eyes up, thinking. 'Well-spoken, quite a soft voice, but I got the impression he could have been putting it on.'

Leon was well-spoken, but I didn't believe it was him. Isaac was too. I turned to see him staring right at me while Daisy, at his side, stroked the white horse's flank through the three-bar fence. His face looked carved from wood, his hair moving slightly in the breeze.

'Everything OK, Rose?' Beatrice's fingers were buried in the cat's fur. 'You're not in any trouble, are you?'

*More than you can imagine.* 'I'm fine.' I switched on a smile. 'I appreciate you telling me about the phone call,' I said. 'It's unsettled me a bit if I'm honest.'

'Me too. It was playing on my mind.' She put down the cat, who darted through an open door into the living room. 'Don't worry though, Rose. I gave him short shrift.'

'I'm so sorry he bothered you.' I was flooded with remorse that my innocent neighbour kept getting caught in the tangle my life had become.

Her face had a glow as she said, 'Oh, don't you worry. I can handle most things, though I probably wouldn't confront anyone in a hoodie.' She shuddered her shoulders. 'You never know if they're carrying a knife.'

'Very wise.' I stepped back onto the path. 'I'd better get going, but thanks again.' I raised a hand in a wave. 'I'll see you soon.'

'Shall I pop round and see your friend later on?'

'I think she'll just want to sleep,' I said quickly. 'She's a very private person, but I'll let her know to knock if she needs anything.'

Snapping a bright expression in place, I hurried back to Isaac and Daisy, aware of movement in my peripheral vision. A taxi was turning into the road.

'Shall we go?' I said when I reached Isaac, replacing my sunglasses to hide my expression. 'I can feel a sneezing fit coming on.'

'You can pinch your nose, like this.' Daisy demonstrated, screwing her eyes shut.

'It's better to let it out,' Isaac argued with a smile. 'Your neighbour OK?'

'Just checking whether or not I'm coming back,' I lied.

He nodded, but I had the sense he didn't believe me. I wanted to ask, *Did you speak to her on the phone this morning?* but he was hardly going to admit it if he had.

'Can I get a drink of water at your house?' Daisy asked, leaning through the fence, reluctant to break contact with the horses. 'Then you can blow your nose and we can come back.'

I smoothed my hands over my pockets, a tremor in my fingers. 'I'm afraid I didn't bring my keys.' I looked at Isaac. 'Sorry,' I said. 'Normally I'd have them on me, but as I wasn't using the car—'

'Does your neighbour have a spare?' He was looking at the house again – mine, or Beatrice's, I couldn't tell. Filled with a terrible sense of urgency – *why was Elise back already?* – I tugged off the sun hat, which was making my scalp itch. 'We're only recently on chatting terms, not at the stage of leaving spare keys with each other. The sun had moved, bright as a searchlight, making me blink behind my shaded lenses. 'Maybe we can stop somewhere for a drink?'

'I've got some water in the car,' Isaac said after a moment's pause, passing a hand over Daisy's hair. 'Come on, bunny. We can come back and see the horses another day.'

'Can I have ice-cream?' Daisy cast her father a hopeful look. 'We can go to Uncle Jonah's café.'

'I'll think about it.' He passed me a smile, while I fought the urge to run to the car and dive inside. I twisted my head as we crossed the road, Daisy calling, 'Goodbye Spirit, Prince and Jemima, I'll see you soon.' The taxi had stopped halfway down the road. Elise must have seen us and asked the driver to wait. I should have known she wouldn't be able to resist a glimpse of her daughter.

Back in the passenger seat, I returned Beatrice's wave with a tight-lipped smile, and Daisy waved to her too. Isaac strapped himself in the driver's seat and adjusted the mirror. I willed him to move, wondered why he was taking his time.

He reached past me into the glove compartment as the taxi idled past. I met Elise's gaze and felt my breath leave my body. Her eyes were wide, alive with anguish as she pressed a palm to the window.

I kept my gaze fixed ahead, glad of my sunglasses. Isaac unscrewed the top of the bottle of water and handed it to Daisy. 'Let's go, amigo.'

My heart pumped wildly as he finally pulled away. I wiped perspiration from my upper lip.

'I wonder who that is.' Isaac was looking in the rear-view mirror. 'A taxi just stopped outside your house.'

My breath faltered. *Was he playing with me?* I lowered my head and made a pretence of looking in the wing mirror. The taxi door had opened, and a leg emerged, wearing a chunky, black boot.

'Beatrice mentioned her daughter was coming to stay.' I was amazed at how steady my voice was, my ability to think up lies so quickly. 'She hasn't seen her for ages.'

'Nice.' He flashed me a glance as we reached the corner and thankfully turned out of sight. 'Family is so important, right?'

# Chapter 32

## *Friday*

I barely slept all night, going over and over the plan, playing out various scenarios – most of which ended with Daisy hysterical, and Elise and me in handcuffs.

I got up at six, sick to my stomach, and stood under a hot shower for a long time, trying to steady my nerves.

There was no point in packing as I'd be coming back to the house at some point, if only to be officially fired from my 'job' having failed to keep Daisy safe.

*My life won't begin again until I have Daisy, and that's down to you.*

I stood by the window, wrapped in a towel, forcing air deep into my lungs as sunlight crept across the garden, picking out the neon-pink geraniums Daisy had told me proudly she helped to plant with Cecilia.

I had to behave normally, or there would be no chance of getting Daisy out of the house. Already, I was fretting she might have one of her migraines or had changed her mind about going to the park, or that Isaac, or Cecilia, might decide to come with us. If that happened, Elise would have no choice but to change the flight or leave without Daisy. But that option was apparently non-negotiable.

I could barely believe Isaac had agreed to me taking Daisy to the park on my own in the first place. It had been such a relief to escape from Chesham the day before – Elise's pleading gaze burned into my brain – even after Isaac's loaded comment about family being everything. *What was he trying to tell me?* The feeling had expanded when we stopped at 'Jonah's café' to find he wasn't there, his day for counselling training, Isaac suddenly remembered. Over chocolate ice-cream for Daisy, and coffee and a pastry for Isaac and me, I'd heard myself say casually, 'Before you came in earlier, we were learning about Beaconsfield today and Daisy drew a picture of her favourite place to visit.'

'The park,' Daisy had supplied, adorably wiping a smear of chocolate from her face with a paper napkin. 'I love the swings.'

'I wondered whether we could go there tomorrow.' I'd shredded my pastry to crumbs, certain I would choke if I tried to eat. 'It could be part of our lesson.'

'Yes, I want to go with Rosie.' Daisy's eyes had lit up with excitement. 'You can push me on the swing,' she'd said, beaming. 'And I can take my ball.' She'd leaned across the table, as though confiding a secret. 'I want to be a footballer when I grow up.'

'Good for you,' I'd said, caught by her enthusiasm.

'It's Rose, not Rosie,' Isaac had reproved, though his voice was gentle.

'It doesn't matter, I'm beginning to like it,' I'd said, truthfully. 'You can come too' I'd added, knowing Isaac wouldn't leave his study on a work day. 'Or Nana.'

'Mum will be at work, if her back's better,' Isaac had said, as I'd known he would. Cecilia had been at home when we returned, looking washed out on the sofa, and went up to bed soon after, dosed up on painkillers. 'And I have to go into Snow Zone in

237

the morning. The potential investor I met with is coming over.' Isaac looked torn. 'I could always put him off.'

'No, I want to go with Rosie on my own.' Daisy had pressed a palm on the table, her expression determined. '*Please*, Daddy.' It couldn't have worked better if I'd planned it, but somehow felt like a hollow victory.

Isaac had tipped sugar into his coffee and stirred it vigorously, as if buying time to weigh up whether it was safe to let me loose with his daughter – the woman he'd found in the attic the night before, going through his wife's clothing. When he'd said, 'Of course, that's fine, if Rose doesn't mind,' accompanying the words with a trusting smile, I'd realised with a blade of shock I'd been hoping he would refuse.

Now, as I dressed slowly and brushed my hair, twisting it into a low bun, I felt the tug of inevitability. Things were in motion, no going back. Elise was waiting, would be up and pacing my house, if she'd even been to bed, willing the hours and minutes to pass, no doubt playing out her own version of events, perhaps wondering how Daisy would react to seeing her again – a mother she'd hadn't seen for a year, believing her to be dead.

*Would the shock be too much for Daisy?*

While I'd lain awake through the night, listening to the sounds of the house, wondering again which of its occupants wanted me to 'do the decent thing and leave' – no signals over dinner, though Lissa had taken a plate to the summerhouse, while Jonah ate out on the patio, leaving only Isaac, Daisy and me at the dining table – one of the scenes I'd played out had been laying some groundwork for Daisy on our walk to the park, asking about her mother, probing how she would feel if she were to see her again. It didn't seem right to thrust Elise's reappearance on her out of the blue, but neither could I mention her mother in front of the family.

In a fever of anxiety, I headed to the wardrobe and pulled out the rucksack I'd brought. Hands shaking, I slipped Elise's journal and earrings inside the front pocket. I would need to fetch Daisy's passport from Isaac's study, and the cookbook from the kitchen, and I intended to slip in Daisy's unicorn, and some of her clothes and favourite books – things that were familiar. No matter what Elise had said about starting over, Daisy shouldn't be ripped away from everything she knew. Elise's memories of Isaac and his family were ruined beyond salvation, to the point where even the mention of Isaac's name provoked a fathomless rage, but the same wasn't true for Daisy. How would Elise deal with the inevitable fallout of her daughter leaving her family behind; her beloved father and Nana, her Auntie Lissa, and Uncle Jonah, even Rocky, her faithful companion and playmate, and the baby cousin she would never meet?

A sob cracked in my throat. I forced myself to run through everything I knew about each member of the family and how they had treated Elise, each in their own way contributing to her desperate actions. If there was another way to solve things, she would have found it. It was this, or letting Daisy go for good.

Maybe, if there was time, I would try to convince Elise to contact the family, to find a way for them to stay in touch with Daisy, even from a distance. Remind her Daisy would grow up one day and might want to reunite with her father, if Elise hadn't poisoned her against him – though I knew deep down that's exactly what she would do. *Poison.* I thought again of the wisteria seeds, and the strange illness that had struck me down the day I arrived; the broken glass in my room, the shove into the stream, what Thora had said about the family, the necklace left for me to wear, and the message on my laptop. So much was wrong here, just as Elise had said. It was like a giant jigsaw puzzle with several pieces missing. Maybe I had to accept there were things I would never understand or get to the bottom of.

I paced my room, fighting a sickening panic. When the blame for Daisy's disappearance landed on me and Isaac decided to take action . . . legally, there wouldn't be a case to answer if I stuck to playing my part, but that didn't mean he couldn't make my life difficult in other ways.

I would have no choice but to go back to Derbyshire, but I didn't want to bring Sarah and Roy into this when they'd been through enough already. I was supposed to have sorted my life out now, or at least be on my way.

'Oh God,' I whispered through my fingers, dropping onto the bed. A bed I would never sleep in again. No more Daisy running in first thing, to see if I was awake. No more lessons, or bedtime stories. I would never hear about her trip to Iceland to visit her great-grandfather.

Blinking back tears, I pushed my limbs into motion. On the landing, I listened for movement. Time had moved quickly, and it was almost seven-thirty. Three hours until I let Daisy go. *Back to her mother,* I mentally added, but my inner voice lacked conviction.

She was still sleeping when I peered round her door, star-fished across her duvet, the disappearing unicorn from the night before peeking from under the bed.

Rocky pushed up from his position at the foot of the stairs and greeted me with an enthusiastic tail wag.

'Hello, boy,' I whispered. When I paused to stroke his head, he sat and raised a paw. 'Time for breakfast, huh?' His face dissolved through a veil of tears. 'Come on.'

I tipped biscuits into his bowl, and after blowing my nose on a sheet of kitchen roll, I re-entered the hallway, listening for sounds upstairs. Hearing nothing, I pushed open the door of Isaac's study to see the passport still on his desk, almost like a test. I would have to wait until the last minute to grab it, hopefully once he'd left for the ski centre.

The sound of a toilet flushing above brought me back into the hallway, pulse quickening. There was a murmur of voices – Lissa, and Jonah, then Cecilia's low tone. I wondered whether they were discussing last night.

Cecilia came downstairs and I shot back to the kitchen. She didn't come in or say good morning. There were rustling sounds as she put on shoes and gathered her things, then the front door opened and closed softly as she left for work, obviously feeling better.

I switched on the kettle, turning as I heard soft footfall behind me.

'You're up early.' Jonah stopped short at the sight of me, scratching his chest through his T-shirt. One side of his face was pillow-creased, and his eyes were pouched with tiredness. 'Guilty conscience keeping you up?'

I looked at him sharply and detected a smile, a trace of humour in his expression.

'I remember helping Isaac lug that trunk into the attic,' he continued, moving to the coffee maker. 'It was heavier than it looks.' He flicked me a sideways glance. 'Considering there were only clothes inside.'

'The wood seemed pretty solid,' I said, deliberately misunderstanding. Was he fishing for information, hoping I'd reveal the discovery of something else – *but what?*

'My grandmother had a trunk like that. It's where she kept her old photo albums.' The kettle boiled. I poured water onto the teabag I'd thrown in a mug. 'There must have been about twenty, all leather.' Filled with snaps of Mum and Sarah through all the stages of their lives, older ones of her and my grandfather, young and in love, and further back to her own parents and grandparents. Sarah had sifted through them after my grandmother died, picking out several to keep. I had no idea what happened to the rest.

'Nothing like that in there?' Jonah turned it into a question.

'No,' I said, pointedly. 'Just clothes.'

'Morning.' Lissa wafted in, hiding a yawn with her fingers. She was barefoot, wearing a burnt-orange dress that skimmed her ankles and clashed with her hair, the thin fabric straining over her belly. 'It's going to be another warm one.' She looked through at the conservatory, blinking as though to clear her vision. 'I'm going to head to the workshop and finish my commission.'

'The wedding rings?' She darted me a guarded look and nodded. 'How's it going?'

She made a so-so gesture with her hand. 'I'll be glad when it's done.' She didn't look at Jonah as she opened the fridge and took out a carton of orange juice, or when he slid her a glass from one of the cabinets, holding it still while she poured. I supposed that's what it was like when you'd been married a while. You developed a shorthand that didn't always need words, though . . . was I imagining a coil of tension between them?

'See ya,' she said, fluttering a wave as she wandered out with her drink.

'Do you want something to eat?' Jonah called after her, something moving across his face as he watched her go. 'Keep your strength up.'

She didn't turn round. 'Not hungry right now.'

The mood was heavy when she'd gone, like something pressing down.

I picked up my mug for something to do, unwilling to move past Jonah to get the milk for my tea. His hungry expression was oddly repellent. After hitching up his shorts he turned back to the coffee machine and began flipping switches. 'Is Cecilia still here?' He rubbed the lines between his eyebrows.

'She just left. How is she this morning?'

'I don't know.' He turned, eyes narrowed. 'I haven't seen her yet.'

'No, of course not.' A flush threaded across my skin. 'Sorry.'

Giving up on the machine, he flicked on the kettle and spooned some instant coffee granules into a *Best Nana Ever* mug, adding a sugar cube with the tiny tongs, and a careless splash of milk. He didn't seem inclined to make further conversation, perhaps mulling over his exchange with Lissa. Once the coffee was made he left the kitchen with a nod in my direction.

I let out a breath of relief and put down my mug.

Isaac and Daisy would be down soon. I reached to the shelf beneath the cabinets and pulled out *The Art of Cooking*. I should take it upstairs now while I had the chance. Checking no one was coming, I opened the book and skimmed a step-by-step recipe for game pie – not the sort of thing I could ever imagine Elise cooking, or Ingrid for that matter. She'd relied on ready-meals and takeaways, and the occasional frozen pizza according to Elise.

As I flipped over another page, a photograph slid out onto the worktop, face-down. I turned it over, and my breath caught in my throat. It was Elise, in the garden, here, at Orchard House. The trees were in leaf, so it must have been taken in spring or summer, the edge of the summerhouse just visible. *She was practically living in there by then.*

It was a head and shoulders shot, and her lips were curved in a smile, hair caught by the wind, blowing around her face, but her eyes . . . they had a slightly frenetic look, as if she was willing the moment to be over so she could escape. It was like looking at a fragile stranger on the edge of a breakdown.

My thoughts flicked back and forth, like a broken needle on an old compass, as my eyes bored into the image, and finally settled with crystal clarity.

*Elise wasn't ready to be a mother, and I couldn't let her leave the country with Daisy.*

I'd believed I owed her this – a returned daughter – to balance the past, and because I believed every child deserved a mother, but not like this. Elise needed professional help before reuniting with Daisy, not to 'snatch' her child and whisk her out of the country to live in a cabin in the mountains. I wasn't even sure how much of her plan was to make Isaac suffer, and while I had no doubt she loved her daughter, she hadn't spent time with her for a year. She wasn't prepared for the demands of a child.

Blood thrummed at my temples, but my mind was clear. I would talk to Elise, reason with her. Explain why taking Daisy from her family wasn't the right thing to do. And it wasn't fair to Daisy to simply reappear in such a dramatic, and potentially damaging, way.

A weight seemed to lift. I felt as if I could breathe properly for the first time in days. Facing Elise would be tough – imagining her reaction fanned my nerves – but I could handle it. And if she threatened to come clean to Isaac, let him know she was alive and tell him who I was, I would handle that too.

'What have you got there?'

My arm shot out in fright, knocking the cookbook to the floor. 'Isaac!' I clutched my chest as he came round the breakfast bar. 'You made me jump.'

'Sorry about that.' He sounded on the edge of laughter. 'You were miles away.'

Flustered, I bent to pick up the book, stars dancing in front of my eyes. 'How's Daisy?'

'She's reading in her room.'

'That's good.' I was surprised he couldn't hear the sound of my heart crashing around in my chest. 'Did you sleep well?' He looked rested, trailing a steamy shampoo scent, dressed in a white short-sleeved shirt over dark jeans.

'Good thanks. You?'

'Mm-hmm.'

He tipped his head at the cookbook. 'Looking for inspiration?'

'S . . . something like that,' I stuttered, opening and closing the book in my hands.

'Planning on cooking for us tonight?' I swivelled at the sound of Lissa's voice.

'You got me.' I scraped the words past a knot in my throat. 'I decided it was my turn after being cooked for all week.'

'I doubt you'll find anything tasty in that old thing.' Lissa pulled a face as she deposited her empty glass in the sink. 'It's about a hundred years old.'

My mouth had dried. 'I came across a recipe for game pie.'

'I suppose I could get Jonah to go and shoot a peasant.'

'Don't you mean pheasant?' Isaac lifted an eyebrow.

'I know what I meant.' They exchanged smiles, their likeness in the moment striking.

'What's that?' Lissa's brow furrowed. Before I could move, she grabbed the photo lying beside my mug. 'Where did you get this?'

'It fell out of the book.' I turned to Isaac. 'I assumed it was a picture of . . . of your wife.' A sense of alarm threatened to cut off my breath.

Lissa threw her brother a knife-sharp glare and thrust the photo at him. 'Can you believe this?'

His lips parted as he stared, before looking at me with a tormented expression.

Fear flushed through me. 'What is it?'

'This isn't my wife.' His voice was strained.

'I don't understand.'

'It's not Ann.' He was shaking his head, his eyes returning to the image. 'This is her sister, Elise.'

# Chapter 33

I watched the rise and fall of Lissa's chest, a tight, cold feeling of shock in my stomach.

'How did it get in the book?' Her voice was hard and angry.

'She must have put it there.' Isaac placed the picture of Elise face down on the counter. Even his lips looked pale. 'I told you, I thought she'd been in the house.'

'What am I missing?' I said, my voice a distant, tiny sound.

Lissa dragged her hands through her hair, wincing as one of her rings caught. 'We should call the police.'

'It's obviously been there a while.' Isaac pushed the photo away, as if he couldn't bear the sight of it. 'She hasn't been back since we . . .' He glanced at me, as if remembering my presence. 'Sorry about this,' he said grimly. 'It's a long and not very nice story.'

Questions punched my brain. *How could he have married Elise's sister? Hadn't she died before Elise was born? Had I misunderstood? What was going on?* It felt like the world had upended. 'Your wife's *sister*?'

Isaac tipped his head back and rubbed his face with both hands.

Lissa watched with slitted eyes. 'I still think you should call the police.'

'And say what?' Isaac's head snapped down, his pupils like

chips of granite. 'I told her I'd take out a restraining order if we caught her hanging around again, and she promised to stay away.'

*Restraining order?* My mind flew to Leon repenting his awful behaviour. Was that why Isaac had seemed so understanding when I explained how I'd ended up in Chesham – because he'd had cause to take the same route that I had? Against *Elise*?

'Could . . . could you explain?' I clasped my arms around my waist to stop myself shivering. 'Is this what you meant about keeping an eye on Daisy?'

Isaac briefly closed his eyes, his lips pressed together.

'I said you should have told her.' The fight had gone out of Lissa. Shoulders rounded, she reached for a chair and wriggled herself up onto it. 'It wasn't fair to keep it from you,' she said to me, swivelling her wedding ring round and round her finger. 'The woman's clearly insane.'

'Lissa.' Isaac's warning was weary, as if it was a topic he couldn't face revisiting. 'I should have said something, and I'm sorry.' He absently laid a hand on the cookbook and took a long breath. 'My wife's mother abandoned her when she was very young,' he said, almost robotically, as if his emotions had been used up long ago. 'She jumped out of the car at some traffic lights one day, and Ann and her father never saw her again. Ann grew up with her father, but when he was dying, he told her that her mother had been pregnant with a baby girl when she left, and that Ann had a sister somewhere, included in his will.' Isaac paused, face working. 'Ann couldn't forgive him for not telling her sooner, and when he died, she hired someone to find her mum and sister, but it didn't go well.'

Lissa made a noise in her throat.

'The sister – Elise – had just got over a suicide attempt when Ann got in touch. Apparently, she didn't have a good relationship with their mother, but didn't fancy sharing her either, with a sister she'd been told had died. On the other hand their mother, Ingrid, was overjoyed to have her daughter back and didn't bother

247

hiding it. Elise couldn't stand it, caused a load of trouble, and in the end Ann left them to it.

'When I met her a couple of years later, she didn't have much contact with either of them, then Ingrid started showing signs of dementia.'

My mind was scrambling to take it all in. *Elise's sister hadn't died.* She'd been abandoned by Ingrid and raised by her father, unaware she even had a sister. Their mother had lied to Elise for years.

A wave of anger rocked through me. How could Ingrid have treated Elise that way, with no regard for her feelings? Pretended the daughter she'd left behind was dead?

*The women in this family are cursed.*

'So your wife . . .' My voice, thin and thready, petered out.

'She wasn't a well woman, though Isaac didn't realise that when he married her,' Lissa said, when Isaac didn't speak, a muscle working in his jaw. 'Like I said to you the other day, she made his life a living hell.' She carried on quickly, ignoring the look he gave her. 'She was totally paranoid, maybe she got it from her mum, I don't know, but although she denied it, I think she was in touch with Elise towards the end, feeding her God knows what lies about us all, scribbling things in her bloody journal out there.' She jerked her head at the garden. 'It was poor mum who found her dead in the summerhouse that morning. God knows why she'd put that heater on, but she'd had a lot to drink.'

'Lissa, let's not go there.' Isaac looked like he wanted to be sick. I felt the same.

'Anyway, there was a scene at the funeral where Elise was accusing Isaac of all sorts, and saying she'd promised her sister she would look after Daisy and wanted access, that Ann had told her stuff about us that we wouldn't want coming out.'

*The funeral.* Isaac's wife had really died. He *was* a widower. I felt dizzy, darkness clouding my vision.

'Elise came to the house a couple of times and because she

was biologically Daisy's aunt, we thought there might be a way to involve her in Daisy's life, but it was obvious it wouldn't work. She didn't even seem to like children, hadn't a clue what to do, or how to talk to her. Daisy's naïve, she liked the idea of another auntie and would probably have loved having her around, but we could see it wasn't right. Elise didn't like it, said we'd poison Daisy against the Lockwoods, and that we'd regret it.'

The scale of Elise's deception was beginning to sink in, increasing the sick feeling in my stomach.

'In the end, we told her to leave us alone or we'd get the police involved, which scared her off. For a while, we didn't see or hear from her.' Lissa took a breath, eyes settling on me for a moment. 'A while ago, Isaac was certain someone had been in the house. We'd got a bit relaxed about security, being so far from other people, leaving the patio doors unlocked.'

'It felt as if someone had been in the bedroom,' Isaac said. 'Daisy's passport was missing, though I didn't realise until later, and someone had been in the garage. There was a footprint, not one of ours. And a photo of Daisy as a baby had been taken out of its frame.'

*The picture Elise had shown me.*

'Mum swore the cookbooks had been moved about too,' Lissa said. 'We didn't think much of it, but that must be when she put that photo of herself in there.'

'But why?' Isaac shook his head. 'Did she want Daisy to find it one day and ask about her?'

*She left it for me to find. Proof she'd 'lived' here. Same with the earrings I found in the garage.* My head was rammed with words, but full sentences were beyond me.

'We thought she might try to kidnap Daisy.' I felt an instant wash of coldness at Lissa's words. 'That's the main reason Isaac pulled her from school.'

'I didn't want to freak you out.' Isaac had morphed into a different version of his earlier, good-humoured self. Old fears had prodded awake, shadowing his face. 'I hoped things had settled down, that she'd given up.' Before I could begin to form a reply he said, 'And I'm fairly certain she has. It's just seeing the photo brought everything back.'

Lissa reached for it, holding it between her finger and thumb. 'It's obviously a selfie,' she said, though I hadn't noticed – I'd had no reason to suspect anything. 'Looks like she's in the orchard. Too scared to come any closer to the house.' She ripped the photo in half, then into smaller pieces, before clambering off her seat and dropping the fragments into the bin. 'We don't want anyone else getting hold of that.'

There was a heartbeat of silence.

'It's a good job Rose picked out that book.' Pulling his fingers across his brow, Isaac gave the ghost of a smile. 'Imagine if Mum had seen it,' he said to Lissa. 'After I managed to persuade her Elise and her mother were harmless.'

The conversation I'd heard outside the garage took on a new significance. So many things did, but I couldn't get my thoughts in order to sift through and make sense of them all.

'I'd actually started to think she might be getting to Rose,' Lissa said out of the blue. 'When you said you found Ann's necklace in your room, and something about a broken glass?' When I didn't answer, she angled her gaze at Isaac. 'I thought she might be trying to get rid of Rose, that she was jealous of her and didn't want her around Daisy, or something deranged.' She issued an uncomfortable laugh. 'I know it doesn't add up, but that's how she's made me think.'

'Broken glass?' Suspicion tightened Isaac's forehead.

'It's nothing.' I shook my head, guilt rushing from every pore. 'I must have knocked it on the floor but don't remember doing it, and I don't know how the necklace ended up in my room, but there's probably an innocent explanation.'

'Another of life's little mysteries.' Lissa pushed a strand of hair away from her face. 'We just want to get back to normal,' she said, darting a look of frustration at her brother. 'For Daisy, as much as anything, after what she's been through.'

'We tried to protect her from Ann's problems as much as possible,' Isaac said, as though moved to explain to me. 'You know, Ann wanted to take her down to the summerhouse to sleep in there with her the night she died.'

A shockwave rippled through me.

'Thank God I said no.' Torment filled Isaac's eyes. 'She'd been away getting treatment for seven months before . . .' He swallowed. 'Before the night she died. So, Daisy doesn't remember too much about her mother. They spent so little time together, other than the occasional trip to the park and a go on the swings.' He glanced at Lissa. 'It's why having my family around has been a godsend. I want Daisy to have fun and happy memories.'

'It's just a shame psycho number two is still out there,' Lissa muttered.

I bit down on my natural response of *You shouldn't talk about people with mental health issues that way. Elise is sick; she needs help.* In a moment of sharp lucidity, I understood how comprehensively I'd been used and manipulated by her. Elise had lied and lied to my face, employing all her drama skills to drip-feed me information she knew would appeal to my sense of fair play, to the mother in me that she knew I'd almost been – to the guilt-ridden nineteen-year-old who believed she'd been the reason Elise had tried to kill herself.

Knowledge was power and Elise had held it all.

A feeling bubbled up in my chest, a burning fury that tore through my veins and torched my cheeks.

'Rose, are you OK?' Isaac's voice nudged through the mist of anger. 'I know it's a lot to take in, and maybe I shouldn't have mentioned it, but—'

'It's fine, honestly. I'm glad you did.' I pushed away from the edge of the worktop, unbelting my arms from my waist. 'I need to go upstairs.' I was already heading out of the kitchen.

'Well, that was a whole pile of awkward,' Lissa said, as I reached the stairs.

Isaac called something after me, but I didn't hear. My head was filled with a rushing sound that must have the blood hurtling around my body. Girlish laughter floated from Daisy's room, reminding me of what was at stake. *Daisy's life.* I'd been on the verge of handing her to a virtual stranger. A woman so unstable, or manipulative – probably both – she'd sought me out and pretended to be Daisy's mother, presenting me with a list of credible reasons why I should take her from her family.

*Was any of it true?*

In my room, I pushed a fist into my mouth to stifle a scream. Tears spilled over, splashing my knuckles. I picked up a pillow and pressed it to my face, shoulders shaking with silent sobs. *Why* had I let myself be taken in? I *knew* Elise, knew what she was capable of. Why had I believed she'd changed, that motherhood had altered her? Because it had suited me to believe her? I'd been looking for change myself and for closure, had wanted to make amends, yet I hadn't done anything wrong. Elise's attempted suicide wasn't even about me, just as Leon's campaign of stalking wasn't my fault.

I swallowed the storm of tears and replaced my pillow, smoothing out the creases. I couldn't fall apart. It wasn't appropriate to be weeping. In the en suite, I splashed my face with cold water to take away the redness, and checked my eyes weren't swollen. I looked more or less the same as I had an hour ago but felt fundamentally different. The anger simmered, but on the surface I appeared calm, the blotchiness from crying fading away.

Daisy would be up and about soon, clamouring to go to the park later on. Elise would be preparing to leave my house, expecting to end the day on an aeroplane with Daisy.

I was shaking again, but with a sense of urgency this time.

I grabbed my phone, keys and bag and ran downstairs. Lissa

had disappeared, but Isaac was in the conservatory, staring out at the garden with a troubled expression, a mug of coffee in his hand.

'I have to go out for a while.'

He spun round, face blank.

'My friend.' I waggled my phone. 'She's going home with her boyfriend today, but wanted to meet up to say thank you, for visiting her in hospital.'

'Of course.' He gave a stiff little nod. 'Take your time.'

'I'll be back to take Daisy to the park a bit later,' I added. 'If that's still OK?' I was guessing it was what he would expect me to say, and to my relief he nodded.

'She can come to the ski centre first. You can pick her up from there,' he said. 'Listen, I'm glad we haven't put you off, Rose—'

'I'd better go,' I cut in. I couldn't bear to hear him say again that he was certain Elise wasn't a threat, that everything was fine, when I knew it wasn't. 'See you later.'

Not waiting for a reaction, I hurried out, almost falling over Rocky lying by the front door in my haste to get to my car. It was time to confront Elise and tell her the game was up.

# Chapter 34

She was in the living room when I arrived, crouched over her bag as she strapped it shut. The curtains were drawn, and in the gloom she looked like a faded sketch of herself with some of the details missing.

Her expression lurched from disbelief to horror when she looked up and saw me. 'What are you doing here?'

I crossed the room and wrenched open the curtains, needing to see her face clearly. It was hard and bony, skin stretched taut across her cheekbones. She was dressed in the same clothes she'd arrived in, and the sight of her long grey cardigan was somehow as disturbing as anything I'd learnt.

She blinked, raising her arm as though she couldn't stand the brightness, or the sight of me. 'Have you brought Daisy?'

I stared at her, speechless.

Driving over, my head had felt fit to explode as it struggled to reassemble what I'd believed was true, scrolling back and forth over everything Elise had told me, comparing her version with Isaac's revelation. I was reeling from the shock of Elise's sister being alive for all those years and married to Isaac. *Ann* had been his wife – not Elise. Elise was Daisy's *aunt*, not her mother. She'd been harassing the family. She'd left items in the house for me to find to give credence to her claims. But vital parts of the puzzle were still missing.

Round and round it went, thoughts layering on top of each other, so by the time I'd entered the house, my jaw was clenched, my head throbbed, and I barely knew where to begin.

Now, I made a beeline for the kitchen where I ran tap water into a glass and took thirsty gulps. Elise followed me, like she had the day she came, when I hadn't suspected a thing.

I stared at her for a long moment. 'You lied to me.'

For a moment, she looked crushed. 'Rose, listen, I—'

'Isaac was never your husband.'

Her eyes magnified into dark pools. 'Look, I can explain.'

I slammed the glass down. 'Your sister didn't die. You weren't married to Isaac. Daisy isn't your daughter.' My hand cut through the air between us. 'What the hell is going on, Elise?'

'How did you find out?' There was bravado in the jut of her chin. 'You obviously messed up.'

'*I* messed up?' Disbelief forced my voice up an octave. 'Isaac saw the photo you left in the cookbook. Lissa saw it too and went into shock. After telling them I assumed it was a picture of Isaac's wife, I was informed that it was, in fact, her sister.' The shock of it hit me again. I staggered through to the living room and dropped onto the sofa. 'I just don't understand,' I said. 'Why did you put it there?'

'So if any of them found it, they'd be reminded of me.' Elise's eyes were cold, but it struck me that if she hadn't – if *I* hadn't been the one to find the picture – I might not have seen so clearly how unsuited she was to looking after Daisy. 'Christ's sake, Rose. I should have known you weren't capable of doing what I asked you to.' Her gaze skipped past me. 'Where *is* Daisy?'

'Well, she's not here.' I looked at Elise in disbelief. 'She'll be going to the ski centre shortly with Isaac.'

'How could you let him have her?' The desperation in her

voice was mixed with white-hot fury. 'You don't know what you're doing.'

I shot to my feet, blood thundering in my head. 'We were about to kidnap an innocent child!' It came out in a panicked hiss. I was terrified Beatrice might hear us through the wall. 'What were you *thinking*?'

'Rose, I promise that what I did, everything I said, the things I didn't say – it was all for a reason.' Anger deflating, she held out her hands in appeal. 'I mostly told the truth, I swear. And I would never have let you get into trouble—'

'When it came out that Daisy had been snatched by her aunt and taken out of the country, do you think I would have stood by and said nothing?' My breath came hard and fast. 'I would never have let you get away with it.'

'But you weren't supposed to know I wasn't her mother – that was the whole point.' Her face opened up, an unsettling smile suggesting it was obvious. 'I knew you'd never have agreed to help if you hadn't believed Daisy was my daughter,' she said. 'You must understand why I did it, Rose. You would have done the same in my shoes.' Her voice became a plea for understanding. 'I didn't have a choice.'

Throughout her speech, I'd been shaking my head, stirring the pain in my temples. 'She's not your child to take, Elise. How did you think you could ever get away with it?'

'Planning.' Something like pride slid over her face. 'Down to the last detail,' she continued, seeming oblivious to my incredulous expression. 'They wouldn't let me see her, or even get close to her. I had to come up with something else.'

'They were willing to give you a chance, but you came on too strong. You frightened Daisy.'

'Oh that's what they told you, is it?' She rolled her eyes, her face a mask of contempt. 'Of course I came on strong. I had every reason to believe that Daisy was in danger, that she could die like Ann did. How was I supposed to stand by and let that happen?'

'Why did you believe that?'

A muscle flickered by her mouth. 'Because it's true.'

'There's no proof whatsoever that your sister's death was anything but a terrible accident, and Daisy is loved by everyone.'

'Ann told me how it really was, OK?' Suddenly, Elise's eyes were brimming with tears. 'Can you imagine finding out after all that time that I had a sister?' Her voice quivered. 'Can we take a second to let that sink in, please, Rose.' Her gaze hooked on mine. 'The sister I grew up believing had died before I was born was alive and well, living with my shit of a father in a posh part of London while we slummed it in Derbyshire, and my own mother never thought to tell me.'

Some of my anger trickled away. It was easy to see how devastating the realisation must have been. 'I get that it was a massive shock.' I recalled what Isaac had said, about their reunion being a disaster. 'It's horrible you were kept apart for all that time.'

'Well, you wouldn't know how it affected me as you weren't around,' she said. 'I had to carry it on my own.'

'You're talking to someone who lost her parents at the age of eleven, so I do understand about grief.' But I knew in some ways I'd been lucky. Sarah and Mum had been close, so I'd had someone to share anecdotes with, someone who had been there since I was born.

Elise sniffed. 'Mum was all over Ann,' she continued, perhaps choosing not to listen. 'She didn't even apologise to me. Ann was furious too, to be fair. At first she said she'd never forgive Mum for abandoning her, or our father for not telling her the truth. It brought us together for a while, but Ann seemed desperate for our mother's attention.' Elise cupped her elbows, seeming to shrink a little. 'Mum clearly didn't want me to be a part of their gang, so I went away. I had the money my father left – an equal amount for both his daughters – so I stayed in America.'

I could easily picture it as she spoke, her delivery a perfect blend of sorrow and anger. 'There was no contact, until Ann got in touch to say Mum had been diagnosed with dementia and needed help. Obviously, there was plenty of money – our dear father did something right at least – so getting her into a home wasn't a problem. Neither of us fancied looking after the mad old crow.' Her words were edged with years of bitterness and resentment. 'My sister and I stayed in touch a bit after that. Ann told me she'd got married and seemed happy. Then she had a baby.'

'She didn't invite you to the wedding?'

'We weren't in touch at that point.' Elise looked blank for a second. 'I thought about visiting, but I was focused on my career in New York. I'd never been that interested in the whole settling down and having kids side of things.' So, that hadn't changed. 'Anyway, I didn't hear anything for ages, then I started getting these calls from Ann, saying she was in danger, that her husband and his family wanted rid of her.' Her voice rose. 'All of that was true, Rose.' When Elise looked at me her tears had dried, and her eyes shone bright and clear. 'It just didn't happen to me.'

It took a moment to digest. 'So you really think Ann's death wasn't an accident?' My mind flashed briefly to the summerhouse and the argument Thora was convinced she'd overheard.

'Of course I did – *do.*' She flung up her hands, cheeks flooding red. 'Do you think I've gone through all this for fun?' When I didn't answer, her voice became choked. 'The last time I spoke to Ann, she was in a terrible state, not making much sense. He'd had her "put away" she said, in order to build a story for when she died. I wanted to come over, talk to the family, but she didn't want that, said I might be putting myself in danger too. She made me promise that if she died, I would get Daisy away from there, somewhere they could never get to her. And then she died.' A vein in Elise's temple stood out. 'Imagine that, Rose. I lost her all over again. Her bastard husband found my number on her phone and called to let me know.'

'I'm sorry.' I didn't know what else to say.

'So, after failing to get access to Daisy, I went away and worked

258

out a plan I knew you would help me with. I got into the house one day and planted some stuff to prove my existence in case you were in any doubt. I knew where Ann had hidden Daisy's passport and the journal—'

'Your mother's journal.'

She bowed her head and pushed the heels of her hands into her eyes. 'I couldn't find Ann's. I knew she'd written one. She told me it was all in there, proof of what they were like, but she must have put it somewhere else. I didn't get a chance to look for it, so I took my mother's and hid it in the bedside drawer. I thought if you read it, it would be enough to convince you everything I'd said was true.' Her eyes looked bruised when she opened them.

'No wonder they referred to Isaac's wife as Ann.' My voice was quiet. 'It was her actual name.'

'That was a stroke of luck.' Her tone had grown tired. 'We were both named after our grandmother. Elise Ann, and Ann Elise.' She paused. 'My mother worshipped her mum, even though she was batshit crazy. I never understood why she didn't like me, and I don't understand how she could have abandoned Ann and pretended she didn't exist.'

*The women in this family are cursed.*

If pushed, I would have said it was in her blood. Ingrid was damaged and so were her daughters. Though, in their case, things might have turned out differently if their parents hadn't deceived them, or if Ingrid had sought help instead of turning to alcohol.

'How did your father get so rich?'

She gave a sour laugh. 'He had a big lottery win in the early Nineties and invested in property. Mum didn't know but wouldn't have taken a penny from him if she had. He never found out where she went.'

I pulled in a long breath. 'None of this excuses what you've done.'

Elise's face seemed to fold in on itself. 'Are you saying you don't believe Ann?' She stepped forward, closing the distance

259

between us. 'If you'd found her journal and read it, you would have seen her marriage was a shipwreck. She even had an affair to get back at Isaac for his.'

'He never had an affair, and you don't know for certain that Ann did.'

'Why would she have lied?'

'Elise, your sister was ill.' I took a step backwards, not knowing how she would react. 'She went away for a reason, to be treated. Paranoid delusional disorder. It means she saw danger where there wasn't any. She thought everyone was out to hurt her, but it wasn't—'

My head snapped sideways, ears ringing with the force of a slap.

'Oh my God!' Elise's screech made me jump. 'I can't believe they really got to you.' She moved to the window and back again, breathing fast while I blinked away tears of pain and shock. 'Jesus, Rose. Don't be a total idiot.' She kicked her bag with the toe of her boot. 'I'm sorry you let them see that photo of me, though I'm not surprised if I'm honest, but it changes nothing.' Her voice was clipped. 'Go back to the house, get Daisy's passport and bring her to the park,' she continued. 'I'll be waiting.'

'I won't be doing that.'

'You will, or I'll call Isaac and tell him why you're really there.'

Everything started to ripple. It was a sign she wasn't thinking clearly – that the loose threads of her story were pulling free – if she couldn't see the flaw in her threat. Isaac knowing the truth meant she would never get close to Daisy.

Dropping my hand from my stinging cheek, I looked at the feverish glint in her eyes, the colour staining her face and neck, and understood there was no getting through to her. Elise had built her own narrative over months, even years. It couldn't be dismantled overnight, maybe never. I had to act quickly.

'He knows already.'

A gasp of shock left her throat. 'I don't believe you.'

'When he found the photo, and I realised you'd lied to me . . .'

I hesitated, mouth almost too tense to form the words '. . . I confessed everything.' I didn't need to force the tears that fell. 'I felt so betrayed, Elise. You should have told me the truth right from the start and I could have helped you in a different way.' My voice trembled. 'I told him you had a flight booked—' I pushed on when she swore and pressed her hands to her mouth '—and he said that if you're not on it, and don't send proof of your arrival, he's going straight to the police.'

Now her skin was the colour of bleached bones. 'We have to go,' she snapped.

And just like that, she was bending to pick up her bag, scooping the phone she'd first called me on into her pocket and tossing my door keys at me. 'Come on,' she urged as I stood rooted to the floor. 'We can message him from the airport.'

I waited for the punchline or the realisation it was a trick. What had happened to her assertion that she wasn't leaving without Daisy?

'I have no proof of anything,' she said, her timing uncanny. 'Seeing as I don't know where Ann's diary is, and you've rumbled that the other one is my mother's.'

I thought of Ann's journal stashed under my mattress at Orchard House, her entries the result of an unstable mind. 'Or even that she wrote one,' I said, relieved Elise hadn't asked how I knew the other diary belonged to Ingrid.

She was by the window, peering out. 'Do you think he followed you?'

'Maybe.' Desperation really was a good motivator, my acting convincing. 'He was livid,' I said. 'He's willing to keep it from the rest of the family, as long as you're gone and promise to never come back.'

She came close and clamped her hand around my arm, 'Promise you'll keep an eye on Daisy for me.' There was a silent interrogation in her eyes. 'Please, Rose, or I'll—'

'I promise.' Her pleading was worse than her anger, but it was a promise I knew I wouldn't be able to keep. I couldn't stay in Daisy's life after this.

'Thank you.' For a moment, it was as if the life had drained from Elise's eyes. She looked soulless. Then, she opened the door a crack, checking the street. 'Clear,' she said, hoisting her bag onto her shoulder. 'Let's go.'

# Chapter 35

Elise hunched in the passenger seat with her bag on her lap, her gaze far away as she leaned her head against the window, apparently watching the Chilterns give way to industrial estates and the M25 to Heathrow.

When I cleared my throat and asked where she was heading, and whether the cabin in the woods, and the friend who was helping her really existed, she said in a monotone, 'I would rather not say where it is, but yes, it's true, and the friend is my partner.' That was a big surprise. 'He would have helped me take good care of Daisy.'

It was hard to imagine what that life would have looked like, how they planned to stay under the radar with all the technology available to a man who would stop at nothing to bring his child home. Someone who loved his daughter more than anything.

'They really do love her, Elise,' I felt compelled to stress.

'So you say.' Still the lifeless tone. 'What are they doing for money?'

'Isaac's got a new book deal, and the others work.' I decided not to mention the proposed house sale, and there was no point bringing up James Parry, a man Elise had no knowledge of. When he'd spoken about Isaac's wife, James had been referring to Ann.

I darted Elise a look and saw that her eyes were closed. Maybe she was feeling the effects of her fall. I hoped she was OK to fly, that it wouldn't be dangerous after her head injury. Even now, I couldn't help feeling sorry for her, glad she had someone to support her wherever she was going.

'We did look alike, Ann and me.' Her voice was sleepy.

'Sorry?'

'The nurse at the hospital, when she thought we were sisters, she said we looked nothing alike.'

'You heard that?'

'Sort of . . . from a distance.' I wondered whether in some part of her brain she'd regretted her plan and had wanted to hide for a while, her unconscious state a shield from reality. 'But we looked very similar. That's why you thought the photo of her with Daisy was me.'

It was more like seeing what I'd expected to, fed by Elise's deceit, but I didn't say anything. I remembered the photo in Ann's journal, of Elise as a schoolgirl. Elise must have given it to her, or perhaps Ann had taken it as a reminder of her sister.

The sky had darkened. There was a sudden downpour, raindrops streaking across the windscreen. I turned the wipers on and tried to breathe in time with their rhythmic swipe. Every flex of my muscles felt obvious, as if I'd forgotten how to move naturally.

I slowed the car, the tarmac wet and slippery as it stretched ahead, striking away an image of my parents in their car in Portugal on the wrong side of the road, and the twist of metal that had left them dead.

When the car swung violently to the left, I thought for a split second I'd conjured something malevolent from my imagination, that I was reliving what had happened to my parents. A scream flew out as I tried to right the car, only for it to jerk sideways again. With horror, I realised Elise had grabbed the wheel and was steering us off the road.

'What are you doing?' I shrieked, trying to unpeel her fingers. 'You're going to get us killed!'

Behind us, a horn blasted. A lorry swung past, followed by several cars. I stamped on the brake, tyres squealing as the car bounced onto the verge and stopped.

Panting with terror, I caught sight of my bloodless face in the rear-view mirror. 'Why did you do that?' I turned to Elise, shaking. 'We could have died.'

'Don't be so dramatic.' She settled back, one hand on the strap of her bag, hair wild around her face. 'I wanted you to know how it feels when your life's in danger.' The words, matter-of-fact, sent fear down my spine. 'And that I'll find a way of hurting you if anything happens to Daisy.'

The rest of the journey was conducted in excruciating silence, the only sound the rain on the roof of the car. By the time we arrived – 'Terminal two,' Elise instructed – my fingers ached from gripping the wheel, and a vicious headache pulsed behind my eyes.

I drove into a bay in the short-stay car park and switched off the engine. 'I didn't ask for any of this.' My voice thickened. 'Why did you come to me?'

She wound a strand of hair around her finger. 'You owed me, remember?'

I opened my mouth, intending to tell her I knew her suicide attempt hadn't even been about me, then paused. It would mean revealing I'd spoken to Ingrid, and I couldn't stomach another showdown. 'And, to be honest,' she continued, examining the split ends of her hair. 'You were the only person I could ask because of your background in teaching.'

'And if I'd said no?'

'I knew you wouldn't, but I suppose I would have found another way.' Her sideways glance was cold. 'It's all academic now, isn't it?' Her voice was compressed with fury. 'Because you couldn't do this one simple thing without getting caught.'

'You should get help, Elise.' It was an echo of the plea I'd made all those years ago, a final attempt to appeal to her sense of reason. 'Seeing a therapist might help you put things in perspective, and to understand that your sister was very sick—'

'Ann wasn't sick.' Elise's fist smashed against the car door, her eyes black with anger. 'You're no better than him, you stupid bitch.'

*You have no right to even see Daisy. Leave her alone, you mad bitch.*

*I could call the police and get you locked up.*

Though I couldn't visualise Isaac composing those texts, at least I understood now why he had. Reminding myself that Elise had in effect lost her sister twice, I said as gently as I could, 'You should try to get access to Ann's medical records and see for yourself.'

'Are you completely dumb?' She eyed me with scorn, hands balled. 'Obviously, they're faked.' She shook her head, as if it was blindingly obvious. 'It was all part of the plan.'

I thought of Thora, and of James Parry, and how they'd been taken in by Ann's story, just as Elise had – me too – seeing things through the prism of her illness, just as Ann's beliefs had been the product of her delusions. It was easy to be convincing if you believed in what you were saying, if you had a disorder that caused you to think the worst.

I thrust open the car door, unable to bear being around Elise any longer. 'Time to go.'

Entering the airport terminal was a relief and a shock. The bustle of normal life, and being around people felt good, but sounds and smells were exaggerated, everything too bright, as if I'd been living underground for months.

I waited while Elise checked in at the self-service machine, thinking how diminished she looked in a crowd with her hunched shoulders and moth-coloured outfit, where once she would have commanded the space around her, drawing admiring stares.

'Satisfied?' She stood in front of a bank of screens showing flight details to Canada, China, India, Malaysia, Switzerland . . . maybe that was the location of the cabin in the woods. 'I'm not telling you where I'm going.' She had seen me looking. 'I'm not risking anyone coming after me.'

'It would be easy enough to find out.'

'Rose, please.' Her face collapsed, all defiance gone. 'I'm doing what you asked. I'm leaving without Daisy, which I swore I would never do.'

'I'll leave when you've gone through customs.'

'You don't trust me?' Her tone grew mocking.

'It's what Isaac wants,' I said. 'I have to be sure.'

A sixth sense prickled, a feeling of being watched. I spun around and caught a flash of movement at the edge of my vision, there and gone.

'It's what Isaac wants,' Elise mimicked.

I swivelled back, jittery with adrenaline. 'There's nothing to stop you walking out once I've gone.'

'Why would I when you've made it clear it's leave or be arrested?' Her gaze narrowed to a razor-sharp stare. 'That's what he said, right?'

I nodded. 'I thought I saw Isaac's car when I was parking, but it probably wasn't his.' I was jolted by a group of women with backpacks on their way to one of the cafés. 'Bit of a coincidence though.'

'Maybe you should take a picture of my boarding pass, to be on the safe side.' Suddenly edgy, Elise tugged a folded printout from her cardigan pocket. She held it out so I could see the time and date, but not the destination. 'Go on then.' Her hand shook.

Obediently, I took out my phone and snapped a picture, jumping when an announcement came over the tannoy, so the image came out blurry. Not that it mattered. Of course I wouldn't be showing it to Isaac.

I shivered. The air conditioning was probably set too high, or maybe it was the lingering shock of the past hour, but I felt raw and exposed. 'I'll take another photo once you've gone through customs, just to be sure,' I said.

Elise gave a slow nod, an expression I recognised stealing over her face. She was preparing to play a part, pulling on a character like a new skin. If only I'd seen it happen a week ago, before she walked through my front door.

'You know what, Rose?' She backed away. 'You were always a terrible friend.'

As she swung around, making her dramatic exit towards customs, I felt again the painful slam of her hand against my cheek. 'Elise!'

She stopped and turned, and I took a photo, then shook my phone at her. 'Just so you know, I've recorded every word, from when I arrived at the house.' The way her muscles fell slackly gave me a surge of satisfaction. 'If you come back, I'll play it to everyone.'

Back on the motorway, the sight of Elise's retreating back as she disappeared through customs sharp in my mind, I brought up Isaac's number using the hands-free system.

'It's Rose. I'm sorry I'm running late, I got held up,' I said, when he answered. It was noisy in the background, muffled voices, and a distant thump of music. 'I'm on my way back and can still take Daisy to the park.'

'No rush.' Isaac sounded reassuringly normal, friendly, and relaxed. Why had I thought for a split second that he'd really followed us to the airport? 'It's pouring down at the moment,' he said. I realised with a jolt the rain was still falling, the view obscured by drops sliding across the windows. 'Lissa brought Daisy to the ski centre for hot chocolate in the café, if you want to pick her up from here.'

'I . . . I need to talk to you later.'

There was a beat of silence. 'Sounds ominous.'

'It's just . . . my friend, she mentioned her boyfriend's daughter's school is looking for a new reception teacher, and I think I should apply for the job.' The lie sat like acid in my throat. 'The money's good and it's . . . well, it's what I'm used to.'

'You're not happy with us.' Isaac's voice had flattened. 'All that stuff about my wife and her sister, like something from a Daphne du Maurier novel.' I imagined him pushing a hand through his hair. 'I suppose it's why I didn't want to tell you.'

'It's not that, I just . . .' Tears blocked my throat.

'What is it?' The twist of anxiety in his tone made me feel worse. 'Has something happened?'

'No, no.' I swallowed. 'I'll see you soon.' I ended the call, my cheeks damp with tears.

I didn't want to leave, but how could I stay? Even if I could get over what had happened without confessing, I would always carry a nagging, low-level guilt, like a toothache I couldn't shake off. Maybe I could offer to stay in touch, check in on Daisy from a distance. Having no contact suddenly seemed unthinkable.

*You're being selfish.* I picked up speed as the rain eased. *You've only known Daisy a week.* Even so, her smile was imprinted on my heart, and the way she couldn't resist calling me Rosie. *We're both flowers.*

Daisy would grow and bloom without me, surrounded by love, and when the topic of her mother arose, Isaac would deal with it sensitively. And if Elise got in touch in the future, demanding to see her niece, I knew he would handle that too. If she decided to call him out on his supposed threat to have us arrested after my 'confession' . . . well, Isaac would be furious, upset he'd been duped by someone he'd trusted to look after his daughter, and that his instincts about me had been skewed, but ultimately he would be relieved I'd done the decent thing and left – just as whoever left that message on my laptop had suggested.

I started as a small white car overtook me in the middle lane, my antennae twitching. It had been a couple of cars behind for the past few miles, tugging at my subconscious. No one I knew drove a car like that, so why would it bother me? Maybe I was still worried Elise hadn't got on the plane. I wouldn't relax until she'd sent a photo once she arrived, but that wouldn't be for hours.

I thought about Ann's journal with a flicker of guilt, but damped it down. Letting Elise have it would only have fuelled her suspicions, given her a reason to dig in her heels, and Daisy would be at the centre. I couldn't let that happen.

I didn't see the white car again but barely breathed all the way back to Orchard House, emotions seesawing between relief that Elise was gone – as far as I knew – and trepidation about what came next. I parked in a blaze of sunshine, but when I stepped onto the gravel, my foot sank into a puddle, and all around was the sound of raindrops dripping from leaves.

No cars on the drive, and the garage was empty. Everyone was out.

I tried the front door, which was locked. I didn't have a key.

I walked around the back, in case the patio or conservatory doors were open, then tried the side door into the kitchen. All locked. It made sense, especially since having cameras installed, that security was a priority, but I felt panicky about waiting outside until someone returned. Driving over to the ski centre seemed as unlikely as flying to the moon, though I knew I would have to go and pick Daisy up, take her to the park like I'd promised. And after I'd spoken to Isaac? I shuddered, picturing myself leaving, going back to the empty house in Chesham. I couldn't stay there. I would give notice to the agency and return to Derbyshire, try to pick up the threads of my old life now Leon was gone. Or move to London, or anywhere – start over somewhere new.

I sat at the patio table, which had been protected from the rain by the parasol, but couldn't settle. I was thirsty, and my stomach felt scooped out with hunger. I took out my phone and looked at the out-of-focus image of Elise's boarding pass. I zoomed in, trying to see the destination, but her finger had obscured it. In the image of her I'd caught, she looked somehow desolate – ghostly pale, lips slightly parted, her eyes dark hollows.

Telling her I had a voice recording had been a long shot, but I was certain she'd believed me. Part of me wished I'd thought of it sooner, but mostly I was glad I hadn't. I didn't need any reminders, our exchange stamped on my brain.

I began to cry, wishing I could talk to my parents, or that I was at the farmhouse, sitting in a bath of rose-scented bubbles with a book and a glass of wine, Sarah's suggested remedy after a tiring day at work.

I wiped away my tears and picked up my phone again to message her. *Fancy a visitor next week? XX*

Her reply was instant. *Who? JOKE! Can't wait to see you. XX*

Sniffing back fresh tears – she wouldn't want me anywhere near if she knew what I'd been up to – I looked around the garden, listening to the burble of water from the stream, hoping the sound might smooth away my discomfort. Something felt off. My brain kept firing random questions – who mistrusted me the most at Orchard House and would be relieved to see me go? Where would Isaac and Daisy live when he sold the house? Would Isaac put Daisy back in school or look for another home tutor? It still felt as though I was missing part of the narrative.

Rising, I glanced at the house, wondering where Rocky had gone. Moving to the conservatory doors, I looked through and saw the apples and pears that Cecilia had picked that morning piled in a bowl on the table. Underneath, Rocky was curled up asleep next to his tennis ball. 'Not much of a guard dog,' I said.

I followed the path to the orchard, where the cooing of pigeons was louder. Right away, I spotted the piece of plywood in front of the gap in the hedge, with a couple of bricks in front to prevent it being pushed over.

'Not very attractive, but it'll have to do for now.'

The voice behind me forced a scream from my lungs. I whirled around to see Jonah walking towards me, hands in his trouser pockets.

'You frightened the life out of me.'

He stopped abruptly, as though a trapdoor had opened between us, looking at me with an odd expression. '*Are* you frightened, Rose Carpenter?'

*Why had he said my name like that?* 'What do you mean?' My pulse quickened. 'I didn't know you were here, that's all.'

'I just got back.' He took a step closer.

'You're not working today?'

He shook his head, very slowly. With his curls pulled tightly into a bun, his face looked bigger, the creases around his eyes more obvious. They held an expression I hadn't seen before – a combination of fear and determination. 'Busy at the airport, wasn't it?'

Fear burst to life in my chest. 'What are you talking about?'

'I saw you.' Sweat beaded his forehead. 'You were there with Elise.'

# Chapter 36

'You followed us.' *He knew. Jonah knew about Elise.*

'I've been doing quite a bit of that this week.'

Icicles of dread pierced my stomach. 'I had a feeling . . . I thought I saw a car, but it wasn't yours.'

'Too obvious after you spotted me the other day in High Wycombe and gave me the slip.' A frown dented his forehead. 'I hired a car this time, just in case.'

I was scared my legs might give way. 'But, why?'

'I know who you are and why you're here, Rose Carpenter.'

A breeze blew and I shivered in the sudden freshness. 'How?'

'I knew the name.' He reverted to his usual, conversational self now the tricky bit was over. 'I think I said it rang a bell at the time, but it didn't hit me until later.' He pulled a hand from his pocket and rubbed it across his forehead. 'I'd stayed up for a drink with Ann one night, not long after we moved in. We got talking, and I don't know how it came about, but she was saying how she and her long-lost sister had quite a few things in common, one of them being they hadn't any female friends. She mentioned Elise had told her she used to have one, at university, a mousy girl called Rose Carpenter, who was training to be a teacher, but she cleared off when the Lockwood legacy became too much to cope with.' Jonah dipped his gaze to his feet. 'That's what she called her illness,' he said. 'The Lockwood legacy.'

Facts were dropping into place like numbers on a slot machine. The diary entry I'd read flashed into my head. 'You were having an affair with Ann.'

'Not an affair.' Jonah's denial was immediate and fierce. 'It's what she wanted; she made that clear. She partly wanted to get back at Isaac. She thought he'd slept with the nanny who was helping look after Daisy, but it wasn't true.' He shook his head quickly. 'I had too much to drink one night, I admit. Things weren't good with Lissa and me; she was desperate for a baby after being around Daisy, but it wasn't happening. We'd argued, which we hardly ever did. Ann invited me down to the summerhouse for a whisky, and we kissed.' His head fell back, and he stared at a patch of blue sky. 'I was drunk, but it was no excuse.' He dropped his gaze back to me, fear stirring in his eyes. 'I told her we shouldn't be alone again, but she wanted more. She said she was in love with me and knew I felt the same, that we had a connection. She had all these plans for us to move away, but I didn't want any of that.' His words rang with conviction. 'I love my wife, I really do.'

'I can see that.' It seemed like the right thing to say.

His expression softened. 'Lissa was suspicious – she's always been the jealous type.' He said it with slight bafflement. 'She even thought I was the one having a fling with the nanny for a while, which I wasn't – she was way too young for a start. Ann . . .' He paused. 'She was beautiful, and could be fun and interesting to talk to, but I started avoiding her as much as possible for Lissa's sake, and she didn't like it.' His voice gave way. 'It wasn't intentional, but things went a bit further one night, in the summerhouse. I'd only gone there to reason with her, but the whisky came out again – I don't touch the stuff now – and we ended up . . on that sofa, we . . .' He stopped, a queasy look on his face. 'Afterwards, she told me that if I didn't leave with her, she would make sure Lissa found out anyway.'

So Ann hadn't made up the affair, which was what it had been in her mind. *What else had she written that was true?* Jonah had cheated on Lissa, with her brother's wife. Because it was convenient? I wasn't buying the whole 'drunk' excuse. The urge must have been there in the first place, or why seek her out? 'Where did Daisy fit into this plan of Ann's to leave?'

'I honestly don't think it did.' Jonah spoke with an air of sadness. 'It sometimes seemed like she forgot she even had a daughter.'

Just like her own mother had forgotten about Ann. *Poor Daisy.*

'I was terrified of losing Lissa.' Jonah's face reddened with the force of his feelings. 'I love her so much, Rose; I really do. I'll spend the rest of my life making it up to her if I have to.'

I felt sick, this new knowledge heavy in my stomach. 'And no one here knows any of this?'

He shook his head. 'Ann used to flirt with me, but to be honest, I don't think it registered with Isaac. He was too busy fire-fighting, you know? Trying to get her some help, keeping Daisy out of her way.' He swallowed. 'Lissa was still suspicious, and I was terrified Ann would let something slip, but I think she enjoyed playing games more than anything else, watching people suffer. Isaac ignored it, which rattled her, and Cecilia could hardly stand being in the same room as Ann, who was really rude to her. She must have known there was no chance of us being together, whether the truth came out or not.'

There was a moment of stillness before my mind veered down a terrible track. Thora was convinced she'd heard an argument in the summerhouse, not long before Ann *vanished and never came back.*

'Jonah, did you kill Ann to keep her quiet?'

'What?' His mouth gaped. 'Of *course* I didn't kill her. I'm not a monster.' His disbelief was evident. 'I can't believe you asked me that.'

'Convenient for you though.' I couldn't quite back down,

unwilling to let him off the hook completely. 'That she was out of the way.'

'She was probably hoping I'd be a suspect.'

'Except she didn't intend to die; it was an accident.'

'I actually believe it was suicide,' he said. 'I think she'd had enough and wanted out, and that's why she put that heater on.' He winced. 'And it wasn't convenient because before she died, she told me she had a journal she'd been writing in at the treatment centre. She had a record of everything that happened between us, no doubt embellished for effect. And she told me her sister knew about the journal and would find it if anything happened to her – it was the sort of paranoid thing she often came out with – and that when Elise revealed the truth, Lissa and I would be over, and the family would break up because people would know Isaac had murdered Ann out of jealousy, and Daisy would be taken away from him, and the shock would kill Cecilia.'

'Wow.' I was stunned by the torrent of words. 'And you believed her? Ann had a diagnosed psychiatric disorder.'

'In the treatment place, she was taking medication.' Jonah seemed at pains to make me understand. 'She was clear-headed while she was there, according to Isaac. The dates in the journal, she said, tallied with her stay there, giving her credibility. Of course she stopped taking the tablets once she was back. I think she preferred being . . . *eccentric*, she sometimes called it. Maybe it was familiar, or she liked the drama, I don't know, but I wanted to find that journal and destroy it.'

'How did you know it really existed?'

'To be honest, I didn't think it did once I'd looked everywhere after she died. It never turned up, so I began to believe it had been an invention, like so much else.' There was a sag to his jaw. 'Until you arrived.' In the beat of silence, I heard a rustle and yip behind the hedge, wondered if Thora was on the other side.

'Did you leave the attic open the other night?'

He nodded. 'I got Daisy to go in with her dad and then tapped on your door.'

My heart sank as he lowered his voice and took a few steps back. He must have heard the dog too and wondered if Thora was there. 'I thought you'd go and look if you thought Daisy was up there,' he said. 'I made sure the trunk with Ann's things in was at eye level, knowing you wouldn't be able to resist. I hoped a fresh pair of eyes might find what I'd missed if you hadn't found the journal already. I guessed you hadn't because I went through your stuff, and it wasn't there. I thought Elise knew where it was and had told you to search the attic, and you were waiting for the right moment, so I made it easy for you.'

'You sent her those horrible texts.' My mind was spinning with the enormity of it all. 'Warning her to stay away.' *You mad bitch.* 'Not nice language for someone training to be a counsellor. How did you have her number?'

For a second he looked thrown by the change of topic. 'She wanted to see Daisy, had called the house several times before Isaac threatened to get the police involved if she didn't leave us alone,' he said. 'I took one of the calls myself, wondered whether she was going to bring up the journal, and my supposed affair with Ann, but she was too clever for that, or too caught up in the drama.' *That word again.* 'She wanted proof, a way to get the family to take her seriously – or to ruin them.' He exhaled. 'Either way, she was a threat, but then . . .' He shrugged. 'She just went away, and we dared to believe it was over, but I'd written her number down, just in case.'

'And now I'm a threat.' It felt important to keep him talking while I tried to work out what his plan was. Because there had to be one. 'You tried to get me to leave,' I said. 'The broken glass in the bedroom, leaving the necklace for me to wear, that message on my laptop.'

His eyebrows lowered. 'I thought if Isaac saw you in a bad light, he'd decide not to keep you on, but he seems to like you.'

He scratched at his beard and gave another heavy sigh. 'I took Ann's necklace from the workshop. I don't know why Lissa had it.' He appeared to ponder for a moment. 'The broken glass was her,' he said. 'She left a list of questions about you in the kitchen to freak you out, and I saw her push you in the stream the other day.'

'What?'

Jonah was still speaking. 'I think she put something in your drink on your first day. I noticed you were a bit off-colour,' he said. 'It's funny, because Ann once accused Isaac of trying to poison her with wisteria seeds when she was violently ill after eating something he'd cooked, but seeing your face last week . . . it made me wonder whether it might have been Lissa.'

My mind reeled. The instinct I'd had, that I'd eaten something poisonous had been right. *And maybe Ann had been right too, but not about Isaac.*

'Like I said, Lissa's jealous.' That tone of bemusement again. 'She sees most females I come into contact with as potential rivals, not that she'd ever seriously hurt any of them.' I thought of Lissa's instant hostility, how I'd believed it was only about protecting her brother. 'She thought I might be attracted to you, like she believes I was to the nanny, and to Ann.' *She was right about that.* 'She wanted you out of our lives, as much as I did once I knew who you were.'

So many things made sense, blank spaces filling in. 'You spoke to my neighbour, pretending to be my landlord.'

A trace of embarrassment crossed his face. 'It was a bit under-hand, but I wanted to prove I was right, that Elise had been at your house. Once I'd phoned round a few local letting agencies and found out which one you'd used, I dropped in and picked up a business card.'

'Lissa doesn't know that *you* know why I'm here, does she?' *The journal,* I reminded myself. *He thinks it's about the journal and being exposed.* He had made it all about himself, scared of losing his wife, their baby. I had no doubts about how vengeful Lissa would be if she knew the full story.

'Of course not,' he said. 'I actually think she's starting to like you too.'

I couldn't begin to unpick that. 'You went to the hospital to see Elise.'

'When you rushed off because a friend of yours had been injured, I knew it had to be her.' Jonah sounded weary now. 'I'd worked out who you were by then, and why you'd tricked Isaac into bringing you home, and then I overheard you on the phone, asking after Elise.'

I knew there had been someone outside the door. I'd worried it was Isaac, or Cecilia, hadn't for a second suspected Jonah. 'Did you think you could talk to her?'

'I don't know what I was thinking.' He gave a self-recriminating shake of his head. 'It was a mistake. They wouldn't have let me see her anyway, so I left.'

'So you've been what? Watching and waiting to see what would happen?'

'At first I wanted you gone, then I thought if you found the journal I could get rid of it.' He narrowed his eyes. 'What was your plan once you had it?' He bunched his lips, then said, 'Once it was back with Elise, were you going to just walk away?'

His voice hardened, and there was a glimpse of another Jonah. Was he the cause of Lissa's red-rimmed eyes at breakfast, the reason she shrugged him off sometimes when he tried to touch her?

'You've messed with Daisy, with all of us.' His voice had a coating of steel. 'You lied from day one,' he said, and I finally understood why he'd confessed. He didn't believe I would tell anyone, and risk exposing myself. 'You're not exactly innocent, are you, Rose?'

# Chapter 37

'I was going to destroy the journal once I had it,' I said, thinking fast. 'But there isn't one.'

Uncertainty crossed Jonah's face. 'You're lying.'

'OK, there *is* a journal, but it doesn't belong to Ann.' Seeing his expression change, I pushed on, an idea forming. 'It's her mother, Ingrid's.' I moved past him so suddenly he recoiled. 'Come on, I'll show you.'

I half-ran towards the house, acting on some instinct I didn't fully understand, grateful I hadn't returned the diary to Ingrid or Elise. I grabbed my bag off the patio table and threw it onto my shoulder. 'Can you let us in?' I beckoned to him to hurry. 'I don't have a house key.'

His brow furrowed as he fished a set of keys from his trouser pocket and moved round the side of the house. I followed and watched him unlock the side door. My headache had gone, and my mind was oddly sharp. I imagined Jonah as a schoolboy with behavioural issues who needed gentle guidance. 'You'll see why I'm not a threat in a couple of minutes.'

'After you.' He stood aside, measuring my movements with a penetrating stare, as if suspecting I was about to knife him in the back. 'I hope you're not messing with me, Rose.'

'I wouldn't dare.' I widened my eyes to show him I wasn't taking all this too seriously but could see it was too much. He'd only known the quiet, sensible, fade-into-the-background version of me up until now. 'Sorry,' I muttered, sidling into the kitchen, the smell of sun-baked tiles, warm bread, and last night's dinner a comfort – as though nothing bad could happen there.

Rocky ambled through, tongue dangling. 'Hello, boy.' I patted his head and he moved to his water bowl and began lapping.

'Hurry up.' Jonah jangled his keys, gaze wary. 'The others might be back soon.'

'I doubt it,' I said. 'They're at the ski centre. I'm going over there shortly to pick up Daisy and take her to the park. They're expecting me.' It felt good to say it, to let him know I'd spoken to Isaac, but he was barely listening.

Something about his nervous energy ramped up my anxiety but I was done with being afraid of men. 'It's in my room.' My voice was still fake bright. I kept hold of my bag with my phone and pepper spray inside, hoping I wouldn't need to use either. 'It wasn't in the attic at all. I really did go up there to look for Daisy and ended up going through Ann's clothes.'

'Where was it then?' His voice was laden with suspicion as he followed me upstairs with a weighty tread. 'I looked everywhere, even in that chest freezer in the garage.'

'It was taped underneath one of the bedside drawers in Isaac's room.' It was a relief to be telling the truth about something, even if my next sentence was going to be a lie. 'Elise tried to get it when she got into the house but didn't get a chance.'

'Really?' There was an alertness about Jonah's expression as we faced each other on the landing that told me he was convinced. 'Can I see it?'

'Obviously.' I pushed open the door to my room. 'That's why we're here.'

I crossed to the wardrobe and pulled out my suitcase, making my movements confident, careful to nudge the rucksack out of sight. 'It's in a concealed pocket, which is probably why you didn't spot it.' I slammed the suitcase on the bed and unfastened the zip. I took out the knickers and bras I'd left scattered inside, momentarily enjoying Jonah's look of discomfort, and lifted the liner at the bottom to reveal the hidden compartment. 'See?' Lifting out the diary, I forced a note of triumph. *Look, I'm being honest with you.* 'I must admit when I looked inside, I didn't see right away that it wasn't Ann's.' *Because I hadn't a clue that Ann existed.* 'It's a record of her marriage to Ann's father, not even a record really, just her reasons for wanting to get away. She planned to jump out of their car at the traffic lights and run.'

'Jesus.' Fully engaged, Jonah took the diary and flipped through it, pausing to study the name on the inside cover. 'It belonged to Ingrid.' He turned it over, then read a few paragraphs, shaking his head. 'Easy to see where they got it from.' He blew a breath. 'The apple doesn't fall far and all that.'

'Exactly,' I said, hating him for the comment. I wondered what his mother was like, what she would make of her son cheating on his wife.

'Do you know whether Isaac ever saw it?'

*Hardly, considering it had been in Elise's possession for years.* I lifted my shoulders in what I hoped was a casual way. 'Maybe she hid it from him.'

'Perhaps this is where she found some of her ideas.' I jumped when he slammed the book shut and tossed it on the bed. 'Why didn't you give it to Elise?'

'She didn't want it.' I knew if I hesitated for even a second, he would be on to me. 'She was furious it wasn't Ann's, said I'd let her down.'

His look of disdain suggested he wasn't surprised. 'So you got annoyed and decided to have it out with her?'

'Something like that.' I lifted my chin. 'I said I wasn't doing her dirty work anymore, that I liked the family, and felt sorry for

Isaac. I told her that if she didn't get on a plane and go home I would tell him she was here, hanging around again.'

'And drop yourself in it?' Jonah pulled his head back. 'I find that hard to believe. Wouldn't she call Isaac and throw you under the bus?'

I felt as though I was sliding down a mountain. 'No, because she hopes one day she can have a relationship with Daisy and wants to stay on his good side. She told me to leave here, and said she never wants to speak to me again.'

He was nodding. 'You know you have to go.'

I nodded, my throat suddenly full. 'Tomorrow.'

'How do I know this isn't a trap, that she's really gone?'

'You saw us at the airport.' I wished he would go. My resolve was starting to crumble. 'I took pictures on my phone of her going through customs, and she'll send me another when she gets wherever she's going.'

'You don't know?'

'She wouldn't tell me.'

'Figures, I suppose.' His eyes crinkled into a squint. 'And you trust her?'

'I have to.'

Jonah seemed to deflate, curling in on himself. 'I suppose this could stay our secret?' He looked at me hopefully in a way that made me despise him.

Trapped words felt like a fireball in my stomach. 'I don't want to get involved in anything else,' I managed. *Go, just go.* But he was lowering himself onto the side of the bed, tucking his hands under his thighs. I heard a noise on the landing and seconds later, Rocky pushed his head around the door.

'You won't hear from me once I've gone,' I said to Jonah.

'I don't want to have to keep looking over my shoulder forever, wondering whether more mad bitches are coming to ruin my life.'

For a second, I thought I hadn't heard him properly. I remembered how Leon had tried to blame me for losing our baby, for the failure of our relationship, and dug my nails into the heels of my hands. 'Don't you think you should take some responsibility?' The fireball rushed to my throat. 'You're the one who had sex with your brother-in-law's wife and kept it from her and used Ann's illness to cover up what you did, you creep.'

'Don't you dare talk to me like that.' He sounded so hurt, I almost laughed. 'I'm training to be a counsellor; I work over-time at the café for extra money. I'm there for my wife and I will be every day, supporting her and our child.' A coil of hair escaped his bun, standing out like a loose spring. 'I'm trying to be a better person every day and don't need someone like you trying to ruin it.'

'What does that even mean?' My breath came in shallow leaps. 'You want to shut me up, like you wanted to silence Ann and Elise?' I pushed out an angry laugh. 'After what you've told me, about Lissa trying to poison me, and the pair of you making me look like an incompetent idiot, a thief, in front of Isaac, hoping I'd leave, or he'd fire me . . . maybe I should call the police.' I didn't give him time to speak. 'Perhaps if you'd kept it in your pants, Ann would still be alive.'

'Making our lives a misery forever.' He gave his neck a rest-less swipe and a fly swooped up to the ceiling. 'Some people are better off not living.'

'That's a vile thing to say.'

He rose and cracked a thin smile, no sign of his usual, mild-mannered air. Rocky growled, low in his throat, but Jonah didn't flinch. 'I think you should leave right now, before they come home.' He knocked my suitcase to the floor and Rocky growled another warning.

'I'm not leaving without saying goodbye to Daisy.'

'Then I'll make you.'

When he took another step towards me, I ducked around him and grabbed my bag off the bed. I pushed my hand inside and felt for the pepper spray, fingers closing around the metal cylinder.

'Just pack and go.' Jonah's tone implied I was being un-reasonable. 'I'll say you had a family emergency, and we'll leave it at that.'

When I shook my head, his hand clamped around my arm, and he spun me round. He tried to press me to my knees, kicking the suitcase closer, but I brought my head up and caught his chin. Grunting he let go and staggered back, then reached for me again. I lifted the spray and aimed for his eyes, kicking him hard in the crotch at the same time.

He let out a roar. Eyes screwed tight and starting to stream, he dropped to his knees, grasping at me as he went down. As I fell, I realised someone had entered the room and was yanking Jonah away. I scrambled backwards against the wardrobe and watched as Rocky leapt into the scrabble of arms and legs and sank his teeth into Jonah's calf.

'Here boy, let go.' It was Isaac, pulling Rocky's collar, dragging him clear while Jonah writhed on the floor. He looked at me, white-faced. 'Are you OK?'

I managed a nod, feeling dizzy and sick. 'I didn't realise you were here.' My mind was crumbling, running in different direc-tions. 'He . . .' I looked at Jonah, unable to find the words to explain what had just happened.

'I heard everything.' A chill settled into Isaac's voice as he looked at his brother-in-law. 'Get up,' he ordered.

Groaning, eyes red and swollen, his face a ball of agony, Jonah struggled to his knees and leaned on the bed. 'She's not who she says she is.' His voice was a frightened whimper. 'You don't understand, Isaac. Elise sent her here. That crazy bitch told her that me and Ann—'

'Save it,' Isaac snapped, holding out a hand to me. I took it and he pulled me to my feet. 'I heard what you said about Ann, and how she didn't deserve to live.'

'But Rose came here for a reason.' Jonah attempted to open his eyes, his appearance almost comical as he wiped his face on the hem of his shirt and tried to focus. 'She was probably planning to kidnap Daisy and give her to Elise.'

I almost gasped. He'd hit on the truth without realising. But Isaac was shaking his head. 'Is it true?' he said tightly to Jonah. 'About Lissa trying to hurt Rose?'

'You know what she's like, mate. She's always had a jealous streak. She wants me to herself, but she didn't mean any harm.'

Jonah was squinting around, peering at the doorway where Rocky sat like a statue. 'Is she here?' He sounded scared. 'Where's Lissa?'

'I left them at Snow Zone.' Isaac didn't bother hiding his disgust. 'I drove back to . . .' He hesitated. 'I was going to take you back there.' He swept me a sideways look. 'I wasn't sure you were coming after our last conversation.'

'I was, I just . . . I needed a minute . . .' I covered my face with my hands, unable to look at him. 'I'm sorry.'

'Isaac, mate—'

'I'm not your mate,' Isaac cut in, coldly, to Jonah. 'I want you and Lissa gone by the end of the day.'

'Gone?' Jonah was pushing to his feet, puffy-eyed and hideous. 'Isaac, you can't. The baby . . .'

'Should have thought of that.'

I lowered my hands. Isaac's face looked set in stone.

'Go and stay with your family in America.'

'But . . . Cecilia.'

'She has Daisy. She'll understand.'

'Isaac, please. What am I supposed to tell Lissa?'

'The truth, or I will.'

'And Rose?' He jerked his head in my direction, voice filled with loathing. 'I suppose none of this is on her.'

'That's right.' Isaac's voice was rock hard. 'None of it.'

# Chapter 38

The momentary silence that fell was broken by the sound of a ringtone. Isaac dug his phone out of his pocket and frowned at the screen before pressing it to his ear. 'Lissa?'

His sister's voice emerged, high and frantic.

Isaac's face tightened. 'What do you mean, gone to the park with Rose?' His eyes met mine, wild with sudden panic. 'Rose is at the house.'

There was a plunge in my stomach, as if I was falling. 'What's happened?'

'Didn't you bother to check?' Isaac spun on the spot, a hand grasping at his hair as his mother's voice spun higher.

'What's going on?' Jonah demanded, but Isaac ignored him.

'OK, I'm on my way,' he said to Lissa. 'Call the police.'

He headed for the stairs, Rocky at his heels.

'Isaac, wait!' I shot after him, stumbling and grabbing the doorframe. 'What's going on?'

'Apparently, Daisy told Lissa you'd arrived to take her to the park.' He'd already reached the front door and yanked it open. 'Lissa was on the phone to her wedding ring client and didn't think to check it was you.'

I felt dizzy, darkness clouding my peripheral vision. *She's going to the ski centre shortly, with Isaac.* I'd told Elise exactly where to find Daisy.

'Looks like you were wrong to trust Elise.' Jonah's voice again, heavy with sarcasm. 'I could have told you something like this would happen.'

'Leave it, Jonah.' I ran downstairs, pushed past Isaac and onto the drive, realising too late I didn't have my car keys.

'Where are you going?' he said, pausing mid-run.

'To get Daisy back.'

'From where?'

'The park.' My voice cracked with tension. 'I'm sure that's where Elise has taken her.'

Isaac didn't hesitate. 'I'll drive.'

I got in the car with him, my blood humming with adrenaline. He called Lissa, told her tersely to come home, and hung up.

*Daisy's too trusting.* I pictured Elise, turning up, wearing a winning smile, seeking out Daisy. *Go and tell Lissa that Rose is taking you to the park now.* And Daisy, recognising the woman who had turned up at her home before, an aunt she was curious about, doing as she was told.

Isaac didn't ask questions, or speak at all, focused on getting the car onto the main road, only to meet a queue of cars at roadworks.

'*Shit!*' He slammed his fist on the steering wheel, peering around as if to find a gap in the traffic that had built up. His face had a waxy tinge, sweat lining his upper lip. 'I can't believe this is happening.'

'Is it far?'

He turned anguished eyes on me. 'What?'

'The park.' I snapped my seatbelt off. 'Is it far from here?'

He pointed to the pavement on our right. 'At the end of the street, turn right, it's a few hundred yards down on the left.'

I was out of the car before he'd finished speaking, fear lending me speed, running full pelt down the rain-soaked pavement, past workmen, dodging dog-walkers and couples, a family trying to persuade their dog to walk through a puddle.

Over the sound of car engines and beeping horns, I could hear my pounding heart and ragged breath as I rounded the corner and ran on, attracting looks of concern. It was obvious I wasn't running for exercise. My lungs were screaming, and my cheeks pulsed with blood, but at last I could see the park ahead.

I hurtled through the open gates and stopped on a wide stretch of grass, panting for air as my eyes raked the area, jumping over newly planted trees, benches, a bright play area and the café at the far end with tables dotted outside. The place was starting to fill, mostly mothers with toddlers heading for the slides and climbing frame, where steam was rising off the metal bars as sunshine dried the rain.

*Where were they?*

I'd promised Isaac I would bring Daisy back. *Please let them be here.*

Scanning the play area again, I spotted a set of three swings set apart from the other equipment, on a shiny black rubber surface. Two of them were empty, swaying gently in the breeze. At the third, a woman with her back to me was pushing a child with confident strokes, a familiar bag at her black-booted feet, long hair blowing around her shoulders. *Elise.*

I froze with indecision, breath catching in my throat. If I called her name, she might grab Daisy and run, though I had no idea where to. She didn't have Daisy's passport. I didn't even have my phone to call the police, or Isaac to let him know Daisy was safe – for now.

I threw a glance over my shoulder but couldn't see him. He could still be stuck in traffic or looking for somewhere to park, or be on his way to the ski centre, believing I was on a wild goose chase.

Turning back, I ran across to the swings, praying Elise wouldn't look round and see me. Drawing closer I could hear her calling,

*Higher, higher,* just as Ann had detailed in her journal that Daisy used to do.

*She's too trusting.* But Daisy had been wary of Elise, was frightened of her, Lissa had said. She might not want to be on that swing, being pushed higher and higher by an aunt she didn't know, who had caused a scene at her home.

Moving swiftly, I rounded the swings, so that I was facing Daisy. She was clutching the rope handles for dear life, pumping her legs back and forth, her expression focused but not frightened.

'Hey, Daisy!' I forced myself to sound calmer than I looked as I gave her a wave and summoned a wobbly smile. 'I'm here now.'

'Rosie!' Her look of concentration dissolved into a smile that wrapped itself around my thumping heart. 'I want to get off now.'

Realising what was happening, Elise seemed to emerge from a trance. She reached for the seat of the swing as it came towards her and grabbed it, causing Daisy to tip forward.

'No!' I cried, as Daisy's hands slipped from the ropes, and she dropped.

Throwing myself towards her, I broke her fall, winding my arms around her as I toppled onto my back. 'It's OK, I've got you,' I managed, somehow injecting laughter into my voice as though it was a game. 'Wow, that was close!'

'You saved me,' she said brightly, scrabbling free, seeming unscathed as she stood, brushing her hands down her blue-and-pink-patterned leggings. 'Did you see me going high?'

'I did.'

Elise seemed rooted to the spot, still holding the empty swing. Though her eyes were on Daisy, her expression was oddly absent.

Following my line of vision, Daisy turned to Elise with a smile. 'She's my auntie,' she said. 'She said that you're her best friend, and you would come and get me if we came to the park,' she said, reaching to tug at my hand. 'Can we go to the café now?'

'In a minute.' I scrambled to my feet, a twinge of pain in my arm from where I'd caught her.

'Daisy!' Isaac was sprinting across the grass, his face alight with relief.

'Go to Daddy,' I told Daisy, but she was already on her way, arms wide, ready to be scooped to his chest.

I faced Elise, took a couple of steps towards her. 'You lied.' My voice shook.

'So did you.' She let go of the swing and I swerved around it as it came towards me. 'You don't think I believed all that bull about you confessing to Isaac, or recording our conversation, did you?' She shook her head before I could reply. 'You always were gullible, Rose.'

'You could have hurt her.'

Briefly, shame twisted Elise's features. 'Yeah, I didn't mean for that to happen. Guess I'd forgotten how swings work.'

'Why are you doing this?'

'I wanted to take her to the park, that's all.' Her face sagged. 'It's not like you would have let me, so I had to get inventive.'

'You followed me back?'

'You didn't exactly rush to get her, did you?' Elise's lip curled. 'Mooching about at the house. Still, it gave me time to pick her up, which was easier than I'd expected.' Her voice was flat. 'Let's hope Lissa's more observant with her own child.'

'And what was the plan?' I said. 'You don't have Daisy's passport.'

'*This* was the plan.' She waved a hand between us, before stooping to pick up her rucksack. 'Give her a push on the swings, like Ann used to do, before you came to Daisy's rescue like the good little teacher you are.'

'That's it?' I gave her a sceptical look. 'You came all this way to push her on the swing?'

'You can't begrudge me that.' Elise's gaze slipped over my shoulder. 'I really am going now, don't worry,' she said. 'You can tell them they've won.'

'The police are on their way.' Isaac was beside me, his voice quiet, Daisy gripping his hand. His face was set as he glared at Elise, the tendons in his neck standing out. 'I told you I'd have you arrested if you came back.'

'Daddy!' Daisy admonished. 'Don't talk like that.'

'Isn't it better to let me go?' Ignoring Daisy, Elise spoke in the same lifeless tone as she met Isaac's burning gaze. 'My ticket's booked, I'll be thousands of miles away tomorrow. Better than having me in the same town, don't you think?' She was already backing away, hoisting her bag onto her shoulder, eyebrows raised in a question.

I sensed Isaac's hesitation but knew that Elise was right. It was better she was gone, than lingering in police custody, with all that would follow – the upheaval to everyone's life, the explanations for Daisy.

'Go,' I said to her, not waiting for Isaac's response, but she'd already turned and was striding away, shoulders hunched, head lowered. She didn't even give Daisy a backwards look as she slipped out of the park and was lost from view.

# Chapter 39

In the end, Jonah packed a couple of bags and booked a hotel for him and Lissa, who was waiting out in the car, stricken at her carelessness in letting Daisy leave the ski centre with Elise, her face blotchy with tears after begging Isaac's forgiveness.

Jonah paused at the front door before he joined her, swaying slightly. 'We've lost our home because of you.' He glared at me with bloodshot eyes, returning to our earlier showdown now that Daisy was home safe. I'd half expected him to be gone when we returned, but he was in the conservatory, clearly having made an effort to restore his composure for Lissa's sake.

'Because of you,' Isaac corrected him, his tone weary. 'And my sister.'

Jonah looked away and managed a mumbled apology without looking directly at Isaac. 'I never wanted this, mate.'

'Don't say anything to Mum about earlier,' Isaac warned him. 'She's traumatised enough after what's happened, and I don't want her dragged into the rest of it,' he said. 'You can tell Lissa whatever you like, but I don't want to see either of you back here.'

Once Isaac had shut front door, after watching Jonah drive away, he turned to where I was standing at the foot of the stairs with Rocky by my side. Daisy was in the garden with her grandmother, looking for butterflies, apparently none the worse for her unexpected encounter with her aunt – unlike Cecilia, back from the bakery, still whey-faced with shock at the news, and struggling to accept that the police had been turned away and no charges brought.

*For Daisy's sake,* was all Isaac could say, knowing it was the only reason she could begin to understand and to not question – at least not in front of her granddaughter, though she'd had plenty to say to her daughter, out of earshot.

'I don't know where to start,' Isaac said to me now, eyes sweeping my face, which I'd tried to keep serene for Daisy's sake. 'Are you OK?'

'How can you bear to speak to me?' Shame curled in my gut. 'I've lied to you.'

'For a reason.' He folded his arms and after a brief hesitation said, 'If I'm honest, Rose, I suspected Elise was somehow involved in you turning up last week at the school.'

I gaped at him. 'Why didn't you say anything?'

'Because I wasn't sure and . . . I didn't want to believe it, I suppose.' He gave a faint smile. 'And when Daisy took a liking to you right away, I told myself I was being ridiculous.'

'But you had a feeling.' Of course he had – they had all known on some level I wasn't who I was pretending to be.

'It's just that you seemed closed off somehow, like you wanted to be friendly, but couldn't quite relax. And something didn't sit right about this friend of yours, who ended up in hospital, with you rushing off to see her. I had this sense . . .' He was lost in recollection for a moment. 'I knew it was more than my sister giving you a hard time because she was jealous. That business in the attic and wearing Ann's necklace . . . and your face when you realised that photo you found wasn't my wife, but her sister. You asking questions, then finding a reason to run off. I couldn't quite get it to work,' he said, 'but I knew you were in shock, and that maybe you'd been lied to, which brought me back to Elise.'

'I was lied to.' I pulled in a shaky breath and let it go. 'Elise came to me just over a week ago, asking for my help to get her daughter back. She told me she was Daisy's mother.' I forced myself to not look away as the words tumbled out, including my conversation with Thora, and pretending to the hospital that Elise was my sister, her conviction that she – or rather Ann – had been murdered, right up to the morning's events, and leaving Elise at the airport. 'I genuinely didn't think she'd come back,' I finished, sickness churning in the pit of my stomach. 'It's no excuse, but she's a very convincing actress and I'm . . . well, she told me I'm gullible and I suppose I am. I must have been to have been taken in by her in the first place.' I gulped in some air. 'I can only apologise for everything, Isaac. I understand you must hate me. I'll leave.'

Isaac had listened intently, his expression hard to read, but now, as if something had loosened, he shook his head. 'Of course I don't hate you,' he said. 'OK, so I knew something was up, but I wanted to let it play out.' Seeing my frown, he added, 'Not in a game-playing way, but because I trusted you.'

'You *trusted* me?' I punched out a disbelieving laugh. 'Really?'

'It's possible to hold two opposing thoughts and for both of them be true,' he said. 'I knew something wasn't right, but I also trusted you to do the right thing.' I felt out of sync, his calm words at odds with my chaotic thoughts. 'I wasn't lying when I said I had a good feeling about you, Rose. I knew straight away you would put Daisy first, and you did.'

'I would never have let Elise take her, not when it came to it,' I said, realising it was true. 'I could see how much she was loved from the moment I met you both, but Elise's story was so compelling – I wanted to help her, *save* her.'

Isaac smile dropped away. 'You know, after Ann died, I wondered myself whether it might not have been an accident. I saw how Lissa was around her, how Ann used to flirt with Jonah, though I had no idea he'd taken it further.' His face was serious. 'But there was an inquest, and I promise you there were no suspicious circumstances. In fact, only Daisy and I were here that night. Mum had gone to a friend's funeral in London and stayed overnight and Jonah and Lissa were doing the summer solstice thing at Stonehenge. It really was an accident,' he said. 'I promise I'm not a wife murderer.'

'I know,' I said, 'and I wish things could have been different. If I hadn't turned up, you'd still be a happy family.'

'I think Elise would have found a way back into our lives at some point.'

I nodded, knowing it was probably true.

'And I would have had no idea what Jonah, or my sister, were capable of.'

'Isn't that a good thing?' I said. 'Ignorance is bliss.'

'No, because I think I knew, deep down. I've never liked their relationship dynamic; it made me uncomfortable. I'm glad I've a concrete reason for us not to live together anymore, and after seeing that side of Jonah, hearing the way he threatened you . . .' Anger flared in his eyes. 'He kept that side of himself hidden.' Rocky clattered over and Isaac crouched to stroke his ears. 'You know I wasn't happy with how things were here.'

I thought of our conversation in the orchard, when he told me that families could be difficult. An understatement, in this case.

'And where do you stop, with the what ifs?' he continued, as Rocky rolled over to have his belly rubbed. 'What if I hadn't married Ann? What if Ann's mother hadn't abandoned her? What if her father hadn't told her she had a sibling? What if she hadn't involved Elise in her problems, and Elise hadn't turned up at your house?' He glanced at me. 'I'd never have met you.' He shook his head and rose, dusting his hands on his trousers. 'Too much.' He gave a tired smile. 'Sorry. It's been a weird day.'

I nodded, feelings jostling inside me. 'Will you and Daisy be OK?'

He looked at me for a long moment. 'I'll make sure we are.'

'And your mum . . . she warned me, to not let anything happen to Daisy.'

'And it didn't,' he said, adding gently, 'My mum doesn't need to know everything, Rose. It's better for us all that way.'

In the silence that fell, our short history and future possibilities filled the gap between us, until Isaac said, 'I think it's time to get back to some kind of normality.' He moved to the door to the garden, eyes not leaving my face. 'Will you at least stay until tomorrow?'

I nodded again. 'I'll stay.'

When Cecilia and Daisy came in with Isaac, I was in the kitchen, cooking the dinner I'd promised: spicy pork and noodles, following a recipe in *The Art of Cooking*, thinking of Ingrid at Graylands Manor mourning her 'lost girls'.

Daisy was brimming over with words, voice lifting with excitement as she described how I'd caught her when she slipped off the swing, making exaggerated movements as she acted out the scene so that, to my surprise, we were soon laughing. It felt strange after everything that had happened, but freeing.

'Auntie Lissa and Uncle Jonah have gone for a romantic trip,' she announced, making a heart shape with her fingers and thumb. I marvelled at how easily she accepted what she was told, and hoped that she would accept them moving to America as easily.

Cecilia seemed unaware of any further undercurrents regarding their departure, and I guessed Jonah had done a convincing job. I couldn't let myself think about the conversation they must have had or deny the crushing guilt I felt when, after Jonah and Lissa had left, Cecilia thanked me for 'rescuing' Daisy. *I got it wrong,* she said, squeezing my hands in hers, eyes shimmering with tears. *It wasn't you I should have been warning.*

We walked Rocky by the river after dinner, the three of us focused on Daisy. I sensed Isaac was giving me space and was grateful, though every now and then we would catch each other's eye.

On the way back to the house, we bumped into Thora in the orchard, looking for Mr Bennett who had found another way in through the hedge, and left Cecilia chatting to her as though they were old friends.

After reading to Daisy once she'd had her bath, I stayed in her room, watching her sleep, knowing I wasn't capable of sitting downstairs until bedtime, making polite conversation.

After dragging myself into bed, I fell asleep quickly and was woken by the ping of my phone just before midnight.

*I'm here,* Elise had messaged, with a video attachment that showed her walking out of an airport into snow, fat flakes whirling from the sky. There were voices, and I thought I heard someone speaking in German, then Elise's hand reached for the door of a car before the image cut off.

On impulse, I brought up the photo I'd taken of the picture of Daisy with the woman I now knew was her mother Ann and sent it. Seconds later, my phone vibrated with a call, and I yanked the duvet over my head to muffle the sound.

'Thank you.' Elise's voice was thick with tears. 'They look happy.'

My eyes filled. 'I hope they were.' I could hear the sound of an engine, imagined a car whisking her into the mountains where someone was waiting – someone who cared for her. Despite everything, I didn't want her to suffer anymore. 'I hope you will be too.'

I heard her breathing into the pause. 'I've no right to ask,' she said hesitantly. 'But would you take some flowers to my sister's grave before you leave? She's buried in St Mary's churchyard.' My throat tightened. 'I know we weren't close for a long time because of . . . well, you know. But she was my sister.'

'Of course.'

'And I'm sorry for what I said.'

A tear rolled into my ear. 'Which bit?'

'All of it really, but especially that you were a terrible friend.'

I closed my eyes and thought of the other Elise – the one with sparkling eyes, who loved music and would drag me up to dance when I didn't want to, who could make me laugh more than anyone and used to light up a room. 'The truth is, Rose, I came to you because you were the best friend I ever had.'

# Chapter 40

*Ten months later*

*Congratulations on the book. I've read it. It's great!*
I cringed. Too fan-girly.
*That is, it's not bad. I quite liked it.*
*Ha ha. Come to the reading tonight. I'll sign a copy for you x*
Isaac was doing a book signing and author talk in Edinburgh on his book tour. *The Long Slope*, the first in a series set in Iceland about a ski instructor turned detective, had been a bestseller, and there was talk of it being made into a TV drama.
*Maybe.*
He sent back a smiley face. It had become a feature of our text exchanges. Him inviting me to things, me saying *maybe.*
*How's the new school? x*
I looked at the kiss for a moment. He ended every message with one, even though I never did.
*Love it. Challenging, but it's nice to be able to make a difference.*
*They're lucky to have you x*

It hadn't been a massive surprise to my aunt and uncle when I told them I was moving back to Scotland. 'I thought you might, one day,' Sarah had said, after I'd been staying a couple of weeks, and life had felt as if it was returning to something like normal. 'It's been long enough.'

Visiting my childhood haunts, including the house where I'd lived during my early years, had been cathartic, the ghosts of the past as settled as they were ever going to be. It had been a small step from there to buying a two-bedroom house just outside Edinburgh that I was enjoying renovating, when I had time, and finding a part-time job at a school for children with behavioural difficulties. It had turned out to be the best thing I'd ever done, despite days that often felt like one, long battle. I'd quickly made a good friend in another teacher, Fran, who had warm brown eyes, a throaty laugh, and wasn't fazed by anything.

*No new news lately? x*

He was referring to Elise, but since our last exchange ten months ago, there hadn't been any contact. I had a new phone number, so she couldn't get in touch, even if she'd wanted to.

*No new news. You?*

*Apparently my nephew is crawling, and Jonah wants them to have another baby, and his mum's driving Lissa mad but they still can't afford a place of their own x*

He added rolling eyes because that's how he dealt with 'news' from his sister. To treat her messages and occasional phone calls with anything other than a passing comment would be to let her and Jonah into his head again, and Isaac didn't want them taking up space.

*Mum's flying out there next month to meet him x*
*How's her new boyfriend?*
*Seems like a good bloke. Not into skiing, which is probably just as well x*
*And she likes her new place?*
*Got a whole new bunch of friends x*

When Orchard House was sold, Isaac paid for her to move into a retirement flat, not far from his and Daisy's new home – the house in Chesham, overlooking the field of horses. It was an easy walk to her new school from there, which she loved, and there was a ready-made babysitter next door in Beatrice.

*Daisy still talks about you x*

I smiled, and looked out at the car park, where I was taking a minute before going into work. It was May, and the magnolia tree in the school grounds had flowered, showering the grass below with petals, reminding me of the day I arrived at Orchard House.

*Tell her I said hi.*

*You can tell her yourself. She'll be there tonight. We're staying in a hotel and she's very excited x*

I missed her too. She would have grown, might have changed, but somehow would still be Daisy. I hoped she always would be.

*Will you come? X*

*Maybe x*

I pressed send and got out of the car.

# Epilogue

*I dug around in the wardrobe, looking for the dress that Daisy wanted to wear. A blue, shiny thing with pearls around the neck she'd worn sometimes, before we moved. It was perfect for dressing up. There were shoes in there too she wanted to try on. Such a typical girl in some ways, though her love of football hadn't gone away. She had potential, from what I could see. Maybe she would play for her country one day – it wouldn't surprise me. As long as she didn't turn out like her mother, I didn't care what she grew up to be. No sign of interest in the piano, but that was long gone, sold to a man who wanted to learn, but probably never would. It was harder than it looked; that's want Ann used to say if I asked her to show me some scales. She was selfish with her talent, as with so much else. She didn't like sharing unless there was something in it for her.*

*As I rummaged on the top shelf, a box fell down, scattering photographs, and mementos from long ago – theatre tickets, plane tickets, my father's watch and . . . bending fast, despite the ever-present pain in my lower back, I snatched up the old tea towel. Why had I kept it? Probably because it had felt safer somehow. I scrunched it into a ball. Time to throw it away. I wouldn't want Daisy finding it and asking questions, or anyone else for that matter.*

*I thought of the last time I spoke to Lissa, her wistful voice as she asked after her brother. 'Is he doing OK, Mum? I miss him so much.'*

*'He's fine,' I reassured her, because . . . he was. In fact, he didn't seem to need us at all, preferred living in that poky house, but Daisy loves the horses – she's starting riding lessons soon – and as long as I get to see that darling girl whenever I can, I don't mind. I suppose it's thanks to Rose, the riding lessons. Daisy couldn't stop talking about those horses, and of course she can see them whenever she likes now. It was a shame that Rose decided to leave, but teaching is a vocation and I understand her doing a job she's passionate about. I'm glad she's still in touch with Isaac. I think he likes her a lot. I've seen the way he looks when he gets a message, so maybe there's something there. She would be good for him, and a good mother to Daisy. I did worry I'd scared her a bit, telling her she would regret coming to Orchard House if anything happened to Daisy, but I think it did the trick.*

*What I don't get is why Lissa agreed to go to America with Jonah, and so soon before the baby was due, but apparently, it had been on the cards for a while, what with his mum being so sick . . . it made sense. I know Isaac was angry with Lissa for letting that woman walk out of the ski centre with Daisy. I was angry too, but it's all forgiven now. Jonah's mum has recovered, and seems to enjoy being a granny, which is how it should be. I just wish Lissa sounded happier. I've never quite got a handle on Jonah, and still can't quite forgive him for gambling away their money. Lissa insisted we stick to that story about getting scammed once I'd paid off his debts, but it never sat easy with me. Still, it's clear they love one another, and I suppose that's all that matters. Maybe once I'm there, Lissa will talk to me like she used to do, like mothers and daughters should.*

*Ann wasn't a good mother. She barely noticed Daisy, until Isaac mentioned divorce after she stopped taking her medication and started threatening to take the child away from him, saying he'd had her committed against her will and had tried to kill her for God's sake. I had to put Thora Bennet right about a few things after we*

304

had a chat, and I know that slimy estate agent Parry was in love with Ann and believed the worst of us. The truth is my son doesn't have a bad bone in his body. He could never have done what I did.

It was easy enough to slip away that night, after the funeral and the wake in London. An easy drive back to Orchard House, the place in darkness, though I parked in the lane, just in case.

Ann was in the summerhouse, where she'd taken up residence, reading anything she could get her hands on, writing in that diary she would hide if I ever went down there to try to catch her out. I knew that heater was faulty, but no one ever used it, had no need to. It made sense she would have turned it on, because it was bitterly cold that night, my breath misting the air, though it cleared my mind, which helped. She'd been drinking and was in a deep sleep on that awful couch under a thin blanket when I crept inside.

She didn't stir when I turned the heater on – I'd practised once before while she was passed out in there so I knew there would be a ticking sound, and a whoosh when the pilot light came on – but she was too deeply gone to hear anything. I stuffed the tea towel I'd brought in the flue, then had a quick look round for that diary, but couldn't see it. She must have hidden it somewhere, or maybe she burnt the damn thing.

After backing out, I made sure the door and windows had no gaps around, then got back in the car and waited there until morning. It was obvious once I returned to the summerhouse to remove the tea towel that she was gone, her cheeks the tell-tale cherry red I knew happened in cases of carbon monoxide poisoning.

Served her right for accusing my son of trying to poison her, with wisteria seeds of all things. His father would have been livid, as was I. I did my best to try to understand her illness, but all I could see was the pain she caused my son, the devastation she would bring to Daisy's life, and I couldn't stand it. Once I'd removed the tea towel, I left and drove back to London. I didn't lose any sleep over it. Why would I?

My son is happy now, and my granddaughter is safe.

# A Letter from Karen Clarke

Thank you so much for choosing to read *My Best Friend's Secret*. I hope you enjoyed it! If you did and would like to be the first to know about my new releases, you can follow me on my socials below.

I hope you loved *My Best Friend's Secret* and if you did, I would be so grateful if you would leave a review. I always love to hear what readers thought, and it helps new readers discover my books too.

Thanks,

Karen

Twitter: https://twitter.com/karenclarke123
Facebook: https://www.facebook.com/karen.clarke.5682
Website: https://www.karenclarkewriter.com/

# My Husband's Secret

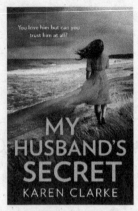

**His secret could destroy them, but her
truth is even harder to bear . . .**

One year ago, my husband Jack left. I've longed for
the moment he would walk through the door and
tell me all he ever wanted was to be with me.

Now he's back, but this isn't the reunion I had dreamt of . . .

Jack has been in a hit-and-run accident. He doesn't
remember we aren't together, has no clue about
his other family, and no recollection of the phone call
he made before the crash – I made a terrible mistake
that I can't put right. All I can do is get out.

Jack is different to the man who walked out and
I'm certain he's hiding something too.

But I finally have my husband by my side, and
with Jack suffering from amnesia, surely the
easiest thing would be to stay quiet . . .

**But can you really trust a man who simply vanished
from your life? And should he even trust me?**

# My Sister's Child

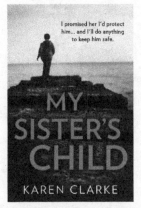

**I promised her I'd protect him . . . and
I'll do anything to keep him safe.**

Five years ago, my sister Rachel left her baby boy on
my doorstep. A little bundle wrapped in blankets.
I loved him. I cared for him. I called
him Noah and raised him as my own.

Rachel was full of secrets, and the truth about Noah
was one we shared. A secret just between sisters.

Now, my sister is dead. The police say it was an
accident . . . But I'm convinced that's a lie.

I owe it to Rachel to uncover the truth . . . Even if
I risk losing the family I've fought so hard for.

# And Then She Ran

**How far would you go to keep your baby safe?**

Grace bundled her eight-week-old daughter into her carry cot, opened the door and ran.

Her life in New York faded into the background – she needed to keep her baby safe. She needed to get as far away from Patrick as possible.

Now, staying in a remote cottage in Wales, Grace is trying to start again. But she can't shake the uneasy feeling that she's been followed.

And then she finds a note. Left on her bed. A tiny scrap of paper with scrawl in bright red pen.

*Keep her close. Anything could happen.*

She's been found. Patrick wants his baby back.

But Grace will do everything to stop him.

# Acknowledgements

I would like to thank the amazing team at HQ Stories, with special thanks to my brilliant editor Belinda Toor for all her insight and guidance. Thank you to Eldes Tran and Helen Williams for a brilliant copyedit and proofread and Anna Sikorska for another amazing cover, and to Audrey Linton for overseeing the process. Thank you also to the marketing team.

I'm in awe of the readers, bloggers and reviewers who take time to spread the word and give lovely feedback, which makes all the hard work worthwhile – thank you each and every one.

As ever, thanks go to Amanda Brittany for her support, and another big thank you to my family and friends who manage to stay interested and always read my books.

I couldn't do any of it without my husband who has somehow survived this process yet again. Once again, Tim, thank you with all my heart.

Dear Reader,

We hope you enjoyed reading this book. If you did, we'd be so appreciative if you left a review. It really helps us and the author to bring more books like this to you.

Here at HQ Digital we are dedicated to publishing fiction that will keep you turning the pages into the early hours. Don't want to miss a thing? To find out more about our books, promotions, discover exclusive content and enter competitions you can keep in touch in the following ways:

### JOIN OUR COMMUNITY:

Sign up to our new email newsletter:
http://smarturl.it/SignUpHQ

Read our new blog www.hqstories.co.uk

🐦 https://twitter.com/HQStories

📘 www.facebook.com/HQStories

### BUDDING WRITER?

We're also looking for authors to join the HQ Digital family!
Find out more here:

https://www.hqstories.co.uk/want-to-write-for-us/

Thanks for reading, from the HQ Digital team